September

THE GERMAN LIST

THOMAS LEHR

September

Mirage

TRANSLATED BY MIKE MITCHELL

LONDON NEW YORK CALCUTTA

 GOETHE-INSTITUT

This publication has been supported by
a grant from the Goethe-Institut, India

Seagull Books, 2013

September. Fata Morgana © Carl Hanser Verlag, Munich, 2010
English Translation © Mike Mitchell, 2011

ISBN 978 0 8574 2 078 7

British Library Cataloguing-in-Publication Data
A catalogue record for this book is available from the British Library

Typeset in Sabon LT Standard by Seagull Books, Calcutta, India
Printed and bound by Maple Press, York, Pennsylvania, USA

For Dorle
and for Fadhil
from whom I can never learn enough

History is the labyrinth of violence.

Johann Wolfgang von Goethe

PART ONE

THE SHIP

September 2001

This world, our sometime lodging here below,
Doth yield us naught but store of grief and woe,
And then, alas, with all our doubts unsolved,
And heavy-hearted with regret we go.

The Quatrains of Omar Khayyam
translated by E. H. Whinfield

And I say to any man or woman, Let your soul stand cool and composed
    before a million universes.
And I say to mankind, Be not curious about God,
For I, who am curious about each, am not curious about God.

Walt Whitman
Leaves of Grass

Our story

is hanging in the air in the night

Sister for you don't bring it to an end its silken thread holds our life invisibly in the darkness whoever cuts it

does not need to have known that

I've always wondered why it didn't bother the king that Dinarzad lay underneath his bed every night and I also wondered what kind of bed it was that had room enough for her to lie under it I imagine that on top it was like a little palace of silk cushions flamingo feathers rose petals a mound of crimson and underneath the dust the bones the cobwebs I've no idea how kings' beds were constructed

in the island realm of India and China

in the Far East where there are supposed to be even more exotic fairy tales than here in Baghdad nowhere is there a better place for giving free rein to your imagination than under my grandfather's massive bed (I never knew him he died a year before I was born he was a sort of king of radio and television) in his house in Wasiriya district where I used to play hide-and-seek with Sami and would often find him under the bed that my grandmother had already been sleeping in alone for more than a thousand nights

on that day three weeks ago when I

at 17

played hide-and-seek again (alone) just for fun burying myself in broad daylight a scorpion in the desert sand while outside in the courtyard the wedding guests had been eating drinking dancing for hours I was once more lying under the bed that smells of rose water sprigs of lavender dried orange peel and mould but my fun was just an escape

before my escape it had come to the point where I could no longer stand the coldly dripping stare (spittle on ice cubes) of the Major that supposed friend of my sister's bridegroom her new husband who takes everything with a smile

I lay perfectly still under the slatted base in the tomb of widowed women I wished Sami were beside me again as a 10- or 12-year-old boy cheerful fearless ready for anything then we'd have secretly tipped salt in the Major's arrack or even spat in his misty drink for a second his glass shone radiantly white in the courtyard like my sister's dress embroidered with glass beads my little dove he said to me as if I were a child and accidentally on purpose touched my breast with his elbow my little dove and in my mind's eye I saw the Kurdish boy at the edge of Saadun Park ripping the feathers off a dove that had been hit by a car off me as if the blood were pouring

out of my nipples

I'm holding my hands flat over them as the slats under the large mattress bend Sister they almost hit my face he calls you his little dove as well Yasmin that voice just as I was about to crawl out from under the bed I must have you today here as a bride it could well be the last time believe me come on Qasim won't notice I'll booze with him until he's incapable of undoing his flies lie down my little dove

and like you I have to spread my legs wide turn my knees outwards put my head on one side as if the springy slats (grey dusty hard) were going to kiss me break my nose and teeth

you two

the beast

girt with the bouncing ribs of a ship's hull

King Death his stake inside you I only saw it as a stone the onyx of a god in a showcase and as a gangling appendage of my brother before he started school he's rocking you (from inside) what does he know of your treasures Sister what a groaning camel you two have become in the desert night a camel with two humps on opposite sides

doves

in the night white black black white

night boarded up with groaning wood don't break the bones of my face my ribs under my shivering skin under the assault of the slats of the

dinosaur ribcage in which you're raging hip to hip I can feel your heart the heart of a red ifrit it could be a ship's keel sailing away above me the whole hull of a ship the slatted base bent into shape fitted together anew enlarged rising high in the air Sister

your shared bed is

the sailing ship of your perfidious love

in a resonant sky behind my closed lids I can see forever as if your dhow had sailed from a harbour in the middle of the desert straight up into the

sky sand dry grains trickle onto my cheeks what can those shapes be moving
in the billowing sails below the sloping yards the wind blows us powerfully
upwards or are you both being drawn up by the lust of the king who bathes
in green oil what's this I'm dreaming it's

nothing it's

just the Major burning

inside my sister

how can she bear it (either marrying the wrong man or letting herself
be used or living between two lies) don't shoot your load inside me she
suddenly says as cool as if she were in her laboratory with a lab technician
a retort in her hand while the

butcher of doves

ploughs through seventh heaven

below me

as I drift along under your keel like the bright shadow of your anchor

are six heavens and seven earths on the back of the bull that has placed
its hooves on the fish in the last water of the black sea resting on the darkness forget

everything forget everything

I

ought to raise my voice now and say: Tell me a story Sister

but you

are in another country

A radiant morning at breakfast in the house on Long Island

with a view of a strip of sand a strip of sea a slim skyline the flag of summer in the white-painted frame of a kitchen window it's a beautifully prolonged summer an it's-still-summer almost cloudless with the promise of bearable heat on this day your skin your bones still glowing with memory with the smell of suntan lotion and grass grains of sand in your ear under your fingernails between your toes

but let's get on with the first story of the first day as you fly along beneath us with your back to the ground under the keel of the ship of the sky

my mother Amanda

(it was two weeks ago) she'd climbed out of her sports car quickly and hadn't put the handbrake on or not enough so that it rolled back down the drive empty and silent as a toy car between a boy on a bike and a yellow delivery van across the quiet street precisely between the gateposts of the house opposite and then into the garage perfectly aligned but much too fast into the workbench full of bottles tins of paint canisters of acids and solvents and the memory of that day is transformed with a deafening crash (the rear wall of the garage perhaps also the row of windows on the side the corrugated surface of the roof like a pond bursting) into a glowing clenched fist

I'm going to visit you through

a tower of fire Sister

as light as a

thought

like a bright white light the laser-

fairy of regularly dancing atoms can dash

through an explosion through a blazing fire through a boiling planet

our flying ship is transformed

into white ash high up in the air quietly sailing more cautiously than anything else in the world it disintegrates as quickly as an idea a story a

life

Sister we see a lot of things wrongly just because we heard too few stories under the bed through the mattress you perhaps only see yourself on the other side in my white skin

as your own dream of the deadly king we need to know all the stories the great merry-go-round on earth then you'll also see the boy with light-brown hair running out of the house where the garage went up in flames as if through the veil

of a dream he was frightened

to death he thought perhaps a war had started

burning oil an angel of fire blowing out the glass facade of the conservatory with a further explosion a messenger who always hits the target but can be driven off again since everyone helps all the neighbours my mother's lover who hurries over the boy's parents the firemen at last who have another easy exercise here

no one has

been harmed we're all sitting together with the yellow-striped knights of the FDNY Eric's mother beside my mother two completely different women with almost the same hairstyle (they both go to the same ladies' hairdresser in the nearby town and in all the excitement they keep giving each other embarrassing mirror looks) the well-groomed plump housewife from the afternoon soaps agitated and pink desperately trying to compose herself on the other hand Amanda from the late-evening programmes of life's TV channel that show cold beautiful female executives but she is a little dishevelled for her and strangely mirthful

mirth is the mail of anguish

says Emily

in my head in my breast

so light and easy and she turns round calmly and disappears in her room without fully closing the door

(spit blood you're injured!)

to me Amanda seems positively exuberant perhaps because she's made a mess of something for once even if it were only for me for I suddenly think that I would like to learn from her simply to admit to an error with such human elegance in her white summer trousers and the mauve T-shirt in which it becomes evident that the skin of her upper arms with its freckles and liver spots is no longer as taut as it used to be with such disarming ease as if she could go on to introduce the friendly stocky man with thinning hair and the markedly casual attire this typical Long Island scriptwriter who looks like one of his own characters with a may I introduce my lover Leslie

in such a disarmingly apologetic manner because he resembles her second husband but is actually less good-looking than him

but her affairs and stratagems don't bother me that much today the smell of burning and ashes from the accident makes everything seem both wrong and right at the same time and you simply can't say what's true any more and lean weary and yet strangely excited into the blue smoky air so that you could easily find yourself against someone else's shoulder in a few quite unimaginable days' time Eric will say to me

just imagine

that she simply needs a friend someone she can talk to when your stepfather isn't there perhaps it's all just a

projection

and with a grin he'll raise a forefinger so liberate yourself instead and come to LA with me

close the door from outside instead of leaving it half open to repel to attract to impose on your irritated environment but now

we're talking to each other for the first time before this we just gave each other furtive glances and embarrassed nods

the nightingale

flies to the rose Sister

he has such nice messily cut hair his ears stick out too far so that he doesn't look too pretty too smooth his fingernails are different lengths (the right-hand ones longer he plays the guitar Watson) no hair in the gap of his light-blue, short-sleeved open-necked shirt

the line of fire engines is quietly parked outside our house the insurance will see to everything he can buy himself a new one my mother says and Eric's left shoulder actually touches me when we eventually go and have another look at the grotesquely twisted skeleton of his bicycle gleaming under the soot you could imagine

being a creature of ashes and charred remains an almost dismembered body which dies the moment a living being that has existed for three seconds or 3,000 years treads on it

what's your name

Eric asks softly

GREETING

My veil, Beloved, is my hair.
 Lift it up and see.
My red lips are whispering you.
 Touch them now and flee.

Happy people should be sensible and feel five times a day (as often as a good Muslim prays) that for them mastering life is

child's play

in that way they would still have a few good times

before their expulsion I breathe steadily I go into the kitchen and make coffee with a German machine I bought only recently at the Ipswich Mall automatically assuming it would probably be good quality as most Americans would have done I must confess (contrary to my revulsion at an unimaginably close future) that I'm glad I have the house to myself again for although I still know too little about Mohammed and Marianne I have long since found

Suleika

and have succumbed to her and am surprised and grateful for the storm she (easily even after three years) sets off inside me for her sudden fits of hospitality calmly pushing aside a few books or a chair lifting an apron her skirt a soft suntanned leg in the kitchen or on the narrow staircase (having an accident there and stumbling like still half-bound escapees from the prison of our college-professor earnestness into the amazed bacherlorish arrogance of my reading-bedroom)

now I'm still

and already

completely alone I get annoyed (for the terrible last time) at Sabrina at a mislaid book I stand (already reconciled) in her room formerly her girl's room since she's been at college in Cambridge she's only rarely been here everything seems unchanged as if preserved in that peculiar state of transition from the chaotic fairy-tale world of little girls (early autograph albums and old Disney comics faithful soft toys the poster of a female rock star) to the in a way secret not at first sight evident order of a young woman (*National Geographic* magazines arranged chronologically textbooks songbooks novels poetry anthologies PC manuals piles of CDs) but there's still the now almost empty space on the bookshelf below which at my ironic suggestion a few years ago she stuck a handwritten label

Stolen from Dad

and there I find my edition of Hafiz the only one that makes a more or less successful attempt to transpose the Arabic metres into German and then

gently

as if by the hand of a girl (it's the hand of a young grown-up) I'm pushed away out of the sealed untouchable realm and turn away happy a daughter who pinches your books is a character from a fairy tale you couldn't even dream of previously I'll put off breakfast it's the almost cloudless morning

of the last day

it's eight o'clock I tie the laces of my running shoes I fiddle with the side-pieces of my sunglasses between my ears and the short hair of my temples (with stripes of silver like a daddy badger she said) and go out onto the wooden veranda with a view across a large stretch of grass to North Pleasant Street the taste of approaching autumn already on my lips I think with anticipation and a certain reverent helplessness or awe of the fifth season which will cover the hills round the town with blankets of fiery foliage (the blood of the Great Bear as the Indian legends call it) with swirls of honey-coloured bright-orange flesh-red purple light-brown maroon

leaves

drifting along the blue reflection of the surface of the streets a rustling sea of flame enclosing the white wooden houses giving them an almost sub-lime lustre as if their painted boards were marble as if their pink bricks and the wedding-cake plaster on the public buildings would last for a thousand years I often get in my car and drive out to the Metacomet Trail or to Holyoke Park I run a lot my longest and most lonely runs in this dreamlessly beautiful season which for me represents happiness suffused with quiet unfathomable despair always has necessarily perhaps just something like a congenital defect of the no actually of any idyll

just as the fine fissures the hairline cracks now appearing in the deep Murano glass of the sky cannot be wiped away cannot be got rid of except by

forgetting them or there are

cracks in the vitreous body of my eye cracks from the future because you can't bear how seamless the past could one day appear to you when I was looking for the Hafiz edition in Sabrina's room a shoebox caught my eye for the first time she'd stuck two postcards on the lid one in black and white of an Egyptian singer wearing a kind of fez probably a photo from the 1950s while the other was in colour and recent a visual pun in an ad for a Californian winemaker headed *Really Dry Red Wines* with a desert landscape below it and in the foreground sitting at a stone table an Arab in a burnous with close-cropped white hair looking at a gleaming red glass an expressive serious man of roughly my age and I didn't think that was mere chance for months ago I'd told Sabrina that I needed someone to help me acquire some familiarity with the East and was thinking of a colleague in the Department of Middle Eastern Studies whom I really ought to approach for cultural support I thought I would need just a glance (not at the contents of the box) a tip a list of books but now I need much more than a colleague I need

Hafiz

(a brother)

on a wooden chair at the stone table the glass filled with the liquid ruby-red blood of the angel who will one day open our eyes at the end of this sleep called life I need someone who will help me to understand all that a

REFLECTION (1)

The skyscape mirrored in my glass
　　Does not reveal its native land;
An ornament of time, of light,
　　The vague, faint pulse here in my hand.

Within my house a scorpion
　　That plunged its sharp white sting of NOW
Deep in the back of its own neck,
　　Till woken at the plane's command.

There on the wine's bright firmament
　　From East to West drifts soft the dream
Of flight, of steel, of oil, of death.
　　The finger writes, the stark words stand:
Blood turns to glass, glass turns to sand.

Tap the glass it's enough to

get onto the other side the thin mirroring surface dissolves and conversely

comes back together as if out of a swirl of splinters within the

face looking back at you which slowly comes to in that white-haired, black-moustached guy (*really dry*) whose lids blearily open who's looking at the peacefully relaxed landscape with rosewood-black waves flowing round it in which he will always be at home wherever he might happen to be

Farida's face

disappears once more behind a (damned subjective) veil

at five in the morning I fall back into cloudier quieter hidden life again look at the mirroring surface as at water as at veiled coolly feverish air in which faces become flounders become other flat fish

Hafiz

thought he was a bird

out of paradise and his body was dust concealing from him the Garden of Ridván the golden tree the jewelled branch on which he was sitting

so then the body of my body's a fish in the absolute substratum namely the water that determines everything even 10,000 years ago and still today let go of me my friend and I splash wriggling into one of the two great arteries of this country whose boundaries were invented by the English (my wife's grandfather lived in Basra and he was asked what it was like when it was conquered by the English but he hadn't seen any Englishmen only English flags and ships and uniforms which the Indians had taken hold of) in whose country it's always raining and which is sea-girt all round which is the reason they can't really understand how pleasant it is when your smiling neighbours in the north play with their knives at the throat of the water and in the south the udder of the gulf between Persia and Kuwait is squeezed they simply thought of oil too much and soon gifted us Mosul together with its raging Kurds and 1,001 senior officials from England and eventually a new king from the Hejaz whom having seen reason we elected after 10,001 rebels had lost their lives paradise is as close to us as in a fairy tale and as the idea that one can very quickly solve any problem with violence or at least transfer it

at least in paradise the streams flow and if we are to meet there then take the other river my brother as a fish as a naval frogman as a tracker carp full of high-tech equipment that extends its telescope eyes and drags its delicate electronic feelers through the mud looking for warheads and tins of chemical weapons take the Euphrates through the limestone and marble gorges in the north (foaming boiling ice-cold between cliffs with the carved figures of the old Hittite warriors and kings and the grandiloquent relief inscriptions recording conquests that were only temporary both scarred with historical bullet marks attesting the artistic sense and the rage of the mountain tribes)

the Euphrates is the great wild mother river but for me it gets too pious in the middle where it flows past the burial grounds of Karbala and Najaf suffused with longing for resurrection whereas on the other hand in the sluggishly winding Tigris I can observe exceptionally male phenomena such as the flash of fighter-bomber cannons on the 36th parallel along the flight-exclusion zone (the gurgling vibration of the water when rocket installations close to the bank are destroyed) such as the submarine-like outline of a whale of the kind that transported Jonah to Nineveh (you can still see the original tail or tooth of the animal there) probably it was only a giant carp such as I am blown up to biblical–Koranic proportions in which the

GREAT SON

and killer of Tikrit has long since been hovering over us

on the water over us the massive cumbersome kalaks made of inflated goatskin swirl along now like the silhouette of HIS militant mother who was in a bad mood throughout her life (she screamed she would give birth to the devil when HE was trying to get out of her) one bad word about her and

you're in an acid bath

with our fishes' lips we're supposed to clean her shining mausoleum

this lousy hole with its clay-brick buildings out of which crawled most of the gang that rules us Saladin was born here and a blink of history's eye later HE following the example of his Nazi-fanatic of an uncle it always ends in rivers of blood give a crazy beaten child a gun forget that he's cunning and unscrupulous look down on him from the elevated perspective of much cleverer and better-educated party members until he sticks the barrel of his gun between your teeth look at the naive blue sky through the hole in the back of your skull sink into the mud

slide mutely over the smashed skeletons through the tendrils that tear on your old iron scales in the desperate meanders of the river until

light

streams into your dull eye and you plunge down through one of the floodgates at Samarra (once the country was sensible enough to build a tower 50 metres high with a spiral ramp going round it five times once it was sensible enough to buy water with oil to dam it up to divert it into huge basins in order to supply the thought-exclusion zone)

I would be able to see the wriggling legs of the boy I once was we would swim in the 1950s in the still-almost-clean pewter-coloured river in the winding meanders pregnant with history of the water in

Baghdad

as a juvenile fish I would see the green growth on the pier of the bridge that plunges into the summer heat above the surface of the water like little frogs we cling to projecting stones each trying to get higher than the other rubbing our dry warm boys' skin against one another enjoying the fact that the other is alive has strength like you and is climbing I see my two prophets clinging onto the stone thin Ali with his aristocratic Egyptian features and Hussein's broad good-natured smile as if it were already the artistic beard of his adult years we're 12 years old the English time is just ending for after 40 years of exploitation and being dictated to the people here finally became somewhat furious they shot the king and his family dragged the dead regent through the streets and recognized the eternal prime minister the best friend of the English as he tried to flee dressed up as a woman lynched him buried him dug him up again and tore his corpse to pieces that wasn't the way an English gentleman behaves my friend but the crazy one they encouraged here in a very un-English way but by now we're used to that

we've grown into old carp

scarred sullen tough crafty cowardly at times already dead as well

and I flap along as a 1.8-metre shabbut and if they were to take me out now I would insist on the venerably perverse method of preparation in which I would be filled with lemon leaves pomegranate seeds parsley and cumin so that (with my head in a vessel full of water my belly wrapped in oil-soaked linen my tail in cotton) I could be boiled roasted and baked at the same time in one piece

they're so artful

at getting rid of us here

continue swimming southwards my contending brother my knowledge-able daughter Muna will tell you something about Babylon and Uruk and Ur the old sorrow the dead dragonflies of Gilgamesh will float towards you on the river but

now paradise lies between us

the alluvial plain in which I would tell you something about Hafiz even though he wasn't an Iraqi

if my alarm clock wasn't going to ring in two minutes' time and I wasn't going to turn it off before it could disturb Farida's sleep wake up and get up Tariq and

go into the kitchen in your pyjamas because this here is

pyjamaland

in the morning (you can happily shoot at the ceiling with your shotgun)

but be quiet when you pick up your doctor's bag on the chest

To fall out of the sky

with billowing sails

I was by the sea again and thought of a possible poem Monday on the Beach (Monday Morning on the Beach? Monday by the Sea?)

your ship

Sister could sail down from the sky and

quietly anchor on the almost smooth still blue-grey shield of the Atlantic I would wait for you here on the beach watch you being rowed ashore in a little boat by

Mamelukes?

Egyptian or Nubian servants anyway black men with massive black arms short silk jackets earrings and turbans faces with make-up gleaming in every pore

Hollywood

as I've been breathing it in while watching television ever since I was a child the tireless flicker of the smoke of thousands of false djinns that never escape from their jar

(they would suffocate in the stinging oxygen

of reality)

you had to flee Sister you needed

asylum

for never entirely obvious mysterious deadly earnest reasons and in a similarly underground way you were related to me a sister (the same age a twin from another body) who lived by my side went to school with me shared every meal with me and slept in my bed to whom as if to a wilful proud shadow with gold chains strings of coins (completely soundless) little bells I had to demonstrate and explain everything I did in an inextricable tangle of joy and sorrow (in order to have a witness to everything and anything who was dependent on me

your permanently mute but absolutely clear negative reaction weighed on me since nothing was good enough for you and nothing could impress you) for a whole year I dreamt of you

the Arabian princess

carried you round with me we were all (Martin Amanda and me) still living together in Amherst I was 11 the Paris trip was still in the future I read too much and was alone too much I antagonized my best friends

with your pride

or the ghost of the pride I took from you which I refused to give

a name

from whose mute stubborn beautiful foreignness I suffered in order to absorb it into myself to get something similar to grow within me perhaps you had to flee because you were the next one a King Shahryar wanted to spend her last night with him and I watched over you I protected your life and read and read so that the moment he found us I could go up to him and demand he spend the night with me and ensnare him in the wonderful

web of my stories

but the impotence the pride the Arabian princess

was me when

I was afraid of Martin and Amanda's separation tried to show them that they would hurt me

at 19 you gradually come to understand that it's almost easy looked at from today

to turn your back on the sea (a better title for the poem?)

to head for the white building our holiday house that's three times the size of our old house in Amherst and that we have to call a cottage because here even more palatial residences become shacks a low grass-covered dune goes up (like the pale back of a skinny African buffalo) towards a higher one on which hedges of wild rose force the path into serpentines

from up there

I look back towards the beach again back to the previous day showers of spray foaming waves silver it was hot and often stormy a bubbly energetic summer-once-more backlit in the dazzlingly veiled air the silhouettes of the bathers moved as if happily hypnotized (they don't hear themselves they don't seem to have any intentions any more) I myself am in the foreground as if I could be even more in the foreground observing myself in the shadowy, almost dazed colours a slim (grown-up) girl in a red bathing costume (that looks almost grey) with wet hair frozen in a sweeping gesture her long arms partly stretched out and her hips sideways on as if I'd just thrown a frisbee across to

Eric

who's coming towards me through the little waves smiling arms hanging down and for a moment I'm horrified as if I really had thrown something that might hurt him hit him in the face or on the neck I kissed we

sometimes hid

lying

behind our mats from the grains of sand blown along from the eyes of other people as if in a straw basket a huge bird's carrying over the sea just close your eyes Eric

while the building workers who've been hastily summoned (a black charred wrecked garage is really out of place in East Hampton) remove the rubble and quietly and discreetly erect a smart new car shack (palatial garage) in the posh last village street before the beach

in those two weeks in which nothing more nor less happened than

the gentle barely noticeable

exchange

of the planet beneath our strip of sand it

feels so liberating and alarming though (for the moment) it's nothing more than an intention a minor escape I'm just cutting the first week of the new term

the Earth won't go out of orbit

Eric says

you know what it's like

damn I think it would have helped it would have been better if we . . .

but you're not asleep (and neither of you ever were? really Sister?) the first time with a boyfriend when you're

bleeding

it wouldn't have made any difference go on admit it it would just have been a little less crazy a little less romantic than this dead certain pledge of ourselves of an intensity and joint pleasure such as never was Sister it's when you leave your pain your pride

behind

leave the corner where you'd hidden it's so absurd so difficult to see when this corner's a big bright room on the first floor where you spent two years in a dreamt-up often dream-like exile with a view of the sea such as I often wished I had when I was a child during our holidays in Rockport

to be able to keep on living

by the sea

the Arabian princess

came back

into me during the time when at 13 I followed my mother Amanda moved into Seymour's holiday house on Long Island in which I was supposed to think everything was wonderful that's Mrs Donally do you want a horse she's a wonderful cook she'll look after you and your horse when we two are in New York City no I cried I want a camel that's what Mrs Donally looks like I'm getting a camel that cooks a horse

but eventually I found the strength to leave this place when I went back to live with Martin in Amherst and calmed down and became normal only

more serious

and that's why I can happily live here now for a while in the holidays or at weekends and I can stay away from here for as long as I like so why

does it make me so nervous I'm

only going to California for two weeks I must come back to my senses I must find something that brings me back down to earth (at least after this holiday) after all that's what I'm

studying

Muna

From our silent

   airship say

   Sister driven by

   imagination and you need a lot of that when you've lost a sister in a
bed above you her legs open coolly receiving the hot white blood of the army
my clear organized superior big sister Yasmin who wrote me so many letters
who went to Paris when she was my age to return eight years later as a qualified chemist as the fiancée of an older man who had already been married
once I wanted

   to marry a pilot I saw in Paris not in the air or at the airport but at
one of the markets where you can hear Arabic almost like at home of course
he took no notice of me a Middle Eastern child of 11 he didn't even brush
against me

   with his blue uniform

   he's a Frenchman Sister an Englishman or a German a Frenchman
they're always just figures of fire of water of smoke

   in the fire

   of our story the pilot looks down on the ochre sea of houses in Baghdad
split by the grey steel snake of the Tigris the domes of the mosques stuck in
the dust like turquoise shells all the time the plane rises to its crazy height
like a bus on an invisible bumpy steep track through a light-blue desert

   the pilot turns his head with the glittering sunglasses he glances out
through the side window he sees

   (as a dangerous dream!)

   our ship

   in the air

   just the two of us would be at the railing for the king would have gone
out to have young men crushed (by young men the usual) he would see us
shimmering in the summer sky the silver sail the narrow silver ribbons in
our light white clothes he would feel the softness

   of love

   for it could have happened once upon a time (or perhaps not) I would
have been a

dancer

for example dancing in the courtyard of an old caravanserai which had
been turned into a restaurant until a flood of banknotes sailed down over
my short veil my shoulders my half-bare breasts my jiggling naked belly (the
Egyptian films from the 1960s sealed in video cassettes as if in slim coffins
in Farida's wardrobe) now the pilot can see me flying in the sky as I did yesterday in the smoke from the hookahs in the sweat

of my frenzy

I've got to be like my sister I've got to be

able to

let go I'm becoming blurred in the air (just like the ship our dhow the
feverish will-o'-the-wisp of my sister's outline) and now the pilot can see his
instruments clearly again (manifold pressure gauge altimeter airspeed indi-
cator gently rocking blue–brown rotating disc the artificial horizon Sami
says did we ever have a different one Sister revolving winking flickering elec-
tronics water fuel quivering white needles on a black background)

the dragonfly Sami says that white thing that looks like a banana

turn coordinator

turn back Sister take the pilot out of the air the dead dragonflies out of
the river erase the aeroplane from the sky

it must be 10 years since a passenger plane flew from Baghdad to Paris
Baghdad isn't even on the Flight Simulator at seven in the morning a sleepy-
eyed Sami swings to and fro over a landscape in Italy outside Rome he thinks
over rolling hills with no houses with no people or trees as if everything
there had been erased by a fury or painted over with yellowish-brown paint
like the streets of Baghdad in that

storm

last week that blew grains of sand into every crack in the house as if it
had been able to simply blow in through the glass of the windows yesterday
with Farida I cleaned the kitchen the bathroom and every other room but
this morning there's only a light breeze wafting round the house that's filled
with a calm saffron-yellow light the old crooked crudely enlarged house of
my great-grandfather in Betawiyn where we moved four years ago when
Tariq started getting less and less money for more and more work and even
though Yasmin didn't come to live with us when she returned from Paris
(with Qasim who needed three years to get a divorce from his first wife even

though it had long since been settled and sorted out with the cadi) here we're more cramped than ever

we wouldn't have been able to keep the bright flat in the new block even if Tariq like so many doctors scientists writers professors had sold his books and those of our great-grandfather

keep flying

on an old blanket on the ground like an itinerant pedlar my crazy clever little brother Sami on the old computer Yasmin's contribution (apart from that nothing but books and video cassettes for me) he clatters away on the keyboard whistling he's dreaming of going to study in America of the girls there he'd drop down dead if he saw a girl like you Sister anywhere apart from a screen

in the bathroom

I wash my face run my wet hands over my hair wash my arms up to the elbows my feet up to my ankles I say the Fatiha I go back to my room sink to the floor on my narrow light-blue rug breathe in the wax smell of the floorboards it sometimes helps sometimes I still manage to say prayers without them being interrupted by other thoughts and I say the Verse of the Throne because I want something splendid and soothing something that can heal everything even my sister's wound

(in her head the thing that has changed her)

and open up the sky over Baghdad again while we just continue to live and dream and sleep

God never sleeps

for you Sister it's still the night of the first day the shadow line wanders slowly across the delicate blue and white of the globe there is Paris there is New York there is Bombay and Peking my father Tariq gave Sami a CD he had from a grateful patient on which you can look at postcard views of cities from ground level as if you were there in the streets I much prefer looking at that than at the Flight Simulator over the shoulder of my brother who otherwise has to be woken

by Tariq who's usually the first sitting in the kitchen in the morning drinking tea or reading or even writing poems before going to work as if he could cure patients with verses

your face he once said to me

cures me of all my ills

we have breakfast Farida insists Sami has something to eat the three of us leave the house together the men of our family I don't say anything about Yasmin to any of them out of fear that they'd think nothing of it or that they had to attack the (influential and dangerous) Major what nonsense I think at the moment it's still bearable in three hours it'll be over 40 degrees a dusty palm tree rustles in the breeze beside a telegraph pole with the torn wire hanging down the drinks seller (SevenUp Mirinda orange and pomegranate juice) shoos a ragged urchin away from his stall I adjust my headscarf lift my foot to cross the drainage channel running down the middle of the street I only need to go 10 minutes northwards to get to school I say goodbye to Tariq and Sami at Nidhal Street since we've been living in Betawiyn with its maze of old ochre and clay-coloured houses with the high thresholds made into benches its narrow streets its intermeshed life we're deeper and more complete as if newly

native

to Baghdad

at that time however we were modern and had a high income we went to a club I wore a short white dress zoomed round the district on my red bicycle I was going to learn to play tennis and we took a taxi on a smooth infinitely long track to Amman Airport and that was how

I went to Paris at 11 abroad for

the one and only time

The University Lodge is a kind of flat-roofed motel looking a bit like a garage on a grassy hill Triangle Street you have to take the orange warning hand of the crossing light seriously here if you don't want to take your life in your hands it's just that here three roads join in an odd way you can't quite see after that everything

goes smoothly no danger between low white and brick-red shops cafes restaurants the Blue Sky Gallery the Toy Box a bookshop a record shop St Brigid's Catholic Church with its free-standing bell tower opposite the Unitarian Meetinghouse

at eight in the morning

it's still quiet the sputtering buses that tirelessly link the five colleges and the residence halls are still almost empty

someone waves to me outside the fire station

I'm still

the UMass professor divorced but no longer unhappy about it early 50s and reasonably well preserved (revitalized) and once more

unsuspecting

on my last run for more than a year

it's being alone with my thoughts my breathing the rhythmic pulsation of the kaleidoscope of my life in memory that makes running so worthwhile for me my last carefree uncensored thoughts of the big chestnut thimble-like smooth nipples of my female colleague from Hampshire College (the smoke-blue house in Spring Street) at the most important crossroads normally busy but now similarly sleepy in the town I always (automatically actually) look to the left down Main Street to the perspective formed by the brick-red City Hall the granite-grey Episcopalian Church which with its stone arches and battlements reminds me of the model-railway landscapes of my childhood while on the other hand the

Jones Library

with its wonderfully old-fashioned interior like something from a Hitchcock film takes me back to so many experiences from Sabrina's early years in school and every time I see the little historical museum behind it I've never been in (probably meticulously worked quilts and scrimshaw old weather vanes with Indians or eagles transoms spinning wheels muskets bearskins and carefully painted figureheads incessantly dipping into the pale seas of oblivion behind the dusty windows of the museum in which we swim past heedless) I see one single scene in my mind's eye needle-sharp in

joyful panic

when Amanda 11 days after she was due

swayed

right here

went down on the ground and sat on the grass until a friendly young fat bank clerk from across the road ran round the corner and came back with an ambulance

19 years ago

Sabrina was born here (the hospital just on the next hill behind the maples and chestnuts still in their summer green) on Amanda's belly her

Mayflower

trembling she raised her damp little head and sought our eyes with a magical black I-want-to-go-ashore look and in those minutes of perfect

threesomeness

I too left the ship and arrived between the Green Mountains and the White Mountains between the cows of Vermont and the humpback whales of Nantucket to the south of HISTORIC Deerfield and picturesque Springfield at the southern end of Pioneer Valley where students are cosseted and tormented here in this university town the centre of which looks after four o'clock in the afternoon as if the entire population had imbibed the most effective elixir of eternal youth from the drinking-water supply apart from only a few token mature grown-ups and strangely fake-looking toddlers that's where I arrived

at least with everything I loved and could see as part of my mature life my reason and the fascination that with Sabrina I was now

finally

half at home in America

or rather two-thirds for at that time Amanda was still a living home her lean neck the sweat in the hollow between her collarbones her ash-blond hair still smooth and cool-looking even after four hours in labour the bright fresh sea in her eyes a morning sea for me she always had that maritime aura it automatically made you think of a clear day of dry salt crystals fresh yacht varnish waxed ropes polished teak burnished brass white canvas shoes of the clarity and energy of a coastal region as on the beaches of Cape Cod or

on that horrible Long Island

perhaps we should have lived by the sea not just spent a few summer holidays in a colleague's house in Rockport but that's just a hindsight thought from a worse future looking down like a tattered raven on Amanda in jeans and T-shirt painting the window-frames lugging the flowerpots out onto the porch pushing Sabrina's bicycle across the lawn under an awning between the garage and the south wall of the house that she cut to shape and put up herself with shears and a straw hat between phosphorous-yellow hedges with a green barbecue apron and a pair of tongs among my colleagues perfectly

false

in that picture as if a meticulous artist (Sabrina as a 10-year-old) had cut her out of one of the large unpublished photo catalogues of life as if she were suddenly missing from a yacht outside Rhode Island in a restaurant on the Upper West Side at a business lunch in her home environment of Palo Alto (the terribly precise silhouettes of her absence) as if she'd been detached from the setting that was meant for her and installed arbitrarily or even with a certain sadistic intent on the wooden verandas outside the sports grounds and in the libraries and classrooms of the little high schools scattered all over these hills and green valleys in order to

test her perhaps

to subject her to a self-tormenting procedure lasting years at the end of which she at last figured out what she was made for (coast city society business) she who had persuaded me to leave New York City with our still unborn child in the belief that New England was the right place that a woman from California and a man from North Germany would be best settling down in that green red and gold ur-America of the WASPs where the Puritans landed the Winchester rifles were invented Cambridge and Berlin rebuilt cod and officer cadets caught the best thinkers and cranberries cultivated presidents and eco-freaks grown witches burnt the first great novels and the most beautiful poems written do you remember Woodstock

for me

for Sabrina (perhaps)

Amanda was right

even here in the woods among 17,000 inhabitants and 30,000 students
SO FAR

in my bubble of still intact today in which I run out

westwards

to the stadium and to the sports grounds of the University of Massachusetts where I'll do two circuits before I'm running along Frank Morgan's garden fence again the high white slats a downwards flickering raster in which I could see the freeze frames of my life or just a

white wall

white map

patches of blood on the white land the exterminated Indian tribes the settlers' villages attacked over decades (Sabrina at eight or nine in the museum of local history in Deerfield looking in disbelief at the massive wooden door of the so-called Indian House in the middle of which the numerous blows from Indian axes had left the unforgotten scar of the attack of 1704 an eye the size of your fist looking back on

relentless struggles

relentless

memories the door

in a glass case

can no longer be opened) there are no white spaces in history what you always get is a blanking out a narrowing down a covering up of the view certainly even when people dig deeper immerse themselves in the relative innocence of the eighteenth and early nineteenth century the idea of looking at Goethe occurred to me when I lost Amanda when she went back to the New York City I'd once set out for in order to live a real late-twentieth-century life a big-city life from which she lured me away (for Sabrina's sake and with the illusion of an idyllic family life which she put more energy into believing than anyone else) only to dump me leave me (shortly after the three of us returned from Paris after that ill-fated pointless trip together) stuck in the hills of West Massachusetts like getting stuck in the

mud season

during which the woods are filled with a grey mush larded with twigs and roots as if something were fermenting in it (the grubby mental mush of a future catastrophe)

after the icy spring in Paris I sank back into the eighteenth century it was pure chance not Amanda's nor my intention I was following the coffin of a colleague born 46 years earlier in Vienna Sigi Ramsauer a splendid Klopstock-Goethe-Schiller-Herder-Hegel-Hölderlin man who was now departing this life without ceremony in the standard funeral drizzle dripping onto my honey-tinted bell jar (the extension of my sunglasses my whole body my diving suit of residual alcohol and a good-morning scotch) without bothering me without really being able to touch me inside my protective clothing which however was then

perforated so immediately it was as if it had never existed and as if stupidly the worse for liquor I were just hiding the bags under my eyes behind my sunglasses in contemptible mourning camouflage

the firm plump hand of the UMass dean simply went straight through (I suddenly saw the fine raindrops on my own suit as the skin of a black cobra) his rosy cheeks suddenly shone out before me and he immediately understood everything don't think you can fool him his forefathers bought molasses in the West Indies by the ton used it to make rum which they sold to Africa in return for slaves which they then exchanged for molasses the

dean smiled in the rain (on behalf of my late colleague as I later learnt)

he talked about the footprints filling with yellow water while the mud squelched under our heels as in the streets of the eighteenth century into which I sank at his handshake as if beneath the mud of whisky and self-pity there were a layer or sphere of a paler calmer gentler world in more subdued shades whispering in softer voices a world of ghostly easy movements the

past

which until then had seemed motionless and inaccessible to me that still peaceful weak still dreaming still thoughtful Germany of minor and minuscule states pretty well squeezed between the cynically gay Prussian boot and the heartily high-Catholic iron tits of the Habsburg mother for me that pipe-smoking contemplative Germany that was only forced to wake up by the harsh fall and cut of the guillotine became a manageable expedition area I found myself by getting more and more lost in it and I took on something of dead old Sigi Ramsauer's gnarled calm at times a kind of premature lignification from which I slowly began to put out leaves again

the past is astonishingly

healthy·

said the dean beaming as if the Germany of Kaiser Wilhelm and even that of Hitler and Goebbels had changed back into its friendly confused puberty full of geniuses and those who behaved as if they were after the years I'd spent at Amherst College the everyday surroundings of UMass helped me find my way back into reality a fat ordinary street cat lying on a low hill a few massive office towers a sad artificial lake the old chapel the massy concrete Fine Arts Center I lectured

on Hölderlin and Goethe went to Frankfurt and Weimar published articles again was invited to give papers at Luisa's suggestion didn't write *Goethe's Lovers* but *Loving Goethe*

don't just talk about women get inside them lend them your voice after all there was a time when you wanted to be a writer dump your footnotes in the wastebasket and talk to me if you think you might need information about the other planet on your pillow and thus it started all over again the game with

women life time

against the shame or embarrassment of adopting female voices against the powerful hypnosis of the twentieth century against our fear of a free unprotected narrative (somehow feminine?) language against (male?) whisky

after all you've brought up a daughter you know how a female human being grows up (at least in principle and in one example) and what a woman is (the professor places her warm ankles on my back)

America became aware of itself

at the time of Goethe's lovers

just imagine riots in Boston with his Friederike from Strasbourg (a lively pastor's daughter dragging a *Stop Bush's War* placard through a cloud of tear gas) come to the Tea Party with Lotte cutting the bread surrounded by her brothers and sisters (get away before she turns the knife on you) his affair with Lili from the banker's family in a Continental Congress Hotel in Philadelphia she gives herself to you openly freely threatening you with a life that is whole

so off you go in the year of the Declaration of Independence to Washington/Weimar to pale Frau von Stein the lady-in-waiting who at 33 has already had 7 children and has handed them over to someone else to take care of and is now suckling you instead of them with her pale milk without ever finding fulfilment with you she then politely avoids you after 50 years' acquaintance with her funeral procession once you ran away from her to Italy finally (at 37) to find a taste for the Young Beautiful Coarse Direct Woman 10 years after Independence real war and real peace with Christiane until the next war there's a Dorothy in the Grass Roots Kindergarten (University of Massachusetts Child Care) who three times a week gives Professor Lechner coy and satisfied smiles as if her work on her freckled statue were the cause of his panting excitement to be in the game always means to sense within yourself the ability to play other games for two years (the mud years from which the dean pulled me out by submerging me into the campus pond of UMass) I didn't look at women at all at 46 and at 47 I'd quit until at a stroke I sobered up and was once more so full of the joys of life and sociable that Sabrina came to live with me to graduate from the high school in Amherst instead of on Long Island

Suleika never consummates her love with Jussuph we are

(fortunately)

not Goethe and Marianne we have so much less of the special torment of creativity and so much more of happy ordinary experiences (Luisa tall and calm among her sweating students explaining Spanish grammar and Latin American fiction tapas and fino on the porch she shoves me out with her knees when Sabrina arrives with David drives my Ford four streets away we're in more of a hurry than the young ones we have I think a stronger and clearer presence in the here and now)

the sultan against his will feared women just as much as he needed them which is what made him think of the Orient (stifling patriarchal air in the men-only cafes)

I run at the moderate pace of a horse-drawn carriage it will be 130 years and only with the help of the United States before the Germany of 1815 will develop a stable democracy following two wars with slaughter on a scale that would perhaps have been inconceivable even to Napoleon Bonaparte who in that year had just fought his last battle and the star of whose *Légion d'honneur* the old man used to wear when he emerged in the afternoon in his dress coat to unbend in the Gerbermühle near Oberrad on the Main he has just been accepted into the Order of the Mad Privy Councillors for his *Orientalismum occidentalem* he looks out from the west window of his corner room in the former mill across the River Main to Frankfurt then goes panting down the stairs 66 years old toothless but slimmer once more bent forward his eyes almost black his mouth sensuously curved at the corners the upper lip sunken he is given a turban of Indian muslin two baskets of exotic fruit a wreath of wild flowers with some lines by Hafiz and later in the evening he reads from his *West-Eastern Divan* and is alarmed at Marianne's bayadère song (death by fire I bear you in my arms from the fire up to heaven the substances that transform a human body into a flame a thousand times faster than tinder

are yet to come)

and soon begins the lyrical dialogue with the actress' daughter the little well-built 30-year-old ex-adopted daughter now wife solicitously entertained by her husband the ex-banker with confused artistic ambitions

Suleika

Present in everything, at once I recognize you

lives on

and if I speak the hundred names of Allah

as Marianne

in ev'ry one resounds a name for you

still as a feisty old lady writing poetry (though never again of Suleika's quality) strumming her guitar (which she could play well nothing's easy Sabrina says) only a year ago I was sitting with Sabrina and Luisa under a chestnut tree outside the Gerbermühle that had been rebuilt in a plain and non-historical style our relationships with women alone can't take up the whole of our lives the old man said in the carriage to Heidelberg they lead to complications that get out of hand to torments and suffering or ultimately to complete emptiness

all those women pseudo-nuns maternally frigid coarse as dairy maids artistically inclined always running away from an equal partner

out of cowardice Luisa says out of cowardice and good sense I say how can you become Goethe if you have to marry Lili Schönemann when you're only 25

at a slow horse-drawn-carriage pace I run round the sports complex that is still completely deserted in the morning air in the summer it only livens up in the afternoon but then in such a concentrated and energetic manner with hundreds playing football and baseball (men's and women's teams separate) filling one pitch after another it's enough to frighten the life out of you but that's the way it is with all large-scale sporting facilities (which I've always found repulsive and that in every country) while here we're trying to arouse their interest in education *we live in the heart of America's education state we stand for freedom and enlightenment social justice and personal responsibility this is where liberal arts education started—and where it's going this is*

Massachusetts

I'm overtaken at a brisker horse-drawn-carriage pace by a model athlete with a ponytail and bare torso I can hear the iron-bound wheels on the bright dry asphalt Baghdad is still far away (the thunder of hazy six-lane Rashid Street jammed with hundreds of rusty dented cars reluctantly driving at walking pace red double-decker buses pulling out into the middle of the stream pedestrians going in all directions rolled-up carpets furniture domestic appliances earthenware cardboard boxes of clothes piled up on the sidewalks water and ice-cream vendors shouting women hurrying past in white head-scarves and cotton dresses or in jeans and pullovers or covered in black abayas) the carriage doesn't need gasoline in 1815 the oil lamps still used fat from whales which will only be saved by kerosene near Kirkuk among the grazing herds of sheep fire almost unused flares up out of the ground the fiery furnaces of the Bible into which Nebuchadnezzar used to throw prisoners still yawning wide

the butterflies of the dead women flutter ghostlike round me

attracted by the flame of Hafiz

I feel nothing I run I'm here in the middle of my times

as if

in my sleep

Hafiz

there are things I can tell you about him but I won't manage to make it a nice story it's

like a false or falsified

interlacing of time and space (we're used to every kind of falsification we read Orwell as instructions for use of the television and as a signpost to the kindergarten) flights of poetic fancy and the best of intentions end up sinking in the morass of the marshes where the Tigris gets bogged down in troubled dreams as twisted and tangled as you are yourself in the reeds and marsh grass of your reflections realizing that the time must come when you'll have to record and evaluate your whole country your state even if you never wanted to in my

sole and real life

I did once actually end up in the marshes but it's better if we meet in anticipation of the area just a little to the south in the paradise near al-Qurnah where the Euphrates and the Tigris join in the Garden of Eden as if the old fish near Baghdad had managed to escape the chefs cooks bakers and barbecues

by taking a 1,000-kilometre flight (let's enjoy the view across to the grandiose folds of the Zagros Mountains)

a fish can fly a long way in Iraq

when the grenades explode or a fat 100-kilogramme gittan along with its personal chef boards the PRESIDENT'S AEROPLANE to hurry over to Paris where flanked by personal guards in sunglasses it will roast over the open fire in the kitchen of a first-class hotel in the traditional Iraqi way for the French PRESIDENT who is delighted that he has sold our DEPUTY (still Nebuchadnezzar's Tamburlaine's Napoleon's Hitler's and Stalin's deputy here on earth) a little nuclear reactor guaranteed for peaceful purposes alone

just as he did 20 years earlier to his Israeli friends who five years after the barbecue party in Paris blew up the lovely new Iraqi reactor but

that's a long time ago another 20 years which of course means nothing in the bloody pulsating avalanche of humanity since

Adam

his tree stands in al-Qurnah here you can take us old fish out of the Tigris and the Euphrates at the same time out of the sluggish glassy surface of the confluence over which pitch-black boats glide here they fish with five-pronged spears sticks of dynamite or hand-grenades so we fly at best in one piece across to the big tree standing stiff and askew withered and bare of leaves hemmed in by stone flags falsely praised by Satan as giving unending dominion but granting knowledge bringing expulsion threatening with blindness all who seek immortal dominion on the Day of Judgement (Saddam my torture-lover: the angel's red-hot iron!)

the dead tree of immortality once it was green it had no snake in the Koran and the woman did not seduce Adam but simply ate of the fruit together with him

though we do not know whether SPEECH here is behaving like a gentleman or whether even at this stage Eve had no say in the matter

perhaps it was green with an Arabic double treble meaning here my Brother there's always something between true and false and there's a story to that

kan ya ma kan . . . It was and it wasn't . . .

a story like the one of our life in which immortality slips away first unnoticed but then slamming the door

once the tree was green and that means Shahrazad can tell the story of the merchant's youngest son and the well-read nursery-school teacher

Farida

lifts up her face in the hot dusty spring in Baghdad unveiled 20 years old

her eyebrow cuts him to the heart

years in the dawn light

vehement silence paradises biting their arms and smelling of musk and oranges how can I put it Brother I cut up my first corpse in the anatomy lecture theatre and became half religious for the Prophet says that marriage is half of religion (he himself was therefore at least a sixfold believer) I fell into that unconditional imprisonment that was my sole and greatest liberation

DESTINY

Your sleep—more joy than I can bear,
    Softly I your cheeks enfold,

Let the tresses of your hair
  Bind me in their handcuff hold.

I was captive all my life,
  Only dying on my own,
For in any paradise
  We will ever be as one.

that's just kitsch of course but for many months I was lonely as a dog in camps barracks military hospitals in retrospect however it's that first year in Paris that seems the worst the year without Farida when I was living in a tiny room with Hussein struggling with the languages the nasal academic whine miles above my head in the lecture theatres my tousled snotty-nosed *Petit Larousse* gabble dashing after the quick blue people in the street the tiny but imperial clockwork Latin of the atlases of human anatomy the first specialist articles in English which seemed sober and soothing like a nanny washed in palm soap by day my Arabic blew away like a design drawn in the sand yet returned with force in my dreams among Hussein's oil-paint ghosts (burning Daliesque camels under the Eiffel Tower portraits of rulers with maggot-eaten faces)

then when spring returned Farida came to Paris after I'd found a flat in the 20th arrondissement where I became the thin Iraqi with the thin wife swotting up physiology with plugs in my ears between thin walls among phlegmatic Senegalese Moroccans with permanent erections and extended Algerian families

the world turned upside down

hardly were we back together again than we got caught up in a demonstration sprayed away with water cannon we were standing outside the Quartier Latin where the students had erected barricades when the police attacked at two in the morning our Arab fear told us they would immediately begin shooting with live ammunition we overreacted to many things and took others too seriously our political scales needed recalibrating from a distance the Baath revolution seemed almost like something happening outside the Sorbonne or in Berlin or Berkeley but we should have known that at home they settled things differently

but already in our blossoming spring

in our deeper powerless more intense life we had been warned and marked when I was 17

as old as Muna is now it would seem infinitely far off today if I could see my youthful figure emerging from childhood in a serious and comically dignified way there among the old men in their dishdashas watching a television in a night-blue cafe on Rashid Street on the screen the body of the president is placed on a chair the camera zooms in on the bullet hole a soldier grabs the head by the hair and spits on the dead face that once painted on red and blue balloons sailed down from the sky to us children the face of the Iraq-first-and-foremost man

Abd al-Karim Qasim

the old men

didn't bat an eyelid I saw the unmoving folds on my grandfather's cheeks neck forehead as if he'd been transformed into a stuffed camel arrogant and cruel as a result of the decades spent studying all those volumes in his house I thought but he had just long since protected himself with a leather binding even his face was closed as if with a flap like the edges of the old copies of the Koran from Africa he possessed the point was to make himself impervious to fear not to react to the horror not to yield to the

theatre of cruelty

whether it was performed in the black and white of the electronic tubes or in the blood-red ochre of unbelievable reality it was years later that we saw

the hanged men in Tahrir Square

on a television in Paris the same wobbly discoloured hand-held-camera pictures as the reports from the war in Cambodia in the window of a shop by the Gare de Lyon flanked by screens on which Asterix the Gaul was fighting as if our country existed on a murky joke planet on which people still really died which was why it wasn't shown so clearly for example the incredibly stretched necks as if in a comic strip of the conspirators Zionists of course the bridge appeared that we'd crossed countless times to get to Liberation Square where supposedly tens of thousands had gathered summoned by radio transported there in buses to enjoy the celebration

just the prelude said Ali just a few spectacular picnic-murders for the people what we don't see is far worse Ali whose elegant pharaoh's head on the lean torso of a man in his mid-20s wearing a T-shirt and Levis is somehow a comfort as if all possible times could be reconciled with one another and touched like a friend since 1968 the PARTY had ruled and things were veiled with images

veiled with words

Instrument of Longing Ministry of Public Relations Special Services in
our country death had set up a palace which stood for the lust the ostenta-
tiousness the ornamental luxury the gluttony and excess of murder

veils of forgetting of disbelief of longing of hope of blind faith

I kept having to remind myself how we

after seven years in Paris (four years after the lynchings)

could go to Orly Airport in the summer of 1974 to set off home

Farida six months pregnant holding a scuffed leather suitcase in a blue
coat a white hair-slide 25 years old so strangely

unassailable absolutely calm

so confident that nothing would ever happen to us (to the three of us)
that's just the way it was I can't explain it we were just innocents with our
stupid belief that the world was our oyster still unbroken innocents with
not yet 30 years behind us rashly trusting in our own strength my scrawny
Tariq-self newly certified like my childhood friend Ali who wanted to work
as a paediatrician in Baghdad as well it was (among the noisy children the
Iraqi women still in their Parisian get-up the pyramids of suitcases packages
bundles tied up with string and rendered unrecognizable with plastic and
sticky tape like torture victims no just protected against bumps bundles of
valuable finds from forays in supermarkets electrical shops furniture stores)
the time of money spurting up out of the earth in black jets of the heroically
nationalized oil industry of the great lottery prize of the OPEC boycott of
the modern apartment blocks motorways schools nurseries hospitals beautiful tanks from the USSR everywhere in Iraq people wanted to

believe

there had been a little lying-censorship-torture-murder temporarily
clouding the picture distorting the prospects but the path was the right one

perhaps

heading towards a country that had thrown off colonialism overcome
self-paralysis found a position between East and West socialist-Arabic-
Kurdish-Sunni-Shiite everything balanced out ground down to butter up the

party faithful

it would recivilize itself since it already bore the oldest civilization within
itself and had invented the wheel and writing it would be quite individual

and yet like France and display domestically the same civilized polity (forget Algeria) that we had had the opportunity to experience one day the child in Farida's womb would study in Paris (a telling erroneous belief) to acquire foreign experience perhaps only for a year

if I

have to find reasons arguments grounds in the jostling crowd at the check-in counter with *Baghdad* above it a word whose normality will one day be as inconceivable as the stupid pride which turns Ali and myself into beaming newly qualified doctors returning home then it was simple powerful reasons with no questions that took us back to the place we came from my country my home town my infirm parents Farida's country Farida's home town her widowed father the graves of all her relations in Najaf and Karbala and the confidence of my own prophets standing before me in cheap winter coats

Ali who was returning home with me was the only one who was really interested in politics had argued through the night with Nasserists communists Baathists

Hussein who had decided to stay with his French wife in the city that had everything (all the surfaces) painters needed was so easy to understand that the separation seemed quite natural more natural anyway than if we had all three taken the same flight home

we fastened our seatbelts people stopped smoking I wondered not worried not really concerned whether one of the books I had packed among my clothes represented a danger (I had the answer and still have it today: I wanted to be a doctor in Iraq and nowhere else)

and could already see as if the flight had hardly lasted an hour the countless diamonds of light studding the smoky veil of dusk over Baghdad

Not a cloud in the sky

   when I look out of the window the day's drifting

   towards the sea the house feels as if

   it were moving with me as if I didn't need to go anywhere to arrive Eric

   I think

   would just have to live here with me and I could stay in East Hampton
too year after year as what wouldn't matter but now I'm packing the blue
rucksack I bought together with Martin in an outdoor shop near Springfield
before we flew to Europe the dust of Berlin Frankfurt Munich Florence
Rome is still sticking on the outside to its synthetic pores I only need summer
clothes for two weeks for

   life

   in California a pullover perhaps I can borrow one from Amanda I'm
already standing at her large wardrobe as if it were in an actress' dressing
room and I can see my mother in her swiftly almost seamlessly changing
roles

   suddenly so close

   I feel that I could put her on like a coat and to make it in her harsher
more serious glittering world it's an illusion right away I can hear her low-
ered voice not even unfriendly bored rather (walk—stand up straight—don't
stay in the corner all the time—relax and open your mouth) I can never get
so far forward within myself

   as if

   you could go up close to the surface of the window into the light the
way you can in this summerhouse

   there's something

   in me of the energy that carries Amanda light as a feather from one role
to another I will perhaps after all learn to be wide awake in the middle of
the day (as she's always demanding I be) I could take the money for the journey from the secret drawer in the kitchen and leave a note but I want to ask
her straight out I want to go through her reproaching me for missing the
first week at college will it just be

she'll ask me (blue suit starched blouse string of white pearls perfect hairdo)

these two weeks in Los Angeles

for that's my own question since she demolished the garage of the neighbours across the road with her sports car (that of a senior police officer of all people) whether it might get more serious I have a physics book in my hand with my rucksack still open I have to do some serious thinking after all that's what I was looking for at MIT this other determination (no designer clothes and pinstripe suits nor professors with mustard-coloured cord jackets and leather bags full of books pedalling their black bikes) to understand the world as a geophysical system as a climatic system as a planet in the cosmos

the boundless blue over the beach

as the scene of the clash between the atmosphere the mainland and the ocean go to lectures read geophysics geochemistry I have to enrol for 'Differential Equations II' and 'Non-linear Dynamics I: Chaos' and register for the trip towards the end of the year

the physics book sinks back down onto the table and with the relief the scruples also appear I have to

break away this is just a holiday and a love and a

question

how it began with *National Geographic* magazines with increasingly substantial tomes (sections of the earth's crust relief diagrams of the seabed the air marbled with isobars) that stay open for a long time at a single page larded with formulas and diagrams and

soothe

me it's more like a meditation on a short text it's not piles and piles of books as in Martin's study or the serried ranks of Amanda's files quickly taken down consulted and replaced in their proper order it earned their respect when I sat quietly at a table with the Earth or in the garden but

no longer

together with them

in Amherst it was my father alone who would commend me when he came home from work surprised to find me not listening to music or reading novels or writing poems in my notebooks the kind of thing expected of me as the daughter of a literature professor but

Shahrazad's father

was a vizier a kind of politician that is more someone like Seymour (the advisor) who's only too pleased when he catches me doing geology and wants to have scientific discussions with me with the result that I (automatically by now) turn into the Arabian princess stare at the floor go into my room switch on the TV and fish out some poems switch off the TV the white land of paper to which I flee

(in which I

appear

coming from above

in strangely meandering rivers of ink) I quite often write on the PC as well the white surface the embossed print the hum of the hard disc while I'm looking for words for a protective cushion when you enter the void so I'm

a poet by the sea (come off it: the stubborn princess who's looking for rhymes)

or the shy daughter

who's perfectly capable of jerking off a panting boy

coming from the Jones Library where I spent so many childhood afternoons clutching a scientific tome as a breastplate for two whole years after I went back to live with Martin I walked through Amherst so sure of success as if it were a kind of

paradise

the point of a permanent auspicious departure that is where you could

stay forever would like to get stuck forever strolling forever down Amity Street to the junction of Main Street and North Pleasant Street through the groups of boys from UMass from Hampshire or Amherst College gathered outside the copy shops pizzerias bookshops parting them like a seahorse going through a nervous coral (I'm not going to touch you again Robert forget it)

one year with a steady boyfriend

the last year (my eighteenth) without David was even better because I stayed in order to go and could make myself taut like a spring

or a nun (Joan of Arc) for 13 months I kissed no one

at least in the awareness of my imminent departure I became much more energetic and lighter (like Martin after he took up jogging again) brighter in my inner self if there is such a thing but you can see the radiance in others as well I was free because I was going to college in Boston in the near future I no longer wanted a boyfriend with a shared room somewhere in a residence hall here (and who then left with no regrets and so coldly I could have slapped his face to go to Texas near where his parents lived with a bigger scholarship) I no longer wanted to be

the professor's daughter that people in the surrounding colleges were already expecting all those teachers who sat me on their lap at the cocktail parties and got me to speak German like a doll with a built-in language module

I didn't want to think about Emily any more either in my last year in Amherst I hadn't been to the Homestead or the Evergreens at all and had only once gone to her grave the idea that I used to like

to work unseen

to write 1,700 unpublished poems as a letter to the world after your death and to live in a house in West Massachusetts as if it were standing on a grass-green little meteor in the

cosmos

of time you don't feel

I don't feel

enough when I'm not moving not travelling not knocking into things and seen from that point of view it was (and it will have been) to my advantage that they tore out my roots when we came back from Paris I began to bleed on Long Island in New York City in

my mother's gardens

there is no soil for me but it (the blood) was a sign of growing up of becoming a woman I found the

restless poem

by Hafiz

black water camels forever on the move the jingling of morning bells pilgrims with no goal

which I actually only read to impress my father and because the Arabic script in the bilingual edition seemed so mysterious there were too many goblets too many taverns too many drunken nights in it

the intoxication of despair

could well be great music but not for 17-year-olds who realize that life for them is not that bad I didn't want to stay in Amherst and become Emily Dickinson it was clear to me that I had to abandon the Arab princess

I stuck two suitably Eastern postcards (a woman singer and a middle-aged man in a burnous drinking wine) on the cardboard box containing my poems and left it behind in Amherst

anyway in this room here on Long Island

the scene of my intoxicating despairs in my thirteenth and fourteenth year

I was only a visitor the rucksack's only half as heavy as it was for our trip to Europe I sometimes used to sit in the living room with the picture window looking out onto the sea and the dunes listening to music and once I came to with a start simply dazzled by happiness because as if by accident I'd sat completely calm and free beside my mother Amanda for half an hour

Eric's sure

to be on time

HEGIRA

Leave your house, tear up your book. And go.
Destroy the things you know and love. And go.
Your heart has broken out so burn it up, and go.
Your god has lost his name, so kill him then, and go.

On the scarred whitewashed wall of the old cinema

the PRESIDENT

has been fading for years right by our school his moustache is frayed and his left eye looks as if it's gradually being eaten away by some disease

but whenever HIS name is uttered

we clap

we sing it every morning lined up in our blue dresses and white blouses he is our father the terror we must worship whose name we only sing never speak it never crosses our lips when neighbours when friends when Yasmin and her husband are visiting us we say nothing about the

PRESIDENT

I'm losing my sister I miss

language I would go mad

with staying silent if I didn't have Huda and Eren behind the ochre walls of the school the entrance to which is so close to that mural (one of millions) every evening on television HE wishes us

GOOD NIGHT

as a threat Tariq says to stop us waking up in his country look at the horse he's sitting on they've chloroformed it so that it can bear him with a wave the PRESIDENT rides off into the sunset that means to the west Tariq says for tonight he's going to take his wife on a shopping trip to London he's been talking to me like that since I was 16 and it frightens me and makes me proud twice a year Uncle Munir comes to see us he's the one who's carried on grandfather's electrical business and he goes over every wall and every cupboard with mysterious devices he's looking for ears we can do that Tariq says a family with built-in danger sensors so he can carry on expressing himself as freely as he likes and making me proud and sad alarm and torment me with his jokes and his despair until Farida tells him off (because of Sami she can sense that he needs his father's strength and composure more than I do)

the dusty mosaic in the inner courtyard of the school showed the Thames and Big Ben on the wall opposite is the shining mosaic twice the size in which Saddam as a member of the fedayeen in a red-patterned headscarf and magnificent robe is swinging Saladin's scimitar at the terrified faces of George Bush and Margaret Thatcher for this is the former English Girls' Grammar School though in the last 15 years it's had three different names and three new headmasters and now even for the senior classes there are only two English lessons a week we should only understand the minimum necessary about

the ENEMY

for the mosaic the parents whose children wanted to stay at the school made a voluntary donation of two million dinars

I breathe

more freely when I see Huda and Eren the benches in our slowly deteriorating classrooms are so old that Huda found her mother's name carved on one the blackboards have had cracks ever since an American bomb landed by the cinema destroying a bakery killing eight customers because they were buying bread against America

when Yasmin maintains that Iraq must defend herself I wonder if that means boastful mosaics cemented on the wall against bombs being or the chance of being dragged into bed by the army in your family home at any time I'll talk to Eren about that only to her she's the only one who can hold her tongue like me her long white neck with the little birthmark just above her collarbone turns in the open collar of her blouse vulnerable and free but Huda will probably say

if she wanted it and if she's willing

staring at me as she speaks with her Indian eyes gradually raising her brows by fractions of an inch until I go bright red and we burst out laughing but I couldn't bear it in this case can't bear it any longer because I'd had to bear the Major in my role as the shadow

of my sister

nailed to the floor

calm down during Mr Baram's maths lessons from tatty 20-year-old textbooks he was a new teacher at the school when we were in third year and introduced himself with an amusing problem: *If a Hussein rocket shoots down a fully manned American spy plane how many Americans will be killed?*

die of boredom in National Determination lessons

we know all that already from the TV programmes that Tariq hates but always leaves on so that we can learn to see through the pictures through the flickering snowstorm of half-truths and lies so that we can talk quietly with the window open after all I am a TV doctor Tariq says since his father paid for his studies by selling radios and later TVs

we see pictures

flung shamelessly and uninhibitedly into our living room as if by a storm raging in the past and swirling tirelessly the blood-soaked bodies of Palestinian families the mutilated heroes of the Gulf War the mountains of corpses of those massacred in the Sabra and Shatila refugee camps the children of our own country maimed misshapen with huge heads and quivering dolls' arms swollen bellies grotesquely twisted legs open wounds that refuse to heal children crippled by the radiation from the uranium in the warheads of the American rockets that landed by their homes when they were still in their mothers' wombs the hatred that struck them even before they were born

Embargoland

is running out of steam the lives of further thousands of children were lost and OIL FOR FOOD couldn't bring them back to life nor the fact that they had only been half killed because the unmerciful madness of the PRESIDENT murdered their other half

is that not all true then I ask outraged

when there's no struggle for truth

there's no truth Tariq says

I wish for a ship

our ship

Sister like Noah's Ark or the great sailing boat of Utnapishtim that escaped from the Flood so we can escape from the waves of fire from the violence together with all the maimed undernourished emaciated terminally ill children we will fly on clean white cool beds up into

the land that

has never existed anywhere or perhaps it has

is it not the case that the man from the Baath Party who sits behind the television set in the school hall trying not to tire as he stares at our faces can see through our skulls as if with

uranium eyes

my sister Yasmin

knows something about radioactive decay about decay in general a sailing ship would be more reliable than the electricity supply the emergency lighting suddenly going out the television pictures imploding the refrigerators silent as so often

when there's a power cut the curtains open again the noonday light falls on the scuffed avocado green of the walls within which we're sitting as if in an aquarium that no one wants to clean any more in our spotless white blouses and carefully mended blue dresses we breathe a sigh of relief for perhaps we would have had to watch the six-hour-long film about HIS early years again *The Long Days* in which HE doesn't bat an eyelid when without anaesthetic the bullet is removed from his leg that (according to Uncle Munir) was never in it

no electricity no water for hours on end often in several districts

the English lesson with Mrs Jadallah who began wearing a headscarf two years ago and who speaks more and more quietly as if she's gradually disappearing all the time her whole manner is like an apology for just

existing

in the last lesson Uncle Mahmud with his resolutely friendly manner his attentiveness to each of us his persistence and precise clockmaker's patience tries to give us a feel for the old High Arabic poems as if a fine priceless piece of silk were going through our hands or as if we were allowed to take miracle drugs in public in the heat of our classroom our thoughts our concentration evaporate Huda's fanning herself with a volume of poetry I can go home with her this lunchtime perhaps even go to see her mother in the National Museum we're already

going out through the school gate arm in arm past the one-eyed PRESIDENT into the afternoon oven of the city with the same white slides in our hair

in the old red double-decker bus that perhaps once drove London more than half the women are wearing abayas *BMO—Black Moving Objects* Sami says the big international hotels (the Sheraton the Palestine Meridian) are on the right then the luxury shops next to them judder past battered red-and-white taxis overtake a Mercedes brand new but somehow unbelievably covered in dust as if for the background to a film we lurch against one another in the sweat of the crowd Huda's Indian eyes roll when the men's eyes alight on us or they deliberately let out loud sighs sometimes she gives me a push to let me feel her breasts her hips just as the boys show one another their arm muscles in our pinafore dresses and sweat-stained white blouses we're Leila and the Wolves I think anyone who plays with them needs the nerves of steel the intelligence the boldness the arrogance

of my sister

we get out at Ahrar Bridge on the right are the old mosques and the Assyrian and Chaldaean churches amid the great souks that we sometimes wander this evening Huda wants to buy a bracelet for her cousin's birthday but we'll go across to the Karkh side and treat ourselves to a sherbet Huda says something I shouldn't actually do if I listened to my father who's always giving me lectures about the millions and millions of microbes in water ices but I've survived lots of sherbets so far

on the bridge the hot breath of the exhaust fumes blowing against our bodies is pushed aside by a fresh wind over the Tigris and I suddenly feel as light as air as if I could fly if I wanted to my Flight Simulator is my head if I just close my eyes for a few seconds the balustrade against my hip is the railing the sea is below me I think that will stay with me for ever

the dreams the pictures the quiet

hurry up they're already honking their horns like mad the old goats Huda says and we walk faster

Outside the Gerbermühle

    in the summer of 2000

    the beer-coloured tables and wooden benches under the old trees beside the River Main they're talking about restoring the building which was rebuilt as a faceless cube in a historically accurate or at least more accurate style (will they bring back the mill-wheel refurnish Willemer's study tune Marianne's guitar and hang it on the wall with pink ribbons attached) there's Äppelwoi the local cider Wiener schnitzel potato salad beef roll stuffed with cabbage there is a

    degree of reality against which

    thought is powerless (and which once there it cannot erase either) for example the absolutely spooky idea that we're now living in the third millennium (the West and the world that goes by its calendar) as opposed to the double reality of Sabrina and Luisa laughing and shaking their heads as they study the menu on the bench opposite me underneath a blue-and-white sunshade completely disparate unrelated in their external appearance so that despite the difference in age the intimacy of their gestures the closeness of their bodies hardly anyone would imagine they could be mother and daughter and the three of us a family although we mostly speak English unless Sabrina happens to read out a German expression she's unfamiliar with from the menu (*gri Soß*) and gives me a questioning look

    the fact that they don't belong together pleases me it seems to offer the best chance of a good life together Luisa (blue-black hair pinned up broad face glowing Goethe-eyes—I think here—long neck over a heavy white bosom) could be taken for a Spanish relative or a teacher of this young American who with a loose sand-coloured blouse light-brown summer slacks her hair which keeps falling over her face tries to make herself as inconspicuous as possible with the modesty or natural defensiveness of young people who don't want to be

    dragged into the light

    the flashlight fire destroying any individuality any remaining humanity

    the small nose the shape of the forehead anyone can easily see us as father and daughter it will not be possible

to save her by forgetting our resemblance

Sabrina still can't believe she really has put high school behind her that we are actually on the promised trip round Europe that next she's going to Berlin to meet her cousin a young woman who's older than her and with whom she can then travel on to Munich Florence and Rome

she's making herself more fragile than she is

I thought (in a still irrelevant still completely abstract moment of error)

she rummages round in my rucksack leafs through my books she's interested in Marianne as a woman who wrote poetry was strangely lost but then taken in (an actress' daughter bought from her mother) I repress the impulse to tell her how eight years after his oriental Gerbermühle days the 74-year-old privy councillor (groaning dashing off poetic notes strutting along in front of the dancers like a turkey wreathed in decorations) whose silhouette Marianne will mourn right to the end of her bloodless though not unenjoyable life brought himself to make the only proposal of marriage in his whole life addressed to a beloved of just Sabrina's age

Ulrike

fades and continues to glow as an

elegy

as the vision of a girl who turns into a young woman Sabrina's hands with the unvarnished nails leaf through the volume of poetry as a child she painted her nails red and silver and blue she was crazy about make-up and glitter in any shape or form once she painted herself as a princess with three gold teeth with gaps between them in her upper jaw

she once had just two little fillings she never had a brace she's found the poem and reads quietly and with concentration so that only Luisa and I can hear (precisely in the middle of her thumbnail is a thin vertical line a discolouration neither Amanda nor I have)

Zephyr for thy humid wing,
Oh, how much I envy thee!
Thou to him canst tidings bring
How our parting saddens me!

Now in German Luisa says and Sabrina quotes Marianne's poem in the original her eyes initially fixed on the page as if she were translating it then she at least looks at the table at beer and cider glasses the cool straw-coloured Riesling in a glass with a green stem the effect of which in my bloodstream even then seemed to take the scene by the Gerbermühle outside time (safely consigning it to memory) Sabrina continues to speak head half bowed while Luisa gives me a contented astonished generous or perhaps even (slightly) forgiving (slightly) superior look it could be that I'm refusing to see the signs of competition between my daughter and my lover Sabrina's German has almost no accent especially when she's reciting or reading something it's

my German a very personal and yet deeply general reflection in her brain for the first five years of her life she talked to me almost always in my mother tongue alone she has a father tongue she has almost every early word from me

visions

signs

green chestnut leaves falling

wasps on a receipt soaked in apple juice that lifts off the table and is now flying past towards the Main a summer-sky-blue river lined on the other side with a row of tall poplars behind which massive warehouses rise their concrete-grey facades looking oddly restrained in the brightness as if already half dissolved (as if they were already memory) on one wall I suddenly recognize an ad for Aurora hugely enlarged and pale like a photograph projected in daylight that sun on a red background which I used to see as a child on the packets of flour in my mother's kitchen

Sabrina's the first to discover the ginkgo trees in the meadow beyond the mill as we walk along the bank towards the city centre and immediately afterwards she finds a little sandstone plinth with no monument but ME in letters of gold

laughing she poses on it

we don't have the camera with us and although we think about it none of us is willing to make the short trek back to the hotel so we go on in the light of early summer towards the arches of the Deutschherrnbrücke large curved hair-slides one next to the other across the Main

behind them the modern skyline consisting of a good dozen high-rise buildings that look as if they've been hurriedly put together the tallest looks as if it's raising an arm in the Hitler salute Luisa says as if it were trying to stop the planes that are

burning

their way up into the sky Sabrina was walking well in front she was now so grown-up that even at my side she kept feeling she was the third that made a crowd and at that moment I was quite glad she was keeping apart from us because I felt the need to tell Luisa how fed up with my work I was a feeling that seemed to have grown even stronger under the trees outside the Gerbermühle it was perhaps just the tiredness which always makes your strength flag slows down the momentum lets in doubts or I was simply fed up

with Marianne

and one more silly toothless love affair of the old man

send a skin flick and a lively Istanbul girl from Frankfurt Central Station 20 years old but done up to look 17 back to him on the storm wind of time blowing out of the future

I felt as if I were myself divorced from all these women and now had to see them again individually and describe them in detail (after more than a century)

eleventh-hour panic Luisa said one night

in one of the olde-worlde double beds in the hotel next to the mill in which we were lying beside one another oddly distant under the massive duvets as if flattened by soft heavenly bodies (Sabrina in a single room on the floor below)

all this sentimental adulterated Eastern stuff this stupid dressing up as Jussuph and Suleika these false turbans these fake quotations from the Prophet scribbled Arabic maxims the sultan's hand-embroidered slippers the evergreen rubber cypress trees the coded pictures made from the bones of the poor old genius Hafiz

relax Luisa said from under her massive cloud

things'll be much easier and clearer in Granada just let yourself drift along

in the storm wind

Ach, um deine feuchten Schwingen
West, wie sehr ich dich beneide:
Denn du kannst ihm Kunde bringen,
Was ich in der Trennung leide.

The silly old joke: Shalom Moshel

my brother Munir said merrily but quietly in my ear when he embraced me at the airport in 1974 giving me a cheerful dig in the ribs before making a respectful bow at Farida's six-month belly

my life has come full circle (the iron collar you haven't yet noticed) the three of us arriving in Baghdad my lonely departure seven years ago everything going differently from the way it was planned or not depending on how you look at it

1974 arriving back

setting off in 1967 I'd done my military service in those exhausting months near Hatra in the north and then the boring time in the south beneath date palms and murals of the heroes of the revolution and colour photos of Abd al-Salam Arif the air ace who let the Egyptian eagle land on the Iraqi flag and crashed in his helicopter almost immediately after I'd been assigned to a unit of the medical corps (because a friendly colonel believed I really did want to study medicine) so I was lucky because Abd al-Salam's weak elder brother and successor immediately showed his non-existent strength by dropping bombs on Kurdish villages in the north recovering from the exertion by watching football matches on television in Istanbul hotels at least I returned from the boredom safe and sound I spent one semester at university in Baghdad

I got married

to the doe-eyed strong-willed stubborn clever nursery teacher a keen reader whom I saw once a week for five months by the bookstalls in the twisting lane of the al-Saray souk awash with paper and binding glue gold leaf ink writer's delusions philosopher's wisdom and tried not to stare at as she bought Camus and Ibn Arabi until she asked me whether we

couldn't

perhaps disappear in a book I thought

but she asked whether I didn't also think

that

our mothers ought to speak to one another

I almost fell flat on my back I was 21 (she was 19) but the

web

of love kept me on my feet without many words our looks needed no interpreter I'd spent years learning French because it had always been expected that I would go to join an influential business friend of my father's in Paris who would get me a place at university a gloomy apartment a rusty old car a wonderful young wife and perhaps even children (and from whom I did eventually take some of those things) now I didn't like that idea at all any more after that one decisive conversation with Farida in the souk but shortly afterwards my father had to tell me he was financially in a poor way since he'd invested all his money from the silk trade in a for him completely new line of business if everything went well it would be two or three years before I could go to France

that meant he had no reason to object to my immediate marriage to Farida nor did he look for any for he could see I was absolutely serious about it and have always remained so if you're lucky then it can happen that you're facing a woman and without a word everything's clear and decided on the spot Mejnun and Leila Khusrau and Shirin Jussuph and Suleika stir within you (and want your life) but I'm for

Jamil and Buthaina

who grew old in love together (after all what was the point of doing a degree one is tempted to ask in this matter)

Farida at 26 self-assured almost aggressively beautiful and perfectly calm and strong bearing concealed under her skin the fruit of our seven-year love Yasmin (who will later claim she waited in heaven for six long years before we decided to leave France and go home) floats straight back to Baghdad on our arrival at the airport in 1974 my sister-in-law Jamila takes Farida's arm my brother goes arm in arm with me how's business I ask transistors Munir says and more and more television sets but not the old tube things any more

not Nasser any more but Sadat Munir says there's lots of things different here as well

1967

radio voices

Ahmad Hassan al-Bakr Frank Sinatra Gamal Abdel Nasser Umm Kulthum

intertwined with the muezzins' calls

something was going to happen there'd be events of historical importance officers who'd only recently had to flee because they intended to stage a putsch had returned to Baghdad

we stuck together the university was a beehive newly wed and hungry for books and discussion I stumbled round the campus I wanted to learn to understand I definitely wanted to study the human body (Farida's incredibly soft white planet every night) I had immediately stopped learning French and tried to read Butrus al-Bustani and Salama Musa the novels of Mahfouz as well as Sartre and Trotsky the more recent Egyptian Marxist writers too but I was and still am pretty unsuited to politics even as a reader I don't have sufficient belief in the possibility of leading large masses of people straight to paradise on earth and all those high-flown trains of thought about nations and their destiny seemed to me like dreams

murderous dreams

of power actually I could and still can only think clearly in detail (the atom the heart the circulation of the blood friendship the structure of medical practices and clinics) or very poetically (the universe love) although I'm always making an effort and learning but is medicine science or poetry Hussein asked or perhaps rather the politics of the sick body he was probably right but I still preferred to read poems by al-Mutanabbi (and by Nizar Qabbani when my feeling of being in love was particularly intense) or the plays of Brecht that the student theatre group planned to put on before we performed quite different things

and finally

the ATTACK

in June

and on the second day of the war

MACK THE KNIFE was standing next to me in the refectory of the Medical Faculty without my realizing it that is feeling more than dislike and distaste as he pushed his way forward and bawled out that the government should not show the least hesitation the Jewish aggressor was to be crushed immediately and finally

Saddam

that one time I was as close to him as to death in the pathology lab I never thought I had anything particularly personal to do with him he had a gun in his belt he was clean-shaven a tall athletic guy he was surrounded by four or five weightlifting types and kept shouting in his bedouin dialect he was said to have bumped off a few opponents already we nodded and turned to other speakers most Baathists saw him as nothing but a brutal thug who had to be eliminated (he was the one who eliminated them) we tried to get a clear view of events through discussions with some professors and lecturers but it was pointless the turmoil drove us out into

the decisive battle against Zionism

we had Nasser

the greatest weightlifter of all the guarantor of Arab unity the leader of the Third World the shining light of the Arabs who had taught us to hold our heads high for

there was no doubt we would be victorious every day we were completely destroying the enemy four days later I was in uniform on the platform and Farida almost fainted from the heat fury sorrow I went

of my own free will

against my will that is I wanted to put up a fight I wanted to coalesce with something higher and more important and if necessary perish with it although or because I was happy and although something inside me resisted shaking its head inside my head and as if paralysed and helpless staring at the walls of my body as it rushed forward amid all the others

we had no call-up papers everything happened so quickly as the Iraqi units in Jordan were overrun many reported to the barracks where they had last been stationed to die young

as Arabs

and it seemed logical if not necessarily wonderful not to survive my friends it was my only war as an ordinary soldier I didn't even leave the barracks as contrary to the reports of triumphs from Cairo Amman Damascus

after six days

AL-NAKSA

THE DEFEAT

was certain after a further six days it was clear that the conflict wasn't going to spread and I should just go home

as if benumbed

for the first time I was met by a furious young wife (the next time will you please die because *I* tell you to) and a letter giving me a university place in Paris that I couldn't afford and

everyone still loved kept their ears stuck to bought and bought radios

raging raving wailing sets they were still roaring in the July sandstorms they'd still won

but it had been different (a genuine German BLITZKRIEG) Hussein's cousin who was living in Frankfurt wrote that in Germany they'd declared Moshe Dayan the reincarnation of Rommel

years later

after all the discussions in Paris Amman Damascus Beirut Baghdad your thoughts are clearer or only less illusory perhaps when some of the costumes and make-up in which they always keep trying to perform the successful dramas of history have disappeared while we refuse to forget that basically there's no alternative to the production and that there's no last make-up to take off no street clothes to appear as if by magic from under the last costume and certainly not the naked truth

today one could say

once there was a dream of a liberated socialist and democratic independent and united modern self-assured Arabia between the power blocks across the borders drawn without consideration by English and French colonialism it was a modern political dream inspired by Europe a kind of EU before its time without the terrible birth pangs Europe caused itself in those two wars with the immense mountains of dead that we bloodthirsty Arabs could only look on in disbelief and in which we were nothing more than a secondary theatre of war a supplier of raw materials at the mercy of forces beyond our control

that dream had

probably already died (if it had ever been possible) before the war with Israel began and now the simple fact (perhaps) was

that the Egyptian PRESIDENT (in debt up to the ears of all his subjects) was annoyed with the American PRESIDENT (up to his ears in the Vietnam fiasco) because he refused to send him any more corn for his bread since he was angry with the Egyptian PRESIDENT because of his fondness for the Soviet PRESIDENT and now the Egyptian MASSES were starving and the PRESIDENT wanted to stop their mouths by showing them that he was still thousand times greater and more Arab than the Syrian PRESIDENT and the grim KING of the Saudis (who would soon flood the stage with his oil) and therefore had locked away the Gulf of Aqaba and its beautiful oil terminal from the Israeli PRIME MINISTER and rattled his scimitar so much that the latter could not but be afraid that his country was about to be attacked or at least could convince everyone in the West that he really was afraid of that while the Egyptian PRESIDENT was probably thinking that he himself was fairly unlikely to be attacked but if he were he could perhaps even win because of the air force he had from the USSR of which the Israeli PRIME MINISTER was probably really afraid since it might possibly even destroy his nuclear reactor so that he therefore took the precaution of destroying the entire Egyptian air force early in the morning in the desert sand

the DEFEAT was painful

to the large symbolic organism of the Arabs

by showing that in reality it didn't exist at least not as a politically unanimous factor promising military success I went back to my medical studies I stopped believing in that kind of pain I believed (a few months later when the veil was lifted) in the deaths of 10,000 Egyptian soldiers who died among the piles of wreckage of Soviet tanks and MiGs I believed in the misery of further hundreds of thousands of Palestinian refugees who dragged themselves across the battlefields to Jordan many driven from their exile into exile from catastrophe into defeat I believed in the reality in the occupation of the Gaza strip of the West Bank of Sinai and that these would be festering sores

but for whom and for what kind of whom

not actually running sores for all Arabs but for the Palestinians and the neighbouring Arab states who were directly affected in the following years

symbolic sores

on the other hand for us the sore of impotence of guilt of our repeatedly injured pride the sore of our inability to help the Palestinians (right up to the present day) like that time in the overcrowded train when I accidentally trod on the hand of an old man who had suffered a heart attack and had fallen down in the crush and whom I couldn't save certainly not with my confused wish to lose my life on one of the supply lines to Syria or simply to be flung somewhere or other even though I loved Farida who was waiting for me at home furious

what I learnt above all at that time was the conjugation of impotence that is to distinguish between the impotence to destroy the impotence to avenge and last but not least the impotence to help which remains with even the most peaceable of us my silent (but final) conclusion was

that the mouths of the MASSES must be filled with bread instead of rubbing salt into their wounds

I began to believe fanatically

that one should bandage their actual wounds instead of soaking them in the blood of the enemy turning them into running sores

I was and still am full of understanding when I hear people bewailing Jerusalem of course there must come a time when our descendants can meet freely at the temple or the mosque (or none of the pains and sufferings would have been worthwhile) Jews Christians Muslims but I tell you

that nothing is right if agnostic old doctors like me can't join in as well with their entirely personal non-opinion their profound unbelief and their absolute desire for cultures and civilizations that really deserve the name

so I was benumbed as I travelled home in that train full of depressed volunteers returning from their non-war and beginning to suspect there'd been a defeat but I eventually became a doctor and I have no single experience determining that but the whole tormenting complex of that return journey will have to serve as a kind of explanation the depression the old man falling down and dying the glances out of the dusty carriage windows at the world that continued to turn and then finally a strange image somehow absolute but actually meaningless and perhaps it was that perhaps that was the sole reason why I ended up in the incurably detached state I'm still in today I saw

five white storks over the inky-blue Euphrates

motionless in the air

for one minute

like a perfect other world like something

that was here yet never would be touched something that was in a certain way final an image of

freedom or love (or of complete harmony? as on a Japanese ink painting on silk)

followed by the tiredness the dejection the feeling of shame when I faced Farida

so what title should I give the story shall we say *The Storks of Hippocrates*?

at least the radios

we sold during the Six Day War

sent me to Paris

for one year previously my father had bought five electrical shops with the whole of his capital

I spent a whole night sitting looking at a mute row of these electronic marvels staring at their polished wooden casing the veiled screen concealing the harem of their loudspeakers the ribbed knobs on the sides the glass-covered panels with the stations the ivory keys for selecting frequencies I leant down and peered through the porous back of one set and switched it on as if something could rise up from the glowing cityscape of valves other than hatred of the Israelis and the supposed Jewish spies in the Iraqi government namely an answer to the question

as to whether I should go to France by myself

for we had hardly packed our cases to go abroad as a young couple fortunate enough to make an escape than Farida's mother fell seriously ill

at the beginning of August we went for one last walk along the Tigris the radios were still raging on

two million Israelis had defeated 80 million Arabs (they wrote in the West as if we'd been fighting with rocks and as if every man and every woman and every child had taken part)

that it was the French fighter-bombers the German tanks the American guns was what we heard at home and from one of the fish restaurants we heard Doris Day singing as she did in that Hitchcock film we'd see years later together in Paris Que Sera we sat down on the river bank we were incapable of thinking or feeling clearly Que Sera was kismet an almost Muslim song it broke off almost as soon as we sat down

there's no question about it Farida said I'll come and join you as soon as my mother's better

I would go to Paris thanks to the radios

I went and because I (the youngest) was the only one who could go to university and in France at that my brothers and sisters began talking as a joke but not only a joke of my friend Moshel who had financed my study abroad

in Paris beside Hussein in our digs

I kept dreaming of the Israeli minister of defence demanding one of my eyes as his reward until Hussein cured me by drawing dozens of caricatures of me and Moshe Dayan the last and most elaborate on a large sheet showing me with my head on my desk arms crossed over it and Dayans the size of mice cats dogs swarming round all with an eye-patch some were flying round my head like bats or sitting in little Mirage or Mystère fighter-bombers (I can't distinguish between those miracles of engineering) and one had set my waste-paper basket on fire another my anatomical atlas

even seven years later it still wasn't a good joke

when Farida and I returned in 1974

we were already one war further on we celebrated the birth of our first child on the seventh day of her life I held Yasmin in my arms she seemed to weigh less than a dove I whispered her name in her ear three times (I believe in people's names) just as Farida's pious aunt had murmured the Fatiha in her ear shortly after her birth the slaughtered lamb was roasted in the inner courtyard of the big house in Wasiriya that my father had been able to extend after his coup with the radios so that there was room in it for two of my brothers and their families the three of us could have had my grand-father's house in Betawiyn but I had already leased a modern apartment at that time my father was 70 and still the great sheikh of his brothers and sisters of my brothers and sisters of my cousins who worked in his electrical shops I had to make an effort not to feel I should apologize for Yasmin's sex but he never mentioned the fact that Farida the little Shiite had landed him with a granddaughter no perhaps he was even pleased about it but above all he was pleased that I had actually come back

as a doctor in Iraq

(the land of endless medical work)

there is warmth surrounding me my brothers and sisters didn't believe I would come back and now their joy is honest I can think fear hope whatever I like I am

for the time being at least

back home once more I can feel the heat the familiar materials smell the spices walk along the Tigris under the date palms stroke the clay-brick walls the carpets the cloths wander across the bridges stroll along Abu Nuwas Street and round the souks with Farida get the feel of the cracked centuries-old skin of the city as if I were touching a mighty elephant with the smell of kebabs cardamom carbon dioxide carbide see how the modern apartment blocks the international businesses the new hotels have settled in and sheathed the home of wisdom the residence of reason the mother of the world BAGHDAD in a concrete-hard glass-hard promise for an undreamt-of future while the Volkswagens Opels Renaults even big limousines from the US are driving along its main arteries

it's the idea that what proved impossible to create for all Arab countries together can perhaps be made to work in a single country an idea for which we close our eyes and vigorously

misread

the unmistakable signs of its imminent ruthless perversion

I sense I'm determined to sense

that my great or my best time is beginning with Yasmin's wonderfully concentrated stare at the blue square of the future floating above the inner courtyard

seven years later

I felt

as if she were directing the same gaze towards me when she looked up from the football which as the fastest of the girls she had been dribbling along and saw me by the school fence

in uniform

again

COMPASS

My country lies between the millstones of East and West.
    They revolve with the power of great catastrophes
    in opposite directions,
    approaching one another inexorably.
If you go to the North, your face will vanish.
If you go to the South, death is waiting in Basra.
    Stay with me.
    Look at the stones.
    Wish for nothing.

We arrived in Granada late in the evening the taxi ride through the narrow streets and alleys seemed to me like a hasty dive through a submerged city illuminated by orange floodlights the time-lapse photography in which it was all filmed explained the miracle by which the crowd always drew back just in time then the high old walls and the magical views over the city at night

the morning light of first awakening with Luisa sliding over me her breasts fruit-heavy and dove-warm from paradise with still sleepy sighs of contentment be a garment for one another (it is said) veil silk robe fur glove black mink sliding over my stomach arching over its find a moist elastic ring amazingly cool at first but then spreading its heat the fire in our bodies flares up

clothed

in

one another

in the bright light from the window whose large heavy shutters Luisa opened even before she appeared

herself

before the gardens of the Alhambra

that we haven't seen yet that's waiting for us out there in the fresh morning air we're still lying together breathing heavily a tiny silvery bird shoots past searching for its golden tree Luisa the powerful body beside me book a room on the second floor six months in advance she says placing a hand on my navel (as if—like all those who live in paradise—I had never been born) and you'll get a genuine Andalusian woman before breakfast

the white shimmer of a network of fine lines on a round bronzed thigh

like light reflected in a pool

the miracle of still being able to love again

our hotel was part of the palace and a mosque that was converted into the San Francisco monastery Luisa has fished the hotel brochure out of the drawer of the bedside table she's very pleased with the belated heresy of our love in a former monastery amid ornate Spanish wooden furniture in a massively commodious bed in which I'm sure a Ferdinand and an Isabella must have gone about their Catholic duty of producing an heir

first of all breakfast and then the East that works much better here than in Frankfurt especially my imagination close your eyes she turns her head towards me so we're lying forehead to forehead a still happy past copy of me and this tall strong Spanish girl whose parents fled before Franco's army from Seville to Barcelona then to Paris and before the German Wehrmacht from Paris to Marseilles and Lisbon and via London to New York we met

as if rejuvenated

in the New World and now as old age appears across the horizon we're going back to be young once again in Europe or rather in the morning garden and palace of the part previously occupied by the Moors so tell me what it's like this Eastern world you wouldn't have bothered with if old Goethe hadn't forced you to with his penultimate love

(to Luisa's forehead) you mean the positive aspect the naive fantasy the gazelle in the morning breeze the djinns that dwarf a mountain and shoulder a whole town to set it up somewhere else and become powerless in a little bottle with a stopper like the past our childhood when we read about them

the absolute tyranny Luisa says the power and the celebration of it in the extravagant splendour of the palaces all those slaves servants eunuchs

the harem (I say)

all those hidden rooms corners hiding places screens caverns chests and wicker baskets clay pots that people hide in flying carpets coloured smoke terrible mutilations

Luisa remembers gigantic birds

the ever-present possibility of metamorphosis at any moment any character can receive a new destiny (merchants' sons into beggars maidens into demons kings into eagles donkeys into dogs) so that human existence blends in one single unfathomable shimmering ornament in the stonework

of time

I read the story of Shahrazad

as a child in Bremen

that exasperating barber Luisa says

who ruins another man's life with his importunate chatter is so

true to life

as is my concern my reawakened concern which I remember just as well that basically still perfectly happy worry that struck me at breakfast on the hotel patio (softly plashing fountain Moorish arcade shimmering orange trees surreal—like holograms—in the light) to be immediately discovered and exposed by Luisa who has two sons from two divorced marriages (Charles who's at university in Boston and regards me critically and Francis who might one day be a good painter if he manages to get away from the New York party scene)

she's 19 my love she's on the pill she's got more sense than my two boys will ever have between them

I can I must trust Sabrina I don't have to shut my eyes to see her in my mind's eye in Munich Florence Rome beside her cousin who's four years older she seems weightless almost ephemeral and that's emphasized by the loose long-sleeved shirts she often wears at 15 and 16 she wore short skirts and shorts and used to adorn herself with pearl necklaces rings bracelets as if to convince herself of her own youth but now

she conceals herself

her guarantee is the strength you've given her

the rest

Luisa says

is a matter of luck and back there in Granada that was a great comfort to me I thought how beautiful Luisa must have been at 18 or 19 and that she'd survived it and was now a relaxed and beaming 50-year-old full of worldly wisdom sitting opposite me out there in the gardens among the walls ruins in the palaces of the Alhambra I was overcome despite the countless tourists poured out by the busload in the inner courtyards round the basins among the pillars slaves to their camera lenses making all the scripts into pictures

the calm the silence the

light

in the myriad form of the filigree explosion of a central apogee on the ceiling of the Sala de los Abencerrajes a divine cobweb honeycomb of the angels if only the universe had such a roof

the palace

takes you out of this world

the entwined ornamentation

releases your soul

the precisely gauged watercourse in the garden

liberates you

that's what he was looking for Luisa says the exotic calm the enraptured splendour the (presumed) immutability of the old East while in Europe freedom and its daemon were toppling the thrones and making the empires tremble after 20 years of war hope defeat devastation the emperor's great boot crushes the dusty old rotten princedoms finishes off Prussia the Grande Armée sucks in tens of thousands of young men and destroys them in Russia

Battle of Leipzig Battle of Waterloo

for decades history played its bloody roulette

anyone who had been polishing the emperor's boots one day found himself having to write the hymn to freedom for the revitalized ailing old kings the next

believe in the immutability of power a non-perishable dogmatic belief that keeps having its successes to celebrate

the palace

survives

at least in this case I didn't really miss Sabrina there on that so indestructible-seeming island of the past I was perfectly happy just to be half of a pair of middle-aged lovers on the meandering path to the throne room if I'd had as much to say as outside the Gerbermühle in Frankfurt or in Weimar I would perhaps have wished Sabrina was with us but the time for giving her lectures was long since past (actually since she was seven when I realized that I could talk to her about almost anything that in the way she looked up at me you could see as in all children the powerful universal interest the guarantee of the complete renewal of humanity through human beings the little Buddha who one day will know everything with his billion-fold brain)

Goethe

should have strolled round the Alhambra instead of Heidelberg Castle during the time of his Hessian-Oriental love

Marianne

his little Blücher as he liked to call her

plucks her guitar

on his last island the GREAT EMPEROR plays with the grey wave of his dead once

he conquered Egypt woke the pyramids from their sleep (232 transport ships 2,000 cannons 32,000 soldiers 175 scholars)

the East

awoke with a groan beneath its sweltering heat its dusty palm trees its crumbling palaces in its cut-off madrasas beneath the body of the ageing Turk in

its own blood (just a graze at first)

imagine the old Goethe bent and white-haired toothless but slim once more standing upright in his brown coat

surrounded by his usual admirers and delighted experts or perhaps with only his art-expert Müller just the pair of them like us going into the Court of the Lions (carefully twisting the stalk of a ginkgo leaf between his fingers) and immediately explaining the proportions of the elegant columns that look as if dreamt up in the sunrise with their floating lace

12 lions bear the basin of the fountain in the middle three (the trinity the complete number heaven hell earth) times four (the divisible but all-encompassing number of the four cardinal points of the elements of the bodily humours) makes the 12 signs of the zodiac while the sum of the trinity and the four quarters of the compass represents the seven planets corresponding to the seven arcades on either side of the Court of Myrtles

that could have been the way he thought and held forth

or quite the reverse cursing all mathematical sorcery indulging therefore in non-quantitative reflections in the face of the lions stepping over the rectangular course of the four

streams of paradise

I remember

a few moments lasting a few heartbeats half a minute perhaps during which the two of us were suddenly alone in the Court of the Lions in the Alhambra detached from the stream of tourists a happy chance that left us (confused) alone in the sunny stone-paved quadrangle between the colonnades with pointed roofs

everything (even the fountain in the middle) is smaller (more intimate) than we had expected

more personal

as if paradise were just a hall flooded with light

with her gleaming black hair her firm bosom her red blouse her black trousers her leather shoes in which she could dance flamenco Luisa seems perfect and complete to me in the silence of the light playing on the arabesques of the capitals of the columns she's in the right place I think for one false happy moment the way you like to delude yourself about the harmony the understanding the tolerance the productive cooperation of cultures in the Andalusia of Arab rule

there is still

the palace and beneath it the sweating groaning bleeding foundations whose longings it reflects in the gold of the inner courtyard—for one more improbable moment of silence—it suddenly seems to me as if Luisa and I had a light

passing through us

(were being scanned X-rayed) that leaves no part of us hidden that flows through our cells to the painful liberating limit of transformation

refugees from the old world a couple soon tiring that had the good fortune to find one another late in life

in the light of a place where we cannot be

our only paradise

not to know yet

what is to come

All these stories you think up

Huda says

it's crazy

under your own sister's bed just like Dinarzad but there's something to
it isn't there after all your sister knows people in the army and if you work
in the oil industry

says my mother says Huda

you can't keep your hands clean the oil

gets under your fingernails round the roots of your hair runs into your
ears your nostrils into your wide-open eyes your mouth just imagine you
were a scuba diver in the oil with a pale naked body diving mask oxygen
cylinder you tell yourself the oil is plants and animals that died millions of
years ago perhaps you're diving

because you've been let down into one of the boreholes at Mosul or
Kirkuk and you (as a scientist) are to see whether there's even more even
heavier and more valuable oil deep under the last well you dive

Huda

beside me on the sofa we've taken off our stiff school uniforms now
we're wearing high heels denim skirts and silk stockings tight pullovers with
glittering threads and bras underneath them which like all these clothes come
from the regular shopping trips Huda's mother goes on to Amman and
Beirut

to console herself

Huda says we've not put on make-up today nor are we dancing as we
often do here in the apartment close to the National Museum that comes
with her mother's job and where we don't have to worry about disturbing
anyone (underneath us just the stone heads from Uruk smothered in wood
shavings in large crates those women with eyebrows that meet in the middle
over the empty sockets 5,000 years without seeing or is it the

goddess of the city Ianna herself looking inwards and sucking us
down into the abyss of early times) or exciting anyone apart from ourselves
when we sometimes spend two hours dancing jigging around jumping in
the whitewashed room with the little window next to Huda's bedroom a

room with no particular purpose because it was once intended as a rest-room for Huda's mother who however never rests our secret bare echoing club in which our walled-in heat sometimes becomes so great that at any moment you expect

SEX

in some threatening or even strangely bodiless form

at your sister's wedding how crazy did you really crawl under the bed like you did as a child or did you make that up as well

Huda wants to know we've put our feet in high heels on chairs in front of the sofa that's against the wall and stare down at ourselves as if looking into another world

I really did creep

under my grandparents' bed in their house in Wasiriya during the wed-ding though only for a few minutes when the idea for that scene came to me no one can really get inside

Dinarzad's mind

who perhaps doesn't want just to hear but to feel as well or lies there with a dagger every night and the only reason she doesn't murder the king is because like him she's become hooked on the continuation of the stories his

lurking tormented accomplice (Tell me a story Sister . . .)

the bit I like best Huda says is the bed turning into a ship and then I tear up the piece of paper on which I've written the story although Huda protests but she immediately understands that by tearing it up I'm protecting myself against everything and everyone

outside

but perhaps even more against my own boundless imagination that sometimes plagues me to such an extent that at the wedding I almost ran screaming among the guests to accuse my sister and the Major (an uncom-monly handsome couple actually) pointing to the bedroom window as if it were going on there behind the ornately carved wooden screen while Yasmin was right in front of me in her wedding dress at the side of her carefully dressed-up Qasim (the Major somewhere far away to the right with another man in uniform)

when I've

made it up it pursues me

until I tear it up

and I've read it I love stories like that Huda laughs her big black eyes sparkle her dazzlingly white teeth make me think once more of the damask of my sister's wedding gown

I almost told it to Tariq and Sami as if it really had happened I dive into the pictures (used to dive

even when I was little)

as if into the dark-green glutinous oil we're in at the moment as divers with the white beams of our torches won't it eat into

our skin

Huda asks and I imagine

just imagine Huda

that you're inside one of those huge tanks and suddenly your torch makes some sparks and quick as a flash the oil all round you bursts into flame in a white or orange ball of fire that builds up inside this cylinder tall as a house and full of shining black liquid and bursts out like an exploding sun

oh come off it it needs oxygen Huda says

shuddering she fetches our chemistry book that describes how the oxygen in the air eats its way into the chains of oil molecules splitting them so that carbon dioxide and water are produced and this immense heat (just imagine the whole tank exploding Huda one great ball of fire but you yourself but we—the divers—are unharmed at the centre of the explosion like being in the eye of a hurricane)

that's impossible ask your sister Yasmin she works in Dora and that's something my mother naturally thinks is great the reconstruction with our own means of the refinery the Americans flattened with their bombs and rockets

I think Huda's mother Shiruk's great though with a guilty conscience (which my father instilled in me no one who has a senior position in the National Museum can keep their hands clean) Huda's mother is something we women in Iraq can be could have been for things are moving back again as if everything were on a dark turntable which is moving into the past even the

PRESIDENT

goes down on his knees (on the prayer carpet) what a revolting farce

my mother cries out at the television

Shiruk is perhaps the wrong woman (but I don't care) for the right idea for what a woman can also be not

staying hidden not ground down by defeats not just clever and tired and gently dismissive like my mother Farida whom Huda respects so much because she's translated books and is such a good cook Shiruk senses that I admire her that I love it when the porter waves us in with a friendly smile through the Babylonian-palace gateway of the museum and she goes round the rooms with the exhibits and takes us to the depositories with the huge crates to the workshops to see the oddly sleepy but assiduous restorers taking a sharp look over their shoulders in earlier times she used to show whole groups of teachers from Kirkuk or Basra round and journalists from Sweden scholars from Tokyo London Berlin before we became Embargoland and Bombdroppingland and the most valuable articles were put in storage to make room for boring political exhibitions but Shiruk keeps getting back to the real function of the museum and it's her understanding her genuine expertise that so attracts me to her work and her person

at school history is often just showing off giving ourself airs

12,000 years ago

the new (the fourth during my time at the school) headmaster tells us there were just little packs of Neanderthals living in Europe Asia and the US but then it happened here (earlier than in Egypt) that *Homo sapiens* arose and invented writing the axle the potter's wheel the chariot the multi-storey building the law

an eye for an eye

carved in stone

with Shiruk it's not this boasting but reflecting a kind of alert observant going back she asks me

what's the advantage for us today that they used such a brittle porous material as clay to build with (in that way they built one layer on top of the other and we can go back in time layer by layer) she shows me a stone cylinder with a hunting relief on it and explains how they used them as personal seals to mark their sacks of grain and she wants us to tell her (Huda rolls her eyes) what it means that as has been shown 5,000 years ago there were 25 to 30,000 people living in Uruk while it was impossible that they could have lived off the yield from the land immediately surrounding the city

four languages and no husband Huda sneers

I can understand her for Shiruk's often away on business and leaves her with relatives but for me Shiruk with her elegant suits her perfect appearance her energetic manner is not at all to be pitied she's often afraid Huda says

when I'm afraid

I sometimes imagine the lions of Babylon coming out of the blue-glazed bricks of the walls on the Processional Way as if out of a summer sky and striding along beside me calm and imperturbable like glowing gold higher than my shoulders as if carved and indestructible framing me with their stone muscles at every step

you have these crazy ideas but then you want to know everything exactly Huda says as we're going across Ahrar Bridge again in the late afternoon to buy the present for her cousin in the gold market the Tigris has turned almost grey the queues of cars crawl forward as slowly as if they were actually moving on scales like snakes more honking I'm going to have to wear a headscarf after all Huda moans even if my mother hates the idea

in the souk of the smiths and tinkers a five-year-old boy is hammering nails straight on an anvil pots and pans clatter on a line above us the money changers with bundles of dinars are standing outside a small international hotel waiting for the few tourists still in the town or the UN diplomats

your sister Huda says a few streets further on calmly and softly as if another ironical remark had just occurred to her

through a swaying curtain of gold necklaces through a gap in the curtain rather I abruptly meet Yasmin's eyes looking down on me as usual she's towering above me raising her carefully plucked eyebrows slightly is it in pity or mockery you're quite pretty Huda once said to me but your sister's as beautiful as a

hawk I suddenly think

as if she were about to hurt me she's wearing a blue dress and has a white cardigan round her shoulders I believe she must weigh less than I do when I'm close to her gazelle-like body I always feel clumsy and somehow tragically slow in the look of the hawk there's

a warning a kind of

mute command

and now I understand everything for

a black hairy hand appears among the gold chains in the window too strong and brown to be Qasim's and yet so close to Yasmin's thin elegant neck (in order to put a string of pearls round it) the green cloth of a uniform the bearded face of the Major

    I dream up
    things that happen

Yasmin's hands reach through the flexible green meshes of the schoolyard fence she's just seven so too young my friend to learn about Mohammad Shams al-Din whom you call Hafiz and anyway she won't learn anything about the true causes of the war in a school in which every teacher has to be a member of the PARTY in a country whose supreme representative equals supreme commander equals PRESIDENT thinks in just the same way as it says in the furious old book of his uncle equals corrupt mayor of Baghdad

God should never have created

Jews flies and Persians

the attack on the Persians is coming now that's the will of the monster that crawled out of the belly of the monster of a PARTY with medals stuck to it as if on a green flypaper

soon he's to get a beautiful new insecticide factory from the German specialists (Leipzig toxicologists laboratory constructors from Frankfurt) he raises aloft 10,000 arms brandishing swords and can already be seen everywhere and as if definitively stuck on every wall in every book in every room on the screens banknotes the faces of wristwatches almost on the arses of the water buffaloes in the brackish canals of Basra and on every grain of the sand clouds of the yellow eclipses that engulf street after street in the summer and only cough them back up into the light of day hours later encrusted in dust

I can feel Yasmin's soft little fingers through the fence and even to myself my (still young only 35-year-old) face seems more terrible than all the fatherly faces of my childhood none of which bent over me expecting me to accept that it is now going to disappear in a war the

veils

the light white tissue over your storm-lashed face

tear apart

the flat in the fashionable new district you moved into with your family the new practice opened two years ago the club with the swimming pool Yasmin used to splash about in with a rubber duck while you had a drink with colleagues while the barbecue smoked in the background and farther beyond it the cranes raised teetering concrete girders into the distant future the PRESIDENT

was swimming in oil (that the party had finally taken away from the English to the applause of the whole country) was giving away refrigerators and television sets supplying electricity sending tractors to out-of-the-way villages stringing the communists along as partners for a socialist Arabia until he

had them strung up

the veils became bloodied at the edges keep your head down read your country's newspapers the rebirth of the Great Sumerian Empire under the true king Saddam

airports schools shopping centres hospitals are shooting up like mushrooms there are new universities already there are higher salaries for soldiers policemen doctors torturers

the best time

is the glory of the development of an Iraq awash with gold and oil and the blood of its opposition leaders

there's a

war that no one wants that at first

hardly anyone

takes seriously for Baghdad is building as if it were an architecture competition as if the mullahs in Teheran would only reply with counter building sites and try to win with the best high-rise block and the swankiest luxury hotel

we're at war

because the PRESIDENT believes that the revolutionary black birds on the Shah's razed palaces are weak a favourable opportunity therefore to settle old scores and to avenge the wounds and frights the great Persian peacock (stuffed right up to the neck with America's magnificent weapons) was able to inflict on us and expect us to accept especially their claim to Sindbad's harbour-river the Shatt al-Arab our sole access to the sea

moreover the mullahs were to be thoroughly frightened and humiliated so they wouldn't give us revolutionaries a counter-revolution and wouldn't put a bomb under our Shiites

in three weeks

the PRESIDENT told us

we'd be in Teheran

two months later I was on the back of a lorry bandaging up the first wounds (still only ones caused by accidents during the deployment) bewilderedly daydreaming that I was going to war with them heading for Sindbad's city no roc no bird that feeds its young with elephants swooped down to bear us off (we were already too skinny and wretched) away from

this game of life and being destroyed together with these still breathing still laughing smoking young men on the hard jolting floor of the lorry to which low benches had been screwed (one or the other of them was to return as a dead body by taxi in such luxury by order of the PRESIDENT whose transport fleet was running low) I wished I could see all that

from Paris on a news screen in the Gare de Lyon or outside an electrical shop full of junk in the 20th arrondissement or

from the senior physician's office in a state-of-the-art Baghdad clinic set up mainly for party officials where I might perhaps have ended up

had not Ali's friend Khalid a PARTY member and outstanding surgeon and still a philanthropist told me that my lack of interest in the PARTY was beginning to become a noose round my neck so that I immediately saw my true talent my vocation my need for direct practical work and

without delay

left the clinic to join a medical practice in which Dr Khalid Yusuf was kind enough to support me and in so doing probably saved me from a prison cell though not from being sent three times on front-line duty in the longest and most obstinate war of the century

see

Basra

once more in the twilight of its reputation as the Venice of the Arabian Gulf

and see

how

(the volumes of an edition of classics beside Abu Nuwas and Rumi beside al-Mutanabbi and Abu Ala al-Maari in my grandfather's library)

Hafiz

(Farida recounts how as a child she used to take tea dates and bread to the Persians who were camping for the night outside the town on their long journey to Najaf and Karbala with their children and their dead) dies

wearing a headband with shining embroidery his entry ticket to paradise

Mahdi give me strength—For you Hussein—Every day is Karbala

in the minefields they drank the wine of death as if they were addicted
to it

young men schoolboys apprentices

children with toys approached waving and with a laugh threw

hand grenades

until they were shot at as well grandfathers and their grandchildren as
if the gates of a terrible factory of a murky school of a gigantic prison had
opened so that they threw themselves with cries of jubilation at the barbed-
wire ramparts and waves

of humanity piled up

for the PRESIDENT

has not taken into consideration the fact that revolutions can set fire to
their children and send them out into an attacking wave of fire and blood

as long as

their time lasts the holocaust of the present for the dazzling illusion of
a better future

but the mullahs do know that and they have realized that nothing can
serve their purposes better than the crushing advance of the bloodroller

a constant stream of martyrs

outside our trenches that were like slits in the clay-yellow wilderness
through which the earth drank blood and entrails I assisted the army surgeon
I had to cut patch insert drainage tubes myself in the light of oil-lamps knees
trembling hands unaccountably steady I could see before me the pale always
just apparently sleepy toad's face of Marcel Cassin as if the angel Gabriel
had given him a video transmission channel direct from an operating theatre
in the Pitié Salpêtrière to my brain Surgical Practice I II III (Tariq! An aorta
isn't the hose of a hubble-bubble! But at least the man can handle a needle
like the generations of carpet makers before him and stands as still as a
dromedary and he's right in that Messieurs for calm is everything and a
suture is nothing less than a visiting card!) thus he was still guiding me I
had to think back (during the nights among screaming wailing soldiers) to
the bachelors' refectory of another venerable clinic where I'd seen Cassin
for the last time across the table from me and once as a satyr falling upon a

masked black woman amid other consultants immortalized as participants in an orgy painted by students who had been commissioned to do it there was a tradition of obscene

pictures

the AYATOLLAH giving a magnificent wave (see the ring on his little finger)

the PRESIDENT with a bedouin headscarf and a child in his arm

in the hospitals he's still staring at the wounds acclaiming him one day he was stuck on the lid of a rubbish bin in the operating theatre and opened his mouth for blood-soaked plasters and bandages (a little finger half a right hand)

keep your mouth shut work keep your mouth shut like the soldiers who have no physical wounds who leant in the trenches as if frozen stiff who could no longer bear seeing mountains of corpses piling up in front of them and went mad

without a sound

one of the dead (enemy dead: as if we'd still be slaughtering one another in paradise for our triumph in the next paradise) a 30-year-old from Shiraz perhaps (or from one of the other towns we'd attacked with French bombers while I with the familiar syringes cannulas bandages compresses medicines from Aventis/Rhône-Poulenc/Sanofi was trying to preserve the life of the instruments of death young men who on the orders of old men were murdering young men like that Persian shot dead almost without a mark on him) had a volume of poetry that slipped out of the breast pocket of his uniform

Persian ghazals by Hafiz and Rumi in Arabic script (think of Hölderlin and Rilke in the trenches of Verdun my friend finally we were catching up with Europe)

My Beloved is a child,
In our games he will one day
Kill me, but the law will never
Find him guilty of my bloodshed.

bleeding children with black turbans

a bleeding child in a green uniform

a nation creates the monster whose childish behaviour murders its children bleeding old men who open the trapdoors for their grandchildren

every nation was afraid of the other nation's monster that's why we fought at Khorramshahr until

the very air was bleeding

I came back I

stood at the same school fence (in disbelief like a dead man) I once more enclosed Yasmin's little hands within mine at almost exactly the same place she was given permission to go home with me instead of having to learn by heart another song to the PRESIDENT the new Saad ibn Abi Waqqas who had to defeat and convert the Persians once again after 1,300 years history always repeats itself as farce that's what I learnt (through Ali) from Marx who had no idea to what extent the farces would be able to outdo the modest originals in murderous frenzy in the July heat I took Yasmin through the building sites of a still rich hammering drilling pulsating Baghdad pulling itself up into the chaotic modern age of latecomers for which the war was something like a TV series something like a storm in another country that the PRESIDENT was suppressing quite by himself on a distant television front I was afraid Yasmin might feel the chill of death through my flesh I was sweating in the uniform of the LUNATIC whom we presumably wouldn't be able to shake off that quickly (one summer later the Shiites tried it in the village of Dujail which was then almost completely wiped off the map)

twice more I went to war

I saw

the faces eaten away by German poison gas and the half-dissolved limbs looking as if they were encrusted with mustard of the soldiers who had not been withdrawn from the danger zone of our own attack in time (soon the Iranians returned with *Made in Germany* gas masks)

when things looked bad for

the PRESIDENT and the next hundred thousand doomed soldiers (I was never wounded it was as if to compensate for the enemy in the war ministry who sent me to the front I had an invisible friend in the war who protected me there) when

THEMANSTUCKONEVERYWALL

sent tens of thousands into the marshes at temperatures of 50 degrees to cut down the reeds so they couldn't be used as cover by the enemy as they advanced (while all the time he himself was creeping around in ever new bunkers in ever more absurd new palaces) when HE sent the waiters in the luxury hotels to the front and required more overtime from everyone finally making a forceful demand for more

reproduction

for more cannon fodder

with terrible timeliness with an irresistible outburst of that mysterious strength to live that was characteristic of her Farida at 37 and 38 had children you crazy heaven-sent children as if she had made the decision to call me back to life in this drastic way or rather not to let me leave it

shortly before you were born Muna

the Americans came to Baghdad and brought new fighter-bombers for the

war of the cities

I couldn't escape I was registered I was under surveillance I was called up

Farida breastfed Muna

breastfed Sami

in the bitterness in the slow disintegration of hope you are given

overwhelmingly physical almost unavoidably absurd

two breathing screaming laughing reasons to live to heal to curse

do not heap too many wishes on the fragile body of a child it says in al-Ghazzali's book in my grandfather's library

and not too much fear Farida said

I saw the burning tankers in the Gulf the balls of fire over the oil platforms and the exotic creatures marked with green headbands racing across the burning black sea in speedboats as they sought the crossing to their promised better home the war threatened to set the whole of the Gulf on fire the fat oil barrel on which we and the Persians were murdering one another and eventually the tanks from Russia the planes from France the money from the Saudis the Kalashnikovs from Egypt the satellite maps of the CIA were joined by

the great international fleets that protected our coast and the PRESIDENT and his OILY discharge

Yasmin dragged your pram across the marble surround of the huge split blue onion that recalled the empty head of the martyr-maker and the four hands and forearms of the PRESIDENT chopped off according to sharia for stealing the lives of a million people were set up in pairs at either end of the parade ground crossing their sabres in a triumphal arch high above the middle

of our life

I let my arms drop Muna that's one way of putting it even before the end of the war I went through life through death with my arms hanging down even though I bandaged plastered sewed worked until I could have fallen asleep on my feet I didn't need to move my arms there was (still is) a kind of liberation a lightness in it the PRESIDENT brandished his sabres in celebration of his victory over his subjects with

gas

over Halabja it was only 10 years later (in Paris) that I read the details of the 5,000 Kurds murdered in one day so much

news

that didn't find its way to Baghdad to our

shabbier poorer life in which I treated shabbier and shabbier poorer and poorer patients helplessly

healing as well as I could

WATAN (HOME)

Pierce your sick heart with the ice
    Burn your bright days—you can see:
No one from elsewhere knows why
    Sorrow will not let you free.

Heat is raw cold here and white
    Blackest of nights still. And the
Noose keeps us bound in our plight.
    Run! Though you stay if you flee.

Eric

will be coming in five minutes my rucksack's already in the hall it's not heavy the course books I've left out seem to lift it up there's mostly just T-shirts and bathing stuff and Amanda's blue pullover

if Eric's on time we'll have half an hour if

I insist on taking the twelve o'clock train which I don't have to but still want to or not when I stand in front of the big mirror in the bathroom I see a slim perhaps quite pretty girl who's just become a woman who to me seems inconspicuous and severe (my tied-back hair) I sit there dreaming with my elbows on my knees and my jeans not yet pulled down beyond the middle of my thighs then I stare at my red panties as if another woman were wearing them the thin strips like wings over my skin my groin a

fire-

bird with a soft curved split

beak

I'm only bleeding a bit so

I have to wonder why I didn't invite Eric round last night after Seymour went to Manhattan it would have been the first time I'd let a boy spend the night with me here in this house and the first time with Eric but it probably wouldn't have worked (or just worked nothing more) in

my mother's house

with the garden going out to the dunes across which her lover stumbles at three in the morning (Leslie slightly drunk and drunk dry) I can't

simply can't do what

she does

Eric says and he's right but this here (the dazzlingly bright bathroom the white staircase the living room with the high picture windows my spacious sky-dungeon my pirate's nest with a sea-view) is the scene of my banishment my puberty-exile the

wooden palace to which the djinn bore me off so that I could spend two years writing poetry in the sand of the dunes and every day a thousand white dashes pauses for thought on the salty blue film of the Atlantic crying talking whispering

in the kitchen with Mrs Donally the chessboard pattern of the floor the warmth and the steady radiant artist's or film-studio light from the halogen lamps in the ground-floor room where I had my breakfast alone with the housekeeper in the mornings and sat through long afternoons and evenings

comforted calming

down more and more month by month

because I could get things off my chest or keep them to myself finally learnt to cook and had so much to tell Iris (Mrs Donally)

she's really interesting isn't she Seymour said who

by that

also very much reduced my resistance to him (my mother's second husband) he liked Iris the way I liked her when I began to understand her a robust and not at all beautiful woman whose daughter had been living in Brooklyn for ages writing crime novels while all her working life she herself had changed employer and town and sometimes even country every three years

on principle because otherwise it gets boring

(she said) a little apartment in Queens where she kept her treasures and three suitcases for her travels were enough

you don't have to be beautiful

you don't need a degree

you don't need a fantastic job

a husband a club a car a religion just

the courage to go out into the world like going into the breakers on a rocky coast it's cold fresh and not without danger but

you learn to swim

sometimes I'd like

to reach that point to be as relaxed as Iris without the need for a framework an organization a science or family living close by (move to a university in California?)

I'm standing in the middle of the living room

in jeans and a light-brown T-shirt in the black shoes in which I can both walk on the city streets for a long time and hoof it on the dance floor it's turned brighter and sunnier so that the sea and the sky look as if they've dissolved like on an overexposed photo I've never been all alone on this spot in town shoes dancing shoes a week ago Seymour had invited important people from his line of business

oilmen

who clinked their wine glasses after they'd gaped at the wrecked garage across the road (scorched earth the usual by-product of their business but here just) the result of

my mother's carelessness

a year ago

I went to Boston with my father and suddenly felt ashamed of his old Ford we'd crammed full of my things that I was suddenly also ashamed of I realized all at once that I possessed nothing or hardly anything so few

things

that I would be very easy

to eliminate I thought that all I had was myself and this apparently

indestructible

youthfulness of being

that I see in Eric too a mirror embracing me in a world that's to be established the abrupt

ejection

leave-taking setting off

a year ago Martin seemed oddly strange to me when he lugged the old PC up into my room in the residence hall and books and piles of clothes the professor in jeans and UMass sweatshirt like a removal man who's come down in the world

he's absolutely interesting

Julia whispered to me (as if he were Mrs Donally) but she meant it erotically and he did actually have a new love life *bella* Luisa it started three years ago Sister at the beginning they were so uptight it's stupid and embarrassing when your father thinks you don't know anything and he's being so discreet and considerate and clever that he can pretend he's living like a monk after six years of separation and is just helping poor Luisa carry her big round earrings but we are the

seers

the spinners of tales in time and outside time the only thing I don't see is

the here and now immediately round me my

glassy feather-light flowing present

instead I have this feeling the walls the rooms have fallen away the places where I was something I thought I knew and everything appears equally distant (the room in Amherst the strange ship's cabin on the ocean of science in Boston that I share with Julia the corner room in the summerhouse the garden the Charles River the Atlantic)

the bell rings and when Eric comes into the hall I'm

so strange and uninhibited for 10 minutes that we tumble across the hall and happily contort ourselves on the living-room sofa until a point comes when Eric senses that it's occurred to me

where I am

now we look as if robbers had tried to tear the clothes off us (and it's incomprehensible why my nipples and the smallish bluish head of Eric's penis appearing over the top of his underpants are still trying to make things easier for them) and we immediately look as if we feel we have to flee (driven by the long midday break in the timetable of the Long Island Rail Road) so quickly do we straighten out ourselves pick up my rucksack and leave the house

Eric

is nothing but completely effortless easy

understanding

it's not necessary to say what I'm gradually coming to see namely that I want to keep things

vertical—horizontal—a seagull on an invisible jittery wobbly swing over the roofs of the wooden houses

up in the air

the promise

of our departure the feeling that everything that the best possible thing between us will happen tomorrow no presumably in three days' time after the Greyhound has gotten to Los Angeles Eric carries my rucksack to the station I can see myself so clearly in the living room of the summerhouse again on the precise spot where I was standing before Eric rang the bell as if I were still there

in another time from which I can no longer

escape

Leave your shadows

it says in the chorus of the first song I wrote for Eric it wasn't a particularly good one but when Eric sings the song it sounds so right and apparently unalterable that I could cry but that's not necessary on this sunny afternoon in East Hampton as we walk hand in hand to the station I'm still excited and tense and content at the same time

Eric's light-brown hair falls over his eyes the gesture with which he brushes it off his face looks awkward because of the rucksack almost like the movement of a deep-sea diver or an astronaut

in the bright summer air that we're swimming

or floating through and it's a fact that now I'd definitely like to be back on the couch in the living room to feel the absolute real thing right down to that subterranean beating twitching of a wild foreign vein inside me

where

does he do I get all this from we just went cycling together threw a Frisbee to one another swam lazed on the beach read to one another sang to his guitar he's got a place for jazz and solo guitar at a conservatory in LA he wants to play in a group he wants to get away from East Hampton from his over-demonstrative permed mother and his father the senior police officer and his older brother who's serving in the army and who's proud to be driving the latest hi-tech tank (STRIKER)

we're not

just anywhere

but in America so

we believe in ourselves Eric that's the way we've been brought up hand on chest singing to the flag of freedom we have to define ourselves and something in Eric's casual yet definite manner tells me he's not only a dream-dancer but will always find ways and means of bringing part of the dream down to Earth

which is what you're studying

he loves saying that and also that the Earth exists even in California yes that I could best do research into it there of all places where it's extremely lively he also said he needs the gravitational pull of my books and my German

Nachdenklichkeit

(I taught him the word)

in the sunlight on the platform

we lean against one another

a flame blazes up in our bodies

breaking like a wave

and joining us as if we had no clothes on no skin separating us

the Long Island train's coming in now the screeching hissing and snarling
of a higher (stronger) being towers over us (only a machine) kiss me Eric

open your eyes

the yellow-striped front of the engine then

a grimy blue iron wall

Just another two miles to run

it took the length of a whole child's (Sabrina's) life before thinking in miles feet inches became second nature to me the office towers of UMass rise up like battlements behind pale raspberry-red fences round sports grounds beyond which the vague figures of a few early athletes are moving college and high-school students as if caught in big nets by terrible trawlers of the air the images

flicker past blur fade into

patterns of light the rain on that day a year ago when I drove Sabrina to Boston

the last time as I can't stop myself thinking

again and again

suddenly stopped the sun broke through with sheer violence and on the passenger window that Sabrina had half wound down I saw outlined in the trickles of raindrops and the condensation

the mirror of a past in this past

the silhouette of the Alhambra as Luisa and I had seen it a month before from the Albacín quarter (sitting on a stone wall beside a white church) massive and yet calm on its base of ochre rock and my thoughts regarding that holiday were the same as what Sabrina said as she watched our house her old school the familiar surroundings of Amherst slipping away namely that she didn't need to go away any more that she could just as well stay a naive idea refuted by a mere glance at the back of the Ford crammed full from the tailgate over the folded-down rear seats to the grudgingly compliant backrests of the front seats with boxes of clothes and books sports bags plastic sacks (Sabrina's ice skates dangerously close to the glass screen of her old PC monitor stuck inside a quilted jacket it was time for a notebook)

once more it's

a day in early September

a late-summer day

colder wetter more dazzling (blinding corridors of light over Highway 90 we join outside Springfield) than this day soon to be fixed in memory of my last run for such a long time my run is

not yet over

the last year has

not yet begun

the border crossings are not even shapes in the mist of the future yet

it would have helped her Sabrina says if having just returned from Europe after the five-week trip she had simply continued travelling had just repacked her suitcases on the pretext of having to check the nearside lane I glance over and am filled with alarm at both her courage her ease and the still girlishly slim body beside me most of all I would have liked to turn right round and drive back home I must reinstal the more sensible faculty inside me that only recently would have preferred to see her go farther away to university (at least to California or even Berlin) than to choose Boston a kind of geographical compromise between the villa on Long Island and the wooden house in Amherst

in Cambridge

where I spent the night in a bed and breakfast in order to prolong our farewell officially however because of the planned lunch on the following day with Amanda

and the oilman

as Sabrina and I always called him as if from head to toe he consisted solely of a shiny black viscous lump or a glistening liquid rather held together by some miracle (of petrochemistry) in human-seeming form

in Boston and Cambridge the early September day of 2000 had turned into a classically beautiful summer's day (exaggeratedly three-dimensional marble cloudlets like flying stones against the background of a steel-blue expanse of sky) to start at university in a new millennium seemed less remarkable to Sabrina than to me (who had often doubted whether I'd live that long)

we benumbed

the first hours with organization lugging cardboard boxes unpacking things putting them away and I tried not to seem too keen so as not to give the impression I wanted to get rid of Sabrina even though the moment I saw the residence hall on the Charles River (one of those sober five-storey buildings that imitate the classic brownstone architecture just a little more angular more transparent so that nothing seems lost and nothing won) I felt the never-to-be-bridged rift which had once closed up again when at 16 she decided to come and live with me in Amherst and graduate from high school there (at home) suddenly so concentrated and committed that her application for a place at MIT was accepted

the rift is nothing more than

the necessarily completely independent life of another person of your own child

your daughter beside you on a pine sofa among half-unpacked removal boxes studying the *MIT Housing Lists What's in the Room: Extra-long bed— Mattress—Desk—Desk-chair—Bureau—Phone—Ethernet-access—Waste baskets . . . What to bring: Address book—Alarm clock—Aspirin or other*

> *pain*

> *reliever*

Sabrina picks up her mobile that's burbling some pop song it's her mother confirming our date for lunch tomorrow the point of which isn't clear to me but I don't want to avoid it either (Amanda organizing another of her demonstrations of patchwork-family harmony that are a real challenge to survive) and when Sabrina hangs up the echo of Amanda's voice in these surroundings takes me back so vividly to the time when we lived studied and made love together in a residence room that I felt as if Sabrina were visiting me not I her in her new accommodation and the feeling has lasted till this day

when we get up leave the room and examine the equipment in the communal kitchen first-year students in the elevator like the ones I've seen in my lectures and classes for so many years seem almost as interesting to me as they probably do to Sabrina (at least they're future MIT-people and not new students at our run-of-the-mill universities)

this illusory time shift

continues as we rumble down to the underground car park I feel like an older fellow student of these freshmen whose parents and friends are similarly lugging cardboard boxes CD players bundles of clothes baseball bats and TVs into the residence on Labour Day

towards evening Sabrina's room-mate Julia arrives an ironic redhead lethargic and plump but with a quick tongue we go to an Irish pub on the campus and although the two young women get on splendidly and chat nonstop to one another I still can't quite get back into my professor age instead

I'm floating in an indeterminate time zone among the students with their flickering mobiles the Guinness ads the black-and-white photographs projecting the life of the Irish immigrants in a semi-ironic semi-glorificatory way into the vague present

the next day Sabrina was already breakfasting alone with Julia and I woke up in my guest house on Harvard Street

suddenly 52 years old with a sudden sense of outrage as if I'd been fast-forwarded into an unbearable age wedding doctorate alcoholism and divorce already behind me (the order therefore immaterial) I'd been fobbed off with my own life even cheated out of it

but when towards nine I meet Sabrina to see how quickly she and Julia have sorted things out between themselves in their double room I can accept myself again the great old comfort of having a child frees me from myself and as I look at the wobbly shelves and little desks I'm overcome with relief

at not having

to live through

all that again

Sabrina would perhaps start her studies with keener interest and higher energy than was possible for me (30 years ago in Bremen) beside the plump witty feminine Julia she seems rapt like a fairy who has sailed down in order to back up her magic powers with specialized MIT knowledge it's Earth, atmospheric and planetary sciences to which she wants to devote herself much to my amazement for a child who's grown up with literature who could read at five and a half and writes poems even today (who still wrote poems as a young woman) perhaps the poetry of the future needs more precise knowledge of the tectonics of the Earth the physics of the oceans the motions of the air

possibly Sabrina also needs the profane modern decidedly nontranscendental ethos of MIT with its glass-and-concrete buildings its constricted green spaces and calculated passageways into bare inner courtyards its modernized brick buildings and revitalized examples of the awful architectural fashions of the 1960s and 70s among which there's sometimes a glimmer of the shacks of the 40s when the radio codes of German and Japanese warships were cracked here it must be a salutary shock or what you might call a far-reaching

coming down to earth

she's looking for here

contact with the technological physical subcutaneous harder substratum of reality that

she wouldn't find if she just kept on going beside me as now

in dreamlike haziness between the well-tended front gardens the red and white blue and pale-green wooden houses freshly painted verandas clipped street trees crimped bushes refined expensive condominiums from Harvard Street to Harvard Square which she does after all like when seen from a cafe table

while she only seems to be doing me a favour when she says she wants to see the venerable campus (of the richest university in the world) and like drunks or people suffering from vertigo we're somewhat bemused by the radiating paths of the Yard I show her the freshman rooms which are similar to hers at MIT but arranged like chickens round the mother hen we polish the gleaming silver tip of the bronze John Harvard's left shoe (like everyone wishing for luck that wouldn't exist if everyone had it) we have a quick look inside the fantastic reading room of the Widener Library and stand looking at the memorial the fresh flowers the oil painting of the former student whose mother established the library after her son had died when the *Titanic* went down

he is said

Judith a 60-year-old colleague who teaches German here and appears as if by magic tells us

to have taken books from Harvard Library with him on the liner without permission

Judith naturally assumes Sabrina is about to start German and literature here at Harvard but then expresses her admiration for Sabrina taking Earth sciences at MIT and tells us the story of the ice cream that always has to be available in the dining hall on the stipulation of Harry Elkins Widener's mother (since it was his favourite dessert)

what dessert for burning towers for the *Titanic* of the air at least a book instead of a library

beside her mother

Sabrina doesn't look so fragile a robust child rather and also slightly defiant a reaction to the fact that Amanda in jeans and a light summer blouse is evoking her own college-girl past (though she's grown thin and wiry in that irritating way that gives blondes of her age a sharp-edged almost cutting look)

to sit

in silence beside Seymour deVries in the front passenger seat of a big powerful yet somehow hybrid or otherwise energy-saving giant Ranger or monster Rover

while my ex-wife and my daughter were on the rear seat merrily chatting away in high spirits louder and louder until they were almost hysterical

was not really a problem (just the beginning of the challenge)

like a yacht in a stream of smaller boats we sailed across Harvard Bridge along Commonwealth Avenue and then back over Longfellow Bridge because Seymour looking for a much-talked-about restaurant took a wrong turn or just enjoyed driving us round the town of his birth letting us float over the Charles River three times so that we could get a feel for the cool glittering compressed business energy of the city its restrained hustle and bustle the coolness of a brawny athletic but well-turned-out banker in a short-sleeved white shirt or a pinstriped lady (matronly but firm) looking up not entirely unseductively from her accounts too many TV films even inside my head it was just the river the roadside parking along the embankment the tower blocks Back Bay

Sabrina (placing her cool soft hand on my shoulder so that it just touched the side of my neck so often like that so casually) reminded me that we had landed here only six weeks ago

on our way back from Europe

a last view of the river then the loops of the interstate the right exit this time and soon afterwards the genteel English small-town world of Beacon Hill Seymour took us round on foot (after he'd managed to park his monster with the help of bleeping mini-computers and thinking mini-cameras) it's deadly boring here Sabrina said too English for words what a load of kitsch

would you have ever moved to a new Germany Amanda suddenly asked and I said of course not after all we were there when Sabrina was six at the Friedrichstrasse checkpoint when we didn't know whether we had to split up into (a) German with green card (b) US citizen and (c) Sabrina and did I still love the woods so much (to which she had taken me

keep it to yourself)

like Thoreau

Seymour said I've never disliked him he's not a Boston Brahmin nor a descendant of the Irish immigrants (the former underdogs who've long since taken over the city) his parents fled from Rotterdam just before the Luftwaffe bombed the city tore the heart out of the centre he looks (blond freckles blue eyes) like a Dutchman (or a Hamburger or Stockholmer) Seymour's our oil-man although there's something pleasantly dry about him that yacht-club air of distinction I always admired in Amanda it would be easier if I could simply hate and keep out of the way of my successful rival I'd be spared this depressing affinity and closeness to the love-choices of my former partner

and I wouldn't need to have these civilized lunches like this one here in a restaurant in Chestnut Street we eventually choose instead of the place known only to the few which proves impossible to find

now I need

I can bear

the last lunch together at which I don't say much and don't even listen properly I presumably share this in retrospect unforgivable lack of concentration with Amanda perhaps like me she was thinking back to the Berlin Friedrichstrasse crossing in August 1988 the matter-of-course way I touched Amanda's elbow back then Sabrina pressed her head against my stomach for protection we joined the line for US citizens and were dealt with very politely

perhaps a flicker of something in Amanda's eyes a short relaxation of her guard for the nostalgic excursion a brief ironic parry as if to an old male acquaintance who for a moment has forgotten his role as friend and looked her too deep in the eyes

there's no air for us

in the past

no matter how desperately the future would like to breathe there would want to have another and better look round there at least I have a very clear image of my divorced wife at that restaurant table opposite me at midday a static and yet flickering reversible figure of feeling which for a few seconds makes Amanda look alive and close in a way that is no longer appropriate only to move her immediately away into the wondering almost wonder-struck distance of a stranger looking at an energetic businesswoman who you can tell from the contrast between her professional make-up and ordinary clothes is doing her daughter a favour one of those outwardly cool blondes whose dreaming body you can't properly imagine even though you were holding it naked in your arms half an hour ago apparently so armour-plated so

invulnerable

now

in the summer

in which I'm suffering from the fact that I can't see Sabrina at the table as clearly as her mother because she's sitting on my left

and from the fact that I

can hardly remember what she said hardly remember her reflections her vehement objections my (nostalgic) abstraction and my father's pride only registered her gestures and the effect her arguments had on the oilman sitting diagonally opposite me the fact that he kept looking impressed looking amused and astonished sometimes even taken aback

was enough for me

and stupidly (later perhaps even) understandably

I can recall exactly the arguments that he (who also went to MIT who devoted his attention to my daughter with a mixture of specialist's conceit and presumptuous fatherly pride which I found hard to bear) quite calmly ironically patiently used to oppose her criticism of the oil-guzzling American society and even today they're pounding inside my head (as if he were already the snow-covered figure in the storm shouting despairingly into his mobile) namely that no one knows exactly how limited a resource oil is but that it was a historical fact that the magic of rising prices kept conjuring up new techniques new sources and could bring about a change in consumer behaviour even in the US

oil is buried deep in the earth it's that simple that difficult (Seymour said)

stick to things that are buried before you in the air (in the vacuum of the past)

Amanda and Sabrina on that bright day I long thought must be one of my happiest when

Sabrina started at MIT

On the way home shortly before I get to my great-grandfather's old house
that defies the heat with its narrow window slits and thick cooling walls like
a little sand-coloured castle or part of an Indian pueblo

Ahmed stumbles into me

chased by his older sister from whom (she assures me indignantly) he
tried to pinch the piece of baklava that was for her so I take the little lad
with me to Farida's kitchen where there's always something sweet for him

when he runs out he barges into me again without a word of thanks
squealing with delight a jolly gap-toothed robber's face and thick eyebrows
the impact of his soft bones doesn't hurt his energetic child's body just wakes
me up and brings me back to

reality

to Farida's kitchen to Farida's unhurried precise movements when she's
cooking

chopping onions parsley mint garlic with a view of the shady square of
the inner courtyard where she grows her ornamental plants and herbs

on one side of the table is the book she's just translating she often gets
up abruptly from her work to begin cooking and cooking

keeps bringing you back down to earth

which is where I want to go at least for a few hours to the

earth of the Earth

for after all the Major is real his strong hand on my sister's neck (and if
she needs it Huda says

giggling

inside my head) and my self-opinionated imagination

oppresses me weighs me down accuses me as if by using it I had brought
about been able to bring about what is really happening I wished it was

nothing

Farida's kitchen

cut up pumpkins knead dough pick leaves chop herbs joint meat wash
rice and bulgur make tea

beside Farida I so often find my way back

to the family

we meet in the kitchen as if at a more real place even Tariq automatically falls into the women's rhythm slices cucumbers tomatoes aubergines cabbage leaves with his favourite knife that he alternately calls The Machete or The Scalpel and in the kitchen even Sami does what he's told without grumbling even if clumsily and sleepily compared with what his fingers can do on a computer stir the harissa you can programme while you're doing it Farida says with a laugh

Yiom what are we cooking Yiom

cooking is always an anchor for the crazy ship of my imagination

cardamom pepper coriander cumin

there's less and less meat and fish but even then Farida knows plenty of recipes today for example it's aubergine soufflé make an orange salad to go with it the one you learnt from Nawal and while I'm peeling three oranges and cutting them into thin slices skinning red onions and chopping them into rings scattering black olives over them plucking mint leaves and drizzling oil into which I've stirred a teaspoon of cumin (was there salt as well?) I've time to ask myself once more which mother I'd rather have one who can play with the wolves successfully or this calm soft pale woman in the green housecoat trimmed with gold braid who used to be a teacher until all teachers had to be party members who used to translate novels for a big publishing house until almost nothing was allowed to be translated any more who has withdrawn entirely to her family her relatives her kitchen and her books

and yet

that's what remains I always think and it often seems to me that Farida sees it like that too and that's where she gets her strength from and her pride there's nothing cowed about her although she has been defeated and limited to the old house in Betawiyn and the houses in the neighbourhood only rarely do she and Tariq go to see old friends (as far as they are still living in Baghdad and not in Amman Beirut London Berlin Cologne)

once my father fought with Yasmin

in Paris

I saw it but didn't understand I was only 11

what's the point of continuing to translate this book on nursing Farida asks if we haven't got half the medicines and cleaning materials any more God bless America what's Huda doing Tariq asks that merry Haddawi with her super-mother the eight-language woman with four tongues and six arms did you know last month they found the skeleton of a king anthropoid ape in Uruk that when reconstructed with modelling clay looked exactly like Saddam

he can sense

the shadow

over me because I dreamt about my sister but then what

do I know

I do the washing-up with Farida while in his room right above us Sami's flying away with Microsoft like

a fly in a glass (the wrong planes desperately attacking the glass screen of his monitor from inside)

Tariq's going out to meet a poet friend and disappears after coffee

we read I don't need to worry that Farida might suddenly begin talking about Yasmin there hardly seems to be a tie between Farida and Yasmin any more so rarely does anyone mention my big sister who had the opportunity to do all the things I can only dream of doing who's now laying claim to my nightmares as well

at night

little Ahmed waves to me from next door (grateful after all) he's sitting on his bed like a shaggy little ghost in his light-coloured pyjamas it's only when I go past the box room where we keep the mattresses for outside that I can see the roof of the neighbouring house the beds of Ahmed Hind Mrs Rikabi and her husband who's rarely there and Yusuf's hammock of course my brother's friend he's just popped up behind Ahmed and grabs and tickles him out of embarrassment because otherwise he'd freeze and go bright red again when he saw me

we can put mosquito nets over our beds (they come from England so Tariq says that Tony Blair is protecting him personally) but when the wind's in the east it's not necessary so then Tariq Sami and I (Farida never sleeps on the roof nor did Yasmin) don't hang the nets over the wooden poles fixed at head height

Ahmed from next door squeals and Yusuf giggles

if we kissed

and rubbed against one another

then perhaps some of the energy circulating inside me tensing me up and making me light as a feather would dissipate I'm floating on the roof in the feverish circles of my imagination as if in invisible phosphorescent rings in glowing colours concealed

beneath my skin

car horns voices scraps of music the rustling of the night

early in the evening the edges of the sky were blood-red and purple

now there aren't many stars to be seen in a covering of a kind of pastel bluish grey a blanket I've no more strength

to fly up into the sky the day we took Yasmin to the airport comes back to mind I was six it was shortly after the war that same evening Tariq bought me a red bicycle in the souk my Paris my easy rolling life for three years I rode round the new estate in the quiet smart district where we used to live

I get on my bike up into the sky

I could have given it to Ahmed if it hadn't disappeared during the move perhaps you can see it from up there Sister in the dreams of the past over our city when your bloodthirsty king has sunk into his dreams and the dhow is floating over Baghdad

it is said

that Caliph al-Mansur spent a night on the bank of the Tigris and never had a lighter more untroubled sleep so that when he woke up he founded the new big city over 1,200 years ago the city of light dreams or

no dreams at all perhaps

Sabrina

MTA Long Island Rail Road Departure East Hampton 11.47 a.m.

we'll meet tomorrow I say

sure Eric says at two outside the Virgin Megastore Broadway corner of 45th Street and we'll go to the Greyhound station together as agreed

the train's about to depart you're standing on the steps

in the carriage now Eric says we'll meet tomorrow even if

even if?

I go with you for an hour today or a bit more as far as

as far as?

Babylon Eric says a friend of mine lives there and he'll drive me back I can't just leave you all by yourself

on the seat beside each other facing the front my blue rucksack on the luggage rack the top bit strangely human like a wrapped-up head a listener from another life just imagine every time you feel heavy you're carrying an invisible listener or even watcher and when you have a load off your mind he floats up onto the luggage rack there aren't many passengers around mid-day it's as if the carriage were just for us (the train the parking lots the rows of shops then more summerhouses) suddenly everything's easy clear transparent almost and without any real

differences

as if we could flow into each other merge like cells or flames or roll out through the metal side of the car onto a summer meadow as if there were actually no speeds at all (forces tensions destructions)

everything (much)

falls away from me because I expected the burden to become clearly perceptible the moment I was sitting alone on the seat with Eric giving me one last wave while in fact he's putting his arm round me and giving me a kiss on my ear

possibilities

are

rooms in a house I walk round tranquilly I was afraid of talking to my mother this evening but not any more I tell him oh Eric I can't say how important it is for me that you're coming with me it seems to me as if it's you who's coming to Los Angeles with me although I'm going with you it once happened that my father didn't go with me

when my mother left him

it's being absurdly childishly sulky I know but I'd still expected him to and when I called him two years later (because I knew he'd stopped drinking) he'd understood and told me not to come to Amherst he'd fetch me

Eric we're nothing (just young)

are we starting

the world

that works no:

things are working out it will

be easy to go to Los Angeles and to see if I could continue my studies there if Eric's at university there at least somewhere other than in New England in the eternal heat the eternal smog in the sweltering gigantic steel-concrete-glass mush of the Horizontal City there's

any amount of geology Eric says earthquakes along the San Andreas Fault also masses of illusions

Hollywood

in the film of my life California in the land of my American grandparents in Palo Alto the wood-and-stone house old-fashioned modern as if from a 1960s film there's a smell of apple cake and memories of solitary but happy evenings with fat novels while my early-rising grandparents had long since gone to sleep an excited calm the certainty that I'd soon be grown up and experience exceptional things for which I could gather my strength here Eric I can say that I was alone in several beautiful rooms with outstanding views

at least we could be together during recess and travel or work together

if you don't want to give up your elite university which I can well understand even though you're a poet perhaps and a great song-writer the deciding factor's what you enjoy I really mean that there's still time to make a decision the way you lift your head up you're Katharine Hepburn again (I'm not at all like her) the classic New England lady at 85 she was still going swimming in Long Island Sound every day even in winter

when I'm 85

I'll be dead I say

famous then Eric replies only people who are famous have birthdays when they're dead will you write me a song about Katharine Hepburn and Spencer Tracy couldn't we become a couple like them so strong and in love and who loved a scrap

we don't look like them and I'm not at all grumpy like Katharine do you want to be a sports reporter always chewing a cigar

of course Eric says right after my career as a jazz guitarist

smooth platforms a drugstore motor-boat rental a glimpse of a regular summer castle with a huge park then trees again closely packed houses an abrupt view of the sea

what I am what I can do

what I want

the questions that I have to spend my vacation dealing with as if with unpleasantly large dogs that have been wished on me for a few weeks run away (dogs made of smoke)

at MIT I'll forget all that again there'll be a schedule exams lectures seminars practicals a rhythm to my life I could go to the West Coast next semester at the earliest

but seen from Los Angeles

in a few days' time

things will perhaps look quite different

I'm thinking of the towns we'll be travelling through for the three days on the Greyhound Eric says Pittsburgh Columbus Dayton Indianapolis St Louis Kansas City Denver Las Vegas El Monte you think you're never going to arrive but I'm sure those are the best kind of journeys or aren't they

suddenly I'm talking

too much

or about what I must talk about it was the internship in New Hampshire at the beginning of the summer in which for the first time I felt both secure and free and as if I could be happy in a real (really existing) job (if I could write poems now and then if I

could spend the nights at Eric's place)

almost every day for four weeks I was with the school children who were visiting the Seacoast Science Center in Odiorne Point State Park and did courses there I helped the smallest ones wash their hands before they were allowed put them in the aquariums and touch the starfish (living cool-rough sand) I climbed over the rocks by the shore with the older ones looking for snails and crabs and with the oldest who were supposed to learn something about the geology of the Gulf of Maine I examined the stones and striations left over from the last Ice Age we constructed fishes in a computer-simulation programme that tested the chances of survival of our creatures (cod's head shark's fins dolphin's tail most died out pretty quickly) we went down into the depths of the ocean in a virtual submarine then collected more crab and snail shells outside in the calmer bays we came across a bone similar to a collarbone that no one could identify I drew with the kids and in the evenings went

alone

with a view to the north over the dove-grey roofs of the visitor centre the wide paths round it the lawns the gentle generous curve of the coast beyond it up a hill as if carried by the evening light I was close to thinking that here on the border between Maine and New Hampshire there could be a

definition of happiness

that would be: children science sea and then in addition exactly

what Eric gives me promises to give me unexpected and complete I heard Emily's lines inside my head

recited by a measured quiet but all at once passionately ardent voice

Wild nights—Wild nights!
Were I with thee
Wild nights should be
Our luxury!

there had once been a gun emplacement on the hill and across the parking lot you can see the mound with the plinths for the 155 mm guns from the Second World War standing in a semicircle (every millimetre noted) on the rear wall of an abandoned toilet the obscene sketch of a naked woman lying down her head formed by *Your Mother* written to make the shape next to it a carefully drawn stop sign with *Stop Bush*! written underneath

we have to find a way

in reality Eric that means

children science sea wild nights

or in unreality we could be as austere shy fruitless magnificent as Emily
I usually hardly care either way but not today and perhaps not for weeks
and months either

you know everything

why's it called Babylon actually

Eric asks close to my ear it was just a pub the mother of the man who
founded the town had to look out at from her house an inn that seemed as
disreputable as the city in the Bible

I go back down the hill to the shore

it's early morning as if

I'd spent the whole night up there like the soldiers of Battery 204 but
also as if going down I'd slipped into

a different

earlier

time and a different

place

we went out together to wake up the shrimps Martin said he stumbles
along beside me in a daze his glasses steamed up any number of dogs race
past us so I keep close to my father's legs all the time the beach is narrow
close I feel at home it runs along a tongue of land lined with fisherman's
houses restaurants hotels souvenir shops painters' studios I can see bare feet
in the mud pale white child's feet that never seem to get cold (Martin says)
the green plastic pail in my hand is already half full of stones and shells the
dogs come closer yet they never bite push brush against me because they're
afraid of Martin there's a lot of questions and I'm specially talkative in the
mornings before breakfast there's a lot I want to know and I often explain
things to myself out loud and even before Martin can find a good way of
putting it I'm coming up with many more big incredibly lovely questions
like golden sea-monsters and fire-breathing Chinese dragons in the dull blue
morning air it was perhaps just our closeness the bigger hand the walking
together that feeling of always getting an adequate

answer (but: what did I ask)

Amanda

is still asleep

we spent three summer vacations in an acquaintance's house in Rockport we can still

tumble into Amanda's bed chilled fresh laughing just about dressed without jackets and shoes and she hugs us seals as she says

with Eric what was will also get better

he throws a new a quite different light on other irrevocable parts of the past

get off with me in Babylon he says jokingly we could go to your mother's together tomorrow morning

no thanks I hear myself say

I've been there already

in Babylon I

remember it

MEMORY

On the pages of your books,
    Water lily, bound and free,
Images of fire are drifting
    Down to pure eternity.

On the way home with my old leather case in my left hand (stethoscope blood-pressure gauge reflex hammer bandages syringes emergency medicines edible or drinkable gifts from patients sometimes a piece of mutton or a whole unplucked chicken things no one would have dared to offer a doctor a few years ago) my white shirt unfortunately very sweat-soaked at the end of the day the rampant mat of hair on my pigeon breast coming out of my open collar however people are still impressed by my pepper-and-salt moustache and the wreath of woolly hair round my skull gleaming in the evening light

in the twilight mixed with exhaust fumes and the smoke from a restaurant grill dreams could rise up out of my tiredness my weariness Muna's flying ship

the ark

in which she wanted to save all those in the country who were beyond help I wish it really were hovering above me so close that you'd only need to throw a rope ladder down I could use her lifeboat every day wherever it was flying now I picture to myself a dhow quietly and slowly sailing through the evening air and the end of the rope ladder touching my shoulder I would just need to make a sign for the critically ill patient to be taken on board

at least I've managed to help a few for example the mother whose husband sold their UN food ration to buy arrack (after which she stuffed her screaming infant with pap made with flour instead of with milk powder) also the mullah with the abscess on his right thigh (*Ubi pus, ibi evacua.*)

I sewed up (without a local anaesthetic) a long scalp wound I didn't need to know how he came by it and simply said

lie down and stay still

to the three broken ribs of a young man

but the girl with acute leukaemia will be dead in a few months because there are no cytostatic drugs for the poor while the 11-year-old with closed tuberculosis could survive if his parents had only the faintest idea of the regularity of a cardiac pacemaker which the sighing fat bodyguard (at least not one of the Tikriti) who didn't want to get down from the chair in my practice urgently needs but will definitely not get (at most in one of his boss' luxury clinics)

I can do something about three cases of typhus because there happens
to be some Chloramphenicol available again after I've seen dozens of children die from it and from vomiting and diarrhoea and from cholera as well

O you our lords and masters!

drink the water of the Tigris until your entrails turn to mud

Lords of the UN!

drink oil until you see that you have not weakened the tyrant but hand
in hand with him have murdered the children of the land he has abused

the ark

would have to be part of a whole fleet Muna the fleet of those who die
unnecessarily which has nowhere to berth which should hover over Washington over Berlin Stockholm Paris

it's a souvenir of Paris

old Colonel Basil said

and handed me a bottle of French perfume still in its original packaging
from Kuwait probably booty from his heyday in the army when he had a villa
in the Yarmouk district where he still lives but lying smoking coughing spitting
blood in a two-room ground-floor flat with six other family members

for him I still have morphine from the hidden reserves I share with two
colleagues and restock whenever something comes from one of the secret
channels occasionally also clean infusion sets painkillers or a box of sterile
gloves usually in return for free treatment or a simple diagnosis that's our
speciality impotent clairvoyance for the

Iraqi doctor

has become a soothsayer of the body my friend a human X-ray machine
with insight into the inevitable that could at best be cured in Baghdad's private clinics or anywhere else

in happier lands

old Colonel Basil knows Leipzig (secret service training under Honecker)
and Paris (delegation negotiating the purchase of fighter-bombers) but he has
no idea why he ended up in Safina six years ago in the precipitous stone bat-
tleship of the secret service rammed into the body of the town

two years in the red section

the floor streaming with blood Basil sthas a video it's on a shelf over
his bed and shows among other things a masked man pulling his bound

arms forward while another is lashing his bare back to shreds with a cable
it shows some prisoners having their skulls smashed with iron bars and
others being thrown to their death from high windows after they'd been
maltreated in all ways imaginable

greetings

from the secret service to the nation

available at all bigger markets and only under the counter for form's
sake for it's meant to be sold and have its effect on the

lower levels

fear however is so old its deep and deepest levels so soaked in blood
that tiredness is almost all that's left and apathy there's a worn-down sleepy
mortal fear which has grown weary of itself as if your head were in a lion's
mouth and the lion and you were both yawning

the ark for Iraq

is the ship of the torturers

you can even get out for good greetings

from Paris

says Basil whom I give the morphine for his half-destroyed body because
without him I would probably not be alive now for he sent the spy who
heard me in a first-aid tent

when faced with a lacerated abdomen curse the

PRIDEOFTHEARABS

on a suicide mission but that was probably not the reason why he ended
up in the ship of the dead but

there was and is no reason

that is the strongest purest most obscene form of power destruction par-
don punishment liquidation torture and promotion

for no reason

for then there's

nothing

between you and the glaring seething sun of power (at best the thin
ether of mortal fear)

two years after he'd been dismissed without reason they gave Basil a
quarter of the pension that was due to him without reason in the same way
as they'd left him with half a life

with the wedding present for Yasmin in my bag

I go out into the darkening street it's been a long time since I've been here close to the old embassy district the images of the wedding return it's just two weeks ago that my eldest child married her pale irresolute long-term fiancé in my father's big old house in Wasiriya where we also celebrated her birth shortly after our return from Paris and everything seemed to repeat itself the warmth the sounds the banquet (only organized with the greatest difficulty today) the guests merry and dulled with arrack and whisky the crush of bodies the familiarity of all the rooms and corners of the house

only now we know can sense through the fumes from the kebabs and smells of the barbecued fish that everything has changed been distorted even without the memory of those who have been lost (my nephew perhaps executed in a barrack perhaps also killed by a nocturnal greeting from George Bush senior

Farida's younger sister Fatima and the whole of her family of five during Saddam's vengeance on the Shiites whom the American PRESIDENT suddenly didn't feel like helping any more after he'd called on them to topple the tyrant)

Fatima often haunts us so friendly so easy so very forgetful

none of us is what we were any more and we try to get over that with our celebrations because we sense expect believe that everything can get even worse in the land

of dogs with their tails between their legs

that we have become (that is the difference no matter what our age

inwardly

we have our tails between our legs my friend we're vicious wretched uneasy with false pride and genuine hatred) in our role as subjects through the fumes and the veil of arrack

I see Yasmin and have to come to terms with the sense of both living closeness and immense distance that this vigorous beautiful young woman instils in me she's getting married with her head held high in the Western fashion she has effortlessly (always I was going to say even when she played football at school and I desperately clutched her hands at the fence) cast off the old Islamic psychological ballast (of course Farida didn't load her down with much) she's never worn an abaya and almost never does any cooking she has become the kind of person the Iraqi women were promised 20 years ago in her everything has become true and false at the same time I don't know

how much how far it's six years since we had an open and free talk together that time in Paris our tender furious abstract discussion before Muna's horrified look

now I can't get through to her any more even when she embraces me in the hubbub of the wedding celebrations and I feel her perfumed body whose sinewy strength comforts and calms me somehow as if it could help her

even in Paris with her career-chemist Qasim she entered the sphere in which an upright encounter is no longer possible she wanted the best (for herself) she wanted to work as a chemist she wanted a career of her own

with Qasim she also brings his uniformed friends into the house who sit at the table and make jokes all those round them laugh at as cautiously as if they were working out moves in a chess championship (a video-rental shop that sold Saddam's speeches as porn and no one ever protested Bill Clinton and his cigar George Bush riding a bicycle in Baghdad)

Yasmin has made a marriage that is so perfectly right for her that she can never be satisfied with it

at the wedding she didn't give me one single uncertain searching questioning glance as if she were trying to tell me that this time she was lost to me without tears not at all like that time

one year after the war

six months before the war

in the summer of 1990 we drove her to the airport

a week before there'd been a joke a mistaken joke by our neighbour Amal about

HEWHOSENAMEMUSTNOTBEMENTIONED

after which she disappeared for three days and then was thrown out of a car outside her house in the grey light of dawn covered in bruises cigarette burns with broken fingers teeth knocked out bleeding womb

new schools new kindergartens new

women for the militia

there still seemed to be money around it was still possible to fly from Baghdad to Paris

that farewell

which Yasmin at 16 thought would be for two or three years while I even then hoped it would last for 10 drained me of all my strength I have never (not even in the wars) felt so heavy so slow so impotent it was as if I were wearing iron armour that was constricting my breath I knew that we should all have gone the whole family

but I was not clear- and single-minded enough there were parts that wanted to go to Paris with Yasmin who was fighting back the tears and who then gave a brief cheerful wave and there were parts that

wanted to stay here

wanted to sink

hold out and by holding out win I saw (as if it were a reason for all of that and the very best as well) Farida's tired and yet so attractive face and behind her framed in glazed earthenware with copies of Sumerian or Assyrian cuneiform script (there's come a time when you'll explain all that to me Muna) the

BUTCHER

as a stupid imitation of Nebuchadnezzar whom he wanted to follow even to the destruction of Jerusalem

on the wall writing appeared that only I could read

it was a little message from the future for me for you Muna namely that I would not manage to send another daughter to study abroad

and we turned round on that warm evening in May took one of the red-and-white taxis and got out before our street to have a little stroll in the shock and happiness of Yasmin's departure and out of despair and happiness I bought two children's bicycles for the amount

I now earn in a month

it's 11 years ago now since we used to go to the English Club in the neighbourhood of the embassy district and drink cocktails the clubs have gone bankrupt the former expensive boutiques are boarded up the only life is round the monstrous building site of the Rahman Mosque with its bulging outer towers that themselves are to house in each of their eight walls further embryonic round-domed structures (as if packed with space shuttles like a pregnant concrete spider) the mightiest mosque in the land of the

MIGHTIEST

erected in the deserted former smart district to butter up the ulema

through the window of a restaurant in Jordan Street

I see jerking from right to left the subtitles of wildly gesticulating TV reporters the cloud of fire and smoke pouring out of the skyscrapers like blooming pith from the stalk of a flower behind the glass of a screen on the counter of a restaurant on Nisur Square a skyscraper a second burning tower I look through the window as if

I'm looking into the open skull of a madman

it's the World Trade Center both towers are on fire and I turn aside for a second as if I could blank it out

but I'm already in the restaurant surrounded by the men close to the screen I didn't notice how I came to be in there and later I will often think I didn't move my feet at all but I can never forget the two thoughts rubbing against one another inside my head like millstones among the restaurant's customers some of whom seem paralysed others more as if they were watching a football match some mutely happy or already laughing as if at the sight of a much-too-big present

that there would be a war

and that inside the tower it must be as it is written in the scriptures which cannot be doubted as in

the fires of hell

whose fuel is stones and people

Something inside you has to

split open

it's not possible to survive if you insist on being made of one piece like a glass ball that's hurled onto the floor it's not possible

even if to start with I remained so incomprehensibly unsuspecting and felt nothing tear inside me I could have followed the plane crashing into the South Tower just as it happened (on the closed unbroken layer of glass) in real time I got back to the house at quarter to nine (at the very minute possibly the very second) I never leave the TV on during the day I don't switch the radio on I'm so

secure so indifferent trusting

so happy with the

world without me

that in the mornings I even put the telephone on mute and thus while I had a drink of water took a shower walked past my desk to the window I remained unbearably calm composed unimpressed by the furious hammering of longing of the despairing rage of a

future

memory and drank coffee and looked out into the garden the first maple leaves on the fading lawn yellow dragon's hands in September 186 years ago Privy Councillor Goethe (in the late autumn of his life) invented a

Suleika

for himself and a little 30-year-old woman responded to him the child of the circus who soared high up into the poetic big top

assume another name to fall in love to live to save yourself so as

not to break into pieces I

became Hatem a cool vain superior profoundly all-encompassing indestructible master

of all he surveys or simply just a nobody in the farthest corner under the ceiling where I was flung up when I stood up from my desk around four o'clock finally switched the telephone on and the answering machine with the oilman's despairing words out of

the darkness

THE TELEVISION

I'm there it's

there

I

(will never be able

to touch I)

am standing

on the flying carpet of glass 500 feet above downtown Manhattan facing the upper body of a CNN reporter who's standing on tiptoe perhaps
with his back to the abyss as well (monstrous ravines open up below you
over South Street or Water Street once you're high up) on the very edge of
the carpet but only concerns himself with me turns to me infinitely worried
leans forward slightly with a sad expression with the

Towers in the background

that disappear reappear and

disappear

we've suddenly gotten much higher up in the sky and can see the Battery
the Financial District the whole of the Lower East Side like a gigantic sombre
ship suffocating under clouds of smoke perhaps bombed shot at by rockets
destroyed by underground explosives tons of which had been concealed
there over the last few months my

mind is a blank

I'm standing on the swaying glass carpet facing the CNN reporter as if
I wanted to throw him off when quick as lightning

the sky parts letting its watery plasma flow into a new radiant blue
square in which the Towers

rise up again and now

and still my mind is a blank

it's time

to split ourselves my Brother something of us must stand above things
above the glass carpet above our despoiled destroyed devastated heart now
it's becoming pitilessly

clear the North Tower with smoke billowing out of a yawning gap in the 80th floor

BREAKING NEWS
AMERICA UNDER ATTACK
TERRORISTS CRASH HIJACKED AIRLINERS   CNN
INTO WORLD TRADE CENTER; PENTAGON   LIVE

right
    out of the blue
    lying on the floor of a stone cave a slim bearded man with Eastern headgear his cheek resting on the palm of his right hand under a blanket casually chatting somehow stuffed with a kind of incurable vanity

BREAKING NEWS
SOURCES: 'GOOD INDICATIONS' OSAMA   CNN
BIN LADEN INVOLVED IN ATTACKS
'WALKING WOUNDED' EVACUATED TO AREA AROU

the telephone
    now I know that Seymour's call goes with the pictures I saw came right from the smoke and fumes came from one of the dazed figures stumbling about in the mist looking as if they were covered in ash in white foam in snow and black feathers cowering on the ground behind battered automobiles

BREAKING NEWS   CNN
AMERICA UNDER ATTACK
HUGHES: PRESIDENT SECURE AT
AIR FORCE BASE IN NEBRASKA
10.26 AM ET: SECOND WTC TOWER COLLAP

the telephone
    he was only about 400 yards away he was only a minute away from the collapse of the first tower he'd tried to get through to Amanda dozens

of times he'd suddenly found himself at the victory parade of terrorism in the middle of an immense column of swirling paper a blizzard with the facades of the Towers shining through and people falling down like teardrops

he saw

nothing

he saw people covered all over with dust extricating themselves from a wall of fog and running towards him yelling

he said (three days later) that immediately before the tremor and the collapse of the South Tower he'd found himself among already battered cars and the bizarrely still undamaged window of a travel agency (*Visit Egypt*) as if suddenly on an island an almost circular area on which despite the ear-splitting sound of the wind or whistling or perhaps because of the unbearable intensity and shrillness of the noise a kind of local or inclusive silence had spread round him with which the ground covered in flakes of ash scraps of paper things (plastics) burnt to bright glittering down like a blanket of snow fitted as did the vault or wall round him it was (for two or three seconds or perhaps five) like being inside a sphere of snow the size of a house an inside-out or inverted sphere of snow rather for the flurries of shreds and debris seemed to be held off by a glass dome it's

the THIRD WORLD WAR THE BASTARDS a man covered feathered in snow or foam shouted in his face as he staggered out of the white wall it's the earth quaking with the

end of the

collapse of the South Tower which he later on kept seeing from the perspective of millions of unaffected people (behind glass shields whose emulsion the twitching beam of the Braun tube hardly penetrates) something like the sudden 30 upper storeys bursting open foaming up in a gigantic graphite mushroom cloud that with lightning speed gets brighter and even bigger taking on the colour of raging water like a huge poodle's head crowning the tower rushing along its sides like an avalanche of smoke tearing down taking everything with it immediately piling up the VOID above it in the sky only then to plunge down entirely on the streets like (he thought down there at that moment)

a sea of wreckage foam and stone

and soon everything assumes a set ceremonial form

a ritual of destruction for two skyscrapers and two airplanes

and 3,000 people I

didn't think

of Amanda I see the smoking North Tower and the undamaged facade of the South Tower and out of the corner of my left eye the silhouette of a plane suddenly coming into the picture which as everyone expects ought to simply fly past the Towers but immediately destroys all distance all expectation by smashing into the middle of the South Tower with such apparent ease as if crashing into the tissue paper of a grey box-kite that immediately goes on fire in the form of two clouds of smoke balls of fire swiftly billowing out as if surrounded by matted disintegrating bowls and the next moment hurling down tons of stone and glass hundreds of body

parts I wasn't thinking of

Amanda I

wasn't thinking

I kept seeing the mercilessly blue sky the merciless aliveness of the peroxide-blonde CNN newsreader in the green suit of fireproof lizards the merciless pausing repeating replaying of the catastrophe

kept seeing time compressed into an inextricable bundle a blood-soaked smoking tangle during which the Towers fall rise again collapse crash down bleed burst into flames disappear in a cloud shine undamaged against the sky once more are left standing as mere stalks tower over Manhattan anew pour down foaming into the streets again

you can't

touch it

in your wooden house 150 miles north of New York in the middle of a life that isn't there any more you stare at the screen in the middle of your living room that isn't there any more that has already flown off broken off like the Twin Towers that you can no more touch than you can

touch her cheek her hair again

the green leather couch the table with the magazines the shelves the books and plants blow up your study that is just an image flickering before your eyes your desk on which you place a trembling hand as if on a cushion of (imagined)

electrons

Martin Lechner: *Loving Goethe*

white ash in 250 sheets I wish it were a

single breath of yours

that would have blown everything away for then you'd be

by my side once more by my side

Hafiz the friend I create for myself out of my despair by splitting up my grief separating my brain from my heart I regard the house the lower storey of the house as

blown up

I watched with a leaden brain that was simply pushing my eyes out of their sockets again and again

and I wasn't thinking I just watched again and again

and again

the infinite loop of disaster

PART TWO

THE TOWERS

September 2002

When your mother dear
Through my door comes near
And I turn to see
What she wants of me,
Not on her sweet face
At first I turn my gaze,
But nearer to the floor,
Beside her in the door
Where, peeping round her knee,
Your dear face would be,
With mischief brimming o'er,
Your father's joy and cheer,
My little daughter dear.

Your father's ray of light,
So bright,
Too soon extinguished.

Friedrich Rückert
Kindertotenlieder (Songs for Dead Children)

New York
A woman—the statue of a woman
Holding in one hand the scrap of paper called liberty
By the documents we call history
And with the other strangling a child called Earth

Adonis
'A Grave for New York'

You draw a line my friend the

strongest line

the cell membrane the last and impenetrable

ground-glass screen between actual events and yourself (the most important fact of all) I keep coming up against this barrier every day in some weeks it runs

right through my work

one of the doctors' nameplates in Saadun Street is mine there are four rows of them one right above the other like a pile of cardboard boxes seen end on boxes of medicines that haven't arrived again and this panoply of nameplates deludes those who see them with the hope that there is help for them whatever their problem and cardboard is what my treatment-box looks like in the concrete 1970s building where the people queue on the stairs that is when they aren't squatting down or lying exhausted on the floor

the line is wafer-thin only a

membrane behind which

the naked armies of the dead push forward (of the recently dead I assume while the others will already have turned away since they were forced to see that their desire to return was futile and set off on their way to the further depths)

but it is also the

strongest the most important separation the one that makes the life of the dead into a play into a film which we repeat mercilessly and more and more confusedly and palely without ever

awakening them

you stay here: faced with a mother who sits a yellow-faced four-year-old girl on the examination couch whose dark panic-stricken look slides off everything as if it were slipping sinking sliding deeper and deeper down no matter where she is and whose bloated belly tells you she has swellings of the liver and spleen which will take her over to the other side of the border in three or four months all I can do is send her to the state Saddam Hospital where it is highly likely that they can do no more than what I could do now that is give the mother a sheet of paper with PENTOSTAM written on it in

Latin and Arabic script so that like so many others with similar signs and sheets of paper she can stand in the streets outside the hotels near the run-down clinics or outpatient departments in the hope of being seen by a smuggler or a corrupt nurse a generous or criminal doctor with a hidden supply an angel or a worker for some aid organization who might happen to know about a delivery of the medicine

in such cases I'm no longer a doctor but a seller of lottery tickets who at his age has had to become familiar with diseases such as kala-azar a speciality infection which had previously been at most associated with fly-infested slum areas of Africa and India places in the

Third World

to which

Iraq has reverted in so many ways with her bombed power stations shelled sewerage systems blown-up fertilizer factories disintegrating school buildings overloaded overfull ramshackle hospitals I go out into the street and I can see

Calcutta in Baghdad

gaping sheep's bellies with the entrails sticking out maggoty lumps of minced meat in the hot sun water sellers with ancient pewter jugs or glass containers like aquariums with dirty ice floating about in them more and more children of school age stealing and begging their way through life of course all this my friend has its

reasons

all the way up to

the UN Security Council whose member states have supplied three-quarters of the arms in the Middle East and are therefore well aware of what we

VILLAINS

deserve

that is hundreds of thousands of children dying unnecessarily from infectious diseases malnutrition and sepsis who naturally are all just victims of the cynical game of our PRESIDENT who has been playing cat-and-mouse with the weapons inspectors for 10 years and diverting the millions that are left into the coffers of his clan into the greedy mouths of his secret services into the towers and cellars of his absurd palaces where he hides while his puppet doubles wave to the cameras (there are no copies my friend Ali says HE's so vain he plays his doubles himself) still

my friend the Iraqis have tried to dispose of him many times already we can quite easily beat Hitler's Germany with the number of our good murderous intentions

war

will come Farida says and with it the day of reckoning but I wonder whether those will be called to account who omitted to loosen the stranglehold when they saw the suffering they were causing through it year after year

in my opinion my friend history asks only one practical religious question

who will judge the victors

my photo of the RULER

from the early 1980s is hanging above grey metal cabinets wonderfully discoloured and faded by now just like its fellow photos in so many places where we know that the only thing we can do to him is

time

in the metal cabinets are the piles of my material with contributions to the next devastating set of UNICEF statistics the civil servants in the health ministry are keen on this because it only accuses the

ENEMY

and not the smuggler-barons and black marketeers who feast and flaunt their wealth in the few top-class restaurants left nor the corrupt officials who following the principle of oil for caviar are doing splendidly out of the sanctions gravy train

at the moment I still have enough paracetamol to supply a woman with a slipped disc an operation would probably not produce an improvement anyway I reluctantly reassure a beanpole in the uniform of the Revolutionary Guards that he's only got diarrhoea and not typhoid as he feared I can spare a little more paracetamol for a 14-year-old with inflammation of the middle ear but no antibiotics even though he's howling with pain his grandfather to whom I recommend the usual household remedies used to be an English teacher and tells me that for years now he's had to feed three families by selling household goods and spices because his two sons were in the army and fell during the retreat from Kuwait

with which (my friend) we ought to get to the beginning (or one of the beginnings) of the story that's coming to an end here on our ramshackle machines in contrast to the young fry of the generation who grew up under the sanctions regime assuming they didn't die from it and had so little contact with the outside world that they had no chance of understanding how all this misery has come to be visited upon us

we old fossils can still remember the

glorious moment

of the victory over the Persians (the split Dome of the Martyrs the cut-off giant sabre-holding forearms over the magnificent street the helmets of fallen enemies fixed like tortoise shells to the concrete base) the

PRESIDENT

had won he had

defended

the Arab world the interests of the West the border of the USSR (with the generous support of all of them) with streams

of HIS

Iraqi blood from

Khomeini's hordes

a million men of his victorious army were still under arms and were beginning to eat him out of house and home while HE was defenceless stuck in the mire of foreign debt holding out his empty hands (his spare pair) to his

Arab brothers

who however suddenly remembered that they preferred to dip their own fingers into their own chests of gold and thinking that the PRESIDENT was now too powerful they (the Saudis the Kuwaitis) refused him further credit and in addition called in Iraq's war debt and what is more sold oil well beyond the OPEC-agreed upper limit so that the price collapsed and the PRESIDENT was finally forced to remember

that WE ought to quickly liberate (from their billions of petrodollars) the people of Kuwait who were under the yoke of the corrupt Sabah clan but finally ready to rebel

all that was at stake on the surface (of the Earth)

was a portion of desert and a portion of sea

a minor backyard affair like Panama for the US or the Falkland Islands for Britain so that the PRESIDENT felt he could assume a certain understanding and certainly deduced that from the legendary discussion HE had with the US ambassador Glaspie at which she thought that HE could surely not have thought that her statement that they had no opinion on an intra-Arab conflict meant they would do nothing if he were to conquer the *whole* of Kuwait (instead of only the disputed Rumaila oilfields and one or two uninhabited islands) and from there might possibly turn against Saudi Arabia after all she had gone on to say that given the troops HE had massed on the Kuwait border HE ought—in the spirit of friendship—to think over his intentions but HE

refused to think

was too stupid (as Glaspie later stated to the US Senate) to imagine what the US' reaction would be if

they had been growing oranges (alternatively dates or cactuses) in Kuwait and a senior US official (no name) later commented in that case Washington would have quite happily

gone on vacation

but as it was it was a case of an attempt to snatch

the fattest oil barrel in the world

and their friend Saddam was suddenly a reincarnation of Hitler and any toleration or unnecessary concessions would be a new edition of the Munich Agreement (Mrs Thatcher told Mr Bush) and so it happened that hardly had

the Kuwait branch returned to the Iraq trunk on our TV screens and hardly had we been able to undertake a few fine raids on the palaces and shopping centres of the Sabahs who had disappeared like lightning and improvise a few artisanal Iraqi torture chambers in garages and cellars than

that diplomatic merry-go-round began

with its genuine horror and grotesque comedy

of the battle of the lies

until the mother of all battles

from the incubator murders (a professional fairy-tale product of a US advertising agency presented by the 15-year-old daughter of the Kuwaiti ambassador in Washington as a supposed eye-witness to the stunned members of the UN Human Rights Committee

312

babies dying

on the cold floor)

to the flagellant theatre of the human shields (visit Iraq smile for the cameras take 20 30 100 fellow countrymen home as souvenirs Kurt Waldheim Jesse Jackson Willy Brandt Edward Heath)

the PRESIDENT bends down places his hand on the shoulder of a seven-year-old English boy paralysed with fear and asks him in Arabic whether he's been given his

MILK

yet)

the milk of death from the cow of international abhorrence poured out red and black

over Iraq and I woke one morning covered in fragments of plaster someone had shaken the whole building by the shoulder (the modern block of flats where we lived at the time today I couldn't afford it but the rent could be going down by now) Farida carried Sami and I Muna who was five out into the street (she hadn't woken up and was breathing steadily in my ear) after the third explosion the sirens gradually started up but we were well away from the districts where the bombs were dropping

what do we have to complain about

perhaps the extent of the destruction the lack of precision of the precision weapons we could ask why so many schools and hospitals were hit and why tens of thousands of civilians died why it was considered necessary to drop more bombs during the first two weeks of the war than the Allies did during the whole of the Second World War perhaps you could talk of the boundlessly self-righteous hatred of the side that was going to win all along who were presumably waiting for statements such as our PRESIDENT'S incredibly cruel announcement in which he said he was hoping for such a bloody ground war that the squeamish Western governments wouldn't be able to stand it in contrast to the

Iraqi people

who were ready and willing to shed their blood to the last drop

when 150,000 Iraqi and 376 Allied soldiers die in one week of the war (the latter mostly through accidents) then perhaps the question of cruelty arises once more which was only asked more loudly by befuddled reprimanded controlled arrested journalists of the

FREE WORLD

when on the

Highway of Death that dead straight road to Kuwait

on which among others the two sons of my old English teacher/spice merchant were burnt to ashes in the same moment

an aerial slaughterhouse could be admired at work

with international TV cameras running (inadvertently)

after which it gradually seemed advisable to break off Operation Destroy-the-fleeing-Iraqi-army but leaving us with the question which for 10 years had continued on its murderous way burning into our flesh of why after so many victims they had not also liberated us from our PRESIDENT (sudden concern for stability consideration of public opinion the possibility that the power of the Iranian mullahs might be strengthened) which would have been easy if you can believe what some US generals said

after 42 days of war

on the mountain of 200,000 or 250,000 Iraqis

our PRESIDENT had now

once more

WON

weregardourvictoryasahistoricduelnotasaconflictbetweenonearmyandvariousothersandyouarevictoriousbecauseyourejectedattemptsatintimidationandrepression

the old English teacher is still sitting facing my desk telling me about his sons while his grandson into whose ear I've put some cotton wool soaked in essential oil is staring irritatedly at my motionless therefore energy-saving ceiling fan

I've stayed in Baghdad (I suddenly think) because people talk to one another here that's a reason you could give in retrospect but at the time there simply came a point when I realized I'd left it too late to flee to join the great

brain drain

that swept thousands of doctors teachers scientists out of the country I was presumably just too slow I can't even really say now why we stayed all I can remember is that at the time torn between fear and rage at everyone like a confused camel on the black scorched desert ground among the gigantic torches of the burning oil boreholes I staggered through life drained by the day and night shifts I had been drafted into until I found

I was once more on the winning side in a war and sent my two younger children to the wrecked schools of Embargoland with a kind of mixture of grief and pride

if the VILLAINS suffered the way we suffered
then I had to stay
at least
as a doctor

PERSPECTIVE

For Fadhil al-Azzawi

I fell from a stork's long beak
    High above Baghdad.
With my father I went to Babylon,
    And my mother took me to Najaf.
I fled from the tower and the mosque,
    The jaws of the lion and the fire of Islam.
Burning, I was devoured
    By an ancient wing-borne monster.

The blue

    in the morning

    it'll be almost a year it's

    September again

    the end of a summer the cloudless blue cuts through the curtains no comes in through a vertical gap between them of course it's not the blue just the brightness the white light on my closed lids the unbearable energy and brilliance of the late summer's day again and again I keep feeling as if I were waking up

    numb (benumbed)

    as if it were possible that the light the brightness the mercilessly unfeeling blue had caught me before all profane sounds and given me a local anaesthetic benumbing my ears I feel as if I were waking up

    on an immense surface the

    Blue Screen

    THE BLUE

    I can only see the word as a threat as pure destructive potential for out of the blue you can only come as a

    bolt

    sending you if you're lucky into a dream that's the best that can happen to me I still can't hear anything eventually just the soft sounds of waves and seabirds and I wake in the morning on the beach in that

    dream of questions and answers

    the strip of sand at Rockport curved like a crescent moon the grey beach the dogs and the seagulls the fresh wind the sleep in my in her eyes her soft hand still a toddler's hand in mine she's six or seven I can't tell any more just after or just before she started school Amanda's still in bed and we walk across the smooth almost untouched sand that the water has given a coat like shining varnish her hand briefly lets go of mine to pick up a cockle a snail shell a stone and returns damp and cool and sandy I wipe a child's cold runny nose it's

    the time of questions

in the quiet the cool air

I just want to go

back I just want to be on this beach

PARADISE

(tell this to the murderers overwrite the so-called holy books shout it out to the world)

is nothing

but a single scene in the past

that you can enter again and again

without realizing you've already been there a thousand times and without knowing what is to come

she looks up and asks (it's as if she's intoxicated infantile intoxication the oxygen she can't stop asking questions)

How did the water get onto the Earth?—There used to be ice, then it melted.—Do you believe in God or in primitive man?—You mean evolution, that everything developed from really small animals over millions of years.—Yes, until the apes came and some turned into humans. Do you believe that?—Yes I do.—But can an ape turn into a human now, in a zoo for example?—Not that quickly, it takes a long, long time.—But some time or other humans were there and were driven out of paradise?—That's what it says in the Bible.—But why were the apes and the other animals driven out? The ones that went in Noah's Ark? And the snake was in the Ark as well, wasn't it? So why do people think it's the devil?

in order to have an explanation for evil I think I say that's all

people want

simple images they can hold on to then all at once

the sounds come with the light I open my eyes the honking of horns the constant drone interrupted by the wailing sirens a rumble not the distant thunder of a storm in another town of a rockfall in a nearby range of mountains but the collapse of the Towers within a few seconds and the tidal wave it set off until the deathly hush of the first night after it during which no one from round the smoking churned-up grey-black wound tormented by dazzling operating-room lights seemed to go out I

go to the window each morning and stare down from the seventh floor at the tangled everyday flashing confusion of Amsterdam Avenue

the simple image

used to be:

Hate-fuelled terrorism declares war on the CIVILIZED WORLD

an icon for

statesmen lining up hand on heart at Ground Zero National Anthem Flag Holy Firefighters Patriot Act War

against Terrorism

the plain the quickest the burning pictures a year ago were clearer were more precise

TERRORISTSCRASHHIJACKEDAIRLINERSINTOWORLDTRADE-CENTERPENTAGONSOURCES 'GOOD INDICATIONS' OSMAMABIN-LADENINVOLVEDINATTACKS

the incomprehensible reality melts in the past in its monstrous scale the still incomprehensible reality is a comfort I dashed

out of the house in Amherst it was already

shattered afternoon

the southern tip of Manhattan had been smoking for some time already black as a supertanker hit by incendiary bombs I drove telephoned got out in order to phone because I was stuck I had no reception was too agitated to drive and phone at the same time again and again screens radio-voices airplanes light as shadows plunging into skyscrapers as if they were thin aluminium pillars huge vomited fireballs traffic jams roadblocks accidents still unsuspecting people telephone booths by restaurants filling stations malls in order to perhaps get more information than with my cellphone all I have is that

THEY'RE IN THERE

driving me mad when I knew that THERE no longer existed (its last sign and memorial the cubes outlined by millions of scraps of paper and small debris a white shimmer in memory of the torn souls of the Towers) at first I couldn't get through to Seymour the cellphone networks in the Financial District had collapsed I didn't know Eric Mrs Donally wasn't in I had two numbers for Amanda's colleagues but got no more reply from them than from her I only got answering machines responding to the engaged tone mailboxes with synthetic voices telling me I was in a queue leading right up to the deepest abyss

THEY'RE IN THERE

for weeks and weeks I had Seymour's terrible words inside my head and those words are never-ending and won't go away those words

spoken at 10.06 on Broadway within sight of the Twin Towers after they'd been hit one minute before the South Tower crumbled Seymour had hung up and set off running only to freeze immediately

for 10 seconds

an avalanche coming down totally against reason a happening belonging to a completely different (geological, alpine) context

a cloud the height of a tower came flying towards him edged as if wrongly drawn or in a stupid cartoon by the hard vertical lines of the tower blocks but then

Goya's Titan

right above you

trampling you underfoot

no oddly enough just sending you to

a deafening booming grey-and-white world out of which figures of ash and smoke stumble vomit fall to the ground as if into a foam of rubble so light it looks as if the sharp-edged shattered objects wouldn't cut you as if all those you're looking for should come stumbling towards you any minute like these coughing spewing screaming cloud-born bankers housewives policemen someone dragged him into a shop closed the glass door just in time before the next cloud front (blacker higher a storm-cannon loaded with bits of debris) came hurtling past and all at once it was night and he was in a cramped drugstore with 15 other people bathed in the light of fluorescent tubes like fish in an aquarium

that's the way they're still there inside us as if enclosed in a luminous internal aquarium Amanda Sabrina that they can't escape from that we protect with our flesh our skin with the last of our

life Seymour

I didn't make it to Manhattan that night I stood beside my car in New Jersey sank after hours in the darkness to the ground on a path along the embankment leaning back against the front wheel and staring across the Hudson the Towers should have been on the far right just a conglomerate of smoke low flickering light seething darkness rising inky-black clouds adjoining the tower blocks beneath the pale sky plane-less over the whole of America that completely cleared-out upper storey over the whole of America such a sky as there was in Goethe's days

suddenly there was nothing but this

I-can't-stay-upright-any-more

as if that were my only problem a policeman spoke to me I drove the car onto the shoulder and must have told him something about Sabrina for he brought me a cup of coffee and wrote nothing in his notebook today I'd like to know his name so many people are meeting now that it's all over to stare back into the past together at the dazzlingly bright shield of a crazy day that even in the hundredth repetition and under the pressure of millions and millions of looks will not yield one fraction of an inch nor lose anything of its mercilessly clear steely blueness

but night had already fallen I was shivering or trembling so much that I got back in the car and continued to stare into the darkness from there until it gradually started to become transparent as if I'd won as if the Towers could now rise again in that long-drawn-out vertical column of smoke initially black and of a dense oiliness then getting lighter and thinner smoke that could still be seen months later over the ravaged ground a veil refusing to dissipate like spectral hands clouding the brilliant views from all the helicopters high above the destroyed complex their penetration into the

DEVASTATION AREA

fed by the glowing hardly extinguishable underground cores three or five storeys deep beneath the rubble of high-density baked materials the kerosene had turned into a blazing bonfire

in the morning light I saw that I'd almost knocked a fire hydrant over the policeman who'd told me to park properly had presumably not noticed I was in Hoboken in a desolate area between football stadiums right by the river and looked across why Hoboken of all places I wondered several times perhaps because I'd once heard that soldiers' saying (Heaven, Hell or Hoboken) finally I managed to make it to Manhattan after a roundabout drive to George Washington Bridge then on foot and with buses the car parked close to City College was stolen because I'd forgotten to lock it that was a relief and made me all the more determined to keep to my decision to stay in Manhattan and to stick it out whatever it turned out to be I found a hotel room which I used as a base for the two days I spent wandering round trying to get closer to

the zone

that monstrous shape of fumes and smoke spreading between the tower blocks like a mushroom cloud that can't get off the ground

IT'S WAR

ACT OF WAR

the front pages on the second day

just imagine Hiroshima an acquaintance (a macroeconomist, a man who takes the long view) said a few weeks later or the area-bombing of cities during the Second World War

why I asked did Sabrina have to die there but he said we must find a limit to the boundless pain something that would put it in perspective

what perspective

what for

I saw the

PRESIDENT (George Bush Jr whom we at the universities had once derided) and was suddenly hanging on his thin lips at least for one day for those few minutes recorded the evening before for the constant repetitions which he spoke with greater and greater difficulty with apparently decreasing strength while

on those same screens the Towers crashed down ever more perfectly ever more expressively from ever more ingenious camera angles

terrible sadness

evil axis

AMERICA UNDER ATTACK

we will make no difference between

those

defend

a great nation

we will be open

for business

tomorrow

good night

there will be war and I want to see their bodies piled up in great heaps said a weedy blond man in a smart dust-covered brown suit beside me

what for a huge fat Puerto Rican policewoman retorted

what for

shortly afterwards I finally got Seymour on the phone we were standing a few yards from each other at an office for missing persons provisionally set up at the roadside looking out onto a street strewn with debris that beyond two police barriers was blocked by a landslide of twisted metal sloping up to the tenth floor of the buildings on either side that looked completely untouched it must have been one of the World Trade Center buildings later on no one could explain why (with the exception of the Marriott Hotel) only those seven buildings that belonged to the World Trade Center were destroyed

we must check their movements we have to be sure

Seymour said and so we began

to share what we knew I was at a disadvantage I'd assumed Sabrina was on Long Island it was the first I'd heard of her plan to go to California with Eric for two weeks and I discovered that Seymour was the last person to have seen her in the afternoon in his and Amanda's apartment on Little Brazil Street where she'd left her blue rucksack and had a cup of tea before (possibly) going to see a friend on the Upper East Side (intending to spend the night at her place she'd told Seymour) whose exact name and address we never did find out

everything had to be noted down established researched we had to cut our way through the black web of uncertainties and we put together all the telephone calls all the available scheduled appointments all the sentences and half sentences of all available witnesses but from the very beginning we had no chance I wish I'd never been in Amanda's office on the 94th floor of the North Tower and never seen that picture of my stressed almost irritated ex-wife looking up from between two computer screens in her dark knee-length skirt and white blouse suddenly smiling because she remembered she'd asked me to drop by and for a moment forgot that we'd long since stopped loving each other then recovered and showed me the

fantastic view

over the Upper Bay as far as Staten Island because the buttresses of the outer facade were so close together to see it I had to go close to the window and to her I saw a shining sapphire expanse in the dazzling light but what is precisely etched on my memory is the dull shimmer of her pearl necklace and her perfectly starched white blouse (some

synthetic material or a cotton–synthetic mixture) the elegant lustre of damask contrasting with her bronzed freckled skin and I'm glad I can remember she was wearing a perfume I didn't know glad I can remember that I didn't recognize it and not the smell itself it's the blessing of imprecision that was given us less and less that could only be granted us (Seymour and me) as far as time was concerned as a dissolving cloud round a point that from the very beginning was precisely determined

8.45: impact of American Airlines flight 011 Boeing 707 on the 96th floor of the northern side of the North Tower

they spent three weeks looking for survivors before the first large pieces of wreckage were taken away those scissor-like bizarre bars of the fragmented lower facade past which the tracker dogs were led over the extruding masonry and steel girders by specialists how many specialists has Death you asked yourself

(one for

every person)

then we saw Ground Zero from close to again and again from the platform that had been set up for the families of the victims but

after three weeks we were past all hope we had groped our way through a tangle of blank spaces (for it was no more than that just our conjectures and deductions and the detours we had to follow that wearying meticulous detective work which appeared to allow us the expectation of good news) we talked to a lawyer from Brooklyn who did some work for Amanda's firm whom she had called at 8.15 (30 minutes to go) from her office as she'd said

until after talking to members of the formerly 22-strong firm three-quarters of whom had been lost (I often came across the families of people who were missing I would have felt like a messenger boy of Death had not all those people been as open and helpful as could be and had I not had long devastating telephone conversations with people I didn't know in Queens Brooklyn Lower Manhattan) we found a colleague who because of a heavy cold had stayed at home on that glorious late summer's day and talked to Amanda on her office landline at 8.35

10 minutes

would have been enough time to get out using the express elevators or just 10 storeys up or down from which so many people had made it

who however very quickly made themselves known who were found in the nearby hospitals every day sent us deeper in the night this time we weren't some of the lucky ones whose friends relatives

wives

children

had escaped there

were hopes that flared up brightly for example the ridiculous idea that after she'd left Amanda and Seymour's apartment Sabrina might have changed her mind and run away and remained hidden until that day or even that she and Amanda had taken the opportunity to free themselves from us (from me and from Seymour OK but why from Eric) and everything else oppressing them and start a new life together

but Amanda had had a completely normal business conversation she'd only been in the office for three-quarters of an hour there was not the slightest reason for her to leave all at once our only hope was fixed

on Sabrina until

Sabrina's room-mate Julia called me

in the middle of October

she then came specially to New York City she'd found her mobile that had got lost in all the excitement of the ATTACK and after she had found it only slowly and reluctantly as if she had to go into an ice-cold room came to understand

what Sabrina's call in her mailbox meant

2001-9-11 / 8.37 a.m.

Sabrina's voice sounds tired but cheerful warm happy determined

(there's tiredness in it there's reason for happiness they were making plans

what else should I have thought)

there was a key dangling from Julia's mobile and a little toy tiger that I found unbearable in the minutes during which I listened three times to the short message

that she was going to miss the first week of semester because she was setting off that day with her boyfriend (Eric, as you know) on a Greyhound the first time she'd be travelling so far by bus she just had to have a word with her mother first

she was phoning from outside her office (by the glass door with the frosted section at stomach height giving you an odd view of the torsos and heads on the other side as if living busts were moving round in there) and now she was going to hang up

See you, bye-bye

Julia (plump red-haired eyes rain-coloured swollen with tears) sat opposite me exhausted at a Starbucks table she wanted to give me the last recording of Sabrina's voice (not even 20 seconds) somehow hand it over rather but it wasn't inside the lilac mobile with the toy tiger and I couldn't be accessing her mailbox all the time

if I . . . her last words . . . Julia stammered

after a mute oppressive minute we had the idea of copying Sabrina's message with the sound-recording function on my mobile but it didn't have one so I bought a little dictaphone and we sat on a bench in Central Park and held the two machines close to each other

you can still hear a blackbird singing in the distance (there are gardens there but not for the murderers) I didn't want to try and record it again but Seymour didn't notice when he held the little silver device to his ear instead of turning the volume up

eight minutes

we didn't need to continue our enquiries it was too unlikely the offices on the north side of the 94th floor had been destroyed immediately it was only half a second after breaching the facade that the plane had reached the core of the building with the elevator shafts actually fusing with the building tearing apart vaporizing itself and everything round it until all that was left were red-hot pieces the size of your fist in the fireball of 34,000 litres of burning kerosine

it's death

in one breath filling the lungs with fire could have filled them but has already destroyed them with the rest of the body before you even feel it

the blue that clear apparently silky blue

appears in the heart of a flame the whole sky of that day (in which I keep waking up and waking up) could perhaps be better explained as the section of a fire of a flame over such a large part of the world where

in September in the city

can you still find

a butterfly

Muna

They give me a glass of champagne after all

I'm over 18 and a second glass won't do me any harm as I'm assured by the exhilarated beaming Qasim the 40-year-old birthday boy sweating in his light-blue shirt as he introduces me and Sami to his guests telling them I'll soon be passing my school-leaving exam with 120 out of 100 I drink

cautiously

I don't say much and when I do

then cautiously as well say nothing about London that's all I ask

my father said

before he put Sami and me into the red-and-white taxi he'd never go to one of his elder daughter's gatherings and Farida also made her excuses but she was all in favour of me putting on the shiny thin light-green dress she bought with me two months ago for the school-leaving party and other grand occasions

such as the victory celebrations when we've finished America off Tariq said dryly

who knows when you can wear it again my mother said with tears in her eyes and pins between her teeth just this one seam she's already filled so many shelves in the cellar with preserves bottles and cans she firmly believes war is coming she almost wants it to come I think all her preparations are going to bring it about

it's so nice to get out of the old house in Betawiyn for one evening

although even there I (recently)

have been getting that surreal floating madly light-headed feeling that has overcome me here among all the people in their finery it began with Sami and me alone in the taxi driving through the darkness past the lights of Abu Nuwas Street in the throng of hooting cars full of singing laughing people three wedding parties one after the other so exuberant as if when they crossed the Tigris they'd go straight into another country or life it only became quieter at Damascus Square and in the upper-class al-Mansur district where we got on quickly before stopping outside that four-storey block of modern flats I'm not accustomed to standing among guests in a short-sleeved knee-length dress with a glass of champagne in my hand

my sister

the beautiful hawk with the amethyst plumage naturally puts me in the shade and also most of the other women in short dresses and suits including a few with hair dyed blond or red I'm clumsier more powerfully built less supple than Yasmin and

yet I float

it's as if I simply couldn't touch the floor once I dreamt I'd been forcibly filled with helium but now it's only the solar buoyancy

of love

Sami too in his black trousers and my father's best dark-green shirt looks happy and at ease he like me will be pleased (not to mention how pleased Tariq would be!) to see no olive green and no khaki not a single officer so at least it looks as if one year after her marriage Yasmin has managed to get the Major's paw off her delicate wiry neck she seems more cheerful more excited sometimes even more embarrassed than previously as she greets and entertains her guests together with that Chaldaean couple who once ran a restaurant and have been employed specially for the occasion and are looking after the buffet the canapés and the drinks (choice fruit juices Turkish beer Iraqi arrack French wine Scotch whisky etc)

my brother-in-law has told a plump lady with a beehive hairstyle that I'm interested in archaeology and ancient history and would like to study it

here in Baghdad

of course but surely with a few semesters in London as well the lady says in her cherry-red suit that looks as if it's been cut out of one of my mother's 1970s fashion catalogues she talks loudly and no one contradicts her she has a positively obscene way of pushing her body forward as if she were trying to get the best place in the hammam and didn't need to restrain herself because there were only women round and I can't stop myself thinking that for dessert she'll sit in Qasim's leather armchair and swell up and spread her legs I can't do anything about my imagination I'm as disturbing and dissecting

as an anatomical atlas and as crazy as

Dinarzad it could well be (and this would explain much) that the king and her sister and all the wonderful stories she tells are nothing more than Dinarzad's own inventions I'm so happy I'm too over-excited

but the laid-back and confident manner of the elegant people here this evening (presumably mostly engineers and scientists from the Dora Refinery) calm me they're so different from our neighbours in Betawiyn who always keep their heads down to avoid the blows of the next catastrophe in a week's time Bush is to address the UN and he'll be sending us new weapons inspectors for us to play hide-and-seek with someone says it doesn't matter what he sends another replies he'll still get it back split into two halves

even into three halves

Iraqi arithmetic my sister quickly says as she goes past them with a glint of mild mockery she's somehow charged up but you can't tell with what she greets a massive fat middle-aged man with a walrus moustache carrying a sack a frightening

but quite nervous

friendly-looking rather anxious

figure

he takes a glass of water Qasim places a chair for him in the wide doorway between the living room and the dining room the sweat's pouring down his round face that looks as if it's been inflated the brown linen bag slips down to the floor the shining polished coconut-like body of an oud appears his fat round fingers hover apparently helplessly over the double strings press down on the fragile neck

all

the voices inside you

however precise however complex however sensitive self-willed tender they may be

will find a place

will be intertwined

woven in the tapestry of life into a perfect ornament

Beloved

I drink champagne and sweet raisin juice I go out onto the balcony stand beside my brother and no one knows I'm hiding you my bare arms my open hair the thin dress the oud-player knows fast lilting tunes as well to which one of the guests is drumming with his fingers on the upturned lid of a pot so very skilfully so exactly right that the virtuoso is pleased

O Love! before we pass death's portal through,
And potters make their jugs of me and you,
Pour from this jug some wine, of headache void,
And fill your cup, and fill my goblet too!

were those not the lines of Omar Khayyam that Umm Kulthum sang in
Ahmed Rami's translation the voice of our old teacher Uncle Mahmud says
inside my head you came Beloved with the sound of an old poem that I was
trying to learn off by heart facing the dazzling sunlit wall of the house next
door how pleased I am that Yasmin is keeping better company than at her
wedding a year ago they're such happy relaxed educated people here what
a pleasant and liberating environment ideal for

hiding something

I lean on the balcony railing in the night in the crush of glass-clinking
guests on my face the spring breeze which only I can feel but they all ought
to see it for how can you hide a laughing heart have you ever been

to Babylon

the woman with the beehive hairdo asks me she must be a bigwig or
the wife of one to talk so loudly and in such a free-and-easy way

to our wonderful festival? no unfortunately not (folk-dance groups
from lots of countries at the fall-to-your-knees-before-your-god-Saddam-is-
greater-than-Nebuchadnezzar-spectacle as Tariq calls it)

in my Babylon there could also be such a darkly blooming tropical night
and everyone would go out onto the balconies as if under a veil of perfume
as here it would be both lively and calm at the same time as in this wide
fashionable street with its palm trees and villas and gardens Beloved we'd
have the same party in my Babylon only

for the whole town

and I would be standing beside you like my sister among the guests I
only have to close my eyes a little and dream myself away to the sound of
the oud as if from the terraces of the Temple of Marduk I'd look out over
the Hanging Gardens and I wouldn't need the magnificent avenue and the
tower I imagine a really peaceful joyful festive Babylon for all in

1,001 years no in 101 years

everyone will be able to go out onto their balcony without poverty without fear without hunger without power cuts a whole town having a party
on their balconies I open my eyes and see

smiling relaxed attentive polite people I can't understand how I can tell two of Qasim's colleagues in such an unselfconscious and ironic way about the long-promised trip to the real Babylon for which Tariq borrowed his brother Fuad's rickety old Opel that he called an old Teutonic camel and drove like a learner driver going wild

the thing that I am hiding

lights up their faces shines out through my skin glows in my eyes raises my breasts no one has ever touched them (they go and see my colleague Ahmed in his garage he makes virgins out of whores with nothing more than a few hundred dinars my father says how can I be romantic as the daughter of that doctor)

Yasmin

the hawk

touches my left shoulder she almost never stays close to her husband as is presumably right and proper for good hosts her slim fingers with the red-varnished nails test apparently playfully (like those of a slave trader) the flesh of my round upper arm

you are

she says and doesn't finish the sentence but lets me see that she

can sense you inside me

Beloved

she's so much more fiery supple elegant than me I've never been kissed! I want to tell her to her face why perhaps

because she's alive

and I just invent the stories but this time it's different her breaking up with her Major is no more real than me starting with you Beloved archae-ology's very nice she says softly giving me a brief squeeze the main thing is to keep your courage up Sister then—

again she doesn't finish the sentence but I imagine that THEN I will also have an apartment like this will be able to invite people round like this (even in difficult and depressed times) I don't need to invent a French pilot an Egyptian doctor an English archaeologist any more (anyway I have an Arab figure) and my own friends will come Huda with her two proud lovers and Eren with a husband and seven children

the elections are in October

I hear someone say shortly before we leave and after the terrifyingly anxious-looking oud-player has put his instrument away in the linen bag as carefully as if it were a newborn baby

oh dear Tariq replies—they'll put a cross in their own blood next to HIS name each one will cast sheaves of votes they'll dance in the streets until the cameras are switched off—my sister says in the spirit of my father I was so flabbergasted that I thought I could hear his voice saying her words I presume you know that HE once wanted to learn to play the oud that great Arabic instrument and HE had the best player come to him but he

could neither play nor speak

out of fear

goodbye little Sister she squeezes my hand so hard it hurts gives me a kiss on the cheek urges me to the door so that I can't see whom she was talking to Qasim takes us out to the taxi all blabber and BO and best wishes to our parents

Ah, my Beloved, fill the Cup that clears
Today of past Regrets and future Fears—

Sami gives the driver our address then sinks down onto the seat beside me he's probably not had such a good time as I did he refuses to speak during the drive I enjoy rumbling along in the night even though the skinny Egyptian driver fiddles about under the steering wheel with a long screwdriver at every red light Tariq used to have a car he sold it rather than his books in

my Babylon

people should just be able to fly or at least get up onto the roofs where they'd be picked up by lovely quiet flying machines made of wood string canvas like those Leonardo da Vinci thought up and carried silently and completely safely to their destination I don't know whether Sami still plays the Flight Simulator since the time he showed me he could even fly a Concorde to Manhattan over the little island with the shining green Statue of Liberty directly towards the closely packed skyscrapers towards the soaring grey Twin Towers Sami has grown apart from me he goes round with his friends a lot and visits the newly opened Internet cafes

you haven't understood anything at all!

he says in a strained voice after we've got out of the taxi in Betawiyn and are still outside the door of the house that's in darkness you who're usually so clever didn't even notice those nasty guys they were

terrible people I never want to go there again but you

never notice anything

what's

the matter with you?

The telephone

it's Seymour it's Thursday 5 September 2002 it's the

259th day since that other call (from that other planet inside a nightmare they all say that as they walk towards the

SITE

they're going out of the city

into a dream)

he wants to know what I've decided whether I want to keep the apartment on Amsterdam Avenue for longer one of the one-and-a-half-room apartments his firm NORTHERN OIL makes available for their workers at a low rent

it's no problem

Seymour says and suggests that in the coming academic year I should give another lecture course at Columbia University who've been very obliging to me as visiting professor and I could talk to UMass about a sabbatical on half pay if I have a minimum of research to show the things he knows about me and about what's good for me

but that's the fatherly way we've been talking to each other

since then

I'll make my decision by the end of the week we'll meet for lunch on Saturday

we'll see then Seymour says the neutral restrained indifferent furnishings of the apartment help me have been helping me for 259 days and nights (no 245 days and nights I forgot the night in the car and the first nights in the hotel)

to stand outside

above all outside myself enough for me to survive Seymour gives me a farewell cough his agonizing badge of honour he worked with a group of volunteers at Ground Zero for three weeks until he was forced to admit that he wasn't up to it couldn't stand the strain any more

stay he says you have to come to terms with it

in your own way it's the only way

that will allow you to keep breathing beneath thousands and thousands of tons of stone steel melted glass

with

METEORITES

among it as they said strange lumps fused together out of the material of the Towers the offices the steel girders the hundreds of kinds of metal and plastics the concrete the stone the fibres the textiles the electrical appliances the cables the human bones turned into strange kinds of extraterrestrial objects (what else are the dead)

breathing my friend tells me what

breathing is (in medical terms the windpipe the bronchial tube the lungs the whole respiratory apparatus)

his cough pursues me his characteristic shallow cough which gets me down because I don't have one the rubble cough the existence of which the authorities are still denying as a new illness as a fingerprint lungprint the sign of an authentic witness lodged in his chest he was actually right there when

the Towers fell

on HOLY TUESDAY

as they call it

while I was running down Amity Street to the UMass sports stadium in Amherst at 8.23 American Airlines flight no. 011 deviated from its scheduled course and flew towards New York City turned practically over my head (nothing no memory not even a shadow) invisibly towards the west to kill my ex-wife and my daughter you have to

comprehend it just comprehend of course there's no understanding which always has a germ of forgiveness that could develop we must I must

comprehend

without hatred without rage (or even with both)

but it's impossible without hands I think and I know why I'd once hidden Grimms' *Fairy Tales* from Sabrina before she could read better and faster I bought a new edition suitable for children because I found the story of the girl without hands too terrible it must have been in the first grade she still sometimes felt very lost and when I collected her from school we'd go hand in hand for a while but she wanted to feel more of me and would hold on tight to my forearm would squeeze it almost hang from it she would presumably have best liked to go arm in arm with me as she did with her friends but that wasn't possible because of the difference in height and later on we never did it why not I can't understand that those hands were destroyed I

can't bear it all I can bear is

the questions when

will my questions be answered (when we have tired where did I read that or when

any further answer will just tire us) Question Number One the official main question of the metropolis

WHY DO THEY HATE US

why did they kill so many of us that's how we must put it for some murdered them without even having sufficient hatred (but then what was sufficient for them) who are

THEY

who are

WE I'm not even an American so all these flags on apartment windows car windscreens doors bicycles telephone masts traffic lights switch boxes TV screens T-shirts buses concrete walls trash cans flower beds signs in front gardens fences facades cups plates caps

aren't mine the

STARS AND STRIPES

although I can understand the great despairing oppressive liberating embrace and although there were times when I would mentally wrap myself in the American flag and close my eyes to find the peace at last that no longer exists in my life I can't rest I have to keep asking myself the most important and most idiotic questions why DO THEY HATE US why was it precisely 111 days to the end of the year why was the emergency number on all telephones 911 why just the seven World Trade Center buildings why do I count

the days why

am I still eating drinking talking writing I (am NOTHING)

am a question and the truly endless weariness at the state of mankind that will never improve I'm an ALIEN in New York I'm the ALIEN in my own life the outsider that existentialist construct we grew up with (that in those days could still come from Earth) am I real now I wake up and for a moment I think I can feel the weight of my three-year-old daughter on me when we slept together in one bed she would often roll onto my belly or back several times during the night it's the Discovery effect you're a shuttle Amanda said I have to go round all day with the impression of that wonderful little weight a man made of sand of glass the fire turns the one into the other

we lived in the East Village for three years eight months after we moved there we celebrated my thirtieth birthday a smoky beer-bottle-fuelled argumentative jazzy party even today I can't look at those streets again the district in which with Amanda I played out our own version of *Barefoot in the Park* more true to life though today it seems to me almost equally Hollywoodesque as a melancholy and semi-hypocritical comedy of a still indigent couple with tragically cheerful aspirations among fruit boxes and fraying wicker chairs the mini ironing board we had to put on the table when we wanted to iron our shirts and blouses I can't stop

my memory opening a window on Amanda's still perfectly smooth bronzed thigh on those morning hours when I awoke looked at the other pillow and could not believe my luck with this young blonde American student sleeping beside me dazed with life drunk the moment my eyes opened leaning over in the shimmer of happiness Amanda's rapid vigorous reaction as if you'd woken a gazelle an antelope sex as if with a strong hyper-nervous naturally shy animal a chase with quivering flushed still almost skinny bodies

the man made of glass

has to

tell himself that it made no difference that we took Sabrina away when she was still floating in her mother's womb took her out of the merciless metropolis (the harsh shrill shabby New York of the late 1970s) having a child's a serious matter Amanda said I didn't become a writer nor a script-writer or dramatist but an assistant professor but even that

made no difference

Sabrina was conceived in New York City and that's where she

left

this earth

we don't need to delude ourselves

we know the time and the place not as a point it's true but still as precisely as a noose going round our neck there was fire and there was an explosion too violent too fast to allow even awareness of pain (I tell myself again and again)

3,000 people 20,000 recorded body parts

we didn't get anything no notification from the Forenstic Department that sorted through 1.5 million tonnes of rubble stone by stone

ring by ring

we had nothing to bury

when in February we decided on a symbolic burial a funeral with no substance with less even than ashes with the alarming sense of a murder or rather of a threatened murder I often found it impossible to believe that Sabrina was no longer alive even when I'd long since given up all hope for Amanda

on that day I thought

the memorial ceremony had the character of an act of aggression as well it was nothing other than the expression of our inability to bear the lack of knowledge of clarity the vague feeling that they might still be there the living banded together for an

elimination

Amanda's parents from California Amanda's colleagues who on that day hadn't gone to the firm that had been three-quarters obliterated (a business specializing in copyright and software licences and that kind of thing I never really understood what they did but they certainly never murdered anyone never harmed a hair of the head of a single Muslim but who cares) countless friends and acquaintances of Seymour Amanda's friends but not her lover so many students from Amherst and MIT and finally Eric whom I might have liked as Sabina's boyfriend I very much appreciated him coming all the way from Palo Alto but I couldn't forgive him for the way the grief was already sliding off him (but how could it not after almost six months and only the memory of 19-year-olds having spent two weeks together) on the Teflon of his

as if

indestructible youth (unscratched youth I really was thinking of Teflon even though Eric seemed to be a perfectly natural open young man who could do nothing about the fact that he had to live happily ever after) my mother my sister Caroline and her younger daughter Lotta Sabrina's favourite cousin all of whom had come from Berlin I can still see my mother's bewildered look

not at Ground Zero but in the completely undamaged bombastic canyon of Fifth Avenue with its permanent vista of an ever-receding future that steel-and-glass dream of urban prepotency with its undiminished metropolitan energy and colossal banality

how on earth could you bring my granddaughter here

her look

seemed to be saying but she said nothing at all she could find no anchor no connection to Sabrina (I don't love my German grandma as much as Grandma Cynthia I can't help it Daddy it's just the way my body is) in the huge largely intact perfectly functioning city my mother was 72 and all she knew of the States was Boston a little of the northeastern coast and Amherst of course in its Pioneer Valley idyll she was looking for an anchor something that could help her understand what connected me to this urban mega-machine why I had brought Sabrina here how I could have fathered her here

I almost said

but she's an American

at 14 my mother had survived the firestorm in Hamburg I think she couldn't cope with the way the vitality of New York City was still intact undiminished even strengthened it just brought out the absurdity even more it was the physical expression of the reverse of the shoulder-shrugging

wrong-time-wrong-place

we kept hearing from right-time-right-place people certainly

sympathetic

it wasn't a war just thousand-fold murder with the heightened absurdity that for individuals

thousands

terror broke out in the middle of supposed peace

my mother had to see Ground Zero she needed to see the teddy bears the children's drawings the letters the flowers and dolls that defenceless unprofessional private grief desperately spread out on concrete blocks like improvised altars in the poorest of developing countries so that she could finally find that anchor and the reality of the actual murder of her grand-daughter and her daughter-in-law the things she had in common with Amanda's parents and the student from Amherst with whom she shared a table after the funeral she'd admired Amanda that only came to me then abruptly heightening my sense of guilt for who knows in what right place Amanda would have been if we hadn't divorced

there's no right place

but there are so many better ones

my sister and Lotta stayed for a few more days they wanted to go to Amherst and Luisa went with them because I couldn't bear it (thought I wouldn't be able to bear it) they were also very German with their

anti-war reflexes

as Seymour called it (I didn't remind him of Rotterdam and how his parents had just managed to flee before the arrival of the Wehrmacht and the SS) because they disapproved of the bombing of Tora Bora and the threatening gestures of the US administration towards Iraq as did most New Yorkers as it happened

the bombs were not the least comfort to me I just wanted a no-holds-barred (no an effective) hunt for the perpetrators that certainly

and that was something that was apparently farther from the

PRESIDENT'S

mind than the moon on which his country had after all landed

thoughts filled with shame and scepticism (the German reflex after 1945 or better after 1968 or even better after 1975) thought is your disease my sister Caroline said (a high-school teacher whatever do they teach there nowadays) as we said goodbye at JFK Airport but I was more preoccupied with Lotta Sabrina's favourite cousin with whom she'd gone on the trip to Munich and across the Alps to Italy before she went to university it was a preoccupation that produced no result at all I scarcely spoke to Lotta I could hardly tell what she was thinking that's something I ought to know from all those years of teaching how difficult it is to understand the world of a young person

who's hardly settled into it himself or herself I still can't go jogging again I stare at the runners on the sidewalk or in Central Park like a dead man there's nothing left but to

drift drift along

through life Amanda's mother Cynthia said a kind of preparation for the great river we'll all end up in the inevitable hereafter a motion that befits us the brightly coloured frivolity of the joggers is unbearable is deeply

enviable (the right time the right place)

I walk to tire myself out to dull my mind I calm myself down with forced marches I don't wear trainers I walk for 30 or 40 blocks in town shoes because I can only accept being a normal stressed inhabitant of this city in town shoes after four months I had to buy a new pair I walk until I'm drifting along I want my body to fuse with the city with its colossal normality with its nervous polite quick despairing crafty inhabitants who after all these years have become much closer and more understandable to me as a

European

than the English French Swedes Spaniards even when I'm with Luisa with just one remark she got me to start teaching again from next Thursday I'll be a visiting professor at Columbia University

they enjoy it

Luisa said

the sacrifice has been made (and limited) and now there is the temptation to assume you're always right and to regard yourself as absolved from everyday matters from criticism from the rules of civilization of international law and to

clear out Ground Zero

like crazy

or bomb the Taliban or mutilate civil liberties in your own country set up brutal prisons outside the jurisdiction of your own courts to legitimize torture to

have a go at

Iraq

why am I still thinking why do I need weeks and months to

understand something

to find the magnanimity not to go to war now Luisa said in the very first week after the attack when stunned I watched a Taliban spokesman on TV demanding proof before they would hand over Osama bin Laden what an idiot I thought who does he think he's dealing with he's dead now and

he deserved it

I thought for his stupidity alone in imagining America would stand it

what do I understand

if I'm full of hate in three weeks I can be as clever as a leading article and reduce the whole world to two columns of newsprint but it doesn't help me I have to sort things out in my own way

HOW I CAME INTO THE WORLD

why I'm still living there (only that of course)

how I could have a wife (an American wife) how I could manage to father a living child why I stayed in America why

I'm still staying there

why do (they) hate (us)

the nights

are restless bright torn I often get up and walk round and round in my cell on Amsterdam Avenue tormented but also with a throbbing head glad that I can't sleep I almost never used to switch the television on certainly not during the night

a film with a gang of rappers the weather map with threatening swirls over the Atlantic a greenish-grey night-time picture of the gleaming bomb cylinders or warheads of a supposed find of weapons of mass destruction destroy the picture with the remote as if it's imploded from outside there's always the immense mass of night that can shoot everything back into the tiny point of light in the middle (the red sun on the forehead of an Indian girl) I can't help giving out a loud groan I have to have a drink of water now I only drink water and coffee I press

my forehead against the cool glass of the balcony door

the rumble of traffic the wail of police sirens the glow of the fluorescent tubes thoughts of Amherst my life there is so far away as if it were a TV series that's long since gone out of fashion Luisa's looking after the house shall I sell it or not I have to make up my mind why didn't Sabrina tell me anything about California why didn't she call me instead of going to see Amanda why

the wailing sirens

TV images again

switching off quickly again I often think of Sabrina's first year the disturbed nights walking round with her until first light I put on some Mozart but she preferred Astor Piazolla (I think)

to take her to go with her out of the world I thought I often walk round again

if I sleep badly I need the nights of a

whole year

When you were with me
    I lacked for nothing.
But then I saw
    That it was unhappiness.
Ever-new delicate figures,
    Sinking down,
Ever just you,
    Suffocated butterfly,
Black and like a charcoal line
    So light.

Your non-breathing,
    The shadows dug into your eyes,
Blind spots on the paper
    Of this bright and scorching
Day.

Will it come to war everyone's asking me will it come to war Doctor as if we were those with responsibility for encouraging a war as a job-creation scheme perhaps or to outbid the embargo with a grand slam do you know what will happen that's obvious patient mortality will be greater than anything we've seen so far perhaps the whole of Iraq will become collateral damage HE will take his chemical weapons THEY their atom bomb and BOOM! will it come to war they ask me they want to hear a fairy story about Saddam's bold men throwing the US back into the Gulf or into burning holes in the desert or they're even dreaming of peace breaking out of our great SOLDIER strolling up to the newly arrived weapons inspectors with a dove of peace on his chest and then George Double U comes over himself bringing a turkey we'll stick into the mouth of our shabbut or up its arse or vice versa am I operating on an umbilical hernia here oh yes that'll be it that narrows down the associative field will it come to war Doctor but please don't tell me the truth after all we're Arab patients so out with your fairy story Doctor everything will turn out fine there will be a war but a bloody fairy-tale war like something out of *A Thousand and One Nights* but let's not forget how this whole thing began my dear Tariq could you hand me a fresh swab you look as exhausted as I feel thanks by the way that was a textbook supra-umbilical hernia directly over the navel and not very inflamed yet thank God the poor mite we'll put all this here neatly back where it came from where was I oh yes the fairy story now how does our great fairy story begin my old friend it begins with the hurt pride the wounded dignity the dented virility of the PRESIDENT think of the living chess set in the courtyard of King Shahryar's palace of the 10 white slave girls and the 10 black slave girls who suddenly reveal themselves as men in disguise as extremely virile Moors who plunge between the fat thighs of the white girls and lie with them from morning until midday just as the king's wife got her black lover Masud out of a tree and commanded him to ride her how does the story end they were all of them chopped to pieces by the sword and hundreds of other maidens in hundreds of other nights until there were no more maidens another swab please just there I don't think we need a net the intestine has only been clamped not torn it'll grow back together in no time at all the point is that the PRESIDENTS fear the PRESIDENT as if he were 10 and a black prick inside their women you see the PRESIDENTS themselves my friend are the

PRICKS of their countries that is of the rich old men and the rich old women of their countries they are the prick and the women want to see one like that so when the PRESIDENT has lost his TOWERS then he has to make sure that here too not a stone is left standing will it come to war what else it arises from vanity and prudence alone my friend quick the needle from vanity and the need to be the biggest and there's something profoundly AC/DC something nancy about having to show the power of their pricks all the time there's bound to be something about it in Freud that Jew whom along with Kafka I like reading best of all because we Arabs really need him just look at these PRESIDENTS these travesties these transvestites of ours always blazing away with his hunting rifle dressing up in his silk suit his shepherd's outfit his fur-collared coat his Assyrian fancy dress his Tyrolean hat his green uniform and then that US cowboy with his horseshoe pitching his jeans and chainsaw his bomber jacket the pilot's get-up from the top squadron the baseball bat all the to-do with the model West Point recruits they always take it very personally their honour their wounded virility the fallen towers the Six Day War the shot-up nuclear reactor that's all just their PRICK and hardly has something happened to them than it's: chop everything to pieces! men women children a thousand dead bodies for one night will it come to war Doctor yes a lovely clean UN war these country bumpkins who murder their own daughters to rid themselves of the stain of a foreigner who's raped them are asking me if it will come to war there's

WAR all the time and

you have to WATCH OUT!

Ali cries as I quickly pull my hand away and continue to be amazed at what a dexterous and garrulous surgeon he's become

it had begun just before we were due to finish work

a taxi driver was one of the last patients he'd been going on and on at me about his swollen groin it was probably just prostatitis and I normally let such people get along with medicinal herbs but I promised him something special after Laila (my old receptionist who's like 10 wolves protecting me from madmen malingerers and moaners) had interrupted the consultation to bring in a young woman with a pitifully wailing eight-month-old

despite her black abaya she reminded me so much of Muna that I almost jumped up in shock no actually did jump up but could explain that to the taxi driver by pointing out that speed was of the essence as the child's umbilical hernia proved I kept him there rang Ali who said he could operate at once if I assisted him and was driven despite everything very skilfully by my prostatitis patient the fortunately short distance to the private clinic in Karrada where my old friend carries out his operations within a comparatively still tolerable intensive care unit the fact that I'm doing this myself with the screaming infant in my lap on the back seat of the car that smells of cold tobacco smoke and kebab fat is probably only a

foretoken

of my concern for Muna that must finally lead to action to get her to London is the most urgent family problem and probably the easiest to solve I've already got Farida to agree albeit reluctantly all I have to do now is have a serious talk with Muna even though her departure would hurt me more than Yasmin's did I was younger then and Yasmin was younger than Muna is now but there's more to it if I'm honest I have to admit that Muna has always been nearest to me (not dearest or is she?) nearer even than Sami whose carefree manner amazes as much as it relieves me Ali sews like a world champion I can only watch in admiration since all I've done for years is little emergency operations in my own place I was completely out of practice for such an operation the little child's belly closes up and now it's just a matter of hygiene a matter of pure chance nowadays but at least here in this private clinic there is a chance

at the end Ali lets out such a volley of oaths about the general conditions I have to look at the tall broad-hipped anaesthetist how trustworthy is she a few years ago no one would have dared do that I don't have to remind Ali that I would have ended up in extreme difficulty after cursing the situation in the country while I was operating if Colonel Basil hadn't sent the spy to his death

but then Ali suddenly says to the anaesthetist you hold my life in your hands colleague and points to the child the door opens and a nurse comes in behind her in the corridor is the young mother in black who reminds me so much of Muna

in the street outside Ali rubs his face with the slim Egyptian features now he's the age that always suited his noble head and his pharaoh looks how long can it be since we jumped from the bridge into the Tigris

why are you looking at me like that old friend am I too skinny are you going to draw up a diet for me

I was reminded of the Pitié-Salpêtrière I say now you operate as well as Cassin but you also talk as much as he used to

the anaesthetist needs something to keep her amused otherwise she'll fall asleep he says shrugging his shoulders but if she should happen to talk to the wrong person

she doesn't like talking he assures me we have it off together once a week and she doesn't talk then either

that's no guarantee

he waved it away—listen I really am making an effort come on let's do our shopping and then go to Madjid's I've got some whisky already you can bring the vegetables

Muna and Sami have been invited to Yasmin's this evening so Farida's alone I'll give her a quick call

give her a call I thought you were married? the last of the romantics Ali sighs

the greengrocer lets us use his phone and we stroll with our salmon-coloured plastic bags through the evening roar of Karrada Street pursued by taxi drivers one of whom we disappoint with a much-too-short journey to the Sheraton Hotel then we continue on foot through the narrow side-streets as far as the Shahid Mosque

you're so cautious Ali says as if I had no reason to be his calmness comes from the fact that he managed to send his wife and two sons to London four years ago and when I tell him that he retorts that I also owe my

SPECTATOR ATTITUDE

to my family situation namely that I have two daughters like George Bush and that Sami isn't yet old enough to be liable for military service if I was lucky the war would be over before he'd finished school Ali gives me an encouraging pat on the shoulder with his light-coloured trousers his thin pullover and his pink plastic bags he has a relaxed holiday air you wouldn't believe he's just finished a 13-hour day just occasionally he lowers his head slightly short of breath I don't know if the anaesthetist is really good for him even if she does know how to keep her mouth shut

earlier (a long time earlier) we used to meet in a cafe in al-Mutanabbi Street or in a bar on Abu Nuwas where nowadays we could only meet secret agents among dozens of prostitutes beheaded by the PRESIDENT who are serving the wine of their necks on order to howl a few panegyrical songs in memory of the poet who was tortured to death by his last patron and who could say of the Pleasures of Baghdad:

He asks me if I'm going to go to Mecca.
I reply: Yes, when the pleasures

Of Baghdad have been exhausted.
For how can I go on pilgrimage
As long as I'm drowning here
In the brothel or the inn?

Since Mecca's too far away and the innkeepers considered too dangerous we prefer to meet privately and in small groups the ideal place would really be the planet Mercury with its furious eccentric orbit on which since 1976 Abu Nuwas has been able to call a fine crater his own it will be there to greet us during the war next May just a tiny black spot in front of the sun's death-dealing life-giving shield of fire quickly

passing

like all the painters writers journalists and the supposed intellectuals who have been scattered to the four corners of the earth Madjid's studio is an exception this is where the

painters' and writers' club

meets old men too bowed too sick too addicted to drink to worry the STATE any more only when the

Hermit Crab

is there do we have to watch out that poet who lives in the poet's house the latter going into exile 15 years ago after months of torture and imprisonment the former being rewarded with the abandoned house for his masterpiece *Saddam's Blossoming* which I can only imagine as a ring of haemorrhoids though the Hermit Crab tells us that for years he has just been a faithful steward of the house for nothing guards it better against being taken over by the wrong person than his presence a false poet residing in the shell of the true poet but the Crab in our club protects us because his presence makes other police spies unnecessary Abu Nuwas who as a homosexual could easily have been arrested (and beheaded) in his own street reaches for the bottle and says:

Drink three glasses
And quote a line.
Good has become mingled with evil
And—may God forgive me—
The man will win in whom the one
Overcame the other: enough!

amid the murky green-and-red glow of Madjid's oil paintings we're sitting at a long table with historic scratchings on the top in front of us overflowing ashtrays bottles of beer whisky and arrack glasses of tea and water there are only five of us today (without the Hermit Crab) two doctors two painters and Jabir the writer and literature specialist who hasn't published a book for 20 years but has written seven books

in his head (as he puts it as if he had an Assyrian clay tablet or a computer hard disk between his ears)

from which he can quote whole passages above all from the invisible volumes of poetry *Ultra* and *The Wars in Paradise* he's a tall gaunt man with delicate fingers and shining brown eyes in a face that's at the same time wrinkled and finely moulded which seems familiar and yet reminds you of nothing so much as perhaps a clever old bat a creature everyone knows about but very few have had a closer look at so quickly does his mind fly

Jabir's working on a new essay Madjid tells me while I'm with him in the cramped grubby man's kitchen making a kind of tabbouleh from cucumbers tomatoes sweet peppers and bulgur

we spend three hours drinking against the war

that will come we're all agreed on that if for different reasons or rather theories Ali propounds his hypothesis of wounded virility again he drinks quickly to relieve himself of the strain of his day in the hospital

winged bulls and winged women their skin gleaming in lurid complementary colours burning mullahs recalling Dali's giraffes stride over glass pyramids hit by aeroplanes making me think of Paris and my friend Hussein who paints in a very similar style

asked for my opinion I just say that my view as a plain and simple practical medical man is that you have to look for the simplest possible theory

that was exactly what he was producing in his essay Jabir says a simple and verifiable theory of power following Hobbes the core of which was that

every nation also every political force or even

every person

sought the moment of power

which meant

that power was used and misused to warlike ends at the moment when it seemed to offer the possibility of achieving supremacy without too great losses for example the way England and France shared the Middle East out between them after the First World War on the ruins of the Ottoman Empire or the way Israel exploited its advantage in the Six Day War and Egypt its own advantage in the Yom Kippur War before Black September in Jordan the PLO believed it was so strong that it tried to seize power and even today Syria manipulates Lebanon because it was only or above all there that moments of power might arise which

OUR MAN

naturally saw

in 1980 when he attacked the Iran he presumed weakened by revolution and Kuwait a good 10 years ago overlooking the fact that with the demise of the USSR one of the great historic moments of the US had come

using the power to act Jabir believes is almost unavoidable

no matter whether it's a so-called democracy acting or a lovely old dictatorship Madjid interjects

or your wife Ali says which gives the younger painter Karim the idea of combining Ali's theory with Jabir's that aggression arising from an insult would increase reciprocally gathering the aggressive momentum of a genuine or imagined right to exercise power as in the case of Afghanistan for example

for example as in our case that we're going to have on our doorstep in the near future Madjid cries but why? do you understand why people in power can behave the way they do can you explain that with a simple theory such as Tariq would like to have he tips some water into his arrack as if all he was asking was what causes arrack to suddenly go cloudy or milky

we drink diligently to find a reason for the great monotonous exhausting crushing horribly reliable constant of history for a theory of

PARTICIPATION

(in history) that always works and takes place

the essay I'm writing in my head Jabir says also deals with that topic

fear? I guess for in my mind there's no other reason

Madjid whose artistic moustache has grown more and more grandfatherly in recent years (bushier greyer hanging down lower at the tips) raises his glass and we clink glasses in order to keep the level of abstraction of our discussion among the blazing canvases as high as possible for up there in the mental circles the conceptual spirals we're following spellbound from down below in the cellars (prison cells) of our bodies that appear to be sinking lower and lower for up there

they'll hardly catch us

it's an old technique deep-rooted from many years of training a collective conditioned reflex that when you (WE

those who've remained here)

are talking to anyone beyond your intimate friends you don't get too specific so that you don't end up

dangling from the fisherman's hook

consequently we seldom discuss the exiles' standard coffee-house topics for example the the unfortunate way the Americans drew back at the end of the second Gulf War leaving us entirely at the mercy of our PRESIDENT's regime of terror or the unfortunate feuds between our nationalist parties in the 1960s and 70s that ultimately paved the way for the Baathists as well as the unfortunate tie of the once so powerful Iraqi communists to Moscow who commanded them to go along with their executioners

in principle

Jabir explains

at a safe height then

in the depths then (Jabir says) where things are actually decided

on the level of our vulnerable torturable

bodies

we called for the STATE the LEVIATHAN that would watch over us from the basics to the supreme heights it would be a pyramid or a tower at the bottom it would see to the provision of essentials (from food shelter clothing to jobs and petrol for your car) then to security (health protection from criminals and terrorists) then to our sense of belonging (your country your state your nation) and finally to meaning (what our magnificent country is doing with its magnificent culture in our magnificent times) all citizens of each and every country (democracy dictatorship forget those labels) would be part of the leviathan of their own respective giant and the goal of those powerless parts that reposed and were disposed of inside those giant figures would be to survive the unavoidable struggles of the leviathans

at maximum profit to themselves

if therefore we'd brought Kuwait home then nothing much would have happened to us and we'd just have got richer (we thought) and if we bomb Iraq then nothing much will happen to us at home either but petrol will stay cheap the Americans are now thinking Madjid says and with that we're back on firm ground we're trying to drink away from under our feet hoping there are no nooses round our necks the guitar-shaped completely absinthe-green body of a

woman in oils

is still pursuing me outside in the narrow alleyways of Betawiyn as I try to take Ali back to Saadun Street so that he can get a taxi while he's insisting on first of all accompanying me (in my state) home on foot he takes my arm while I'm trying to hold him up with the result that we probably look like two old dancing bears who for some mysterious reason are brushing off the layers of whitewash from the old houses with their backs or shoulders finally we manage to walk in a more or less straight line and get round to talking about life in general and women (the anaesthetists of existence) in particular when on the left a view through to the Abu Nuwas and the Tigris opens up and I grant myself

a pause and declare that I will stay there and wait until the bombs have fallen and Harun al-Rashid returned whose personal physician I propose to become and finally

get into such a state of ecstasy

or in the grip of such yearning and such longing for Farida (who is fast asleep in our bed five minutes walk away) that I quote one of my old poems and Ali does finally escape into a taxi after all—but what should one say in a state of sobriety

SOBER PEOPLE

Sober people frighten me.
They stop drinking and start murdering.
They intoxicate themselves on sacred scriptures,
Allowing no contradiction.
The less hypocritical they are,
The more terrible their lie.
A sober man's stomach has nothing but
Acid and blood.

Goethe's Principal Works I (concentrate on the text first of all get them to read what they're reading about)

don't you read

any newspapers at least yesterday's

Luisa asks on the telephone

Traces of Terror—News analysis of President Bush's decision to seek approval of Congress before taking military action against Iraq

no Schröder Luisa says she means the

GERMAN CHANCELLOR

who said in an interview that the American administration would be making a terrible mistake if they declared war on Iraq he himself was against such a war even if the UN Security Council voted for military intervention

he's right and he wants to win the election I'm sure Bush understands that in the longer term Luisa says

I read the newspapers every day I read for an hour in the morning I watch the TV news for an hour every day I drift with my head slit open along the

full channels I

drift

into the so-called incidents (which kill the children of other people in other places) I saw

Black Hawks over the Hindu Kush

I saw the ring of Israeli tanks outside the miserable headquarters of the

PALESTINIAN LEADER

at Christmas a Christmas tree had been put up over the

PILE

as only the building workers called it now and I met Seymour there

what is

the question what do I really understand when I get everything re-explained to me every day as if I'd woken up with no memory of that morning

Luisa (on the phone): she'll come on Sunday to stay with me for two days if I ask her to I have to answer some quite clear explicit questions am I going to spend another year in Manhattan am I going to keep the apartment will I actually be in a fit state to give my course at Columbia will I

be drifting towards something or more and more away from everything

please come

at least I can say that to Luisa (after a year) for my grief and the energy with which I ask myself the

decisive (what do they decide)

questions will not be reduced by my attempting to rescue my Indian-summer love or will they and would it be a bad thing if I were to fight against this mood

it's like a clouding over a dulling a weariness which started way back when I tried to make Goethe's women speak and thus came to Marianne and the *West-Eastern Divan* only now everything is grounded in hatred in impotent grief I'm afraid that the Middle East will never really interest me indeed that I can only loathe it now can only see the oil the blood the lunatics who set off bombs and make airplanes into bombs

but we have no right to hatred there is no right it's just

so easy so natural so disgustingly

human

make a billion Muslims responsible for a few hundred madmen I don't want to do that and yet cannot stop myself from despising whole countries for their backwardness their aggressiveness their miserable economic performance their inability to make proper provision for the health the education and prosperity of their inhabitants

for days on end

then once more fear weariness exhaustion

the oppressively guilty conscience of the gas-guzzling nations (just go down onto Amsterdam Avenue and across to Broadway or to Riverside Drive the night's full of noise everyone's hooting bashing into each other and poisoning the air they breathe swearing getting injured or even killing themselves with their blasted stinking wheels

I wasn't much interested in old Arab culture when I started reading about Goethe and Marianne only the architecture and the mysterious script I'd always wanted to be able to decipher and a few poems perhaps

germanish?
skewed/influenced by history

or the tales from the *Thousand and One Nights* Sabrina loved reading so much

WHY DO THEY HATE US

THEY the hate-filled terrorists WE civilized humanity

the simple picture on all the channels but what does the accurate one look like I spent a whole evening arguing with Luisa and two distressed students from Amherst who'd known Sabrina for years

until we wrote it down

Islamist terrorists largely of Saudi Arabian origin attack the US at a place that represents their economic world power with a strike that costs the lives of almost 3,000 people

add: in such a spectacular way

creating a historically lasting symbol of the vulnerability of the US exposed to the thirst for vengeance and gloating of their enemies

so profoundly and indelibly that a war of the only remaining super-power as a counter-symbol is virtually unavoidable no matter whether it stirs up further terror or not for

we're playing

CHESS

my friend the old oriental game with the castles like towers (deep inside which we are helplessly stuck) towers commanded by

KINGS PRESIDENTS CHANCELLORS LEADERS I have to ask specific questions so

WHO hated us so much I have to melt the suicide pilot out of the wreckage the meteorites baked in the mass of the PILE as another lethal insane ALIEN and

dissect him

until he becomes understandable

but he refuses to do so for months I've been staring at the gruesome neat composite pictures of the

11 SEPTEMBER 2001 MURDERERS

those portrait photos in vertical rows of four or five as if they came from one of those passport-photo machines with mirror curtain and revolving stool in the special multi-portrait format though which with a single flash leaves nothing but ashes behind (but that too is just a merciful illusion for a short time before the Towers collapsed you could see in the blizzard of paper on the plaza of the World Trade Center human torsos lying with strange sashes the safety belts of the airplane seats) and spews out to news agencies all over the world thousands of the strips with Middle Eastern likenesses that dry in the blast of words produced by the international hot-air blowers

We are a group of young men from various Arab countries. For some time we have been living in Hamburg in order to pursue our studies. We would like to start training to be professional air pilots.

that was the email my daughter's murderer sent to flight schools in the US a pretty absurd will dating back six years was also found but that's not enough direct words (though I did manage to have a look at his final-year dissertation on town planning at Hamburg-Harburg Technical University)

apart from that and above all

pictures

of the 19 men of whom 15 came from Saudi Arabia with an average age of about 24 a German newspaper called them

blame? BOYS

they could simply be just a football team from the Middle East I stare at them they stare back most of them with not unfriendly looks and only given a criminal touch by the muddy colours of poor photographs and faded copies (colours of mould and decay) Atta the chief terrorist the senior at 33 looks at least 10 years older and with his clenched teeth seems to be sucking saliva he'll eat himself up you think and his name is the same as that of the cleaning product of my childhood that corrosive white powder that foams up red when you put it on a metal scourer and thus tear to pieces the faces of young women working mothers unsuspecting business people

with my hatred

I

can't get through the surface the actual perpetrators these 19 who carried out the atrocity are only the facade the athletics team of death doped up with specially chosen verses of the Koran and hypnotic killer chants massmurder sportsmen who can be trained up anytime anywhere and the words I read about them are masks just like the rogues' gallery photos just as out of context or embarrassingly private as the holiday or family snaps of the chief terrorist who always seems to have a spoonful of the homonymic white scourer in his mouth even as a little boy (would you have strangled him there on the beach of Alexandria in the summer of 1975 between his smartly dressed elder sisters with their equally forced smiles if you had been there and had been granted a vision of the horror to come no because no glimpse of the future can be certain) he is said to have cultivated a Nazi outlook the Jews control America and all the other evils in the world as usual and no woman was allowed to shake his hand and even after his death no one was to touch his prick as it says in the will he wrote five years before the attack and presumably intended for a less dismembering martyr's death (the people washing his corpse were to wear gloves when working on the genital area who can write such idiotic rubbish in their last will and testament why on earth was this provision in the suitcase that just happened to remain at Logan Airport was it intended for the angels) he never watched TV which actually ought to have improved him never listened to music was taciturn sullen ascetic pious disciplined and according to the reported conclusions of Spanish investigators a repressed homosexual which explains why he so enjoyed teaching and preaching to the little boys his professor in Hamburg found him focused polite and quick to learn

among the other terrorists there were also some more fun-loving and (initially) communicative types one had even got married and wasn't considered unhappy

so we learn that

a pervert is necessary as leader (certainly an idea worth considering but what is it that drives the others into his arms especially the ones that appear to be happy)

in order to see inside his head they tip out a pile of propaganda material from a student hostel in Hamburg-Harburg from the pathetic German ordinariness of the offices of Islam AG that he set up

books pamphlets leaflets tracts from all possible Arab countries martial videos and cassettes in which calls for jihad can be heard against a background of machine-gun fire

and they quote the most stupid maxims prejudices and the most absurd dietary rules out of this or that booklet with the aim of

insulting the murderers

but what use is that

I asked Seymour during all those months in which he carefully archived all the newspaper articles that tried to reconstruct precisely how the CIA the FBI the Transportation Security Administration Border Protection etc failed not forgetting the German police and Federal Intelligence Service given that three of the four suicide pilots came from Hamburg (we just have to be glad Mohammed wasn't German) for the future it's certainly important

HOW THAT COULD HAPPEN

there must there will be a congressional report Seymour demanded (there will be such a report some time in the future when further unimaginable events have occurred and it will establish the main problem namely

lack of imagination)

do you really want to live in a country where there was no way something like that could happen Luisa asked

also the posthumous investigation of the terrorists

a PI Sam Marlowe kind of job

since they entered America at the beginning of 2001

only gives us the surfaces of the surfaces because we cannot comprehend the relentlessness of the murderers from externals

but at least you can say that in the last days before the attack by staying in shabby hotels in Las Vegas among striptease bars porn-video stores liquor shops with bars over the windows cheap gaming casinos a three-dimensional walk-in projection of their caricature image of the degenerate West they were already familiar with from all the rabid pamphlets in the Olympic Gardens Topless Cabaret people stick dollar notes in the strippers' garters among the maritime junk (sharks swordfish miniature lighthouses and plastic lobsters in mock fishing nets) one poured vodka cocktails down his throat while the other (Atta) tried to get drunk on cranberry juice and spent hours in a large video-game booth where he played one virtual game of golf after another to get the high score

the shimmering sham green a coarse pattern of pixels so intensely luminous that his brain keeps having to project red complementary colours onto the screen a bizarre foretaste of the meadows of paradise where 70 virgins who will receive his purified body will only touch his penis (he has to go and have a pee again that damn cranberry juice) with rubber gloves while

no one there can beat Allah's high score for

God is the best player

and golf is death it's the beginning of the Asphodel Meadows on which the old and the moribund head for the abyss in slow motion the rich in their actual bodies the poor faced with whining machines but similarly only with the fragile single body that has been lent to them it is perhaps an irony even Atta felt there's

no point I can find nothing (or very little) on the surface of the dozens of journalists' reports which read as if they're deliberately fragmentary deliberately dirty scenes from 1970s thrillers

dirty play

while the subject is the absolute purity of mass murder

they found

in the car of one of the suspects in the wreckage of the plane brought down in a field in Pennsylvania as well as in that suitcase that wasn't put on the plane at Logan Airport and that contained the memorable will

a book of

SPIRITUAL INSTRUCTIONS

according to which I should imagine cleanly washed perfumed killers meticulously free of all superfluous body hair who went in shoes tied as instructed and with plastic and/or carpet knives hidden about their person through check-in directly to paradise their hearts already open welcoming death at any minute praying unceasingly and reciting verses from the Koran working themselves up as if they'd swallowed a messianic iPod hammering the sound of absolute unscrupulousness into every cell of their bodies

hit them

hard on the back of the neck (in the knowledge that heaven is waiting for you the angels are already calling your name and have put on their finest garments for you what kind of heaven can it be where angels have to clothe themselves but that was in our children's Bibles too) for

you are following the eternal path the path of 100 per cent obedience for

the time is ripe

to do

what is right it says and without question that's true for each and every one of us but suddenly I hit upon a sentence with a devastatingly all-embracing reason

for we have wasted our lives and now the opportunity has come to devote ourselves to God and to obey Him

if

I don't understand now

I'll be wasting my life on my sorrow and so

I read

for hours on end piling up books on the floor of the apartment stumbling over them at night without getting annoyed often simply making my stumbling an excuse to switch the light on and continue reading

study

the dispute of the Arab or rather Islamic countries with the West in let's say the millennium that's just finished (an easy exercise for a man who at any time can account to himself for 3,000 years but not for someone like me who lives from night to night asking myself what hardly manageable masses of reading I actually require of my older students) let's start with

the trauma of the Crusades

that to the other side presumably often seems as close as an everyday military threat (repeating itself every day) but to us has already sunk into the depths of the era of Hollywood Technicolor films in which there was good and evil on both sides (the democratically apportioned balance between aggressors and defenders still ought to bother us) and into an awareness that rises to the surface now and then like bubbles that the hundred years of fanaticism with which the popes consolidated their position and the emperors and knights tried to get rid of their sins by committing mass murder in foreign lands was nothing other than a pointless and criminal enterprise

the Crusades started the way wars almost always start with

fairy tales

that is with invented horror stories about the atrocities of the other religious communities and cultures (alleged desecration of Christian holy places in Jerusalem purported maltreatment of Christian pilgrims by the Turks as well as invented Jewish machinations)

they were instigated by those who instigate most things namely by people in power who felt the reins slipping from their grip in this particular case by Popes Gregory VII and Urban II in their struggle with the imperial power

they were carried out by calculating clerics nobles desperate for redemption muddle-headed knights and fanaticized or pressed peasants from the most disease- and famine-ridden areas of France and Germany

they ended in bloodbaths in the loss of the holy places in the whipping-up of jihad fervour among Muslims in the outbreak of animosity between Latin and non-Roman Christians in the split with Byzantium and the conquest of Christian Constantinople by Christian Crusaders in the hatred of knights and soldiers for the clergy and those in power

the dialogue between cultures the interchange with the other world the transfer of Greek–Arab science came by other routes namely via Sicily and through Italian merchants in Venice and Genoa via

Andalusia

Luisa where only two years ago we noted but with no particular emotion all the conventionally cheerful *De-la-frontera* place names and other *Reconquista* signs perhaps because it is so long since the border was effective today I sometimes think I would defend the Spanish coast sword in hand and the massive bulk of the

cathedral for Charles V with its double circular cloister

sited within the area of the Alhambra a straightforward piece of domination architecture from the early sixteenth century that was never finally completed because of the revolt of the Moors who had remained in Spain after the *Reconquista* and who after the capitulation had been promised freedom of religion only to be subjected to forced conversion soon afterwards to be deported or left to the tender care of the Inquisition

in retrospect then the cathedral which seemed so out of place when I first saw it exudes a reassuring strength (but what use is that) just as the early Renaissance which created such colossal architectural structures

calms

and comforts me as does humanism and the Enlightenment for Europe developed those from her own resources and I will not give up one iota of those for that particularly extreme variety of Islam that wants to spread its rigorous tyrannical mindlessness over the whole earth and that

MURDERED MY DAUGHTER

(calm down who

are you talking to think

instead of

hating)

the *Reconquista* here

has

its Saladin there

but then its new Ottoman dynasties and in the east the Safavid princes from the northwest of Iran I go into this as precisely as possible if I can't find something on the Net I go to the Public Library even if it's just for a definition or a picture or a sketch it's only the relentlessness no: the adequacy

of my own answers

which helps numb my grief and give me a good night's sleep now and then

now where was I?

for 3,000 years we didn't exist at all

once upon a time there were

3,000 people

what remains what remains for us (Luisa says) but grief and shame a targeted hunt for the criminals and insight into our own guilt

what remains I dreamt I nightmared

that the aged Goethe had come and wanted

to marry Sabrina

LONGING

When first your flame blazed into life
You had no need at all of death,
A welcome guest in any world,
Brightest dawn your every breath.

Your eager face with radiance shone—
Too soon came your adieu.
The pale shroud of my dust alone
Conceals your image from my view.

Butterfly, the icy fire
That sent you to your doom,
Will die with you, for in the sky
There's neither grave nor tomb.

Now deep within the earth you lie
As phosphorus none can see,
But when one day a flame am I,
I'll find you inside me.

The afternoon light (warm almost honey-coloured)

immerses

Sami and me in its glow so that the

house next door seems strangely transfigured (as if that were necessary) immersed in the softness of early evening it's as if everything were dissolving in the

tea of the air

it's (still) quiet on this Friday the weekend calms Baghdad down like a a cloth being thrown over a wild parrot's cage

little unkempt Ahmed his merry plump sister Hind and Yusuf the eldest who's slimmed down now he's 17 are sitting across the alley while

you

are still standing between a fig tree and a little ginkgo bathed in a very special invisible dazzling (dazzling only for me) warm radiance of sunshine that the nightingales butterflies painfully bright iridescent birds of paradise metallic hummingbirds in the seraglio of my breast

are fluttering towards

my grandfather's old house and that of the Rikabis are so close you could easily jump from the roof of one to the other we can chat across the gap as if we were sitting together at a table without being disturbed for there's a locked gate barring the narrow access to the rarely used side-doors and we've been talking across this closed-off alley for decades (Tariq says) as if the ground had just opened up and swallowed the table we were sitting round across a little 10-foot-deep abyss while we stand by the parapet or simply sit on it like Hind and Yusuf and Ahmed

like Sami and me on our side while you're still standing among the ornamental trees and bushes lovingly and expertly set up tended by Abu Yusuf as if you were counting the ginkgo leaves (no leaf is like another people say) or trying to see through the rear walls of the tall buildings on Saadun Street that block off the view of the Tigris in the summer you arrived as a soldier in your green uniform exhausted tired and relieved because you had your military service behind you and could now stay with Abu Yusuf who's a distant relative and is renting a room out to you cheaply for the whole duration of your studies (I would wish)

you already look like a student (in jeans and a sky-blue shirt) come and sit down (Beloved!) on the sunlit wall beside little tousle-haired big-eyed Ahmed we sit here together two or three times a week with nothing round us but aerials clothes-lines fluttering sheets colourful housecoats black abayas nappies smoking chimneys plants in the roof garden Abu Yusuf's a gardener they say he even plants things in the president's palaces he's transformed it so cleverly with plants and bushes that it seems to be set in the maze of all the other mostly very ordinary roofs like an ornate Persian miniature so you really ought to be wearing a suitable robe (silk brocade gold a turban with exotic feathers) a fairy-tale costume it's

your reticence that slightly defensive yet concentrated friendliness it's your shining light-brown eyes behind the thick round glasses it's your measured way of speaking of gesticulating it's your powerful round shoulders your big but soft and nicely shaped hands your teeth when you laugh those little white spots of calcium with your high cheekbones above them that give you (like Huda) something of an Indian look it's your patience and your cautious movements it's

a blaze of blossoms inside me a thorn a naked hard tempestuous slave's body in my sweat-soaked bed dreamt up and terribly wrong for you would be gentle and patient and soft it's the wish

to be precisely here in this place it's a whole real (wholly real) existence a burning longing for this place at this time and its immediate almost daily fulfilment often I want to do nothing but just keep sitting here

opposite you

beside my brother who always has something to talk argue about swap with his friend Yusuf plump 10-year-old Hind and Ahmed in his dishdasha or his shorts and striped T-shirts are like midget clowns or chubby-cheeked cherubs buzzing round us among the little orange trees and the washing on the line

I talk about Babylon and the new finds there and you about football (with the boys) and about the Abbasid period while Sami swaps *Star Wars* and *Terminator* videos with Yusuf and CDs by *Massive Attack* or Madonna (that he lends me now and then)

the magic word

was spoken a week ago it was a mistake by Sami but the two children had been called down into the Rikabis' courtyard and the four of us speak

178 THOMAS LEHR

freely among ourselves so my dear nervy gossipy brother could well have let something drop about Tariq's plan to send me to

London

to study while you are to study administration and data processing at Wasiriya at the insistence of your uncle who's financing your studies but it will

no longer be necessary

Tony Blair will come over personally with his friend George Bush Yusuf cried

I hurried to assure him that it wasn't certain it was just one of my father's ideas and neither of us knew what we were more afraid of the prospect of being apart or the vision of a war London was the word that gave you a fright and opened up your heart to me for a sight that was like plunging into a sky that will never let us go again we

had already been there once

all our paradise needed was a

returned look

the moment of response which now

recurs whenever our eyes meet no matter for how short a time yesterday

American or English bombs fell on a military installation to the west of the city again you could be in Uncle Ibrahim's living room in London watching them shooting the crap out of us on his television Sami said with a giggle

even now today when the two children we're not supposed to talk in front of are there he goes on again about the Americans having newfangled bombs and hi-tech weapons sitting quite happily at their computer monitors in Washington they could use a joystick to guide rockets with camera-heads to Baghdad right onto this roof for example or they could even

depopulate the whole of Baghdad

so that all the buildings were undamaged and just the people went up in smoke (five million little piles of ash) or vice versa

you say

shaking your head and laughing all the buildings would disappear and all the objects and we would be left empty-handed and could start again from scratch they've also got miniature drones small as butterflies or bumblebees that fly slowly round the streets and fire through windows or explode and recently a kind of deadly thinking dust as well—stop! I keep having to tell Sami that he mustn't talk about the war or the president in front of the children Tariq reported to UNICEF that more and more children were suffering from nightmares and insomnia that they only drew pictures of the war flinched at every loud noise

but Ahmed claps his hands in delight when Sami talks about the fantastic American weapons he thinks it's all a game and his brother as well probably they think nothing bad could happen to them beneath the monitor screen of the sky at worst they would lose some points

the Baathists and the Zionists and no one else

Yusuf says then everything would be OK he swings his curly head to and fro and grins now his face with its big nose merry eyes is very much like that of his 10-year-old sister unlike Sami he hates the Americans even though he does watch Hollywood films with him all the time but you can't take him seriously he says the oddest things and smiles as if he were the last person to believe what he's just said for two years he's been gazing at me adoringly he wants to give me bracelets and chains he makes in his goldsmith's apprenticeship

I'll show the Americans I'm going to be a bodybuilder Ahmed declares and gets his sister to feel his fat little biceps which she does with good-natured expressions of respect at the same time giving me a questioning glance as if I as a woman could give her a clear explanation of what all our brothers' talk about war means

I don't know and just sit here beside Sami on the parapet in my green housecoat with gym shoes on my bare feet we breathe laugh talk feel fear argue in the warm sun so incredibly

undisturbed

it's simply beyond belief that for a year now they've wanted to attack bomb eliminate us it's been settled since 9/11 my mother says the moment she heard about it she said WE're the ones who'll have to pay for that and no sooner had she said it than

the PRESIDENT appeared on television

to tell us that at last the Americans had experienced for themselves the pain they together with the Zionists were inflicting on the Palestinians every day which seemed to make sense to me until Tariq said that would make

365 x 3,000 dead per year in those well-known Palestinian skyscrapers I
said it wasn't the number of victims but the fact that something had finally
happened to the Americans in their own country to the civilians as it did
over here not just to the soldiers they sent out all over the world

there's something in that Tariq replied but just imagine a girl (this with
a screen in the background on which boys' choirs once more perform the
song Saddam's Pulse of Life) a girl of your age in the World Trade Center

she wants to go to university like you or has just started

you could have met in London or Paris

at McDonald's or Starbucks I think we'd argue about the Palestinians
we're defending and the Israelis you're defending about the embargo the
wars of the past and the one that looks as if it's in store for us if I can believe
what people say

if I were in London (where I don't want to go any more

Beloved!)

then on the screen in living rooms student residences cafes I'd see

the flames over the burning body of Iraq and Baghdad in ruins like in
a Hollywood film and I wouldn't be able to believe it just as when you're
asleep or half-asleep you can't believe a bomb's falling on the city at least
not unless it happens in the immediate vicinity and the walls of the house
tremble I sometimes ask myself what you can believe even badly wounded
and dying people (Tariq says) can't believe it we're

sitting here in the early evening sun unbelievers in the religion of death

I don't want to go to London if you're all going to stay here it's

just one possibility my father said he still needed to have a good talk
with his brother Ibrahim who's been living by the Thames for 10 years now
he wasn't going to make the decision on his own I was to think it over but
I don't know anything I'd just like to sit here and watch as all the doubts
and misgivings simply melt away feel it rather

whoever kills a man

kills all men

you quote to the two excited boys from the Koran and they're impressed
(for a short while at least) because unlike them you have been in the army
it's such a good thing there's this place here between the old houses these
benches out in the open air where you can talk undisturbed as if you were
sitting opposite one another on an open double-decker bus for generations

the Rikabis and the al-Khayyats have been chatting here and twice already we've talked here alone I don't have a suspicious father or a domineering brother I've not been promised to some cousin I'm enfolded in the trust of my parents

so speak

Beloved

you can wait until the muezzin's finished and then talk to me in the eventide peace and calm (after the children have gone and Yusuf jumped across to our roof to go to the computer and television room with Sami) in your measured and precise way this year

I want to be kissed by you

even if it took you five weeks to realize that you don't have to flee from your roof when there was the chance of being alone with me up here (I'm a modern girl my father's a doctor and his colleague Ahmed makes hymens in his garage would you faint with horror if I told you that) I really must go to study abroad my sister Yasmin told me in order

to be able to become grown up

before I get married

what could I learn in London when all the ruins are here in Iraq apart from the treasures stolen and carried off by European archaeologists Yusuf once asked me and you pushed your glasses a little higher on your nose and said

truth and scientific method

so what's behind your question when you ask me again what it is about Ur and Uruk and Babylon that grips me so why I want to study archaeology and ancient history the times before Mohammad and Ali when not a single word of God had yet been spoken clearly I

wanted to say that I'm still waiting for Babylon for the cheerful worldly glamorous free centilingual Eastern city of the future free from fear and anxiety the way I dreamt it in that night on my sister's balcony there we could take one of the Da Vinci flying machines and fly

into a bed (above the clouds)

but what can I say to you now when you're giving me such attentive and amazed and (I also think) embarrassed looks shall I simply say what I thought before I got to know you namely that I didn't want to be in Uruk or Assur or Babylon at the time of their vanished glory but to find out more about those cities to study and understand them as a scholar

you say approvingly and without irony so all at once I find it easy to see myself in the role of an energetic and focused museum director among restorers model-makers glass display cases showing visitors round talking with fellow specialists in an Italian suit or sometimes in jeans blouse and unbuttoned white coat it's

Shiruk

Huda's mother

I suddenly begin telling you about the impression she made on me when I was only a child it doesn't scare you in

New Babylon

there won't be a Baath Party any more and kings rulers tyrants warriors will only be there as martial reliefs on clay tiles while the lions and monsters will run fly round in beautiful open-air enclosures

but now to you (Beloved) I can sense you getting nervous and being tempted to look over your shoulder although no one here will think anything of it if we have a chat in the evening sun sitting on the white walls over the little drop to the way out between the houses neither my father nor Abu Yusuf (the calm gardener who's seldom there) will tell us off I know a lot about you from my mother she's on very good terms with Umm Yusuf shy pretty Mrs Rikabi among other things because Farida comes from a Shiite family too and all the Rikabis are Shiites I not only know that your uncle's financing your studies but also that Saddam had your father and your elder brother murdered 11 years ago when George Bush senior encouraged the Shiites in the south to revolt then left them in the lurch when the army attacked

on my mother's bookshelves

there's a postcard-size painting of Ali the radiant young hero with his beard and large eyes Farida's religious in a way I don't quite understand she told me the painting was a souvenir of her childhood in her devout family we visited my grandfather in Basra three times before he died and I was very impressed by the oil paintings of the 12 imams he had in the living room of his old house beside the canal 11 looked almost the same as if cloned radiant bearded young men robed in green with big shining eyes filled with the light coming from their direct descent from the first among them the twelfth

Mohammed al-Mahdi

who was saved in the cellar of his house and carried away to a place of great seclusion (my grandfather told me while Tariq preferred to go out for a walk) had in place of a head just a beam of shining light between his shoulders a little exploding sun until he returns

my grandfather told me

we will not recognize any government not even that of the mad ayatollahs of the Persians who have fallen into the sin of power what do you believe Beloved

what do you believe

the one who asks first gets their answer first

tell me what you want to hear

everything

then I want to hear everything as well you say with a laugh throwing your arms out wide (fly over the roofs with me Beloved)

OK then I don't pray very much and I'm a SuShi I say

a Japanese raw-fish cake?

you can laugh but what do you expect from an atheist Sunni father and a Shiite mother who goes to the mosque three times a year to admire the carpets she says

the fact that you give such a beautifully shocked and I think slightly admiring laugh suddenly gives me something of my sister Yasmin's hawk power a feeling of courage strength originality

I don't ask what you believe

I wait

until you tell me you only managed to put up with military service by believing that suffering was a part of us the best part perhaps how can you bear the uniform of the man who murdered your father and your brother on your skin why didn't you flee how have you managed to preserve your shyness your friendliness your uncle's more or less ordered you to study administration and data processing it was probably better like that although you would have preferred to go to a hauza

15 hours a day studying for 10 years before you—

can get married I know you say blushing I'm definitely too old for that

and 40 years before you'd be a great teacher yourself do you really want to be one of those mullahs or even an ayatollah you'd have been interested in the studies themselves philosophy where you learn about the great philosophers as well as logic mathematics metaphysics rhetoric on the other hand though you'd also have been interested in the Sufis al-Hallaj or Rumi in a hauza you'd certainly have been too tied down to find out what you really believed or how you could make progress in the faith

so what now I ask abruptly and with an emphasis I wouldn't have believed myself capable of it's still Yasmin's power inside me something of that Babylonian energy

it's not bad now

you said and then there was a power cut lasting three hours throughout the district my parents were reading quietly by the light of candles and gas lamps and I try to calm my wild racing heart by sitting down next to my brother

whenever there's a power cut no television no computer Sami remembers his interest in calligraphy he's been practising the scripts since he was seven and it calms him down too you wouldn't believe that this excitable fidgety boy was capable of something like that he's mastered several styles and the most astonishing most delicate lattices appear with precise amazing flourishes he takes the long angular Kufi script turns it upside down and makes an arch on which the vowel marks are entwined like flowers on a rose trellis difficult to decipher in the candlelight: mim damma nun fatha alif maksura . . .

Muna and Nabil

MY KING

You haven't slain the giant in our land.
The bull of Heaven is still trampling on the people.
Your great city will never be built.
Your crown is mere air.
No one fears your name.

Your kingdom will not come.
Your will is no command.
No desert resounded
With your word.

Nothing runs through your hands
But my life.

Unfortunately he couldn't come that afternoon (Seymour said on the phone) but now he had not just permission but strong medical advice to take up jogging again

so he'd call for me the next day Sunday he'd never manage it without me I was to buy myself some running shoes he knew I hadn't been out jogging for a year and that gave someone with a heart problem like him the chance of keeping up with me

without Seymour

I wouldn't have bought the shoes and presumably not without Luisa's message either that she couldn't come until Monday but could make up for it by staying until Thursday (and therefore also for the

ANNIVERSARY

Is everyone late because it's approaching inexorably?)

the running shoes I bought in a hurry and with a sense of shame a pair of jogging pants and a grey-and-olive (camouflage-coloured) T-shirt from the bargain counter in the same shop

are all in the hall as if

dropped there by a child I find it difficult to forgive myself for the spurts of joy I felt despite the rushed casualness of the purchase without Seymour I couldn't go out running he's well aware of that but it has only now occurred to me that the reverse might also be the case and not for the ostensible reason of his lack of self-discipline but as with me in order to be able to bear the feelings of guilt why

are you still alive

the question that becomes louder and louder as soon as you seem to be getting back to the normal life that you neither can nor should ever have again you're forcing this idea on yourself Luisa said during one of the nights when once again as for the whole of the last year I was incapable of sleeping with her I can't have sex any more I just throttle my penis now and then wring it out in a corner of my bed or trembling in the shower just to be left in peace nothing more

he'd started psychological treatment Seymour said and as well as that (I couldn't stop myself feeling contempt for my tough constitution it's as if it makes the suffering implausible—for whom—if you're in fine shape apart from your erections) he'd had to have a heart operation three weeks after the funeral service it was a minor affair for the specialists of the

New York Presbyterian Hospitals (*we can see things*

many others can't)

that castle complex of ivory skyscrapers on the East River bring your mother for we don't just cut open thoraxes we see the person (*can see things*)

as a whole

Seymour was alone

in a single room I was his first visitor who apart from guest professors and students could go and see someone in hospital in the morning (a cold sunny March day uncompromisingly beautiful with a harsh light sculpting every wrinkle every pore) he didn't look as tired and grey as in the preceding weeks but strangely fresh even if in a somehow unhealthy or embarrassing way as if he'd treated himself to an affair that had been a bit too much for him the affair of his coronary arteries with one of those tiny sophisticated balloon probes which released their constrictions or agglutinations I pretended I wanted to know more about it but Seymour didn't insist on explaining it he wasn't to blame just as he wasn't to blame for (wasn't the cause of) Amanda's separation from me seven years ago now for just a moment it seemed to me

as I looked out of the hospital window as if out there the harsh sobering spring light of our last trip together were shining again a Parisian blue through which Sabrina had marched along behind us pale and mute arms permanently folded a helpless witness in whom we kept trying with decreasing effort to whip up some sight-seeing enthusiasm even if we'd stopped bothering to preserve the facade of a normal happy family Seymour was

a fortunate circumstance (for Amanda) such a different man that even now I find it impossible to imagine it was the same thing the same people we'd lost but that wasn't the way it was she must have been quite different (I told myself again and again until I no longer believed it) to be able to live with him that Boy Scout then ace footballer then MIT rowing captain extrovert good-humoured energetic cooperative sociable and positive in the sense of being in relaxed profound accord with the heart the soul the living principle of his country of its political system with no loss of biographical energy without the heavy weather through waves of abstraction a

German of my generation made of coming to terms with the Federal Republic he was an affirmative pragmatist still with a distinct touch of youthful charm his patient's shirt like a roll of patterned kitchen paper gave him or was given by him a sporting air even the cannulas stuck in his powerful brown freckled arm looked appropriate or desired as if the drug of his own character were pouring back into him from the Presbyterian's ego reserve no way was he going to miss seeing the

Tribute in Light

from close to or best of all he wanted to watch from Brooklyn or Jersey as Sabrina and Amanda rose as firework dragons in those blue fluorescent columns of light which had been conjured up over GROUND ZERO in place of the Towers by batteries of floodlights

touching frightening solemn an unpleasant reminder of anti-aircraft searchlights and on cloudy nights science-fiction-like because of the artificial blue as if something were shooting downward through the darkness into the destroyed Earth there was nothing no figures in the beams but

in an impersonal technical way we still found it comforting

two weeks later when we were standing beside each other at the Battery perhaps because the chaos the pain the shattered debris that had by now quickly been flattened suddenly seemed transcended and removed preserved in

organized light the church-window light of a resurrection perhaps or at least of a

transport

as if by powerful laser beams carrying everything to another planet to another sphere at least

it often (today for example with his jogging idea) seems to me as if Seymour wants to take our loss in a sporting way to be a good loser (of his wife and my daughter) but it's not that simple nor is it that easy to understand or explain him when I went to see him in the Presbyterian in March we talked together for two hours

he wanted to know how I was

coping (COPING)

how my thoughts were going what they were about I'd just been reading some of the things written by the Islamic theorists of terrorism available in English things which were said to have been the greatest influence on the BOYS from Hamburg-Harburg I was surprised at this often very calm pseudo-scholarly hatred addressed in very kindly tones to the BROTHERS when I read the books and pamphlets the fatwas larded with quotations from the Koran references prayers lists of arguments encompassing compressing the word of God the course of history the condition of mankind the moral degeneration of the nations into a few repeated formulas and platitudes into a tunnel a funnel getting narrower and narrower

(the BOYS the simple fact is that 50 per cent of the population of the Arab countries is under 18 and that the Islamist enthusiasts among them don't read these books but prefer to wait for video clips of bin Laden)

at the end of which there's nothing for it but to take up the machine gun put on a dynamite vest cut a stewardess' throat push down the control column of an airliner with 90 passengers on board directly above the southern tip of Manhattan and zoom over all the high-rise buildings the district a compact chevron the tip of the island larded with rhombuses cubes squares they think of as empty like the spear-shaped circuit board of a supercomputer hitting the Towers is easy because they're so prominent because they're just waiting for it a load of nonsense but so many journalists wrote that at which point Luisa remarked that ever since the Tower of Babel a portent of disaster had been built into the foundations of every grandiose architectural project and also anticipated visually since the establishment of the Hollywood studios we always like to see spectacular designs come to a spectacular end

but Sabrina was so restrained and

quiet

the blue as if molten as if boundless the kerosene of the sky

that makes everything so unreal so sharply unreal like a huge model exact down to the very last fraction of an inch in the summer light

jihad

is a duty and it means (for all these murderers preaching in kindly tones to their murderous brethren) nothing but the armed conflict each and every devout Muslim had now to engage in

a duty

allowing no choice

yes that's more or less the way I see it Seymour agreed on his sickbed always the same old story

but one that ends in real deaths (I countered) and why did we even need to question it was it just because of the pseudo-historical argumentation that there was and always had been an Islamic zone (dar al-Islam) out of which the intruders in the shape of the Israeli state of the US Army in Saudi Arabia in Iraq and in Afghanistan had to be driven (following this or that recorded anecdote from Mohammed's life or in accordance with this or that fatwa of this or that scribe from this or that century) a defence fantasy that has been inflated into a persecution mania and was derived from historical eruptions such as the war in Afghanistan or the Second Gulf War which were all put through the same Koranic mill and interpreted as an assault on all Muslims as hate-fuelled attacks by the West on the everlasting mediaeval house of Islam the phantasm of those who believe they hold the truth but which could only be derived from complete ignorance of political developments and actual conditions

they declare that jihad in its most violent sense is the duty of every individual the war against the infidels is to be pursued in their own countries as well I claimed at which Seymour started to cough so badly it made you think he was in the Presbyterian because of his obstinate 9/11 cough and was only wearing that clownish penitential robe for that reason what is it they see in us in these houses

(the person as

a whole)

that the deed itself is their goal was what had struck me most that it seemed to be a matter of indifference to them whether they actually came any closer to their declared ultimate goal the theocratic Islamic state on earth the perpetrator himself as an individual immediately enters paradise utopia he becomes a martyr he's made it all they're aiming for is as many acts of violence as possible which will sow doubt and confusion among the enemy and ideally create a chaotic or even apocalyptical scenario in which God will intervene if sufficient jihad energy has been released the deed murder massacre

that's the way it is Seymour said in a strangely relaxed tone that's the way terrorism works that's the way it's defined I suspect it's a spiritual home

it's something that saves these people from the torment their own thinking could bring and relates everything the whole of politics the whole world all unhappiness and every idea of happiness directly to their own lives implants MEANING as if a bomb were exploding inside their heads all the time

with the result (Seymour said) that they can kill 3,000 New Yorkers without scruple and even rejoice over the deed

so immeasurably distant from us I thought tensed up in a grey-upholstered visitor's chair on the right-hand side of the oilman his obligatory cheerful patient's nightshirt its childish pattern was proof that they were taking responsibility away from us here in their jihad against bodily evil Sabrina had once imagined that the oil-people who came to visit Seymour didn't have arteries and veins but metal pipelines of varying sizes it had come to the point where we had to talk openly about

OIL

it was absurd that I'd never questioned Seymour about his experiences his knowledge his opinions on a subject he'd been involved in all his life he'd had precise and lengthy discussions with Sabrina about it they'd taken the same subject at the same university even if over 25 years apart I couldn't stop myself from wondering why she'd run away from language and her great talent (the gift for poetry that I wanted her to have and spoke about less and less for fear of imposing something on her)

while as far as Seymour was concerned nothing other than oil would ever have occurred to me precisely because with his sportsman's aura he didn't at all look that kind of person but as soon as you knew it it was clear to see like patches of crude oil on white canvas these managers couldn't be any other way somehow all of a piece with a viscous shine and fused with the whole system (which one? the system of the industrial exploitation of the earth's resources) but how?

now I wanted to know

to find out whether despite his knowledge his intelligence and the important positions he had held in the course of his career (1974 his first appointment as on-site geologist at a small-time drilling outfit in the wilds of Oklahoma then co-owner of a firm of geological consultants in Houston then a spot market trader with too little success going back to his area of expertise to the North Sea with Royal Dutch/Shell then with Exxon/Canada and so on until a well-earned summary in his résumé: *various engineering and management positions with increasing*

responsibility)

whether he had perhaps spent his time at the house of oil wearing a kind of patient nightshirt stretched out in their sickbay or poking round in the earth without trying to justify what he was doing I'd already assumed that he did think about that but now I was interested in knowing exactly what his thoughts were indeed so interested that I clothed my question in the outrageously precise statement that

after all oil was always involved no matter where no matter when he took it as a stopgap move with the pawn (c2 to c3) and pointed out that there was any amount of oil

here

he presumably meant the source of the heat in the radiators in the room the synthetic fibres in our clothes the colours of the furniture the TV set the curtains the material of the flexible tubes going into his arm the inert carrier for the highly active drugs flowing through the cannula directly into his beating heart

everywhere the

devil's tears (another nice expression of the businessman Rockefeller he explained) are flowing

but how I asked could you make the devil cry

by catching his cat Seymour replied (Amanda's love light as a feather and prickly the pink blotches on her breast the perceptibly hard breastbone between nipples red as a fly agaric) he regarded me almost with a kind of pity (knight d4 to e6) the US legislation in the middle of the nineteenth century when they still had the production record regarded the hidden crude oil as a wild animal that hunters were after so that even today an undeveloped field is called a wildcat the black cat that is pursued to depths of between 2,000 and 13,000 feet where it gets caught in tectonic traps wedged in faults crouches under gigantic domes of salt or is enclosed like a huge cube-shaped lake at the intersecting surfaces of

disconformities

until after 50 million years of peace and quiet the rocky roof is broken through at a stroke by the all-penetrating rotating intermeshing steel heads of a roller bit studded with tappets and arranged in 120-degree segments

drilling technology

alone was a fantastic affair the racket of the drills accompanying the music of the earth that was what someone once called geology which would mean that extracting petroleum was its

rock 'n' roll

at which he gave me as an unmusical literature mole a somewhat pitying look that the earth looked on in silence as the petrol fumes befuddled it rhythmically but

without the oil

I said defiantly without the number one drug in the engines tanks syn-
thesizing boilers of the industrialized nations such streams of blood would
never have flowed that burning scorching mingling of dead prehistoric life
turned into juice over millions of years of that greenish-black pungent energetic corpse-broth with the bubbling wine of vulnerable living human bodies
would have remained the inborn curse on the Arab countries

you should go to the Middle East more often have you ever actually
been there (no I'd never felt the urge to and how could I go there now) at
least to Egypt Lebanon and Israel Seymour told me you shouldn't just watch
CNN or read the *New York Times* I'm no historian my friend but I'd say
that oil just works as an amplifier neutral you could say it's like advances in
technology pure power energy in forms of decay pure solar energy stored
up a preset from the cosmos sunk in the Earth's mantle it was a long time
before we realized what it was Lomonosov was the first to suggest its
organic origin from a sample of Baku oil then Faraday discovered benzol in
1824 we had to learn the complicated method of processing it by fractional
distillation step by step to produce lubricating oils gas oils light crude oils
and benzene breaking down the long chains into which millions of years of
fiery Earth-time had placed the light into that black devil's soup and that's
why with a sense of power and of light the first oil tankers were named after
gods or godlike prophets

Zoroaster Buddha Spinoza

Spinoza doesn't strike me as very appropriate here I objected to which
Seymour responded with an account of the comparatively high ethical stan-
dards of the Nobel brothers who for a long time dominated the Russian oil
and the Tsarist arms industries and oil at least had financed the infrastructure
of many Arab countries and the armaments madness as well and at the risk
of sounding banal he concluded that all it left us with was its technological
ambivalence and the political control over it

but now I went on persistently we keep on attacking the House of Islam
(they say) because we want the rest of the oil

we attacked Saddam Hussein within the framework of a UN resolution
after he had invaded and occupied Kuwait contrary to international law
Seymour replied calmly of course we wouldn't have done that if they'd only
exported dates (he said quoting NONAME the anonymous bigwig in the
US administration) *oil is too important a commodity to be left in the hands
of the Arabs* (he quoted again this time Henry Kissinger whom even I had

heard of) moreover America didn't need Kuwait's oil and even Saudi oil was only a factor

but a huge one presumably I objected how else can you explain the unparalleled operation by which shortly after the World Trade Center attack more than a hundred Saudis living in the US who belonged to the ruling house or the bin Laden clan were bundled off home with the help of the FBI

he raised his arm with the cannulas fixed by two narrow strips of plaster presumably to say point taken I didn't want a political argument with him in that state especially since all I had to offer was what I'd read in the papers my conjectures and prejudices and the little I'd read up in my anger and grief as I searched for

adequate (for what)

answers (for a wound)

are we stealing the oil I found myself asking a moment later

Seymour shook his head (I didn't even know whether he was a Democrat or a Republican) it wasn't just oil he said much more was at stake in the Middle East namely a fundamental conflict between three world religions and the existence of the modern state of Israel

but the oil is the most important factor for us

you can't run your car on Jesus' sweat he said patiently we're not stealing it but

we insist on being able to buy it?

no one out there wants to drink it he assured me so we just have to stop anyone stopping them from selling it

WE I said though not really emphatically perhaps because I was thinking less of the great martial collective of the

TOWER (the castle)

in which we all were whether we wanted to be or not casting its destructive or protective certainly powerful shadow over the chessboard of the Earth

than of that lunch in Boston with Sabrina and Amanda that uncomfortable embarrassing foursome Amanda had set up in order to square the circle of her life or to give Sabrina some encouragement for the coming semester I now recalled Seymour's discussion with my daughter and quoted his statement from it that

oil is always buried in the earth

damn deep in the earth he corrected me and that's the whole point you can't just go and take the black gold off some natives by force or by bartering a few glass beads for it pour it into bars and keep it in safes there was the upstream and the downstream loading shipping processing refining worldwide distribution of the products to millions of consumers in difficult market conditions and under strict government regulation only

the SEVEN SISTERS he explained (without that once-upon-a-time tone though still irritatingly cheerful and flushed so that I told myself off for having got him worked up and assumed that any minute I'd be chucked out of the room by a real sister—*we can see things*—rushing in) the seven big oil companies were the only ones who controlled the business who already had decades of experience before significant oil deposits were found in the Middle East and who moreover (warding off a possible objection from me with

knight to c6)

couldn't just do as they liked not even in the US especially not here in New York City he made another odd gesture with the arm through which he was

on stream (the oilmen's cry of triumph when they've caught the wildcat by the tail)

as if he were reminding me and the whole town outside the window that it was in New York City in 1911 that ESSO the supposed anaconda of the Rockefeller conglomerate was chopped into pieces by the anti-cartel machete of the Supreme Court

we I said (WE so as not to exclude myself from the matter) certainly push our oil interests through by force against those who attempt to stop us from buying it by attacking us or others that is the Islamists that is Saddam Hussein we collaborated with him and at the same time with the mullahs in Iran and we collaborate with Saudi Arabia without taking account of the political situation there as long as oil exports are OK

we can't change the situation by force Seymour said we have to work with what's there we didn't found Israel nor instal these regimes in the Arab countries

but we support both sides we arm them to the hilt even though they're mortal enemies and now we're standing in the ruins

of the Towers Seymour added it's OK you can say it only I don't believe it had to be he'd joined a citizen's action group whose aim was to break the Bush administration's resistance to an official enquiry into NINEELEVEN he read out a newspaper article about the Jersey Girls to me those energetic abruptly widowed housewives who were demanding information about the death of their husbands in the Towers and seeing these reports and uttering the standard phrases for a few minutes we once more found ourselves in that happy crazy state in which we could believe

all of that

had nothing to do with us or only

in a literal way

Seymour could sense my resistance to losing sight of the wider political framework so stressed that the framework was nothing but the sum total of all the little direct concrete causes and in the total account derivation reasoning historical causality I seemed to be striving after he advised me to start out clearly from the conditions which were concrete and obvious which took us to the failure of the American secret services on the one hand and on the other to the concrete history of the perpetrators that is where did the Islamists come from Egypt Jordan the West Bank Saudi Arabia and they met

in Afghanistan

I said exhausted and perhaps looking more wretched than him in his bed surrounded by oscillographs I looked at my hands as if there should have been shining black splotches on them I felt like Goethe at the filling station but I was anything (mediocre) but Goethe and HE (as a minister and former chairman of the Ilmenau Mines Commission) would surely have been fascinated by the drilling records the gas pumps the refineries and those colossal divine or philosophical tankers ploughing through the oceans with 50 million gallons of oil in their bellies which they spewed up now and then when they felt sick or broke up on a reef Sabrina had definitely argued with Seymour about environmental disasters he missed Amanda (I suddenly thought)

in a more immediate painful way not just as the subject of a melancholy memory that had healed

I felt sorry for him in a way that was difficult to define however now the door to the sickroom did really open and it wasn't the nurse who came in to tell me off and throw me out it was

the twins Charles and Emma Seymour's children from the marriage with his late wife elegantly dressed concerned well-brought-up 26-year-olds right place right time

check

or perhaps not

we had no (more) moves to play when I left the room I took the elevator in the wrong direction and went up to the roof with a male nurse who wanted a cigarette and let me go with him after he'd asked me presumably because of the expression on my face if I'd

lost someone (a good loser

again) when I said yes

he asked no more questions just stood beside me smoking through the yellow metal bars which split up the view of the Hudson like the bars of a monkey cage until you press your hot face between two of them I could sense the male nurse's mute pity halved by professional tiredness and obtained by devious but half-genuine means by me and then forgot it as I looked down at the

March-grey river

you could see far away across the roofs and over the big bridge to Jersey and also to the southeast over the initially stone-armoured giant lobster that is Long Island views out through the pain as if through a partition completely transparent but several feet thick I recalled similar and even more distant views (from the World Trade Center with Amanda when she was pregnant in November 1981 the Towers were only five years old I had no idea that one day one of us would work would die in such a monstrous edifice that student of almost doll-like beauty in a bright red 1970s parka with a fringe of fur round the hood her stomach protruding in a soft oval behind glass several feet thick)

the views with Sabrina at 11 from the Empire State Building where did King Kong climb up I'm the

father ape

behind yellow bars

below me a hundred open hearts in the operating rooms I don't want to eat

the bananas of war that George Bush is throwing me

I had always found such views of the gigantic compact mass of buildings that is Manhattan alarming and exhilarating at the same time they told me I had no business to be there had nothing to do with the place that there'd be no pity for me there (the slight grey-faced nurse had finished his cigarette and was waiting for me)

and yet on the other hand there was always the sense of freshness of the grandiose that carried you away

America

a new beginning new air new skies by the mighty bright blue Atlantic the anthem of generations of millions

Walt Whitman, a kosmos, of Manhattan the son

a view across to fish-shaped Paumanok on which he was born I met up with Sabrina on Long Island just once (but I didn't go as far as the lobster's claw to East Hampton where the sight of Seymour and Amanda's summer residence might perhaps have cut me up after all)

Sabrina (at 16 or 17) liked the simple but well-thought-out wooden house Whitman's father had built with his own hands she would love to live there she said in the little outhouse with the white door and the two freshly painted windows

we (WE)

could then move into the main building

she immediately glossed over her mistake with a smile and a brief wave of the hand in front of her eyes as if a leaf had fallen just in front of her or a spider's thread got stuck in her hair

again and again I went to see poets' houses with her today I can't remember why it's not the houses that are important it's the country it's the people

One's-Self I sing, a simple separate person
Yet utter the word Democratic, the word En-Masse

to be no more and no less than all the inhabitants of the country

why only of the one (because it's new)

the nurse touched me on the shoulder nurses on the battlefields in the military hospitals at the bulldozed ruins of the Towers I could have learnt another trade instead of visitor to poets' houses the superb Whitman had managed it but would I have been able to bear it

I went to see Seymour three times in the clinic (more often than his children) and neither of us was surprised at that

It's quite some time now since anyone consulted me about an afternoon nap but I can remember this or that *regimen sanitatis* of Galen or Maimonides according to which you should eat in moderation and get up after a meal instead of lying down and if possible neither retain your urine not clamp your buttocks together and Ibn Sina also warned of gout colds and headaches resulting from sleeping during the day if you had to then you should restrict yourself to half an hour with your belt undone and your shoes off but with your feet covered and in as dark a place as possible usually I agree with him but

I felt so rough after the meal with the power- and painter-philosophers that I spent the whole of yesterday with an empty throbbing head despite the miracle cure available to me (two litres of water and three aspirin) it wasn't until the evening that I really got over it and my (truly astonishing) strength back in the night that's just past when Farida suddenly fell upon me or rather took me

to her bosom

like an old teddy bear but I performed pretty well and presumably because of that had a restless night again and consequently found the four necessary weekend house calls very heavy going so that completely against my usual habit and better knowledge I fell into my bed exhausted

it's a strange undefined half sleep in which I'm less immersed than elevated it feels as if for hours I've been in a precarious state of suspension as if at any moment I could plunge down but am too tired to change even the least element of my situation I'm enveloped in a peculiar dull grey void but it's not really unpleasant it's even liberating it's simply an absence of (irksome) shaping as if I'm floating in a grey cloud with nothing else in it and waking up in such a situation is wonderful my friend you progress through cotton wool layers of indefinite nameless stuff into a similarly very diffuse self as if you could make a surprise visit to yourself and to the rest of the world as well from the perspective of the

Flying Man

whom Ibn Sina again (your Avicenna) invented to give us normal minds an idea of how little is needed for consciousness to develop we only have to do without arms legs ears nose eyes mouth for once and imagine ourselves suspended in the air for a moment (without a wire or rope of course)

there we would sense ourselves perceive ourselves imagine ourselves

but with what?

with our soul Ibn Sina believed he had proved

on our return to ourselves we feel our self as this or that and I greet my return with an amazing flying erection for which I presumably have to thank the memory of an even more amazing event with a tender madame smelling of jasmine flowers and musk thus we have time memory and wife what more can you want I think I've been married to her for thousands of years and we have hordes of descendants but where yes where

that's when the glass pyramids come to mind

and I see burning mullahs striding over them

Madjid you crazy bugger didn't Ali prophesy that the Shiites would hang you the moment the Americans had put them in power now where was I

flying

oh those mullahs and Muslims but what can I tell you about the believers my friend it was 40 years ago when I was last in a mosque after all I'm a Parisian no an

ARAB

an Arab in Paris my friend that's where I portrayed it

the exotic bogeyman

once more it's an almost unbelievable 25 and 30 years ago and I'm hanging half asleep at five in the morning from the straps dangling down in the night bus on my way to the early shift in the Pitié-Salpêtrière already dozing after a 24-hour stint drained but freshly showered and too well dressed to impress people as a carpet weaver or a drug dealer behind my eyelids the camels trot across the Empty Quarter shepherd dogs bark beside the cold campfire I stagger out of the virtual tent over cold sheep bones into the wonderful wastes of silvery sand and sea-blue sky through bad-tempered rattling scorpions and refractory rams (*Votre billet s'il vous plaît!*) and suddenly HIS VOICE comes thundering down

drowning me in his

never-ending all-argument-rejecting inexhaustible inflexible jealous threatening thundering angry opinionated enticing cursing crafty overbearing ultimate imperial eternal

SPEECH

the whole night through (I keep holding tight to two plastic straps)

and another night

and a further 999 nights the relentless call of the great voice the universe is text the cosmos words my brains my blood nothing but flowing script in my language which is HIS language (I greet an incredibly fresh incredibly shy incredibly 24-year-old Ali who gets on at the Children's Hospital stop and people turn half annoyed half asleep towards us our throats choked by God's consonants

sabahu l-hayr kayfa l-hal ana tayyib al-hamdu li-llah)

in my dawning morning-blue internal atmosphere there appears

the black stone the Stanley Kubrick obelisk

with black Berbers riding round

Abraham lived here Mohammed lived here if you're

looking for the root you're still standing in an old desert city in the heat the dryness the harsh salty air the glaring sun among the herds of camels outside the cold wealthy city houses among the merchants dealers preachers slaves in the souk 1,400 years later (during which we continue to quote the SPEECH as it echoed down from the sky and was written down with precision and immense respect for the words that would only become comprehensible in other worlds and other immense times) tens of thousands of pilgrim pelicans still meet here camping round the stone piling up in gigantic fans like the curves and grandstands of a huge stadium their bodies remote-controlled by loudspeakers on pylons bending down rhythmically in the floodlights in the surges of the SPEECH transported here in overfull buses tipped out of the sky from the perfectly managed hajj flotilla of Saudi Airlines

it spread out from here

the fire of the new religion of the world with war and blood and zeal (nothing new under the sun) everything (even then) is marked by conflict and fighting and power the fireball that almost instantaneously became state and power and organization the religion that like Alexander set out to sweep away the old empires or like Christianity to smash the Imperium Romanum to expand in the jihad over the whole of the Fertile Crescent as far as Babylon and Basra over the Persian highlands western Egypt Tunisia and even to Spain

as a new IDEA unambiguous but tolerant

clear and definite

you can ask yourself what

it means to YOU (personally)

are you French because one of your maids beat the English because you invented the guillotine because you overran Europe with the bloodroller of *liberté-égalité-fraternité* because you landed in Egypt in order to count the stones of the Pyramids because Jean-Paul Sartre explained (I saw him distributing leaflets on the Champs Élysées a fat little old man standing in front of the glass Sphinx of his books) that you have to be free before life casts you out (where to)

and finally Cordoba Cairo Damascus and

my Baghdad

the new city the round city of al-Mansur and Harun al-Rashid the caliphate and the palace here my friend we should have been storks Nietzsche and Heidegger with the frog Hitler in their beaks after all you're a genuine German my friend with genuine German fairy tales often coming from the French high above the domes they would spit out the frog so that a few of our officers could find it and already they were on their way to the Reich Party Rally in Nuremberg

imagine these storks and more than a thousand years without a word of release (Ali knows it he claims it's called AMERICA in the language of Kafka)

let's stick to the time of the first palaces when people in Baghdad could sleep incomparably quietly even the Jews who wrote their great Talmud here and had their important academies

when the light of Rome had long since gone out and that of Europe was not yet lit (our favourite restaurant Farida behind the Place de la Bastille)

let us once more take a stroll

in the palace with its basins and arbours diverse gardens domes fountains quiet rooms magnificent halls hidden treasure chambers white elephants and harem ladies Nubian slaves Turkish guards leaping eunuchs (choose the right life the body into which you are cast) silver and golden birds on a tree turning and tinkling in the wind

poets doctors scholars

when the Syrian Christians translated the works of the Greeks into Arabic the Indian mathematicians gave us their numbers and we gave the

Persians the dance forms of our poems my colleagues swore the Hippocratic oath in its full ancient wording

if each man

is the sultan in his own palace (robot slaves papier-mâché elephants electromechanical panthers tireless harem ladies *Made in Hong Kong*)

I want to stay in Baghdad and so I dream of

waking to the calls of the golden birds to the splash of the fountains to being cooled by gently waved ostrich feathers early in the morning

as an Arab

but I think I must be something else as well and it's late in the afternoon and evening's already approaching and I wake for a second time but

at least still in Baghdad in an utterly real Iraq

by the river I wake at the side of my wife who is walking slowly and calmly and with whom I was chatting without really noticing until she spoke that

shocking sentence

that I'm now desperately trying to remember although with it she tore me out of all my dreams daydreams worries about which she's now talking again as if nothing had happened I must have misheard she seems as friendly and relaxed as before as always she's talking about Sami who hangs around in the new Internet cafes and possibly doesn't exercise enough caution during the games they play there with real and virtual watchdogs and about Yasmin who's annoyed with us because we didn't go to her husband's fortieth birthday party although we had made it clear that although we are forced to look on powerless to do anything as our daughter surrounds herself with scientists who occupy too high posts not to be in the Party and those army officers we had to put up with at her wedding in the old family home at least we can

keep our distance

as long as we at least still have the space to make a kind of geometrical statement

if we send Muna to London there's no guarantee she won't develop in the same (patriotic) direction as Yasmin in Paris but

the times are different

I assure Farida who at the moment doesn't seem to remember the shocking sentence she spoke I only wish I'd heard what she'd said before that sentence it must it presumably would have been an unreal condition (if each and every one of us in Iraq can have a good safe sound sleep)

we go down to the Tigris by the streets and alleys we've known for 50 years

they've never been more melancholy rotten tumbledown than now let's take it as a mark of courtesy to our own ageing bodies which in contrast have retained more vitality and powers of renewal we've remained vigorous too like that woman coming towards us carrying the old plastic canisters her abaya wide open beneath which a lovely long violet skirt and a shining pink blouse can be seen we

simply go on living

and go on walking

by the river

we have a cup of tea standing outside a tiny cafe with chipped tiled walls covered over with James Dean posters so much is like a withered crumbling yellowing copy of the past in a glass frame we can't afford to be thinking every time about our historic walk in 1967

when you sent me to Paris

and the fish restaurants were all still open and Frank Sinatra sang on those radio days which seem so unbearably beautiful to me despite the lost war that I have to understand why

it's just that ocean of future

and the crazy certainty that we can sail across it to the other side that is so full of promise or even the illusion bursting at its logical seams with happiness that we have already done so and returned to the present to see how things are

Farida at 19 giving my shoulder a squeeze to give me the strength to go on ahead to Paris 'Que Sera': worthwhile jobs happy children intellectual exchange a nice apartment holidays abroad books friends discussions going to concerts and plays

how could we not be

so depressed in the stormy bloody times we've had to live through instead

Farida at 54

looks across the river scenery bathed by the setting sun in strangely unreal colours with hints of violet and gold with an inlay of black palm trees the sky purple and orange the high concrete walls watchtowers domes massive facades with barbed wire edging the presidential palace shimmering romantically on the Karkh side

we don't have to stay here

I say

mainly to do something to combat the after-effects of the terrible sentence which she perhaps didn't say after all I bring up the possibility of fleeing the country at least once a month in our nocturnal discussions in bed for at least I unlike so many teachers and professors have never been out of work and have managed with our economical life in my grandfather's old house to put enough on the side so that if necessary we could pay a smuggling ring

it's only here (Farida says) that we can be healed

only

when we see that stuff over there (a glance at the palace complex with a magical wash of sunshine and peppered with ice-cold searchlights) blown up and if we survive it and we will survive it

her shoulder-length black hair is still almost as shiny as it was when she was 19 and for me her face that has become strong and round looking both motherly and resolute at the same time with touches of fiery girlish energy and softness keeps turning transparent like a veil through which I can see the 20- and 30-year-old

old men are sitting by the river smoking and a younger one is proudly shaving himself in the right-hand and only remaining wing-mirror of his dented white Toyota Jeep two boys are trying to strap on roller skates from the design they could be ones from my own childhood

when I said

that I don't know if I should stay with you

(this time I can't reproach myself with having missed consciously registering the terrible sentence)

I was thinking that it would probably be easier for us to bear what was to come if we weren't together she adds with a (fortunately) concerned look because she could no longer fail to notice that she had cut me to the quick she can tell from the way I look that it has just occurred to me that basically it was always she who had determined the direction our life took

from that first remark she directed at me in the book market to the birth of Muna and Sami right down to the present day we have children as you will recall

they're grown-up Tariq anyway it's just something I've been asking myself for what is going to come will be as serious as a life-or-death operation you know all about that but it can be better to—

amputate? do you think so?

we keep walking for a long time that evening always southwards as close to the Tigris as possible I just can't stop walking and several times reach out to grasp Farida's firm round upper arm I need to hold onto it to get the idea out of my head that she suddenly wanted to sleep with me yesterday because she was

thinking

about amputation

we could go out for a picnic again I suggest out of pure contrariness or simply because in the dusk on our right the bronze contours of the little island in the Tigris are emerging the one we call the Isle of the Gluttons (gluttons with strong nerves who don't care when the Republican Guard comes to check that they're not aiming their barbecue grills at the palace or even— as used to happen quite often—the FIEND himself comes put-putting along with a case of whisky for the picnickers)

Babylon our expedition there was a great release Farida says it really did me good

I've lost sight of her

that's the simple bitter truth of the last few years during which I was simply happy to survive the amount of work I had to do watch the children growing up and once a week meet up with my fewer and fewer friends to drink to our losses after two years as a French teacher at a Christian school she'd only worked at home as a translator until there were hardly any commissions any more at least not interesting ones we live in a house that she keeps spick and span smelling nice neat and tidy lovingly furnished and decorated

without thinking who it is that keeps it in that condition

since Sami and Muna hardly need her any more she's translated lots of things only for herself or for us Blanchot at the moment she tells me when I finally ask her about it he's an author of

disaster

who starts out from the premiss that we're permanently in a state of great unhappiness even though disaster never quite seems to strike—oh forget it

with you

I've been happy

in an unhappy country

A RARITY

Without a time or place for love
    Some couples went their separate ways.
For us the night, an honest thief,
    Took only hours from our own days.

At any time, then, I could find,
    Your heart at least, if not your eye.
What others scarce could wring from death,
    I gleaned like dew from dawn's clear sky.

Laugh, if you like, at me, the fool
    Who only won one woman's love—
A love for which you cannot hope,
    Gift of the wisest God above.

Sunday 9 August 2002 early morning on the almost silent Amsterdam Avenue

I'm writing in my book of random (raging) thoughts (*Are you alive if others are alive?*) the stammerings of

a man who wants to know

no question of wanting to understand I'm only (that's it only) looking for the kind of answers that satisfy me (as well) my raging bewildered often simply exhausted step-by-staggering-step search that can't stop Seymour told me that they call them

NEWTS

or PIGS

those automatic investigation and cleaning systems they put in hermetically sealed oil pipelines so that travelling slowly doggedly they can meticulously check the state of the pipes millimetre by millimetre in the frozen steppes of the Siberian tundra I'm travelling (stuffed with flashing hi-tech equipment surrounded by darkness close to suffocation) along my tunnel pipe to

Afghanistan

again tonight and now over my open books perhaps just because I spoke to Seymour about it on the phone no definitely also because our plan to go out jogging together this (Sunday) morning fills me with panic I can well remember March 2001 when the Taliban destroyed the statues of the Buddha in Bamiyan (my TV-vision not the view that freezes you to the bone from an ice-encrusted plain up to the immense barrier of rock in the Hindu Kush in which the 120- and 180-foot-high statues in their niches look like dreaming stone soldiers in little sentry boxes) I saw the barbarity and couldn't understand the hatred any more than

I could understand six months later how the press and the US administration had been able to identify Osama bin Laden in his Afghan terrorist camp so quickly as the wirepuller (the old acquaintance that he in fact was for them)

all the connections with Afghanistan suddenly so plain to see revealed in all their shocking clarity and extent as if we ordinary citizens had for years not noticed the pillars of highway bridges in our gardens

it took me an effort before I could think clearly again (just four weeks after the attacks) already American bombs were dropping on the Tora Bora cave complex in Nangarhar (Enduring

Freedom)

and at the end of November the Afghanistan Conference was held on the Petersberg near Bonn and I wondered why in Germany and then learnt something about the Niedermayer-Hentig expedition which in 1915 tried (unsuccessfully) to persuade Emir Habibullah to go to war against Russia and British India in 1924 the German-language Nejat High School was founded in Kabul which became a training school for the Afghan elite in 1937 direct Lufthansa flights between Berlin and Kabul started dams bridges Siemens hydro-energy installations were built warm relations established between the true Aryans and the even truer (original) Aryans who at first presumably had no idea of their racial good fortune

when I started working on my thesis in Berlin I occasionally went to see some former fellow students a couple who thanks to an inheritance had found themselves with a townhouse in Lankwitz and the opportunity of which they took frequent advantage to become globetrotters without having to worry about the expense I stared uncomprehending at a frayed red wall-hanging a headdress made of gold coins dented kettles and gilt hookahs souvenirs brought back from a two-month journey round Afghanistan and they were equally uncomprehending

about my desire to go to the US soon even though the Vietnam War was over only when they met some students on Stanford University's Berlin programme did they feel they could understand

cherchez la femme it's because of that blonde Amanda Afghan Beate declared with a laugh in her Lankwitz home we'd slept together after a fashion two or three times in her narrow student-hostel bed (slipping down or out of it all the time) and still got on together I'd run away from this bold robust red-haired globetrotter for fear of losing my head (I felt I had to protect parts of my cerebrum for whom for what) it was indeed because of Amanda that I wanted to go to the States again as became clear to me then precisely because we weren't an item it was only occasionally (for a minute or two) at parties or in the dimly lit old cinemas in Kreuzberg that I thought it was possible the impossibly pretty Californian might be interested in me

the first time Amanda kissed me was in the Lankwitz house in the semi-dark beneath the Afghan wall-hanging

such playful ornamental links

arabesques that turn into nooses to hang you I can't accept that I refuse to acknowledge these insane unnecessary cynical tricks of fate

the German poet through whom Sabrina came to know Hafiz (the book she stole from me)

had lost his three-year-old daughter and his five-year-old son around the end of 1833

I listen to Mahler's setting the

Kindertotenlieder

Rückert wrote more than 400 poems after the death of Ernst and Luise all I have is Sabrina's cardboard box with the two postcards stuck on the lid (the old man drinking wine in the desert and the Egyptian singer) and the idea the assumption rather that she found poems a comfort at five in the morning

I become

a stranger to the world in this jogging kit bought unthinkingly that I've put on in the dark to sit at my window on Amsterdam Avenue in it like a clown (did I want to make myself look ridiculous?)

back then

it wasn't Amanda I should have desired loved followed to the US (it's not a journey I thought back then it's an arrival)

but that Lankwitz globetrotter Beate to Afghanistan not of my own free will but willingly in a dark spiral of premonition Mahler composed the song I listen to again and again six years before his daughter died

You must not cling on to the night
But drown it in eternal light.

you can hear it: a still distant light you're already caught up in its suction a light that

threatens to consume everything

what does it matter if I sink back (previously my intellectual's fear of travel my inability to plunge into the light) to

Afghanistan

I spent that night travelling and hardly had I closed my eyes than the globetrotter turned into Amanda Amanda into

our daughter

we had journeyed together so often it seemed natural to me to go round the Afghanistan of the 1970s with Sabrina

impossible

absurd not giving a damn for anything (for all those poor damned souls there) I often think I

burdened

her with the

EARTH

because she started that difficult and (to my mind) dry course at MIT as if she'd been forced by Amanda and me into those dead places

to me Afghanistan seems to be nothing other than the harsh dominion only relaxing for brief moments of peace over people we could have gone there Sabrina we can travel the place of tourists

is almost solely

the past

I hear the songs for the dead (fear of suffocation at night) but I

continue to breathe I go with my daughter I shake my head at her severe hairstyle combed back and tied in a braid (it's too thin to wear open she says) at her unwieldy blue rucksack with the straps that cut into her shoulders

we would have hired a car a Skoda or an old Japanese jeep from Pakistan we should have taken camels or horses I'm reading about the horses of the Buzkashi riders foam spraying from their mouths and nostrils their bodies whipped until the blood flows pale-brown sweat-gleaming black granite-grey soot-coloured coats over their quivering muscles the contorted dust-streaked weather-beaten thousand-year-old faces of the Turcoman riders beneath their fur caps and red pirates' headscarves the short curved whip between bared teeth

they behead a goat and the one who drags it (round a post far out in the steppes) farthest is the winner the Buzkashi horses are supposed at least according to the Chinese to be of divine origin but is there anything the Chinese won't believe the steppes remain

with their ruins as if they had never been new no

promise of a future of a past we visit Herat enclosed in its green valleys in the northwest that huge sand rampart of a citadel storm-lashed and rain-washed for 23 centuries that Alexander the Great had built we circumnavigate the whole country we follow the rivers farther to the north through the grey mealy golden haze of dust that gets into every pore and crack into the corners of your eyes your nostrils ears under your fingernails streets of dust mountains of dust houses of dust people of dust on dust-yellow dromedaries and clay-yellow donkeys it's the dust of the loess from which the houses and irrigation channels are formed life and death consist of dust in

Balkh

once the mother of cities whose outer walls like half-eroded dunes or the crumbling sides and towers of termite mounds remind you that 800 years ago Genghis Khan destroyed and flattened the city where Alexander had married 1,500 years before

ancient crumbling cities smashed to pieces razed to the ground sinking back into the dust

ancient fearsome conquerors from the East

the Burner of the World

the Scourge of God the Scorching Sun of Satan

Genghis Khan

whom Timur Lenk succeeded Timur the Lame spared the poets thinkers craftsmen architects (for that reason perhaps appears in Goethe and Hafiz) but drowned their cities in blood built huge palaces mosques fantastic gigantic edifices on the trail of destruction of his unceasing chaotic campaigns through Persia down to Baghdad where they filled the Tigris with

blood and books

as we stand outside the mosque in Balkh its beauty releases us from the icy dreary mud of the surroundings a truly miraculous gateau of a glazed-earthenware dome turquoise filigree spray-cream of the centuries turned to stone

a cockfight in the quagmire round it a circle of 200 men with turbans and caftans with pyjama stripes

the beauty the fruits

of Afghanistan don't think of sandy deserts gorges crazy warped drifts snow ice dust mud stone clay alone but also of

blackberries almonds

pomegranates grapes apricots all the

celebrated fruits their fragrance pervading 2,000 years of poetry (sing the praises of the fruits instead of the despots) the exquisite interior of Afghanistan sturdy thick-coated dromedaries striding across rivers that steam in the cold climbing endless mountain paths through icy clefts over rocky plateaus and white moonscapes loaded with lead chests containing the famous melons packed in snow that were being taken to India because their taste is said to have made the emperor

weep

with happiness

you come in through the door

out of the thin blue night air of the Hindu Kush were you to come in through the door in every place it wouldn't help to keep

my mind a blank for example

by travelling alone without books without writings which I've often imagined as a journey to one's doom (at night on Lexington Avenue at a fruit stall bathed by daylight bulbs in the gleaming eternal sunshine of paradise: Hey, *what's up man? You're looking tired. Take an apple. It's free.*) birds flowers fruits

time's harlequins

in the relentless superhuman strength of places the wretched mountain village in Nuristan where I would go without you (could have gone at one time today I would probably quickly be kidnapped and a problem for the German Embassy what's the point of this planet full of idiotic criminals why should one dominate it)

without any of you

I mean including every person I've loved in the incompatible childish quivering nocturnal stupid fusion of Amanda Sabrina and Luisa

it's nothing more

than an intellectual's old romantically false yearning namely to reach a place of complete

rejection

(by language by closeness by responsibility)

13,000 to 16,000 feet above the sea that isn't there to a place where the world is nailed up with rock and ice

in the 1970s the years before the Soviet invasion I saw such places in my friends' photograph albums

shaking my head

incapable of understanding what they were doing there where I

now

wanted to lose myself faced with icy cliffs in the Hindu Kush in a village in Kafiristan (the high out-of-the-way land of the unbelievers that was only Islamized around the turn of the century and who knows how completely) all the dwellings are rotten grey wet as if tipped out down the steep mountainside directly above the raging torrent are huts made of heavy wood beams and clay with large stones baked into it clinging to the slope huts rotting in the wet and cold black with smoke connected by steps and bending walkways of rotten planks you're lying there

sick with a temperature ready to go even to this as if frozen vertical heaven

if that were the price of

Sabrina rising from the dead even if she could only rise

as an Afghan and

was not allowed to say a word to me (how did I come to think of that a pact with the devil what else but even in my dreams that Faustian effect is the only one that seems realistic)

a girl leaning against a wooden doorframe with the snow swirling down as if everything were to be buried within minutes but she's watching her friends or sisters plodding towards her through large driving flakes like scraps of foam laden with wooden baskets sweaty exhausted their feet in worn-out boots blue with the freezing cold

you

could come back as the daughter of a caravan guide as the third child of a young Turcoman mullah as a Pashtun shepherd girl you could belong to the Hazara people and marry into a family of smugglers (opium Kalashnikovs vodka mobile telephones satellite dishes and laptops from Taiwan) or be the favourite child of a garrulous interpreter in Kabul who presents you to an attaché at the British Embassy as an unveiled high-school student educated at top Western schools while two streets away all the women are still going round in burqas buried under pieces of cloth transformed into textile ghosts wrapped up in disinfection suits against the inner plague of femininity

the carpets

it says in one of the guides I've borrowed to find you again in a past that never was in the land that sent death to you

reveal

woman's beautiful soul

wrapped up covered buried among

the revealers

old women are squatting round a low table where steam is rising from teacups in one of the black yurts clinging like Chinese parasol mushrooms to the yellow earth of the steppes at the foot of the rocky slopes on the snow-encrusted subsoil of the high plateaus what are they talking about what

is the Pashtun schoolgirl reading she's squatting outside with dust-grey hands bare dust-grey feet wrapped up in her layers of clothes that look as if they've been daubed with thick oil paint beside a wall of unbaked clay bricks with the (unveiled) face of a Tuscan Madonna what

is going through the mind of the young woman cosy inside her sack-like quilted coat with a blue-grey turban billowing round her head and shoulders like a wave of cloth as she delicately bites into a carrot so firmly

it's

suddenly when I'd already forgotten why I was looking at photographs

Sabrina's eyes staring at me with a kind of

mute horror or just

with a particular question what can a look tell you when you don't know anything else I abandon the nonsense there is no price if you're prepared to pay with your life I cannot imagine any situation for a woman in Afghanistan from which I would not want to free Sabrina and surely that shows

how little I understand or want to understand

when I look at pictures when I remember pictures when contemplating the old dead towns of Afghanistan and Persia I sink into reverie on a bench outside the Public Library in sunny Bryant Park surrounded by lunching bankers and dozing students with their books and computers slipping off their laps I see ghosts of the women

living burning torches death-veils drenched in petroleum in which the
bride rejects for good the husband who has been forced on her

the ghosts in the razed beheaded ruins of Shahr-i Ghulghula the city of
laments half buried in 100-feet-high mounds of sand in dunes that move
with destructive force the moment you look away six inches a night I imagine we'd sleep there and the next morning

just your arm

would be covered in sand we would have journeyed on

Sabrina

in another

happier immense branch of the universe

on the border (with Iran)

my daughter would be given back to me for an hour perhaps

we'd visit Timur's tomb in Samarkand we'd cross over from the grandiose
luxury hotel for tourists through a ring of poverty-stricken dwellings dusty
streets fermenting rubbish curious disparaging bored looks follow the German
and the slender (never again) fragile figure at his side

that is completely shrouded in a black cloth not as in a chador or a
burqa

but as in absence the black cloth of the present flowing close-fitting and
tenderly close to her former body only like that

only completely protected

was she able to walk with me for an hour before us now neatly exposed
and preserved like a gigantic anatomical preparation from the body of
another age is the tomb-mosque of the art-loving limping mass murderer
what is it we want from the sublime mausoleums where power is mouldering
here beneath a wonderful round dome with fluted ribs shimmering like a
silk balloon in colours that have turned transparent over 700 years

we don't go down into the crypt to the broken slab of rock that was and
is unable to prevent Timur's eternal resurrection

literature

Sigi Ramsauer said (the blasted drizzle at his funeral in Amherst the
mud the dean using whisky to draw me out of the mourning veil of a loss
which seemed dreadful to me

but at that time

Sabrina and Amanda

were alive

though only in another town and together with other people—in one
of my lectures the poetic contest between Uhland and Rückert on whether
it was better to lose one's love to death or to her infidelity which in my opinion Rückert lost with the nobler argument but the poorer poem)

literature talks to the powerful

as soon as they're dead said my late colleague at UMass

we can't go any further we turn away from Timur's mausoleum from
the necropolis the fine black cloth round Sabrina's body is so terrible invis-
ibility is such a terrible price to pay for her close and perfect contours for
the complete harmony of the feeling of walking along beside each other the
way the slimmer lighter body of my daughter is part of me stored deep within
my cells

there's no bench no block of stone we could sit down on

there's no word

we may say to each other we

can just walk along the dusty streets between the wretched houses as
far as the fields bounded by stone walls

in the distance

beyond a row of pale crumbling roofs

children's kites soar up

how could it happen (as if we were asking ourselves that out there in
the fields by Samarkand as

if we had escaped) that

we came to New York City to Manhattan to that island in the river narrow as a spearhead that looked as if madmen had laden it with gigantic
stone columns larded it with monstrous glass towers with avalanches of
metal pouring round them the city of cities (before the true monster cities
arose which themselves keep fading before their pursuers from the future)

a surviving

city

at least Sabrina I don't know any more

I can't say any more this here is just

a dream

Yesterday I could hardly get to sleep because of the talk I have to give at school and I woke today with my heart racing one hour before I had to get up though the shouts of the children next door would have woken me anyway it must have been Hind and Ahmed

the world began

with a quarrel my father couldn't remember the story of the creation but it amused him to hear that humanity came into being because Tiamat and Ansu got annoyed at the way their divine offspring were romping round and therefore decided (as a noise-prevention measure) to do away with them only Marduk was able to prevent this and as the saviour of the gods from the original gods he created heaven and earth time and mankind in

Babylon the city of his temple

so that is where everything begins

therefore it's not surprising that I'm interested in it but Tariq always tries to find out exactly (like you now, Beloved) where my interest comes from and what it might mean whether it's serious and 'scientific' you'd think he was afraid I'd want to disappear into Uday Saddam Hussein's magazine *Babel* among sports reports picture puzzles blonde models the leading article on US imperialism by al-Dulaimy (Uday again) all the glossy ads for watches jewellery luxury cars as if we were all millionaires in Dubai or Milan or in a palace like Uday as a

murderer torturer rapist

in a white suit in my opinion he's the true Babylonian I mean from a biblical viewpoint Tariq says where do they all appear in Daniel or John the Boozer?

Huda is to give a talk entitled How Did the Zionists Falsify the Historical Reality of Babylon? she's looking for an opportunity to annoy her mother again but I only want to talk about the site of the city about its architecture about the reconstructions that have been carried out so far about the excavations and what remains to be discovered

tomorrow we're going to Babylon

my mother suddenly said six weeks ago

the three of us (no Sami) went on the trip something we hadn't done for ages and Farida had agreed that on the three days that Tariq had taken off we wouldn't go and visit Karbala and Najaf as well he said it was going to be a

purely heathen holiday

it was impossible to tell whether he was just dutifully fulfilling a promise he'd made me more than a year ago or was looking forward to the journey at least a little bit Babylon isn't heathen I said *Bab-ili* is the *Gate of God* for 3,000 years there've been temples and ziggurats and the top of the tower is said to recall the summit of the mountain where the Ark landed after the Flood

good old Utnapishtim wouldn't have had to swim at all if he'd roared away from the Flood in this rocket Tariq said in his brother's rusty old red Opel I was in the back seat dreaming reading handing out water or fruits and flatbread to them from the picnic basket Farida had filled to over-flowing she was wearing a long-sleeved burgundy dress and like me put on a white headscarf when we got out (to keep off the dust and the natives as Tariq said) I also wanted to see Ctesiphon without being crammed in with a class for once and hurried on by irritated teachers and they had no objection

Tariq and Farida in the front seat more and more talkative

looking happier and happier and younger and younger it was as if they couldn't resist their good mood as if it were created quite automatically by the rickety old car that didn't have air conditioning of course so that we let the wind cool us down actually we didn't need to stop that soon the oilfields and the Dora Refinery slipped past we didn't even mention the fact that Yasmin worked there somewhere do you remember Tariq said at our first stop that little red elephant in Amman a fat old flap-eared thing on a stand outside the Roman theatre and you were already too old to have a ride on it but you loved it and I had to photograph it five times with this historical Soviet camera (he handed me his camera from the former GDR)

of course I remembered the elephant I'd called it Hannibal and had wanted to gallop on it up the stone rows of the amphitheatre like the tow-ering waves of an ocean of marble cliffs that odd connection old dented red metal (the elephant or the Opel) and the ruins or relics of grandiose archi-tecture leads to a feeling of freedom of mobility

in space in time

not to have to be careful about anything the metal's already dented the palaces are already pulled down the temples haven't had any gods for ages

in Ctesiphon my parents are standing under the great stone arch of Khosrau a gaunt man in his mid-50s with a high forehead black-and-grey moustache burning dark eyes animated gestures his shorter slightly plump wife on the other hand has a calm refined manner always looking as if she were just coming out of a quiet room and were dazzled by the sun

they slowly turned right round looking up they were

discharged

I'd done that I'd taken them out of the clamps of their everyday life in Baghdad Farida's everlasting work in the kitchen and on her books Tariq's 12-hour day in his cramped crowded practice on Saadun Street they looked round in wonder in the leisurely fashion of tourists I walked towards them as if I were seeing them for the first time were they still in love did they still have hopes did they still have sex together was there still something they wanted to achieve did they want to live in Paris again what did they talk about with the few friends they still had in Baghdad

this vaulted hall's called the *ivan* that's how Russian those old Persians were did you know that the shah was a Cossack

you and your jokes my mother exclaimed

take a photo Muna

then we were on our way again crossed the Tigris drove along the motorway to the south to al-Hillah across the sweltering stone desert alongside a canal dust devils swirling in the distance like miniature tornadoes Bedouin and their camels resting in date groves close to the water green with algae on the bank a child was balancing on a tyre lying on the ground once we could have come

from the west

across the low bridge on massive stone piers when the Euphrates still flowed right beside the city wall on the left would have been the immense tower one of the wonders of the world the seven-tiered ladder between heaven and earth and on the right behind the battlements of the wall and the outworks the big temple but now the entrance was to the east past a sleepy doorkeeper through a half-size copy of the Gate of Ishtar with its blue tiles its daisy arch its elegantly striding white dragon and golden lion

the Germans carried off the original

to Berlin I know Tariq said they can have Nebuchadnezzar III as well and send us a reduced copy made of fake tiles but where's the immense tower now where our languages were confused

from a mound of debris

we saw stuck in the marshy ground water the remains of the foundations the over-2,000-year-old wet footprint of Etemenanki the tower a huge area like the green-and-brown scar of a gigantic brand or as if the tower had sunk into the ground and only a few turrets were still visible eroded and overgrown with grass which must have afforded a magnificent view when they still rose 90 metres up into the air I wanted to have you at my shoulder Beloved as I looked out over the newly restored city gleaming in its blue and gold but

for 10 years there'd been no more excavation or building work done the guardian said there were hardly any visitors of course no more tourists had come since the war

it reminds me of Ground Zero my mother said who actually made the tower collapse who razed it to the ground I suddenly recalled the girl of my own age my father had invented to stop me gloating Xerxes I said out loud he broke the statue of Marduk but Farida didn't hear my answer she'd been attracted by the shabby little museum that had been set up here on the ruins of the Esagila temple (so that it couldn't be reconstructed any more) for Ali's son Amran and seven of his companions who had been killed in Karbala

bones burying walls

that's quite interesting Tariq said and I think my mother was a little put out because she could sense that the two of us wouldn't have let Amran hold us up in our search for Marduk (I don't pray any more)

today

as I'm turning over and over in bed with the prospect of having to stand up in front of the whole class in two hours' time and tell them about the old city (the centre of the world)

the emptiness

in Babylon

seems to be explained solely by the fact that you weren't with us Beloved of course you would have agreed with my mother and refused to disturb the remains of Amran Ibn Ali but in your considerate and conciliatory way you might perhaps have thought up a kind of subway tunnel or an inspection tube

my parents followed me

along the Processional Way to the north beyond a wrought-iron barrier you could see the bitumen-encrusted road surface the first asphalt in the world as a foundation for the stone slabs of the royal roads pitch of Ereshkigal the goddess of death welling up directly from the underworld crusted oil from hell even thousands of years ago

then in the partially rebuilt Southern Fortress we found ourselves in quiet narrow passageways between neatly reconstructed walls and arched gateways the completely empty courtyards opened up and you kept being a little startled as if the priests warriors officials scribes merchants slaves whose conversations and negotiations had filled the places a moment ago had been cleared away quick as a flash by ghostly hands immediately before we crossed the threshold

Mene tekel upharsin!

Tariq declaimed

in the throne room of the rulers of Babylon that was only a big stone podium in the open air with a threefold arched gateway as high as a house behind it leading to nothing but a smoothly finished wall a kind of *mihrab* of the kings vertical and unexpectant without the curvature of niches you find in mosques the past is nothing but

stone and imagination

but the PRESIDENT

has had his name stamped on every tile

in every wall there's one stone praising HIM in Arabic script as the successor who rebuilt it I'd like to get my father to understand that it's not these violent rulers that interest me that for me Saddam is not a cultured Babylonian but only a brutal Assyrian overlord that I'm looking for something else a future perhaps

in the depths of time that no one can touch

when we walked along the Processional Way once more we came to the remains and partial reconstructions of the Ishtar Gate in its original place at the northern entrance to the city the blue glaze had gone from the tiled walls and the reliefs of the dragons of Marduk and the bulls of Adad that had once been painted seemed to merge with the stones or to appear on the grid of their joins as if on a cracked protracted system of coordinates of historical

hallucinations

I touch one of the sacred animals on the shoulder and you

Sister

coming from the Pergamon Altar in Berlin take one angel's step down the corridor of the centuries to Babylon and place your hand on the same spot as if we were looking at our reflections through the stone

beyond the expanse of rubble on the other side of the Northern Fortress the ground rises over a glacis a hill with palm trees in precise rows to a palace of the

PRESIDENT

who insisted on using this vantage point to dominate the past as well extinct burnt-out ground to dust though it was the oversized arched windows and narrow firing slits of the staggered facades in the pseudo-Babylonian style inspire terror and bewilderment as if it were impossible to say for what species this structure was created for a kind of gigantic wasp perhaps or the dragon-snakes which according to legend are supposed to live in the ruins of the city

eventually we took photos of ourselves

(tourists

in our own life)

in front of the famous lion of Babylon that huge massy sculpture standing on the head-high prism-shaped base with its paws on the shoulders of a man lying on his back and just looking up for a moment before biting his head off

the national monument

my father said Iraq prostrate

the view of the palace had put him in a bad mood and his interest in my explanations declined noticeably

you have to understand him Farida said shortly before we went to sleep that evening in our hotel room he's worried he finds it difficult to switch off you mustn't think he doesn't take you seriously he's delighted you show such precise and scholarly interest in these things

because the hotel in al-Hillah had only one completely furnished room left Tariq had insisted we women take it while he made do with a bed in a room that had been stripped bare and so I slept (as I hadn't done for years) beside my mother she was pleased at my keenness to go and see old Babylon for myself for my big talk and told me that all I needed to worry about myself was getting on at school as ever they would be there for everything else so

I ought to have had a good sleep but I didn't even though I wasn't yet letting you burrow into my heart into my brain into my breast as you did later on you had only recently moved in next door and you weren't yet much more than the friendly young soldier who wrestled with little Ahmed (to his squeals of delight) Farida snored a bit and I was too old simply to snuggle up against her back and drift off to sleep as if into a large soft black blanket and I thought that perhaps I would soon have to help her even though I had no idea how

the body

that could comfort me

had not yet been born inside me in my longing for you

Beloved

when we drove on to Uruk the next day I was oddly cheerful and that infected my parents too and they suddenly began singing songs by Umm Kulthum in the car

on my map

the ground plan unfolds its rectangular dragon's wings over the Euphrates and I draw in chalk on the cracked and fissured slate of the old blackboard in our classroom I sketch the course of the Euphrates and the outer walls the position of the gates the location of the bridges and the temples the square base of the tower I speak freely fluently as easily as if

under remote control or as if in a dream

of myself about

Babylon

my classmates' faces look as if they've flattened into weary water lilies against the pond green of the ravaged walls at the end I hand round photocopies of the drawings of the city done around 1912 by the Berlin architect Robert Koldewey they include perspective views of the southern palace and for a few seconds I have the absurd feeling that my classmates can see me and my parents there as well reduced to tiny pinhead-size figures in ink walking up and down in front of the hatched walls

all that was left now

was to point out once again the significant role of the Iraqi excavations and reconstructions and it would also have been appropriate to repeat in full the quotation from our PRESIDENT'S historical book that I had placed at the head of the written version of my talk

itiswrongtoregardhistoryasavoidorassomethingpriortoIslamthatwehave-tobeashamedof

in my oral introduction

(itisnecessaryforouranalysisofhistoricaleventstobecompletelyinlinewith-ourBaathistviewofthedevelopmentoftheArabnation)

thus our history teacher gives me the top mark with a deduction of a few points

Bravo! really almost

like my mother Huda assures me during the break perhaps the day will come when you too can take people round a national museum that's been cleared out sorry

and tell us something about h-i-m! Eren breaks in we want to know all about him

yes is he a real man now or what? there's a mocking gleam in Huda's Indian eyes several times she's told the joke in which a woman to whom it's pointed out that she's about to go into the men's lavatory asks if Osama bin Laden's in there since he's the only real man in the Arab countries

none of us has any idea

what makes real or fake men I think that perhaps they lie on top of us like the Babylonian lion on top of its fallen victim perhaps

the day might come when I'm

the lioness on top of you one afternoon in the museum archive Huda showed me the bronze plaques from Babylon on which powerfully built men are lifting up buxom women on their pricks

Ishtar as the winged

queen of the night

is standing with the claws of an eagle on the back of a lion flanked by large owls her uplifted hands bearing the rod and ring the insignia of power fertility and love she's wearing nothing but her jewellery and her naked body

(her round shoulders her firm arms and legs her very slim waist despite her soft stomach her full breasts with large nipples even the navel high up on her abdomen and the precise curve of the folds of skin between the groin and the pudenda) belongs to me

Huda's mother Shiruk gave me the photograph as if that was how she saw me and cast a spell on me turning me to stone the baked-clay relief (49.5 by 37 cm) is in the British Museum

so with that I'm already in London (Beloved) when (six long weeks ago) we left Babylon to see Uruk my father's mood improved no end perhaps because there are no palaces there any more no mausoleum no neat and tidy reconstruction just the piles of rubble the flat-topped mounds and eroded remains the oldest walls of Iraq deep in brass-coloured soil

here you really wish you had a spade! he cried and in the evening we talked about lots of things about things we'd never talked about before it was in the garden of a restaurant we were given a table in a particularly quiet spot under a leafy roof (after Tariq had told the owner what he could do about his eldest son's inflamed eyes) Farida was very taken with the cuisine and for the first time in ages they talked about how they'd met in the al-Saray souk and about their time in Paris and then the conversation got round to London and that they wanted me to leave Baghdad to leave Iraq for a few years at university it would be a great relief for them and the best opportunity for me

what could I do

I had to say if you want that

and now I think it's still a long time until the autumn of 2003 more than a year

Beloved perhaps you could also come perhaps your uncle could finance your studies in England as well but of course I'm not going to say a word about that now (before our first kiss) you've got little Ahmed in your lap and we're both listening to his bodybuilding chatter and you congratulate me on a good mark for my Babylon talk it's another mild warm evening with a bigger redder sun veiled by sand but one day you will

take the same jump

as Yusuf when he comes to see my brother Sami who's just appeared behind me I see you give him a friendly wave but then the expression on your face changes something's wrong

you've got to come! at once! why

are you always talking to him! says

my little brother I can't believe it and turn round I've never seen him in such a state he's deathly pale his lips even his hands are trembling all I can do is give you an apologetic smile then my brother pulls me up very clumsily what's the matter with him what can be so urgent

in the living room

my father's sitting there his elbows on his knees his head in his hands

my mother's writhing in pain on the sofa as if there were something digging into her insides

my brother-in-law Qasim sits up when we come in but only slowly it's as if there's an invisible force in the room pressing everything down onto the floor as if an invisible leaden medium had been spread everywhere it can't be I think something's wrong no matter what it is no matter what Qasim says now this here

cannot be allowed

to happen

Stop indulging in fantasies

Seymour says

he means: if you want to understand Afghanistan then understand

power

the bloody swathe it cuts through the

shadow forests

of time

look at Kabul and if need be Kandahar look at the centre for that's what's important otherwise there are just a few access roads that matter and the most important mountain passes and trade routes

Greek Persian Mongol conquerors have occupied the country

and fallen faded melted away in bitterly cold winters 1842 the march of the British Army of the Indus 16,000 people of which one single man escaped Theodor Fontane wrote his Afghan poem (literature bowing

before the unknown warriors)

the statues of Bamiyan Seymour says I'd forgotten what they look like what if they'd become Buddhists there?

now he's the one with fantasies

Buddha left Afghanistan on the way to China

Mohammed stayed

it was only Islam the most aggressive obstinate patriarchal religion that was able to put down its roots in the barren rocky ground a religion of Bedouin tribes for Pashtun tribes a strict carapace heavy repressive internal armour dungeons for the soul strongly lit through a mask of the tiniest holes over the banished face is nothing but the amorphous gleam of

Allah's

absolute sea of light or

the fist of the men

the soul dances in the weave of the carpets

concrete things

Seymour says it's

concrete things the connections are political

countries I say are more concrete than politics they are the stage that always remains the icebergs the rivers the steppes the immense plains the sheer incontrovertible permanence of the landscape its torn fractal nature the deserts that's concrete and the sediments incrustations the scars the seal of tradition I want to know why death came from there of all places and not from somewhere else

they had too much of it

Seymour says they had to export some

1.6 million at the end of the Soviet invasion

he made the remark casually but then we're both horrified at the extent of that war because we now have a different relationship to the victims having learnt something about how inconceivable it is from our own experience (from the experience of those we loved) 3,000 people in the Towers and still (almost painlessly) hypnotized by the shining Hollywood pictures that composition of blue sky grey steel spurting concrete breaking steel girders dawn-red fire balls and the brief soundtrack of the repeated cries of horror of a few passers-by

Sabrina

doesn't appear in it

1.6 million people (estimated, by whom?) hundreds perhaps thousands of children without hands the colourful butterflies sitting quietly on the bare ground greetings from Brezhnev (he was capable of tears former German chancellor Helmut Schmidt told reporters) what did it mean when eight million Afghans that is half the population at the time were fleeing what did that war mean at the beginning of which the USSR simply wanted to make short work of the little would-be Stalin who'd flipped his lid (50,000 or 100,000 political opponents murdered in one year when we're talking about

NUMBERS

Ground Zero's almost

NOTHING)

Carter was furious d'you remember Seymour asked he had trusted Brezhnev

I remembered too little about the Asian side of 1979 perhaps because I was finishing off my doctoral thesis perhaps also because I was still living in Berlin and people there were counting the number of American and Russian intermediate-range missiles and pinning their hopes on a partial peace on the continuation of the process of disarmament in Europe and were not so much concerned about the horrors in the Hindu Kush which

caught up with us (so few of us) a year ago today

Seymour takes a few steps in my

his apartment (made available to me through him at such a cheap rate) in a burgundy tracksuit with white stripes that had become clearly too tight and looks to and fro between the window and my books maps notes while I tie my running shoes he asks still casually if I've made up my mind yet and I

say equally casually

I'll stay if that's OK with you

for another year

which means I have finally decided the matter on this Sunday morning I really must rent out the house in Amherst now and Seymour's not surprised he seems pleased or at least not displeased

we go down by the stairs to get loosened up and go out into the warm Sunday morning stand undecided which way to go and already short of breath on the sidewalk outside a deli window two guys past their prime one powerful and corpulent could have been an athlete at one time in a faded tracksuit that looks as if it's shrunk the other thin bespectacled in a brand-new but poorly fitting jogging outfit let's start by walking to the park Seymour says and as we walk the short stretch to the east along 81st Street we pass a liquor store with its grille down selling wines from all over the world which reminds us that neither of us drinks any more (I for five years he since his heart attack) two semi-fossils dressed up in sports gear that they could

exhibit here in the

MUSEUM OF NATURAL HISTORY

as sober men

departing this world you recall all the wonderfully unreal display cases in the museum in the past few months I've so often thought of my visit there with Sabrina when she was 11 that the memory seems as if dead and preserved bathed in an eternal Disneyland summer by gleaming halogen lamps so I prefer to imagine Seymour and myself being presented to the public in a glass case there just as we are now going over the crosswalk past the queues of waiting cars and a mounted policeman or waiting briefly (and for ever) by a soft-pretzel stand as

9/11-FATHERS/HUSBANDS

we go through Hunter's Gate into the park still not running for Seymour's still stuck in Afghanistan as well he starts talking about Bear Trap Reagan showed no scruples in his choice of anti-communist tactics he wanted to give the Russian Bear a bloody nose and see it bleed for a long time even if its Afghan opponents had to sacrifice a hundred lives for every Soviet soldier killed it wasn't American blood yet only money and the Stinger rockets which were soon bringing down one Russian plane after another

thus (Seymour explains) we built up the reservoir the human reservoir together with Saudi Arabia and the Pakistani secret service a constant supply of new blood for the mujahideen and eventually for the Taliban as well available from the masses of the largest wave of refugees since the Second World War that flooded Pakistan and Iran

thus (he points to the Delacorte Amphitheater with a few hip hop dancers tying themselves in rhythmical knots at the bottom of the steps) the

adventure playground of Afghanistan

came about through the destruction of the central power structures through the stream of more and more weaponry and money coming in the Egyptian radicals who fled following the action against Islamists after the murder of Sadat set up their camps in caves together with their power-hungry brethren from Saudi Arabia that was using the billions from its oil revenues to educate thousands of radicalized students they had no use for at the Wahhabi universities and was glad to be able to export the most extreme extremists among them to the training camps in Peshawar

so there they were sitting round in their caves reading the Koran starving freezing training shooting off a few rounds losing a few of their brethren in this or that skirmish and cultivating the legends of martyrs that they were as good at as they were at collecting money

14 years ago we could have met one of their most influential theorists and fundraisers personally here in the park Abdullah Azzam whose works were found in the cardboard boxes of Islam AG left behind by the Hamburg-Harburgers (*Join the caravan!*) the imam of the jihad a father of eight driven out of the West Bank by the Six Day War after an academic career in Cairo Amman Jeddah to devote himself entirely to the

Defence of the Muslim Lands

he could have crossed Central Park in September 1988 just when Seymour was turning his attention from Alaska oil to Gulf oil (his Middle Eastern period began at 40 he'd buried his first wife who'd died of lung cancer and found the 13-year-old twins so difficult to manage he'd sent them to boarding school) perhaps Sabrina and I had seen the fundraiser and spiritual foster father of Atta & Co a bearded man in a respectable western suit somewhere

here

in the broad meadows of the park perhaps in the

SHEEP MEADOW

where the children of the hated empire lay like half-naked shorn sheep in an evil caricature of his paradise

while he

coming from Islamabad and having entered the US with no problem even though he was well known in Pakistan as a preacher of violence (violence towards the right people) he visited the Muslim student fraternities thanked them for the donations they had collected exhorted them to pray (furiously) congratulated them on their fantastic T-shirt message campaign

Help free Afghanistan

and walked through the hell of ignorance the churned-up sea of damnation the (sheep-meadow-green) heart of darkness to open an account at the Independence Savings Bank in Brooklyn by which every donation could be channelled to the brethren when he saw Sabrina (candy floss on her six-year-old's cheeks her sticky hand) he was just recapitulating a few lines from his leaflet: *Customs and Rights of the Jihad: On the execution of old, sick, blind, infirm unbelievers—those versed in the law are not in agreement on this question, two different opinions have been expressed. Some, for example the Hanifites and Malik, put the old men in a group together with the women and children. In this they base themselves on the hadith handed down by Abu Daud from Uns, who had it directly from the Prophet . . . We come to the following conclusion, though God knows more than we do: Anyone who can be of use to the unbelievers or others is to be killed whether he be an old man, a priest or an invalid . . .*

faced with the immoral female citizens of New York in the meadow he could only be proud of at least having shown the Afghan women:

As far as the communist women in Afghanistan are concerned, they are to be killed whether they have taken part in the war or given advice, whether they live in seclusion, whether they are alone or in a group, for their ideology combats Islam and harms Muslims.

all these offended killers

they all come from the experience of great impotence if under varying conditions to the same conclusion these Palestinians driven out from the West Bank who can do nothing against Israel the escapees from torture in Egyptian prisons who can do nothing against the authoritarian pharaonic state the pampered millionaires' sons from Saudi Arabia who can do nothing against the supremacy of the ruling families and nothing against their attachment to the US

when Afghanistan had completely collapsed and was coming more and more under the control of the Taliban they needed new goals soft goals vulnerable goals

what use is that to us Seymour says we've understood some things yet we can't do anything we sit in the tower we go round inside it we drive our cars we sleep but we're still in the tower that's a good image you brought it up yourself in the absolutely indestructible tower of power it even rhymes shocked that it's vulnerable after all at least in one place

where Sabrina and Amanda were I add unmercifully and we lower our heads as if to order and head off towards Cedar Hill it would be easier (I think) if we could pray like those murderers the

father of the terrorist ideas could have come up here as well it's over 10 years since he walked round the den of iniquity that is New York to return flush with money to Pakistan where his brother bin Laden welcomed him warmly only (in the opinion of several unfathomable unseen unnamed experts) soon afterwards that is at seven o'clock on the morning of 24 November 1989 to send him and his two eldest sons by means of a bomb in his car to a paradise we find it impossible to imagine in such a case namely the elimination of a chosen one by an even more chosen one or vice versa

Help free Afghanistan

his chiselled thoughts of hatred survived and returned seething in the brains of the death-pilots to New York the pyramids of skulls Timur Lenk erected to commemorate his victories were provided for the terrorists by the international television channels in the form of a film icon repeated again and again (line the sky with gold leaf for this Everlasting Explosion in the tabernacles of your living rooms a twitching bursting

relic

caught up in its martial cycle)

I'd like to tell Seymour about the towers of silence those circular structures the Zoroastrians built on the tops of hills where they exposed the dead abandoning them to the birds that eat carrion why

do you collect the terrors

is it to bury this night

in other nights

eventually we sit down on a bench which has a good view out over large parts of Central Park I'm still moved by the edges of the park most of all by the area where the treetops coalesce into green banks of cloud so that the classic ivory skyscrapers behind them with their towers and domes look like the outliers of a magnificent unknown city in the middle of the jungle

two denizens of the jungle on the park bench in their sports gear like sad gorillas escaped from the Museum of Natural History shortly before they could put us to sleep and stuff us but part of the anaesthetic did get into our veins producing this leaden feeling in our arms and legs

in our heads in our hearts

Seymour (who earlier had stretched his legs out in the sun and with a patronizing air put his arms along the back of the bench like a professional gymnast doing a crucifix is leaning forward with his elbows on his thighs there's something helpless and vulnerable about his broad burgundy back beside me too big a target I think but we're just two guys

out for the count

in the tower of the superpower

whose central command we're allowed to elect only to look on helplessly at what they get up to

will WE attack Iraq I ask Seymour in a loud clear voice definitely he replies with a shrug of the shoulders staring at his trainers you just have to listen to Dick Cheney on TV

but are you in favour? I ask more forcefully than necessary

I'm not sure I've been away from the Middle East for too long I'd have to

he says breathing heavily looking up towards the western edge of the jungle

trust this administration I don't of course but there's a chance I think an opportunity for the Iraqis to get rid of the monster perhaps the only one if they know how to grasp it but I don't know: are you in favour? no against of course the German reflex action some comedian said you know the world has changed when the best golfer's a black guy and the Germans don't want to go to war but

he falls silent and I say nothing either it's as if we're both listening to the course of the discussion that ought to follow that is repeated mechanically like a music box in dozens of TV studios for example with the quasi-official AMERICAN position YOU are so clearly against the war that YOU leave YOURSELVES open to the criticism that YOU always leave it to the US to defend Western interests while the most YOU do is to give some money but never YOUR blood and beyond that we have to ask YOU how well YOU remember YOUR own past when YOU say that nations ought to get rid of their dictators by their own efforts and then please ask YOURSELVES how genuinely YOU are interested in the security of Israel YOU are supposedly so concerned about

I have arguments against that

which Seymour is equally familiar with

so what

decision will the PRESIDENT make (of whom neither of us thinks much though I have to confess that I don't know that much about him)

when I started at university in California it was the time of the

Saturday Night Massacre

I finally say

Nixon

dismissed his subordinates right up to the solicitor general (heads rolled though not in Iraqi fashion) to avoid having to hand over the tapes of secret conversations in the White House the

MADMAN

had bombed Vietnam to a ceasefire the war claimed (from whom)

58,000 American

2,000,000 Vietnamese lives

as I was driving along Palm Drive to the main building of Stanford University (that strange monastery facade the big red-roofed campus buildings round it something between an Indian town and a huge Benedictine abbey the long covered walks and green quads I never fell in love more often went for longer runs slept less read as much) the humiliating retreat of the superpower from Saigon with people on the roof of the American

Embassy clinging on to the landing skids of the army helicopters was still in the future

you arrived at the moment of total crisis and exhaustion Seymour said back then and again now

as if you had a season ticket for American traumas he could have added but he refrains our mid-20s lie buried in that Vietnam and Watergate America at two corners quite a long way apart in the graveyard of youth (my post-Woodstock feeling on the West Coast while the MIT graduate with a wife pregnant with twins was an REMF organizing oil for the army) which has been turned over by the plough of time and the bones have become so mingled that looking back we can hardly sort each other out

on the other hand the immense pressure of a hundred ceilings collapsing on top of each other left almost with everything in the same place it packed the floors close together like playing cards the unimaginable compression of the towers

the pile

looked at from the point of view of the volumes the expert on FOX explained

the Towers consisted almost entirely of

air

I feel the urge to tell Seymour that I'm frightened of starting my guest lectures at the end of the coming week that I'm afraid I won't be able to bear the students their youth their arrogance their cheerfulness their curiosity their perfect fresh faces

the exaggeration

of being alive

Seymour looks up when we hear military-sounding cries from a female voice approaching 30 seconds later a dozen young mothers in sports get-up come running up the hill past the bench where we're sitting commanded by a female aerobics coach with a paramilitary look instructing them to push their baby buggies in which one- or two-year-olds are sitting with their left hand and raise their right hand in the Caesar salute we could have laughed we could have cried seeing these young women we could have plunged back into the despairing happy tombs of our times as young fathers (I was the only one who had loved Amanda when she was pregnant)

what d'you say about them Seymour asks suddenly giving me an insistent look

I forgive you
I almost said in that moment

I heard that you ask'd for something to prove this puzzle the New World,
And to define America, her athletic democracy

I say instead my brain's full of quotations an occupational disease like Seymour being plagued by the crude-oil share prices

it's a hard time and a good time he replies the athletic time I mean when you're young work like crazy and have a beautiful unsatisfied apparently still completely healthy young wife with little children he'd become a father years ago but even the beginning of the good time (his wife Phillis pregnant with twins my arrival in Palo Alto) was connected with events in the Middle East even if we didn't particularly concern ourselves with them the terrorist attack on the Israeli Olympic team in Munich had happened only the year before now cars were queuing up at the empty filling stations Seymour heard early on about the secret deliveries of oil the Saudi king Faisal had allowed for the US Army the embargo

he says was really an odd thing that won't happen again when you look at things closely you wonder whether there has ever been a good time back then a lot more people died in war what does your Goethe say

history (Goethe said) is a mishmash

of mistakes and violence

I imagine (Seymour says) he wanted to be left in peace

like all of us he adds it's a global attitude people want history to leave them in peace (and woe to anyone who pesters them I add

or rather don't add)

Goethe Seymour says and starts coughing that peculiar shallow debris cough that gives me a guilty conscience every time I hear it

ACE inhibitors the oilman explains after a while during which he's been pressing the palm of his hand to his mouth it's probably a side effect I'm eating any amount of pills like a canary its seeds when I ask more specific questions about his state of health he's pleased and on the defensive at the same time in his tracksuit he reminds me of an ageing boxer recalling his defeats with a touch of self-irony

his days

(with Northern Oil)

were numbered he said he'd been unable to work for almost as long as I'd taken the sabbatical in order

to finish your book about Goethe's women? he asks dubiously but without the least hint of malice or condescension he occasionally looks across at the paramilitary jogging women who have once more come into view in the distance with slight shrug of his shoulders as if to suggest that we

in our state

wouldn't know what to do with women any more anyway

I won't finish it I can't get inside the heads of his lovers any more my course will deal with his works alone I need something impersonal

Goethe Seymour says again (it has a touching and comic effect on me to hear him hoist the difficult German umlaut out of the depths of his throat together with the weighty name)

his *West-östlicher Divan* he goes on giving the name in German Goethe he'd learnt from the cultured Saudis Iraqis Persians he'd met in the oil business was very interested in the East indeed some had even maintained he'd been a Muslim

and I think (suddenly turning towards me) that

now today here in this place

the students will ask you if there's anything in that

Goethe was an Arab

I say impulsively surprising even myself what did I

mean by it there is after all a certain similarity in the historical situation an analogy or structural parallel if we remember how things were in that Germany consisting of small states (if you forget Prussia) confused fossilized in need of reform weak hesitantly urbanizing burdened with tradition provincial Christian monarchist wallowing in the Middle Ages nostalgically bemoaning the disappearance of the Holy Roman Empire conservative and authoritarian that was overrun ploughed up by the rationalist great power from the West exploited for geopolitical ends squeezed economically modernized with harsh territorial cuts and dragged into the great war against the power in the East

at least when we look at the late nineteenth and the twentieth century in the Middle East as a whole under the burden of European imperialism and the Cold War

Seymour didn't know that Goethe had admired Napoleon (as he did almost all so-called greatness) then he would have been a pro-West Arab he conjectures when I tell him a great poet in his own tradition and language who however had regarded it as inevitable that the East would become part of the modern world with which he (Seymour) has probably provided a better formulation of the reason Goethe was so keen to pin the emperor's *Légion d'honneur* on his chest or not what is

truth

in the poem which

comes about with us

the great peacock of a poet who put on even greater airs in contact with greatness

Power that o'ermasters—this, admit,
We cannot from the world expel,
Converse with men of finest wit,
Converse with tyrants suits me well.

has his Erfurt moment (1808)

one morning when the

EMPEROR (40 putting on the fat his tight avocado-green pod of a uniform burst open half way up his breastbone his broad arterial-blood-red sash the combination of white jacket and white trousers with something of a fencer's or a romper suit going down to black knee-high boots his face below his Raphael-putto hairstyle fat and almost square his piercing eyes his long nose his horizontal mouth set in a too-large whitish frame of bulging fat or even dully gleaming soapstone)

receives

the 60-year-old

M. Göt

so that he can remain standing to watch HIM

take his *petit déjeuner* and

triumphantly rearrange the world as

HE believes and can admire all the officers who keep going in and out and interrupting the monologue of the emperor as well as his rather insignificant remarks on the poet's *Werther*

Goethe (I told Seymour) did not write a play for HIM did not accept his invitation to go to Paris nor did he concoct any arse-licking articles on the imperial circus Napoleon put on with the tsar he remained the minister of the poor statelet that an arbitrary act of the

MIGHTY ONE

could have deleted from the map

a Jordanian then Seymour says

we're left to enjoy the uncertainty of the scales: cynical conservative opportunist far-sighted observer the latter would certainly have been aware that the tyrant's brutal expansion was no more the last word of history than the iron liberation collars of the Congress of Vienna his neoclassical Dorothea marries Hermann but still keeps the ring of her first love who died for the revolution

was he an American as well?

Seymour wants to know I mean Goethe

his view was that America was better off I think because it had been spared the old demons of history

old demons Seymour says that's us and

we

get to our feet in the midday sun

but don't turn to dust can't jog and probably ought to go our separate ways or to eat something perhaps in a restaurant by the lake we'll soon come to but nothing seems appropriate so uncertain what to do we shuffle along beside each other for another quarter of an hour in our sporting fancy dress which reduces us apart from a house key and a 20-dollar note to what is left of us if Amanda were to see us now (I can't help thinking) she'd find us ridiculous but thinking of her mockery and the way it could suddenly turn into kindness or warmth as we walk together in the late-summer sunshine of the park which is putting on its Sunday peacock finery with

an absolute explosion of life

suddenly makes me miss Amanda in a terribly direct sensual gaping way

this wouldn't have happened if she'd simply

vanished

a few years ago (when she left me I keep forgetting why)

Seymour seems to guess what I'm thinking as we say goodbye at Hunter's Gate he suddenly says something about his psychiatrist or analyst with an

abrupt urgency so that his burgundy tracksuit makes me think of a film
about boxing again of those scenes where the coach gives the shattered hero
the decisive tip for his inevitable

rebirth

his therapist he says had put an idea to him which had perhaps not
occurred to me or perhaps it had because I was always thinking things over
but anyway he wanted to let me have it namely

that the most difficult thing was

to forgive yourself—what

well it was perhaps still to come or had started very slowly

to forgive yourself

because your grief grew less month by month

year by year

ELEGY

How can I sing without you? You who were my breathing.
    Closer than my heart, lighter than the air.
How can I sleep without you when silence is yawning?
    My breast is of stone, a tomb of despair.
They say the dawn brings life, for me it brings on dying.
    If there's no light for you, no more can I be.
How can I end without you? Only by your side,
    Will I not walk alone, for you invented me.

Muna

The wire grids that the bomb came through look like a large tattered basket-ball net or a torn steel fishing net showing the shape of its trajectory round the edges of the gaping hole in the ceiling of the bunker through which white daylight falls onto the bare floor wires as thick as your thumb stick down into the gloom like the tentacles or antennae of a cynical power from above ground that has taken it into its head to explore the darkness with rusty old instru-ments a 10-metre-long strip of sheet-metal cladding is like a necktie wrapped round one of the concrete pillars covered in burn marks I don't want to see the

shadows

on the walls they say they're like negatives of the people who sought shelter in the bunker burnt into the concrete by the lethal flash of the bomb

mute and leaden

with this terrible new heaviness of my body

I only look at the gold-framed photos of the children the women among the bouquets of real and artificial flowers the pennants with verses from the Koran the toy animals and other little memorials

the hole

is gaping inside my head inside my bronze head the white light is burn-ing me out inside like a welding torch I'll have to stay here I think but soon I won't be able to breathe I'd already be suffocating if

Huda and Eren

weren't staying close beside me supporting me whispering in my ear gripping my upper arms

everything was wrong! I can't stop myself thinking all the time the whole of my previous life before this during which I had been here already (two years ago) with the same class the same teachers who gave us the same description of the events they're giving us now I keep thinking back to Qasim's birthday party back to those now completely incomprehensible high spirits back to the fact that there wasn't a single army officer among the guests

the phantom

of my beautiful happy strong

sister

BUT NOTHING'S HAPPENED SO FAR

Eren says imploringly she knows about that from her Kurdish family from things that have happened in Sulaimaniya and Raniyah in the north

the first time we climbed down into this bunker I was 15 I was devastated I was stunned when they told us that the people's boiling skin had burnt into the concrete huge water tanks had exploded they said and the water immediately turned to steam I was full of hate for the Americans who (so they said) had deliberately bombed this air-raid shelter in which (so they said) there were 1,000 people or 500 (so others said) or 300 (so they said farther to the west) three numbers three times so many lives destroyed

anyone who kills a man kills all men

you say against the background of the Rikabis' little paradise roof-garden the smell of decay in the bunker permeates my every fibre I can hardly stand I see that the whole class has gathered round Mrs Khadurri and Mr Basim who are telling them once more the story of how the al-Amiriya bunker was attacked on the morning of 13 February 1991 by American stealth bombers this guided tour this prescribed school outing by bus the inevitable jollity as we all get on as if we were going for a picnic or to a football match although they knew that we'd only be driving a short distance then going in twos through the white-framed entrance to the bunker (a stylized rose painted at the point where the two arms of the frame meet)

even yesterday

I would have felt it was only a tedious repeat but now

it's like a return to another life in which everything is much heavier the torment more profound the eyes of those who were killed are so ghostly so shockingly restless in the photographs as if they suddenly recognize me as if they knew that I no that something

some part of me

has entered their world that my belief has changed that I now believe

in the possibility of destruction

that's the difference that's why it's a new more fearful life I'm going to suffocate here Huda (your fingers are still gripping my upper arm firmly and if your grip relaxes I'll fall) I remember that two years ago it made me furious when I heard that the American government had never apologized for this attack with so-called precision weapons what I feel now is no longer anger but only the

weight

of bleak dismay nor can I bear the way that now with the prospect of a new war they're tormenting us with the horrors of the previous one (I'm sure that on the anniversary of 9/11 we'll be told to march

in anger

as part of a demonstration of various schools with the slogan we can understand your hatred of terrorists but

you

are the terrorists) this al-Amiriya bomb has fallen three times in my life the first time I was only six when the war broke out we moved to the big family house in Wasiriya and my mother dragged me out of the tangle of cousins who were allowed to go on watching the horrific pictures at which I began screaming in outrage I'm sure we'll move back to Wasiriya if bombs fall on Baghdad again the family unites for catastrophes and celebrations I

could always just

be lying in a bunker like this under the shattered surface of my country I'm falling back again only the day before yesterday I was

a princess in Babylon

do I always have to endure

what I foresee I saw the Major at the wedding inside my sister's body and I came across him in reality with his hands on her neck and precisely because he didn't come to the celebration in al-Mansur (neither he nor any other officer) I believe everything came from him even if yesterday evening my trembling pale weeping brother-in-law Qasim claimed he had no idea couldn't understand it

for no reason

his wife has been

arrested abducted taken away

like so many people we know all about that from this or that person who knows someone it has happened to it

could mean anything

Tariq said we'll find out we'll start right away I'll ring everyone who might know something who might be able to tell us something I can't simply sit here doing nothing I'll explode I know someone important in the Baath Party I've been treating him for ages perhaps he can find out where they've taken Yasmin there are cases in which

something

can be

arranged

from the deepest shadow of the bunker comes (I'd almost forgotten) the black woman who's been living here for 10 years she shows everyone who'll listen or give her some money the pictures and the remains of her husband and her nine children she'd only gone out of the bunker for a short time to get something two years ago her pale face her hollow cheeks her shaking movements gave me a fright now all at once I'm looking for something

in that fright

a clue the sign of

strength perhaps the secret of the ability to bear such dreadful things for so long but all I feel is that weight pulling me down again I'm like a diver who keeps going down until he's used up the last of his oxygen NOTHING'S HAPPENED SO FAR I haven't

collapsed

in the cold and dark of the bunker my friends take me up into the daylight my mother Huda says knows so many people in the Party we'll find out what it's about these swine I breathe

the hot dusty air I listen

with indifference

to our history teacher's talk about the causes of the last war which hadn't happened in our 20-year-old schoolbooks that mother of all battles that was brought about by the Kuwaitis' oil intrigues those aggressive incursions our leader had to stop which gave US imperialism the opportunity to stick its oar in Arab affairs and

starve us out! slaughter us! humiliate us!

as if we were redskins!

Mr Basim suddenly roars hardly a moment after we've sat down in the bus we're familiar with his furious outbursts that's the way it always is when he starts talking about the UN embargo the millions of starving Iraqi children the bombed schools and hospitals he finds it easier to get those things off his chest in fits of rage always in the same words like a mechanical bird and the next moment he can be gentle and thoughtful again this time it was more a signal for the bus driver to set off back I'm so seldom driven anywhere (the big exceptions were our excursion to Babylon and the taxi drive to al-Mansur) that I can hardly repress a feeling of pleasure and relief the wind coming in through the rattling windows cools us the horns of the cars and the roaring engine of the bus make such a noise

that I could stand up and perhaps without anyone hearing shout out

THAT MY SISTER HAS BEEN ARRESTED

then I would perhaps feel better like Mr Basim dozing in his seat he actually has a child's face with a moustache are we to spend all our time enraged or exhausted is that

what's coming now? not only for me but for all the others as well if there's a war

only Huda and Eren seem to be really close to me (the pretty well-developed daughter of a Baath Party career woman and the shy intelligent Kurd who wants five or seven children) I travel on the bus like a sack of flour I walk among my classmates like a ghost I hate myself for my weakness for so far

NOTHING'S HAPPENED

what will happen to me if they torture or kill Yasmin I'm in a daze like the rest of the family when they heard the news Tariq Farida Sami Qasim they all moved as if in slow motion like lead puppets in their own lives their sense of impotence got them down until Tariq leapt up and ran out of the house

our task

the task of the final-year class

is to

describe a place where we would like to spend a day after our visit to the bunker it's supposed to give us fresh heart it's a present from Mr Basim like the fit of rage he gave himself you should calm down that's important he told us for over the next few months there was a pile of material to master it almost sounded as if he were apologizing for the whole excursion I'm

cooking (alone) for my brother who's lying curled up on his bed unapproachable not hungry refusing to do anything I find notes from Tariq and Farida that they have appointments but would definitely be coming home late in the evening or some time during the night

I sit at my desk I stare out of the narrow window at the wall of the Rikabis' house a roughcast surface like old snow the place where I would like to spend one (the) day (of my life) lies immediately behind that wall I call it

Switzerland

because of the glacier colour a

fly lands on the ice and freezes to ice at 40 degrees in the shade our bones freeze at the thought of the place where our sister is

the family

is a single unified body an injury in one place affects all the other parts I realize I feel that now and I write Babylon but I see

Paris I write Babylon

2,600 years ago

how incredibly grown-up and superior Yasmin was to me in those days

at the end of my one long journey in the summer of 1995 when I was allowed to fly to her together with Tariq via Amman the elephant to ride on I liked so much outside the Roman theatre I can see it like a photograph in my mind's eye I also remember the long wearing journey on the road across the desert very well and the joyful sense of freedom on my first flight I wished Sami could have been with us and had been allowed to have a peep into the real cockpit although the pilots also train on a simulator it was so

unreal and yet indisputable as if on a

LIFE SIMULATOR when father and I arrived in Paris Yasmin whom I'd seen at most once a year since I'd started school looked like a Frenchwoman to me she was wearing patent-leather shoes and jeans and a black short-sleeved blouse I touched and held and kept grasping her slim bronzed arms which embraced me patiently she was a marvel a

gift I thought a person who comes into your life with the freshness and intoxicating rightness of a birth

(like you

Beloved

behind the glacier ice from which

the fly suddenly takes off again

I would so love to be lying beside you now as I used to lie beside my mother but couldn't any more in that hotel in al-Hillah near Babylon snuggling up to your back without fear without expectation)

I see my sister again as if

newly born as if

rescued

in a past by the lifts of the Eiffel Tower or in one of the old parks in the Louvre in the Métro on one of the sightseeing boats on the Seine in her student hostel at a street market I think she's so beautiful so fiery so proud she takes me to museums something I liked even in those days the stone above all as if I'd known even then that it would have been better to transform ourselves into unfeeling marble

the stone-weight of my sister pushes my upper body forward I dream of the collection of sculptures in the Louvre and of the Musée Rodin and of the kiss become stone everything can be resurrected on polished marble plinths beneath wonderful glass roofs on beautiful smooth staircases our life like those park statues brought in from outside in the Cour Marly

I didn't say much during those days in Paris I thought that my patience and my silence were perhaps my greatest strength (they still are) my father and my sister were having discussions and arguments all the time as we swam through the dynamic streams of traffic in the French city often without a specific destination

Tariq was fighting (I assume today) he wanted to convince Yasmin she should stay in Paris and do a doctorate or find work I couldn't really understand why they were arguing nor what they were arguing about I only kept hearing my sister repeating

but Iraq! but Iraq!

and she was backed up by Qasim whom she introduced to us as an older fellow student at first I didn't particularly like him I was put off by his long skull and thin arms you couldn't tell whether he was monkey-like or an intelligent being out of science fiction but he was very charming and he let us have his large and meticulously tidy room in the student residence I kept taking my father's hand because I could sense he was losing the argument with Yasmin and would then let his thoughts

wander lost

in dreams after all this was where he'd studied and lived for so long with Farida this was where he had become a doctor from here Yasmin had come back to Baghdad in her mother's womb perhaps the return of the city appeared to him like a colossal dream despite all that for at moments when he thought he was unobserved he would check its details and shyly disbelievingly feel the green-painted wrought-iron balustrades the round marble tabletops in the cafes or the newly printed pages in the bookshops

he drank wine in broad daylight and

presumably remembered things he couldn't or wouldn't talk about

Yasmin sits relaxed

at a table in a bistro she's smoking she's crossed her legs and pushed her sunglasses back onto her shining shoulder-length hair so perfect

so unharmed in the glass pyramid of the past

I could go up onto the roof

it's only a staircase no one's bothering with me no one will stop me I could see you and pour out my sorrow to you I could tell you that I don't want to be in any other country than the one where my family is that now of all times I could never go that now my family will need all the money it's got to rescue my sister I

sit at my desk

I ran

for 10 minutes

after I'd said goodbye to Seymour at the edge of the park and stood alone in my jogging kit on the empty Sunday-morning sidewalk of Columbia Avenue

I set off

at a trot round the next block and could hardly stop even though my pulse immediately shot up like that of someone out of training the man out of training I've become then

standing

at my desk

I looked out of the window waiting for my body to calm down for the inevitable flames of pleasure in movement flickering inside me to die out a few weeks ago I pinned a note above the books underneath the windowsill

I don't feel. I just investigate.

in order

to help me

I will need thought even more than before for now that I've given Seymour a firm undertaking to keep the apartment for another year my decision is (finally) irrevocable for me as well although it was so already anyway because of the guest-professorship contract with Columbia for the academic year that's about to start help the students to think help them to see help them to ask

I can do

no more than that the

fewer answers the better what should I tell them about Goethe and Islam if they should find that particularly interesting at the moment as Seymour thinks I can definitely say he would have abhorred any kind of terrorism that he liked neither uprisings nor revolutions any more than wars he liked peace and quiet which could according to his advice as a statesman best be brought about by paying Napoleon his tribute of blood as quickly as possible that required quota of young male flesh that HE could send to be chopped up at any place in Europe he chose (there is nothing to forgive I too

was once a young man)

Goethe was a man of order and of the centuries (millennia) who believed it was pointless to try and undertake any action against the

GREAT DEMONS

of his age even after the Battle of the Nations at Leipzig he still believed Napoleon would be victorious for 20 years he'd seen his prince fight this way and that as a Prussian French and Russian general so he sought

sleep (to sleep through history) sought an overall view

a standpoint beneath which nothing would change

to lose the weight of his own existence

in a far-off land

was that what it was at 65

on the telephone

Luisa wants to know whether she shouldn't bring the manuscript about Goethe's women with her the next day after all it's been lying on my desk in Amherst for a year now

no I've

had enough of you I say and I'm almost as amazed at that as she is it's ages since I said anything like that what gives me the right and yet for a while after she's hung up I'm happy about it

Luisa once said that it seemed as if it were enough for me that she was my Christiane because like Goethe's wife she looked after the house and saw to everything for me in Amherst I haven't been there for a year

there are firms that will completely empty pack up an entire house deposit its whole entrails in containers that's as comforting as the existence of brain surgeons or morticians (nurseries laboratories for blood tests) or crematoriums earthly

crematoriums

I must bury

Goethe's women

precisely because they were stories (fiction) or just stories they're not good enough of course I had things like Thomas Mann's *Lotte in Weimar: The Beloved Returns* in mind and tried hard (to become a writer after all)

too hard

I just think

you ought to be standing in front of a blackboard

Amanda said a teacher I think that's the best thing for you she said it in a quite normal tone with no special emphasis during a candlelight dinner so simply and firmly I found it impossible not to believe it was

the truth

coming from her

was Goethe a Muslim?

will the students ask me that it could be he was a poet and therefore

all kinds of things

he devoted no more of his time to the Islamic/Eastern business than to many other things I'll put a unit together from the Mahomet fragment he wrote when he was 23 via the translation of Voltaire's play with the same title he was forced to make for his prince to the magnificent *Divan* of his old age will I do that?

my restlessness before Luisa's arrival

in the late afternoon (of my life) I've tidied up the apartment so thoroughly that apart from the desk it looks to me like a pair of neatly pressed trousers actually the way it was before I came the effect being

that I could imagine the apartment and the house in Amherst that is soon to be stripped completely bare

without me

there's an unbearable coldness in the idea of being eliminated it's like the ceremonial removal of the last debris from Ground Zero in April the deathly dignity the graveyard dignity of the exposed cleanly disinfected wound on which the soldiers strutted round with their meticulously ironed Stars and Stripes Band-Aids rituals that seem helpless and crazy given the appalling incineration

but

what can you do Seymour said just discharged from the clinic on that April day breathing heavily and supporting himself on me and his son as we climbed up onto a wooden viewing platform

I can't

not live

as long as I'm breathing it's not a matter of

forgiving myself for something nor the feverish impatience that grips me at the thought of Luisa's arrival we've seen each other six or seven times over the last year the first couple of times she stayed with a friend then we took expensive hotel rooms whose flowery comfort and Cadillac-like spaciousness made us miserable and had us huddling up together in sexless union as if we were having to spend the night underneath a bridge

the last time (at the beginning of August)

Luisa slept here and I stared at her body as if it were white impenetrable stone the breathing smiling patient statue of the greatest sculptor who was mocking me with perfect closeness and absolute futility

the paralysis (I now think) should presumably be put down to the question I omitted to ask namely why

she's still together with me whatever it can mean when people behave like a couple except in the

decisive things (I know Luisa . . .)

at night the

TV

at first just to suppress my nervousness and impatience and fear they're showing a documentary on Islamist suicide bombers which I didn't actually want to see but then I'm taken with

a woman an Englishwoman an

expert

the subtitles call her she keeps appearing among other male colleagues (historians political scientists psychoanalysts specialists in cultural studies orientalists journalists) whose know-all loquaciousness is almost unbearable this English expert also mostly says only things that sound familiar to me and are hardly more profound than the analyses of the others she talks about the lack of education about the sense of political impotence about authoritarian upbringing about Islamist brainwashing about confused individuals searching for transcendence and redemption

once she calls the murderers

simply just

CHILDREN

without wanting to excuse them she says but that's not what grips or provokes me not the almost maternal understanding of a bird-nosed 40-year-old brunette in a grey suit gleaming like an umbrella an almost unattractive woman actually with a slim upper body abruptly spreading out at the hips which are several times caught as the cameraman clearly directed by me (interactive TV) pointlessly pans to the seat of her red-upholstered office chair it

arouses me

which I find disturbing and look for a reason

until I have to admit to myself (almost with a laugh) that that's all there is to it she simply aroused me (female intelligence combined with an unconscious or habitual but definitely incidental lascivious element)

I can think of nothing more inappropriate than that

on the night before Luisa's due to come

I go out to calm myself down at night on Upper West Side I walk along the streets as I did in the most wretched times of the days when I was a student only without craving and hope and a future I head south along Amsterdam Avenue to Broadway which I follow to Times Square and often as far as Madison Square Park it's making my way into a more and more turbulent and compressed urban zone into inaccessible twitching and flashing life when I'm really over-tired it becomes something like

sliding

in the crowd

on light and noise

Manhattan crowds, with their turbulent museal chorus!
Manhattan faces and eyes forever for me.

in the spectralized darkness it's like going deaf being enclosed and strangely insensitive and radiant as if

the whole city were

a film of the future

reduced to the size of a thimble set in a

piece of glass

in one of the prisms that in 1805 Privy Councillor Johann Wolfgang von Goethe lifted up to the sun in his Weimar garden to test out his theory of colour

light over light

they say it says in the Koran what was Goethe looking for in Islam what shall I tell the students a few of whom are perhaps among these young exhausted high-spirited (unnaturally reddened) faces drifting towards me in the reefs planted with fluorescent tubes

that God did not exist as a person not as an individual figure in any way similar to humans

that God was inseparable from nature and the cosmos

that God had unerringly determined the course of events nothing put us in a position to change it or to fathom it even approximately so in that case

God

is my daughter's murderer

and I cursed Him and took refuge in my atheism

which every two weeks sends me to one of the 100-year-old neo-Gothic or semi-Byzantine New York churches mostly to the Cathedral of Saint John the Divine (because it's close or because its pure immensity gives me air to breathe the non-usable space the spiritual superfluity the cool void a meaningless expanse above the pews that isn't immediately fought over by bankers dealers agencies furious local residents unscrupulous speculators politicians desperate to improve their image psychiatrists looking for clients

at Ground Zero

I wanted there to be nothing but a single glass coffin so

I'm

just like all the rest) and I pray for Sabrina

to NOTHING

without

words for that's the only way I can believe that my supplication will be heard that my unexpressed plea will find unthinkable fulfilment in the

night I lie in bed finally tired and worn out from a three-hour walk the echo of the city vibrating inside me but already distant it's as if I were falling away from the noisy surface into an abyss it must be ecstatic that final

letting go

and being split up I sometimes think I could manage it that

transition

if I were only capable of taking that letting go beyond a certain point but mostly it's only sleep that comes or a sudden pain or a vital impulse and now despite the long walk and all my efforts it's the English expert whipping up the remnants of my male energy again to a rather tormenting

question mark

let's have one more talk about these women

(Luisa says) the following afternoon which has suddenly and finally come going on the subway and the bus to meet her at JFK Airport was liberating and almost timeless just drawing aside the curtain of reality out in Queens the shabby wooden houses and overgrown playgrounds still flags in almost all the front gardens a huge almost completely toothless black drunk came into our subway car and sat opposite us and spoke to me because he assumed I was a tourist coming from the airport namely a

Russian

whom he felt he had to tell that it was only rich people who'd died in the World Trade Center anyway and their relatives were being stuffed full of money while they were still doing nothing for the poor

Luisa's holdall

is still in the short hall of the apartment as if

she hadn't decided to stay yet as if it depended on our conversation over a cup of coffee in the little kitchen whether she'd stay here or not or on what I had to say about

Goethe's women

for she'd had another look at my manuscript she said after I'd asked her on the phone not to bring it she could understand that I wasn't ready yet to deal with something so personal as the literary portraits of these middle-class women from the late eighteenth and early nineteenth century but it would be a pity actually Goethe's biography was like a light you could shine on the dark women's world of those times and you could see the strong stubborn forbearing and devoted kind of people they'd been even the most middle-class of them such as Lotte with her twelve and Lili with her six children or the cold and frigid emotional disciplinarian Frau von Stein who had to bear seven children by the duke's master of the horse before she could fulfil her destiny as a female porcelain figure

in the end

I said over the little table with the reddish top separating us as if we were sitting in a street cafe

I found it depressing the way these women would have disappeared without trace had they not found a place in Goethe's novels or poems or anecdotes about him this darkness in which millions lived and billions still live Luisa said even though they desperately try to illuminate themselves with the flashlights of their digital cameras that was a good approach no a good exposition

in the end I've contributed nothing new to the flood of writing on the women who loved Goethe

but you have Luisa breaks in I reread the preface your trinity hypothesis makes sense that is that there were three women in his life who had serious literary consequences Lotte Marianne and Ulrike and three who really loved him namely Christiane Bettine and Marianne and three whom he only truly and honestly loved namely that beautiful but giddy girl Lili then his bedmate Christiane (for 28 years) and finally the elegiac Ulrike as the 17-year-old folly of a 72-year-old

two of them appear twice I realize with an involuntary flicker of interest

oh yes Luisa says as you see: his wife and the one who came after her

for a couple of seconds across the gleaming tabletop on which our hands lie among the coffee things without touching there's the bridge of a common tension and pleasure which formerly used to send us straight to bed and into each other without hesitation horns the wail of police sirens still strong bright evening light over Upper West Side orange windows shining sloping roofs fire escapes a rust-coloured rocket-shaped water tank on the building across the street when you look from the seventh floor we'll go out

that's best Luisa says it's my treat

in the hallway we walk past her black holdall as if it belonged to someone else who intends to spend the night here but whom we prefer not to talk about

over the Italian dinner

without wanting to we get caught up in a lengthy political discussion (better than talking about Sabrina better than bringing up the question I really must get round to asking Luisa now that I can't help noticing how good she still looks at 49)

take your time don't hurry

the young waiter says to suggest to the people at the next table that it's time they thought about paying

now

is the last good time for Luisa

what's stopping her I wonder why's she still bothering with me she's lost a few pounds yoga and jogging she says (in such terribly casual tones) are better than sex she looks like the artistic director of a flamenco group whom you can fall in love with instead of the most beautiful dancer because her relaxed maturity and her deeper warmer humanity have a stronger allure the fire inside her blazes up because she's thinking of the

PRESIDENT

who as she says wants to prove to his daddy that it's possible not just to pen Saddam in but to shoot him dead who is kneading together the desire for revenge the sense of impotence and the despair of several million people with the cold and calculating oil-power politics of his friends to create what appears to be a thoroughly just cause a heroic democratic-Christian mission for the Big Lonesome Rider what a load of shit

but (I say)

the students are depressed Luisa breaks in because they know what it means when Condoleezza Rice says that Iraq is a problem and talks about people in the administration talking about a change of government

WAR

has been agreed on and we're

already in the middle of the usual preliminary farce she says furiously (at which I can't help feeling guilty it sounds to me like an aggressive response George Bush perhaps deserves but which ought to be directed at me as an impotent sad

anti-cowboy what should I—)

Seymour says it could perhaps be a chance for the region things could develop they way they did in Germany after 1945

do you really think that? it's just an argument for you Germans

Saddam would love to be a kind of Hitler and Iraq (I begin)

will be plunged into civil war that's what almost all the experts no one listens to are saying do you really agree with Seymour have you been meeting that often

he's not at all sure above all he's

what?

depressed I ought to say but just shrug my shoulders she finds it irritating I think (at last) it becomes clear to me that there could be something hurtful for Luisa in my odd brotherly complicity with the husband of my murdered wife she could feel shut out of the exclusive club of the true rightful mourners in the summer on the

wooden benches outside the Gerbermühle on the Main

Sabrina leant on Luisa's shoulder perhaps she

could have

sensed the maternal energy of a much older friend I don't know I never asked Sabrina my daughter lifts up her head on one of those uncertain pane-of-glass reflections of the past which

cut the present in two she raises her head to recite that poem

NEWS

Tell me, wind, what news you bring?
    Chilly wind, what tidings, pray?
For all will sound the knell's dread ring,
    I come to blow you far away.

as far as Afghanistan was concerned I wasn't sure perhaps the aim is to make good the harm that's been done to the country through the years of support-ing the mujahideen and the Taliban through the brutal (at the end of the war even in agreement with the USSR) stirring up of the conflict the arming of both sides

that may be the aim as YOU see it Luisa said but in the end the aim is to exploit the hysterically heightened demand for security and obtain a strategic bridgehead did Seymour not tell you anything about the pipeline across Afghanistan and is it not of interest that almost every act in the supposed war against terror can also be seen as an act exerting strategic control?

let's stop

I beg and an argument supporting Luisa's argument occurs to me that is Immanuel Kant's interpretation of the French Revolution as a *historical sign* that the nations will need again and again to remind them that they got rid of their ruler by their own efforts as a kind of permanent inner spring-board to democracy

and there's also the Spanish lesson Luisa says that even dictators even-tually die and it's possible to find your way to democracy without civil war and terrorism

now I'll

drink a glass of wine with you Luisa

I suddenly say just one glass and only with you I can manage that

don't bother she replies gently and so I have a tomato juice

what oppresses me is the TOWER I then say I mean the state the country as a castle in a game of chess that looks like a tower and behaves in a different way from what we wanted and want as a

LEVIATHAN

Luisa says we know about that and about what Hobbes goes on to say to justify his assertion that the state of nature would result in a war of all against all you can see it quite simply in the behaviour of the kings and states towards each other and right down to today it doesn't seem to make any difference whether domestically they're democracies or dictatorships

I find that very interesting with regard to my work I say and have difficulty explaining what I mean

what I've been straining over

all these months all these notes and books rummaging round copying out extracts

it's

just an attempt to understand I say

in bed

it's often like sinking

into ashes

deeper and deeper into loosely fitted layers it's like floating sliding down almost falling with myself becoming lighter and lighter but something radiant still hits me and I open my eyes as I plunge down the blue of that day flares up again and again through the flurries of black grey silvery white flakes even though I reach denser and denser sootier and sootier levels I open my eyes once more

will you go to the

MEMORIAL SERVICE

Luisa asks softly (Pataki quoting Abraham Lincoln Bloomberg quoting Franklin D. Roosevelt Seymour Amanda's parents Amanda's colleagues perhaps students from MIT and Amherst)

with you

I'll manage that

Luisa

Welcome to Iraq! The cradle of civilization

    tipped out in front of the lions

    welcome on the first page

    in the first book of the first people to cut the first characters

    into the skin

    of the first victims

    welcome to the home of NebuchadnezzarAshurbanipalHammurabi-
HarunalRashidSaladinandSADDAMthegreatestofall

    MESOPOTAMIANS

    see

    the beautiful blue tiles in downtown Baghdad on which Nebuchadnezzar
lowers his gaze before HIM

    marvel at

    his mighty palaces in which HE

    hides like a pursued beast of prey

    smell

    the death-sweat of his imprisoned enemies of his doubles of his food
tasters and murdered sons-in-law

    admire the black stela showing HIM receiving the insignia: pistol pincers
electric cable and hammer drill from the hands of his gods NapoleonHitler-
Stalinetc

    ASSYRIANS like him

    on his triumphal relief

    the lions shimmer

    with Kurdish enemies in their jaws

    the bulls

    boring into the entrails of the Persians

    the dragons

    on the piled-up skeletons of communists and democrats

    40 Scud rockets on Israel

carved in marble and already he's greater than Saladin

a god of the gods

a human being among all human beings

let Ishtar open for him the gate

of HIS

dead

let everyone bring

him his deservèd

present

during the night in that bare hotel room in al-Hillah I could still find words for my hatred and wrote on the back of old menus on the ravaged palimpsest of Babylon while Muna and Farida were sleeping in a bed together

now

I just stare speechless at

one of those terrible pseudo-Assyrian portraits of the yellowing PRES-IDENT over the sickbed of NONAME the Baath Party man who could count on me making a house call but not so fast he says

let's go outside

and I support him as he hobbles down in his pyjamas to the courtyard of his dilapidated old house I hardly know how I manage to support advise treat someone for two days I've been going round like a robot to stop myself rolling round on the floor screaming beside my wife who's crying silently

crying and sitting petrified in the kitchen

since Qasim tumbled into our living room to tell us Yasmin had been arrested abducted rather (I've never liked him and it was only now as he was close to collapsing that I overcame my reservations for the first time and gave his shoulder a squeeze)

does it look as if it's personal NONAME asks taking a nervous puff at his cigarette which he really shouldn't be smoking given the state of his cardiac valves it would have been best he told me if I'd said

nothing

from the very beginning

and only looked for Yasmin indirectly in a personal matter (Qasim had indicated something with the Major that wedding guest who with all his khaki friends was worrying the whole family he could be a disappointed lover have had his advances rejected or even—he didn't dare make clearer insinuations in Farida's presence) patience was essential you had to

probe

but you had a better chance if you had someone with tact and diplomacy working for you I

stake strong painkillers

a third of my secret stock and learn the name of a lawyer I should go and see privately or in my position as a doctor

before that however

my old patron Professor Dr Khalid Yusuf comes to mind

his name no longer meant anything in the swanky clinic for living Assyrians who are kept alive by the triumphant progress of Iraqi medicine over the last three millennia and he didn't live in that villa in al-Mansur any longer either but I eventually find him in a shabby little concrete cube of a practice in New Baghdad which resembles mine right down to the queues of patients on the stairs

let's go outside

Khalid says I need a break anyway and nods to his wife a gaunt woman with a headscarf who must once have been very beautiful and who people say has become his mainstay since he was stupid enough to refuse to be a member of parliament and compounded his stupidity by refusing to punish a deserter by amputating one of his feet when he was sent to a military hospital in the north

the smooth round stump of his forearm gleams

in the sun on the balcony

a friend did it an old colleague with great surgical skill I could rely on he says with apparent unconcern a legacy of the professional coolness of the former star surgeon to whom Saddam's lottery which for 30 years has had our heads rolling round in its drum spewed out a lousy ticket

she could be in Baladiyat in the women's prison if you

probe

(the same word I have to be prepared for more and more re-evaluations of my terminology) and

pay

at the right moment in the right place

you have a chance the former senior consultant tells me what did they do with the right hand they cut off are they setting up a collection one asks oneself but of course I say nothing his moustache covers his upper lip it's only from the lines round his eyes that you can tell he has to contro himself

I'm going to be sick for two days

I told Laila who has enough experience to put my patients off get rid of them also to patch most of them up almost as well as I could myself

the lawyer (prober) has a house near Wahda Park it only takes me half an hour to get there on foot walking often and quickly is my only fitness training and for years it's given me a lift and brightened me up between house calls and even in a certain way reconciled me to my unattractive accursed sad magnificent city split by its snaking river that net of (more or less) meaningful attentions to the human body the mesh of which I weave with my doctor's bag in my hand received with respect and goodwill my help sought or at least comfort or approached for free advice

is torn matted riddled with holes

the sharks have ripped it apart I stagger rather than walk what Ali said about my

SPECTATOR ATTITUDE

is pounding in my ears in my brain Farida looks across the evening-grey Tigris to the palace on the Karkh side wishing she could see it blown up before her very eyes (now more than ever)

Saddam is murdering my daughter

Bush will kill my son

that's the game the PRESIDENTS play and I'm left over like a tattered old ball a handful of boys are kicking round on a building site future recruits for the president's son's team he has them treated with batons and iron bars if they don't score enough goals

dozens of patients came to me who had been

away

for a long time until they returned with badly deformed bones damaged internal organs incurable nervous complaints acid-scarred skin from that

foreign land

that can border on our embargo lives everywhere under the earth or behind barbed-wire-topped concrete walls the system of caves and bunkers of the beast that has eaten its way into our flesh like a metastasizing cancer

the only solution left is

treatment by the US Air Force I can tell myself a thousand times over that I ought to have overcome Farida's objections and my own lethargy or fatalism and arranged for us to flee the country but Yasmin would still have stayed here she always did what she wanted ever since she could perhaps because I left her at the bars of the school playground all those years ago when I had to go to the first war perhaps because I sent her to Paris for five years when she was only 16 I couldn't keep her there when I tried to years later I keep going over the memory of the vehement arguments we had (with a frightened Muna in tow) on the Métro in the Jardin des Plantes and in front of the facade of the Institut du Monde Arabe that she insisted on showing me to

remind me of my

roots

while I was still somehow or other managing to live in their blood-soaked thicket

you yourself (Yasmin cried) took me away from Paris even before I was born

to Iraq

she wanted to get married in the place where her birth had been celebrated my bright future son-in-law told me in a pizzeria with a view of the Bastille Opera and today I have to fend off the desperately self-justificatory impression that the opera behind its barricade of glass reminded me of nothing more than those grandiose enclosed building complexes (also designed by renowned international architects) that promote the welfare of our country in their multiple function of palace prison torture chamber and arsenal of chemical weapons

eventually we celebrated her marriage just the way Yasmin wanted in the courtyard of the old family house in Wasiriya she was indescribably beautiful and alive and she had completely slipped away from me all I could do was gaze at her in wonder with a kind of humility and hope as if your child's adulthood were something like a birth leading year after year decade after decade to the light of death

the lawyer

is not one of my patients

he's arrogant and cheerful as an immortal until I tell him that I have a very private question regarding a member of my family in a

foreign land

at which he becomes very human and full of sympathy and says

let's go outside

that's obviously the new motto of our nation

Dear Iraqis—let's go outside

while George Bush bombs the terrors of our country to smithereens

supposing you first of all sorted the victims into groups on football pitches in stadiums or other clearly delineated sections of all the desert that we have at our disposal infants schoolchildren adolescents of both sexes women (civilians) men (civilians) soldiers and could no had to shoot them bomb them to bits in five minutes one after the other before the eyes of the world before the cameras of CNN and Al Jazeera and that was the entrance ticket for victory

who

would enter?

it's very good that you pursue your question

privately

says the lawyer who God forbid doesn't in any way concern himself with people who have disappeared been imprisoned abducted for that is the only way in which we have a certain chance of success and so that

your family you understand . . . (will survive?)

it's the nicest of the three

outsides

here: a traditional well-tended courtyard with plants and flowers and a fountain gently splashing (away the conversation?) in the pleasantly cool atmosphere it's

like a magic chest

you need patience and this or that key

for half or three-quarters of the savings I could have used for our flight or Muna's studies in England or to smuggle Sami out of the country it will perhaps be possible to find out for certain where

Yasmin

is being murdered

REFLECTION (2)

I sought my face in the mirror—
    It melted away.
The glass is a blade,
    Its glint a sharp ray.

Clenching my fists, I see
    Twisted faces appear—
Grimaces of the dictator
    That the mirror blindly draws near.

And if I were to break it,
    The shards would come down
Like a sentence of death
    On my child asleep on the ground.

He

    only comes to with difficulty

    in this place as if he's benumbed (no: partly erased poorly made or even forged faintly sketched simply thought up) he raises his head with its narrow skull its high forehead edged at the top in a heart shape (almost Mickey Mouse–like) by his thick greying hair its sharp nose the sides of the nostrils drawn up in the odd way you see in wood-carvings of some Inca gods (making his readiness to accept blood sacrifices more understandable Luisa says) its thin lips which he hides when he's excited or angry by sucking them back into his mouth

    this place here

    must be alien to him all the

    searing dazzling

    white the sharp-edged

    paper

    he hardly feels

    our questions or perhaps he's irritated because we don't ask any questions we've already condemned him and just stare at him stunned or immediately turn away from him no camera no

    teleprompter just this

    mute black-on-white this snow-and-ink silence with no

    advisors

    he screws up his eyes as he often does as if he were standing speaking

    into the sun or a storm in the black eye of which (*abubbleIliveinabubble*) he's still stuck

    when will the war start

    inside his head

    it's a personal question as well Luisa even if you say he's a nonentity or has become a

    nonentity

    through the way he acted the whole administration nothing more than the puppet theatre manipulated by a collective subterranean leviathanesque process in the people in OURSELVES to which there was no alternative a purely automatic setting-in-motion of the infernal mechanism of

vengeance

and of the compulsion to restore the superpower aura of the United States of America for which the confused hunt for terrorists in the dusty mountains of Afghanistan did not suffice (especially as they didn't find the chief villain there) instead the

SEX APPEAL

of a great swift victorious efficient war was necessary (in an entirely different place of course with predictably low losses on our side and those consisting anyway of young HEROES with the average age of graduates in zinc coffins or black plastic body bags)

SHOCK AND AWE

is less of a strategy than the desired result of the manner in which WE want to be seen by YOU

so be afraid of us

once more so that we don't have to be afraid ourselves if he'd wanted he could have stopped this process (of reassertion) instead of commanding it of executing it with solemn martial fervour but he was determined

to make a big splash in history

which he perhaps imagined as a gigantic patriotic novel for 10- to 14-year-olds but only after the

MISSION

fell to him did he really see an opportunity

so far he'd only won the election

with a closer result than any candidate before him with

fewer votes than his opponent

solely thanks to the ruling of the Supreme Court that stopped the more precise recount of votes in Florida and to the Americans' strong desire to be united to form a single team even if you have to go against your principles and would soon get your son sent back from the East in a black plastic bag he was the

PRESIDENT

who at the beginning of 2001 could casually put his feet up on his desk in the Oval Office of the White House the Resolute Desk made from the planks of an English ship at which the presidents have sat for 120 years and if you wanted to reconstruct the popular photo showing John F. Kennedy sitting at this clumsy piece of furniture in 1962 while his little son has pushed open the front door of the desk with the eagle carved on it and is peering out you could imagine the 65-year-old G. H. W. Bush enthroned behind the desk-top and underneath it the young George in his early 40s in the cuckoo-clock door (and he would almost have had the sense of humour to reconstruct the scene if he'd ever liked JFK) this quite ridiculous yet strikingly successful

succession

(nothing succeeds like succession)

explains how he got HERE

a shadow

who wanted to overtake the original and presumably put him in the shade in an Oedipal admiration-pursuit-obliteration biography (too much psychology Luisa) but just consider (you say) the grotesque series of copied stages in his life same school (but Junior wasn't as good) same university (once again Junior wasn't as good only head of the cheerleaders instead of captain of the baseball team) the repeated training as a fighter pilot and active service (instead of being shot down by the Japanese or in his case by the Vietnamese simple pseudo-combat training flights and life in the sun on the California–Mexico border) the attempt to make his father's oil millions again in the same city

ending up bankrupt in

Midtown Texas a shy severe disappointed wife five-year-old twin daughters and again and again the

whisky bottle I'm

quite close to him there Luisa at this point I meet up with George in a bar with a hyperactive socializing guy who would probably no certainly have wanted to have less to do with a book-guzzling shrinking German violet than I did with this hollow-seeming extrovert gambler who most of all wants to meet people and lead manage command something anything in order to find a kind of distorted father-mirror-self-image we could have slurred along to ourselves only not the same words (and not at the same time either for my two whisky years only came when he'd been dry for almost 10) he presumably also needed

different words different people

to get him out of the honey-coloured spicy smoky syrupy suffocating autumn mists molten golden lead in your brain your arms legs and instead of the resolute dean of UMass and the relieving burden of a scholar's legacy with all the book-weight of the nineteenth century (Goethe-SchillerHerderHegelKleistHölderlin) under which you learnt to breathe again just as a Sherpa no longer feels the weight he's carrying after 10 no 20 months of training

during the depression among the exhausted oil pumps of Midland with their heads hanging down

he came across

a Bible group of 120 men in check shirts and met the outdoor guy with the stubble and a 10-foot cross on his back an itinerant preacher who'd just put his burden down in a corner of the Holiday Inn cafe ARE YOU SURE YOU'LL GO TO HEAVEN IF YOU DIE TODAY GEORGE DO YOU WANT TO GO WITH JESUS OR

go on being dead without Him at which

George AWOKE and continued awaking and one year later the family friend came

the great TV preacher

GOD'S MACHINE GUN

that had already shot the way to Vietnam clear for President Nixon with its rattling salvoes of words

and in the course of a walk on the beach showed him

THE WAY

to the Resolute Desk instead of to the resolute dean I can understand that Luisa this sudden

return to health

but for him it was more namely

JUSTIFICATION

REBIRTH as they call it since then he has lived

a dreamless life

in the great connection God America faith democracy the Bush family the friends who collected more donations for God America and the Bushes than had ever been collected in any previous presidential campaign

he had (unlike me at the time)

a wife a Methodist librarian of life who stood by him who surprisingly turned out to be even tougher than THE ENFORCER (his mother)

either Jim Beam or me

and that's how he managed to get out of the neck of the bottle went to Washington now and then as

ONE OF THEIR MEN

in order to get the majority of evangelical voters to support his father in the presidential election thus helping him to win

at which his father's friends supported HIM provided him with fresh loans and took him into the baseball management business where they used him as a front man until he had acquired a reputation as a smart operator and made his first million with property speculation in the course of a stadium extension he'd become presentable credible as a penitent sinner a family man a simple believer and COMPASSIONATE conservative

he now became someone namely governor of Texas who

four years later

on the day he was re-elected gathered the believers who supported him and declared to them that

Godwantsmetobepresident

so now at 45 he's sitting at the Resolute Desk perhaps still dazed by the speed and good fortune of this (basically predestined) rise to the centre of power as if in the dead eye of the updraught in the Oval Office the pupil in the eye of the American eagle is at the centre of the carpet which every president (as he himself proudly and tirelessly points out) can change himself in order to leave his own mark he will hand the task over to his wife and

have the sun at his feet a shining yellow sunburst round the central eagle

and this shows HIM he explains to visitors as

(nothing other than an)

optimistic guy (his sunny temperament) sometimes he will get up to pat the busts of Eisenhower Lincoln and Churchill (the war hero he admires a loan from Tony) as if they were big dogs and steel his will with an insistent look at the oil painting that he had hung there the title of which he used for his autobiography and which shows a westerner on a horse galloping up a trail in his repeatedly expressed opinion a man determinedly fulfilling his duty and carrying others with him (*A Charge to Keep*) which the painter however intended as a

horse thief on the run

(whom the others are trying to catch)

HE was fine HE was sitting pretty

the sun shining through the glass of the tall white-framed doors onto the sunburst carpet of the sunshine boy cheerfully tilting his chair back with his heels on the desk no one could overtake him now there was no need for him to be anything more than

the forty-third president gaily picking up the phone and greeting his paternal predecessor with

Hi 41 this is 43

and apart from that perhaps he just felt the need to nail up the outer gate of the GREAT RANCH to the hostile un-American world and as head lobbyist of the evangelical Christians to evangelize the government's work as far as possible and to give a few good sermons as well (*From Jim Beam to Jesus*)

when

THE AIRPLANES

smashed into his skull which we can't help opening up investigating

inventing Luisa it's just a post-invention on a living subject or rather during the subject's lifetime in which (as such) you've been unable to believe for ages (but then what are we) in the

lifelong

moment of our impotence

HIS defeat (like ours) is the death

of almost 3,000 Americans and the Towers' collapse that he

will learn to adopt

as an enraged proud father of the nation racked with pain during those minutes in that elementary school in Florida as his chief of staff bends down to his right ear

second plane hit the

the little black girl with the tight braids and white dress looks up at them in astonishment 16 schoolkids the teachers the bodyguards the flag the blackboard

second tower

his press officer holds up a card (immediately noted down by the press for us)

DON'T
SAY ANYTHING
YET

he remains motionless as if a reflection of the raging kerosene fire had completely burnt out his inner self in a fragment of a second

with a stony expression

in the worst catastrophe

he learnt when he was only

six

at the death of his little sister from leukaemia

you have to keep a stiff upper lip you have to start laughing again soon you have to

cheer up

all those who have been hurt

(talking to the TV cameras his white-haired mother recalled how as a seven-year-old he refused to go out with his friends since he had to play with his mother who was in mourning: *So I realized that this caring little boy was looking after me and not me after him.*) he made jokes clowned about with an

unquenchable unfeeling uncanny

charm with that stony optimism that fuses with his body with the mask of his face

confronted with the deadly attack

now not even

POWER

seems (for several terrible hours) to be

of any use

the greatest military power in the world that put as much into its defence budget as the next 13 states together all its airplanes its stocks of bombs the deployable bodies of a million soldiers its bases all over the world its huge fleet with its floating fortresses aircraft carriers nuclear submarines its satellite surveillance system its superior communications technology its military think tanks its secret services with tens of thousands of agents the logistical capacity of this enormous hierarchically organized machinery

helplessly grasping thin air hitting out wildly stuttering the

POTUS (you the chess king)

has to be taken to safety they consider hiding you in the NORAD fortress inside Cheyenne Mountain but then they decided they'd rather hide you up in the air in the hysterical wasp's flight of

AIR FORCE ONE

on which you're now phoning like mad

discussing measures feverishly fitfully staring at passing clouds in your suit your starched white shirt locked in the softly hissing cabin surrounded by bodyguards and advisors likewise telephoning likewise locked in swept up into the air deinstalled removed it

must have been a mortal insult for him Luisa

before he

became the avenger determining things (determining ground conditions) these are the airborne moments during which he rises from a kind of self-help-Methodist-president to

GOD'S COWBOY

with all the red-blooded wrath that goes with that *Looksasifwe'vegot-alittlewarhereIgotthatfromthePentagon*WE'REATWARANDSOMEONE'S-GOINGTOPAYFORIT, Dick

Cheney

safe inside the PEOC (Presidential Emergency Operations Center in Washington we imagine it as a kind of underground safe a concrete-walled steelplated armoured protective cube insulated with aspic synthetic resin polystyrene glass wool egg boxes straw and fireproof down-filled cushions) so Dick

already knows who's

going to pay during these hours at the

birth of the MISSION

the PRESIDENT is catapulted up onto the pedestal of a HISTORIC president of a WAR president (he can't possibly remain just a terror-victim president) he must seize the moment that bathes him in the limelight of history the

WAR AGAINST TERROR is the martial armour-plating of the wound (Luisa says) as if they were pressing bare weapons-grade steel on an artery spurting blood what's the point hardly anyone in New York City wanted that at least not that many or at least no so many of those I got to know personally and met there watching the

PRESIDENT OF WAR

holding a white megaphone balancing among construction workers policemen firefighters on a mound of debris at Ground Zero wearing brown and dust-grey (appropriately) he promised to

HUNT DOWN (the escaping horse-thief) in the

sunburst of the historical moment he will be

raised up to the glory of his father of THE FATHER WHO managed the collapse of the USSR and the fall of the Berlin Wall the smoothly oiled wheels of

history

of the father who extinguished the torches blazing up to the heavens in Kuwait who vanquished the dictator but also of the father

who wept, George, who actually wept (Brezhnev-tears?) when he had to send

OURYOUNGMEN (and women) off to war

what I want to know Luisa is exactly how it came about and not so much because I'm against it but because I'd like to know how it works how it's possible for US to suddenly find ourselves at war again almost without noticing did HE want it straight away

and why did WE follow HIM (we couldn't prevent it from looking like that or how else could an Iraqi for example see us)

two months after the collapse of the Towers and still high on the glorious bombing campaign in Afghanistan he summoned his secretary of defence and requested him

todowhatisnecessaryinorderto

DEFENDAMERICAifnecessaryby

gettingridof

SaddamHussein

WE might think that was that and now he was looking for an excuse for the war against Iraq but is it that simple Luisa? I imagine he was still suffering from

shock

the worst that could happen to an American president had happened to him the gaping wound in New York City the 3,000 dead he had to prove right away that HE was the greatest of all guardian angels HE had to re-erect the SHIELD

he's surrounded by his father's old advisors like a group of grumpy irascible aggressive old uncles who are just waiting for him to go one step further than his father and not just beat Saddam but remove destroy crush him

but

the secretary of state (the sole chief decision-maker with direct experience of war) can see no convincing reason for the attack no necessity and no authorization acceptable to the international community all that would have to be found

your immediate concern is (you explain cautiously)

TOHAVETHEOPTION

the installation of a

red button

which would allow you to eliminate the Iraqi dictator as soon as that

was necessary

after all: *Thisistheguywhotriedtokillmydad* (as you have several times publicly declared recalling the failed attempt on the life of the ex-president by the Jordanian secret service in 1993 possibly though not certainly instigated by Saddam Hussein)

however

the OPTION doesn't exist there is only

op 1003

an out-of-date ponderous massive plan of war (another old uncle from the time of the Second Gulf War) so there's no way you can order the attack only the creation of the option the installation of that special red button which if it comes to the crunch gives you the chance

to eliminate

the Iraqi

however

that would start a

war or at least almost it's

as if a gigantic rock that can crush your enemy (and incidentally his country) in a short time had inevitably inexorably been pushed forward to the very edge of the war zone until it is resting in all its ominous glory as if on a sabre-edge as if it's about to tip the scales and has in fact already done so while people (even you yourself) still thought it could easily be stopped or broken up pulverized or simply shoved into the huge drawer of unrealized government plans

the obstinate 70-year-old

secretary of defence

with his nutcracker head glittering trifocal spectacles and a philosophical turn of mind (*there are things we know that we know, there are known unknowns, that is to say there are things that we now know we don't know, but there are also unknown unknowns, there are things we do not know we don't know*)

who is perhaps also recalling his time as special envoy of the great STAR-WARSPRESIDENT in Baghdad 18 years ago now when he provided the

FRIENDLY RULER

with helicopters and CIA information and more and more fighter planes so that he could attack the FANATICS in Teheran

so this secretary of defence now knows they will have to take all that away from the DICTATOR again as if he were a disobedient child and he sees to it that there are more and more new and more quickly realizable plans that are vigorously checked discussed optimized (faster neater smarter)

the important thing is

to be very 'kinetic'

says the chief military planner (Tommy) standing in uniform six foot three inches tall with tired eyes behind the president like the Grim Reaper behind the smart Western-series Death suitable for pre-watershed viewing

that means

to send JOHNNY crying wolf over however long a period of time we have

(that is: Iraq, the media, world opinion and US the public)

that is leave them in the dark about whether we're planning an attack or just building up a THREATENING ATMOSPHERE while we are in fact planning an attack but in such a way that the president's immediate entourage or even the president himself (as a Johnny) doesn't quite know whether they're still planning or have already started a war the way it roughly works (the philosophical secretary of defence will explain to a journalist) is that someone says something and someone else says the opposite and the president leans to one side and then to the other until he

ALONE

decides

or announces something like a decision for what role Luisa does all the psychology play that we keep pulling like rabbits out of a magician's hat out of the books meticulously examining the mechanics of power if HE is merely the realization or a kind of AVATAR of a structure namely the gigantic grey (brain) matter of North America then we might just as well accept what he is publicly reported to have said

HE

just wants to have the option (that was what he always said which proves his skill) and until it's time for that he gets people to work on the rhetorical stylization of danger (THEAXISOFEVIL)

I'mnotgoingtowaituntilsomethinghappens

he announced at the end of January 2002

though he has no problem telling the French president and the German Johnny in May that

therearenoplansforwaronmydesk

despite the fact that for months he's conferred with his chief planners about Iraq every week and

large airfields and fuel stores are being set up in Kuwait a command centre established in Qatar and CIA agents are roaming round Kurdistan with suitcases full of money while the army is having protective suits against biological and chemical weapons made in

September

at the end of this tragic year Luisa that I've probably only survived because of you and at most because of this absolute

need to understand

the concerned secretary of state with experience of war abruptly comes

out of the refrigerator

(as he says) and with regard to Iraq with regard to an internally broken impoverished chaotic country has suddenly discovered

the CHINA-SHOP rule:

you break it—you pay for it

and later on the president will claim to remember having heard that but maintain that at the time he was more preoccupied with PROTECTING AMERICA

for which now

in September before his address to the UN on the anniversary of the attack he can only find in the storm cloud of reasons for war one reason that will attract international support because it follows the most profound logic of the trauma and leads to the *worst-case scenario* to the total horror not to have recognized and averted which no politician no newspaper editor no director general of television no diplomat and statesman would want to be accused of namely an

attack (on US) by the AXISOFEVIL

with

W E A P O N S O F M A S S D E S T R U C T I O N

the existence of which in Iraq the secret services cannot quite confirm but they always underestimate say RiceCheneyRumsfeldetc the UN inspectors are easily hoodwinked assuming they're not actually lying

what else could HE do however

he had at least to find a few friends who did exactly what he told them on that

Saturday when Seymour rang me to put off our run there was the COJONES meeting

they were a foursome: Tony Blair and George Bush

in Camp David and the president asked the prime minister whether he (his boys) would be up for it

The sensitive, orbic, underlapp'd brothers, that only privileged feelers may be intimate where they are

if it were a matter of putting a stop to Saddam's game to which Tony immediately and unreservedly replied that he (they) would at which Bush assured the prime minister's colleagues that their boss possessed the equipment of virility although they believed it was the case

thattheBritshavenoideawhatcojonesare

and thus my friend

we finally ended up at King   .

Shahryar's palace

but of course all that is a

DEMOCRATIC process (among men)

when the Italian TVmillionaireprimeminister's staying with him

HE explains to him (presumably unnecessarily) that

inourcountriesweleadthepeoplewemustnotfollowthepeople

so he keeps inviting congressmen and senators to the White House for robust

briefings

(THE GUY's got weapons of mass destruction THE GUY's got chemical weapons THE GUY'll use them THE GUY could have an atom bomb within six months THE GUY could set off an attack with biological weapons in 45 minutes) until on 10 October the House of Representatives empowers HIM

to deploy troops in Iraq as HE thinks fit and proper

that means war Luisa said and it was the thought in the minds of not a few of the Columbia students whose disturbed questioning sceptical looks I had learnt to bear who had started to

carry me along

a soft medium malleable yet self-determining composed of highly attentive young people whom we damn well ought to be strengthening goading into thinking for themselves turning into awkward citizens so that even when they agree they know

what they're doing what's being done or supposedly being done for them

once in this mood of elation that seemed purely physiologically determined or generated and that rid me of my grief for half days or half nights as if I were living in a present with a past changed for the better by just one day I was with Luisa so natural in her smiling patient depths

the president's only three years older than me

we no longer have an excuse for not understanding anything one of my students brought a newspaper report according to which HE in his capacity as

commander-in-chief

had had himself inoculated against smallpox (for the in this particular case extremely unlikely case of an Iraqi attack with biological weapons so that not too many VIPs had to be immunized what about his wife his daughters) at times the undergraduates show the apprehensiveness of children or

politicians

it was over Christmas that

IT was (finally) decided many said (afterwards) I kept reading this phrasing in completely non-ironic reports *WouldyoudoIT* (Bush to Rice) or *We must do IT* (Rice to Bush) or *DoyouthinkwehavetodoIT* (Bush to Rumsfeld) as if otherwise there was only either vulgar slang or Latin words for IT

the troops in the region (at Christmas) are almost complete the weapons inspectors are still agonizing the French are against the Germans and the Russians even more so you've received the weapons report from Iraq agreed with the UN which has arrived on time 11,000 pages of half-truths and three-quarter lies you have to check it and what's more you simply

can't be bothered

with any more diplomatic delays dull sluggish peace tediously drawn-out negotiations the whole UN hullabaloo of which you don't think much anyway and when the French Foreign Minister (a snotty-nosed little multi-lingual aristocrat who's said to have written an adulatory biography of Napoleon) announces his veto in the Security Council you decide

to put on a UN performance of your own

wowing the viewers on television screens all round the world the

GENERAL WITH NO CLOTHES

(that he would have been if we'd tried to kit him out in his logical proofs and powerful evidence instead of his dark-blue suit) had to be prepared for it and it'll be quite some time before you forget the pleasure of those 12 minutes on 13 January which presumably ended more or less like this:

The White House, Oval Office. President Bush in his traditional chair by the fireside. General in civilian attire in the seat of honour for foreign guests.

President opens his arms as if he were about to hand over a tomahawk or a large dead fish.

PRESIDENT. AreyouonmysideColin?

General swallows. He sits up straight in his chair.

GENERAL. I'm on your side, Mr President.

PRESIDENT. Thenit'stimeyouputyourbattledresson

Close-up of President's resolutely beaming face. Music starts, discreetly, as if an echo from the future theatre of war: When Johnny Comes Marching Home Again, Hurrah! Hurrah! *Cut.*

on 5 February 2003 the curtain rises in the UN and we see the GENERAL in the show he will soon describe as a blot on his life he presents

fuzzy evidence laboriously fished out of vague-to-unusable CIA material during days of meticulous searching the imitation anthrax tube from the props cupboard the difficult to interpret satellite snapshots of industrial plant the PowerPoint graphics of alleged mobile bioweapons laboratories supported by a few dubious-sounding witness statements photos of Iraqi rockets it was said could fly as far as Israel (taken before they were forbidden by the UNMOVIC) scraps of bugged conversations from tapes of uncertain origin in which you were supposed to be able to hear coded arrangements between Iraqi officers about removing evidence of production centres for weapons aluminum pipes that could have been used in uranium centrifuges vague reports highly enriched with supposition of links between al-Qaeda terrorists and Iraqi agents

a PILE of evidence Luisa said a pile (repeated in Spanish) people are always impressed by PILES

just as an old army trooper, I can tell you a couple of things

the Powell buy-in

I refused to accept

the signed ticket full of holes to the war (you'll be in the VIP box for the blue-eyed boys)

I wanted to

leave the US and three weeks later I had to for my mother had collapsed she had already been in intensive care for two days when my sister finally called me on the way to JFK Airport I was thinking that now there was no time nor place for me the past beneath the bulldozed debris the future a wrong war the present an apartment by the grace of Seymour too cheap and not permanent the ghost-house in Amherst

a cramped noisy hotel behind Adenauerplatz in Berlin (at least that was something I could change)

the exhausted face of my sister on the other side of the hospital bed this sense of

being catapulted back

into our childhood among the tubes and machines our mother's smile that at odd moments once more seemed so close ageless and warm as if we were still living in our cramped tenement in Bremen the unremarkable family of the commercial college teacher Ernst Lechner now

we're in for it

in the long days and half nights in the hospital

that was

often the only distinct feeling the only clear thought I had you have

to make decisions

like the

PRESIDENT who is now absolutely determined to drive out his blood-thirsty opponent from Dodge City (a running gag in the Bush family) and who's now only listening to what and whom he wants to hear

survivors of the German concentration camps advocating the attack

generals promising a clean war: *we do no*

body counts

Iraqi exiles according to whom the victims of the attack will soon turn into rejoicing liberated citizens the only minor fly in the ointment is a

papal envoy

but you show him the garden of peace in the incense-shrouded future beyond the war what has to be done never seems clearer than in the hours in which IT is done

everything simply works it

was just waiting for the moment the cowboy's horse gallops off only the painter's brush of the future can pin it down

on the Azores in the middle of March

the blue

of the decision

a boundless sky and clear

air

the president of Portugal's invited him and Tony's there and that Spaniard Aznar (*always have a moustache beside you*) balls and beard and beside the 135,000 US soldiers there are already 200 Poles under arms outside the oilfields representing the NEW

Europe

it's a stroll scarcely a line dividing the blue of the sea from the crystal-clear air

48 hours for the bandits to leave Dodge City

back home

there's just a

pause before the attack

the hesitation before the beheading a truly personal act in a certain sense (but basically one you've already rehearsed with the more than 150 death warrants you signed as governor of Texas) in which two F-117 stealth bombers and 36 Tomahawk guided missiles set off for a country seat to the south of Baghdad where they suspect Saddam his sons and his wife (and a few

collateral victims)

are

this decision is taken on the evening of 19 March 2003 in line with the ultimatum after you've asked each member of the war cabinet whether he would also do THAT (every one of them would ALSO DO THAT)

but on the morning of the same day the

ORDER TO GO INTO ACTION

had already been given to the commanders from the operations room of the White House via a secure video link with the front almost the same dialogue repeated 10 times

PRESIDENT. *Haveyoueverythingyouneed?*

COMMANDER. *Yes, Mr President.*

PRESIDENT. *Canyouwin?*

COMMANDER. *Yes, Mr President.*

so then: *ForthesakeofworldpeaceandforthebenefitandfreedomoftheIraqipeo-pleIherebygivetheordertocarryout*OperationIraqiFreedom.*MayGodbewith-oursoldiers.*

this is the true

    cannibalistic moment

    in the PRESIDENT'SLIFE that greatly feared greatly longed-for HIS-TORICAL moment in which you

    have to take the first young body in your teeth and tear it apart like a

    quail (Luisa says)

O to resume the joys of the soldier!
To go to battle—to hear the bugles play and the drums beat!
To taste the savage taste of blood—to be so devilish!
To gloat so over the wounds and deaths of the enemy.

but of course above all there will be that solemn state-burial-like glossy black-and-white photo in which

    you and

    God (the latter as usual scarcely recognizable unless he's taken the shape of a little spotted dog that's standing blurred behind you in front of a bound-ary hedge) goes

    walking all alone shortly after you gave the order to attack

    Itwasveryemotionalforme

    Iprayed

    as

    I

    walkedround

PART THREE

PARADISE

June–September 2004

Thus time passed between order and confusion, preservation and destruction, plundering and paying; and this may be the reason why war is so particularly harmful to the psyche. You are daring and destructive one day, gentle and creative the next; you accustom yourself to catchwords designed to excite and keep alive hope amid the most desperate circumstances; this produces a kind of hypocrisy with a particular character of its own that is distinguished from the priestly, courtly or whatever other kind there may be.

Johann Wolfgang von Goethe
Campaign in France in the Year 1792

Nothing ever happens in my dreams.
No wars breaking out.
No parades marching on festival days.
No ships arrive,
and no robots leading repentant dervishes to Paradise.

Nothing ever happens in my dreams.
The street is empty as usual
and I have to get home
before the rain comes pouring down.

Fadhil al-Azzawi
Miracle Maker

Sabrina

When she makes

(works out)

a poem

in the dream-fields of language in which words are to be handled in a completely new way to be greeted as strangers each one even the most well-worn and well-known as a new arrival that

is capable of anything and

needs to be touched and

weighed

for a long time

this is the state

in which you lose yourself on purpose (with purpose) it's almost like a deliberate fainting fit (or the beginning of one) or taking off the armour the diving suit of our thick-plated metallic linguistic shell to become sensitive once more vulnerable like

the first new skin

over a terrible burn

shhh!

and better still look with great sensitivity and extreme concentration out of the room through the window with no glass or the half-open door as if from another planet at the earth at the most ordinary things the little cupboard a blue rucksack a bouquet of roses the young fruit trees the birds in the sunlight

When you lie with me, when you lie with me—

the neat little wooden houses of Babylon out of the windows of the train

Eric gives me one last wave behind the glass under the glass my hand on the dusty pane of the compartment window in the car of the Long Island Rail Road I

never imagined that

the Arabian princess I invented by observing myself when I was little as a companion in my loneliness would talk to me and write poems I've no idea why she's just occurred to me again in these first happy minutes of being left on my own perhaps because without someone as an audience you can't really believe in happiness or in unhappiness

When you lie with me, time stands still—

thinking about a poem is like being drunk in broad daylight I want to give Eric newer and better lyrics perhaps we can look for a new tune on the Greyhound tomorrow what

do I want

not to have to ask myself that question for three whole days I might manage that during this holiday

Babylon (*a great place to live and raise a family with convenient*

train service to

New York City) glides past perhaps the morally outraged mother of the man who founded the town had that last two-storey wooden house in mind whatever the decadent morals of the time can have been in my mind's eye I see the saloons of the more or (mostly) less realistic TV Westerns filth and encrusted mud falling off riding boots as they go up the wooden stairs the trail leads to the room of the notorious Kitty who is undoing a silver buckle on the garter of her black frilled dress (all those pretty girls buried in the mud alone with their syphilis) on my last visit

to Babylon

I was in a bad mood

säuerlich my cousin Lotta said I didn't know the German word or had forgotten it we were on the Berlin city railroad heading for the Museum Island the elevated track literally cut the massive late-nineteenth-century buildings in two you travelled through on a level with the windows I headed with Martin and Lotta for the oppressive facade of the Pergamon Museum that was hemmed in on either side by the walls of the other museum buildings and this sense of being walled in or threatened with being shut in by grey walls reminded me of Böcklin's *Isle of the Dead* (the figure shrouded in white standing up in the barque is so horrible because it's standing and makes you ask yourself whether all the dead must be so completely shrouded and heroically composed as they journey to the island that hardly seems to have room for a few dozen of them)

Hitler

my father said

bought the picture in 1933 and hung it in his house in Berchtesgaden

it would have been better if I hadn't mentioned it I thought then no one would have sprayed a swastika on the rock of my Isle of the Dead and I didn't see that Martin regretted his remark

really regretted it

Lotta my understanding blonde warm-hearted sensuous German cousin who was so often in high spirits told me as we stood at the checkroom of the Pergamon Museum it wasn't as bad as she thought after all I'm used to my father and his very German way of insisting on getting to the ur-German root of anything German and soon he was at it again for instead of immersing himself in the display of the magnificent Pergamon Altar the market gate of Miletus and the lions and dragons on the blue tiles he was reading a leaflet about the expedition to the East in the days of the Kaiser (as was to be expected he was fascinated by the fact that it was the Germans of all people who had discovered the great role Babylon had played and in the course of 18 years of excavation had uncovered the foundations and ruins of the city)

through an internal window on the second floor I watched him in the exhibition from above (visitors went down a long walkway or along a series of corridors leåading into each other) he went back to the Ishtar Gate again and then followed the Processional Way as far as a glass display case and Lotta came towards him slowly from the right

she stopped beside him and I suddenly thought

that she could be his daughter just as well as I that she

could be me

and I had a feeling of depression and at the same time a presage of a great relief in museums you can often get this kind of

extraterrestrial feeling

it's the way they open the door to so many epochs and civilizations

times stands still
outside our door / outside our room

in one of the outside pockets of my rucksack I find my travel notebook and start writing and slip off into the memory of my own hasty Babylon with Eric this morning it's good to put it off for one day and one night with time enough (that is as much as we like)

wild nights
should be
our luxury

in Los Angeles we'll have the apartment of a friend of Eric's brother all to ourselves I can

escape

to my grandparents if I like I ought to go and see them in Palo Alto any-way I've gone on and on about Cynthia's apple cake to Eric and I'd also like him to see the room where I spent so many weeks of the holidays with my books in a solitary past that becomes precious and oddly worth protecting at the very moment that I'm losing it

and it's too soon to use Eric to get over everything (is that it to heal the past

with a person

in the present)

you haven't that much to complain about

Princess

the years when you slept alone in your bed at most tormented by an imaginary king and a sister who couldn't see you will soon be over no one seems to give it much thought but it's true that you (as an only child and as someone who does later find partners) had to spend the loneliest of nights during the first 20 years of your life

why don't I ask Martin whether he's in favour of my trip to California why haven't I even called him so far

he'd simply say he approved after all he wanted me to study in Califor-nia (or even in Berlin)

my mother will put up more resistance she can show me that I really must

make up my mind and can open the door for me behind which there's nothing at all I'm getting no farther with the poem

so I swap my notebook for the CD player and dream closing my eyes

your eye is
memory

and listening until the train finally gets to Manhattan

time is just memory mixed in with desire

(Tom Waits sings would she hear that)

the Arabian princess in the stone heart of Babylon the great entrance to the city of the towers

here

Martin once showed me the red-brick building with the black accordion of the fire escape on the front where they spent the first seven months of the pregnancy we even went up the stairs to the third floor there still wasn't an elevator and I thought I could almost feel Amanda's weariness as she lugged me up there however apart from that everything had been renovated and was hardly recognizable

before Amanda and Seymour moved into the apartment in Midtown I'd only been to New York City twice and over the last four years I've just become used to being here quite often without ever feeling at home or particularly liking the city but I learnt to adapt to it as now on the busy underground platform of Penn Station or coming out into the labyrinth of cavernous streets the maze of hoardings the yellow taxis and pedestrians in a hurry its deafening reality gives me the brief adrenaline rush I need to move swiftly and purposefully so that everyone looks on me as a real city dweller or an experienced traveller

only when Lotta came to see me here two years ago

did I suddenly feel pride in Manhattan I went with her on foot on my favourite walks from Penn Station to Barnes & Noble and then along 34th Street towards the Empire State Building (you should stand outside the entrance and tip your head back to shoot up into the sky like a rocket in three mighty stages and on seven window tracks Lotta did actually get dizzy) we sat under a sunshade in Bryant Park drinking milky coffee and didn't even have to visit the temple of books that is the New York Public Library as would inevitably have been the case with Martin Lotta far preferred to drag me round the boutiques of the fashion mile the luxury shops of Fifth Avenue and almost every floor of Macy's

paradise!

she cried (only half ironically) I imagine her (perhaps a little paler or on the edge of turning transparent in a kind of fade-out) with her shopping bags laughing as she strolls tirelessly round a never-ending mall for months and years not sleeping in no danger eating nothing but strange ethereal sky-blue ices and quenching her thirst on peculiar clinical soft drinks served by dependable

angels

of sales assistants unbelievably smart fantastically polite young women and men who show her superb shoes skirts pullovers jewellery without ever being pushy and if you make an inadvertent movement which would expose you to a slight collision with their body you feel nothing but the yielding softness of a curtain or a down-filled cushion

only your mother

could get in touch with you with a special ring-tone

you're coming to Manhattan? what was that message you left in my mailbox? you're already there? you're going away? tomorrow afternoon? listen I won't be in I'm away on business and I'm spending the night in East Hampton it's more practical but I'm going straight to the office tomorrow we can meet there around nine if you can manage that then we can talk go out for a meal with Seymour be nice to him after all you're grown up now bye

with the call you wake up as if you were

falling

onto the unframed sky-high glass-hard picture of Little Brazil Street ONE WAY NO STANDING AT ANY TIME GET DREAMS MILK CHOCOLATE YOUR WORLD GET ORGANIZED MOVIN' OUT CUT YOUR a confusion of surfaces masts cladding automobiles strips windows like welding flames between them spurts of sunlight the only escape is upwards to the quiet top edge of the canyon beneath the cloudless sky

from the kitchen you can see a high-rise with a dark reflective facade and a side wall covered in advertising hoardings that go up 10 storeys (HSBC—SAMSUNG—COCA-COLA) plunging down onto miniature taxis toy buses insect people crosswalks construction-site debris while the view from the living room shows a group of compact sombre towers with striking stepped roofs metal-cladded fortresses exploding into the sky you have a lovely view of the Empire State Building from your bed King Kong will wave to you every morning

what should I say

to Seymour

who hardly have I made a pot of tea suddenly appears before me looking with interest at my blue rucksack that I've leant against a kitchen cupboard he hasn't much time he says he's just come back for some documents am I planning to be away for long

tomorrow? so soon? to California? great he says pour me a cup of tea too will you he sits down at the table with a view of a 15-foot-tall black-haired lapdog (HSBC) his fair sun-bleached hair and the bronzed freckled skin of his face and his powerful forearms coming out of the precisely rolled-up sleeves of his blue-striped shirt clearly show that he has a wonderful sailing weekend behind him it's just that

my mother

won't be sleeping with him tonight

I don't know whether he knows that so I quickly say that I'm only there briefly to leave my rucksack it's convenient because I'm meeting Eric (the boy from East Hampton whose bike Amanda smashed up) tomorrow afternoon at the nearby Virgin Megastore and this way I can buy a few things unencumbered before going out to a girl friend on the Upper East Side where I'm spending the night

Amanda said you were going to sleep here—

I'm grown up

I haven't forgotten that so now I'll behave as if all that concerns me is the planned dinner

I'm sorry I say and now that I've successfully resisted being taken out to one of his special restaurants I do actually feel slightly sorry for him and I admire him for the inner calm and composure with which he takes everything I'll never be able to be as relaxed as he is perhaps it's the decades of practice in business that helps him keep his nerves so well under control that he can cope with all my mother's moods and whims and sudden nights away (has he tried to bribe Mrs Donally to secretly take photos of Leslie creeping

through the dog roses of his summerhouse which she would never do of
course which would then give rise to the strange and absolutely incomprehensible fact that we both like this unprepossessing and sensational housekeeper very much) I mean should we talk about what's left of their short
marriage I can only stare in wonder at the zest and craving for life the
discipline and strong nerves of these people in their 50s they seem to me like
giants with the skin of an elephant or rather with a splendid arrogance as if
the whole world were made for them I

just want to go

outside the sun's shining down into the deep canyons of the streets
and on the parks I can't understand my mother risking her marriage with
Seymour for a short stocky unattractive and only moderately amusing
scriptwriter (or is that over is that why Seymour's so calm) what should I
say I can't offer him comfort that would be ridiculous in contrast to Julia
who thinks my father's 'interesting' to me older men are like a different
species of mammal (bigger and threatening) I want to have as little as possible to do with them especially when they put on the paternal act but Seymour's had practice with his twins and quite often manages

to involve me in long conversations and discussions

(is he wondering now how to go about it even though he claimed he
didn't have any time)

mainly by talking about the subject I'm studying as if after one year at
MIT I knew anything about

the Earth

out of which he's spent his whole life

sucking oil although he looks as if he'd only been sailing round it all
the time someone (he maintains) has to look after the bloodstream of this
magnificent pile of buildings you can see out of the window (GET REAL)
break through the Earth's crust with drills which nowadays eat their way
through the layers of rocks with outspread arms like octopuses to suck up
the black nectar Martin told me Seymour's family had to flee Rotterdam as
Hitler's army approached the whole city centre had been bombed and he
believed a person like Seymour needs an image of organization and power
to find his way back

to his roots

(Rotterdam as an industrial centre the panoramic view of the system
of islands bristling with chimneys the huge ships floating between them like

toys dozens of massive white tanks arranged in parallel rows linked by a Laocoön-like network of precisely controlled pipelines along the 20-mile exit canal of the Maasvlakte Oil Terminal that handles 40 million tonnes of crude oil per year)

what are my roots what makes me think of that while I'm sitting here drinking green tea with my ultra-successful relaxed stepfather

as you get older

he explains and I can't say why I'd really like to be back outside in Bryant Park or Central Park

you find it much easier to take abstractions seriously as effective and absolutely valid abbreviations of reality

paper barrel

that's what they call the right to oil purchases they send halfway round the world from their notebook monitors in some airport lounge

my paper roots   .

dissolve in the conversation with this realist even though I cling to the Earth with the help of MIT's differential equations and computer simulations I fear (I wish) I can never become as real as Seymour he often expresses all the things I could accuse him of and says himself he's an

old-fashioned man

a man of the old over-exploitative system of seeking out sucking out burning off the Earth's irreplaceable resources sick with *morbus* Prometheus with the mark of the fire disease on him locked into the macho world of oil pumps production platforms supertankers and its exceedingly real-man

Arab connections

special relationships

since 1945 when Franklin D. Roosevelt on a short pleasure cruise along the Suez Canal gave his guest Ibn Saud who had set up his tent on the deck of the cruiser *USS Quincy* an airplane and a wheelchair

hydrogen engines solar cells geothermal energy

Seymour (often) says that's what you think will be the answer and perhaps you'll be right in 30 or 40 years' time

what arguments can I use against him I keep having to remind myself that these things these political and historical complications do really (abstractions as abbreviations) have something to do with me whereas he seems to have become so fused with the colossus beneath the colossus that his dreams probably flow through pipelines and drive tiny turbines inside his head with the help of which he will be able to live three years beyond his allotted time I can only hold on to

what is coming

the future is my corridor

actually a bare black endless passageway the horrors of which are only veiled by the warm glow of this or that island we assume is near and that we will safely reach so I sink back into the present and try to get out of defiance and defence and just

breathe

freely

Plath | *I'm nobody! Who are you?*
Are you nobody, too?

in that case I can only wish you all the best it's a good idea to have a go at something unusual and if you don't try out this or that at your age you'll never be satisfied

Seymour says

when I get up to go and quickly put my teacup on the draining board I feel embarrassed

at suddenly having told him so much about Eric and my planned trip and my grandparents in California when we say goodbye he just gives me a light encouraging pat on my upper arm

for a moment I stand

without my rucksack

down on Little Brazil Street

in a daze

with a 30-foot-high open mobile phone in front of me the gigantic black lapdog into whose eyes I was looking from the kitchen has

risen

I've no girl friend called Mary with a spacious pad on the Upper East
Side where I could spend the night

 as a crowd rushes towards me (set off by the changing lights)

 I almost feel like going back up to the 23rd floor to confess to Seymour
that I just wanted to get rid of him

 however I turn in the opposite direction from the one I originally took
the dark passage of the future is full of faceless people I've got two or three
phone numbers of people I know from college it's only 18 hours to my ren-
dezvous with Eric what's more it's a

 lovely summer's day

WHEN YOU LIE WITH ME

When you lie with me then time stands still
 And blind outside our room.
Its eyes are filled with memory,
 Its ears with our last tune.

And when it parts its leaden lids,
 We're not there any more
For I am on my way to you
 Down the future's corridor.

Once every day you lie with me,
 Let time flow on again,
The present sweep away the past,
 And I'll stop asking: When?

Count the days calm down no

order your days by going through them cross out

three years from the calendar day by day it's

1,001 days since Sabrina died

it was from the notebook in her blue rucksack that I first learnt about her imaginary Arabian princess Luisa on the other hand knew about this childhood fantasy she mentioned it to her quite casually during a barbecue evening when they were talking about literature and the tales from *The Thousand and One Nights* which had suggested to Sabrina a sister living in fantastic symbiosis with her

such imaginary companions

were nothing unusual especially for only children and

no cause for concern

Luisa said to calm me down as if it were still important

today she would have been 22 years and seven months old and when I glance at the *New York Times* on my desk

Mr Bush and his political advisers embraced the legacy of the late Ronald Reagan . . . Mr Bush heralded the late president as a 'gallant leader in the cause of freedom' and lionized him in an interview

I could imagine that it's decidedly healthier to be president of the United States (and to die at 93 in Bel Air, California) than to follow the JOIN-THE-ARMY call of some recruiting sergeant outside a supermarket at 19 and then appear among the

22-year-olds

in the almost-daily newspaper column that is more and more coming to resemble a league table for some sport usually listing four or five American soldiers who have fallen in Iraq

Bush praised Reagan in Normandy

where he had gone yesterday to attend the commemoration of the sixtieth anniversary of the Allied landings for the first time a German chancellor also took part so Schröder embraced his *brother* Chirac and in the military cemetery of Colleville PRESIDENT Bush demonstratively shook the hands

of the (old) EUROPEANS as a sign of the continuing inviolable alliance for
freedom in memory of that great selfless military operation that America
was at all times ready to undertake once more for her friends without as
was widely emphasized in the press

specifically mentioning Iraq

how can you ever hope to escape from the unrelenting mechanism of
history that again and again puts you in a state of impotent apathy with
which you now look at the announcement of the deaths of so many who
were hardly 20

I spent the whole war

that is those 21 days that had optimistically and fraudulently been des-
ignated the actual military action

in Berlin

at my mother's deathbed

I wasn't indifferent to what was happening on the monitors in the wards
or the smokers' day room that resembled a cynical infernal saloon (a field
hospital) and that I often had to go past

when I got back to my hotel in the evening I would zap back and forth
between the German channels and CNN often staying awake till two or
three in the morning until I was benumbed as in the apartment on Amsterdam Avenue so that out of pure exhaustion I eventually fell into a sleep shot
through with vivid memories of the television pictures (I can't imagine hell
without screens any more) I watched the pale German newsreaders trying
to respond to the events with a kind of mortician solemnity while the CNN
people seemed as always to have been born just for this event hitting the
balls back with the concentrated breathlessness of a professional tennis
player before serving their hectic pictures over the BIZBAR

STRIKE
ON IRAQ
PENTAGON. 'SHOCK AND AWE'
OF OPERATION PUT ON HOLD
NETWORKING FIRM LINSKYS FOR $500 CNN

at the beginning it was always the same camera positions (a street that
had been almost completely cleared out and an emerald-green night shot of

government buildings by the Tigris) fixed long shots from the roof or top-floor windows of a hotel in Baghdad where most of the journalists and camera teams reporting from the Iraqi side were housed until finally they could show the spectacular hit on the Defence Ministry a monstrous truncated cone the crest of which under the assault of rockets and bombs exploded thunderously sending a shower of debris up into the orange sky where three or four suns first glistening then black with smoke seemed to be setting and although my sister and I tried to keep the news from her the excitement of the war got through to my mother and she imagined she was once again living through the Hamburg firestorm though in an updated version and told me to get Lotta and Sabrina to safety and to remind my sister who was never careful enough to think of

something nice

in the storm

she said that was the most important thing to hold fast and she smiled uncertainly think of Christmas Martin of your best Christmas of the guitar and the book . . . that book . . . Brehm's *Life of Animals* (condensed edition) you always wanted

put your head between your knees use your hands to protect yourself think of

what the Iraqis were thinking under the hail of bombs and what the soldiers were thinking as they fell on Iraq in that wave of men and munitions 160,000 so-called willing volunteers from 36 nations during

OPERATION IRAQI FREEDOM

in the sand in the air by day and by night an immense hammer coming down unceasingly with no need of sleep of rest that was the idea of the great charioteer and then in Baghdad in three days yet it was to be a

smart

operation elegant and modern a hyper-precise hi-tech campaign the full force of the titanic steam-hammer driven by extremely sophisticated control circuits technocratic opium for the impatient grumpy old men in Washington pouring out unrestrained curses on the rest of the unwilling democratic world quickly in quickly out like the old warhorses and the young bravos who painted shark's jaws dripping with blood on their pilot's helmets

and screamed: *Yes, I want to kill fucking Iraqis!* at the camera

tearing enemy divisions apart from the air before what was left was cleared away on the ground all with a casual flick of the joystick or a click of the mouse cutting open whole districts hurling houses cars trees body parts through the air but always

precisely

calculated coordinated communicated

war as the continuation of computer games with devastating means tearing your opponent's organs of attack and defence to pieces in a split second thought through by intellectual-looking youthful generals with actual PhDs digital technicians of death who set up their central command in a tented city in the desert of Qatar dozens of crop-haired men in camouflage uniforms at their laptops making a kind of military Internet cafe the

Joint Operations Center

in which everything fuses with the speed of light and radio and on a god's-eye screen the size of two doors the data from spy satellites remote-controlled flying cameras high-resolution radar screens and the CIA turn into shining pink yellow blue and orange symbols on the green and brown background of Iraq at any place and any time (the trifocal glasses of the defence secretary slip down on his nose and the

PRESIDENT'S face

dissolves into a kind of Mickey Mouse mask with a grey hood) even in the darkest night with all our living and dead (instrument) eyes for us YOUR land is

green

like a gigantic murky moss-grown aquarium in which we can swim round at any height we choose to set it on fire at any place we choose though of course it's not swimming but the

flight of the owls of Mars

invisible (almost)

soon we'll only be sending YOU stealth warriors avatars of old men with two PhDs who from their hospital beds in Washington or Los Angeles with shaky micro-movements of their arthritic fingers on their touchpads will slaughter you in complete silence out of what you think is the empty air on the ground or in any storey of any (for US transparent) building

only the VILLAINS! of course and

then with greater precision than

in that most complex of MURDER(BEHEADING)ATTACKS in history with which WE after long investigations by the secret services opened this

OPERATION

with those two Stealth Bombers and three dozen cruise missiles which with great precision only hit a dozen civilians in a non-fortified building instead of the PRESIDENT'S FAMILY in their underground bunker

that's war for you

says the general

says the major says the colonel says this or that soldier facing the cameras of the future with a clear eye and steady voice in the soft light of family-viewing documentation but also on some roof or other in Najaf as he watches Private X chucking charred body parts into a plastic sack at the same time hearing someone say defiantly that war's not a clean and hygienic business apparently they can cope with that (at least until they send them back to the post-traumatic psychiatrists on the home front) but

they're happy to forget the particular characteristic of current West–Middle East wars namely the unclean victim ratio of one to a hundred or one to five hundred as a condition of the hygienic distance the media allow which presumably makes the wars possible in the first place everywhere we see so much effort and money and technology for the paucity of thought and excess of action

of the one-eyed men

in the right eye

of the Apache helicopter pilot there is

an electronic simulation of his hostile environment the

MONOCLE

replaces the telltale glow of onboard monitors and displays during night-time attacks everything he needs is reflected in the round disc the size of a watch glass it takes years of training to master this schizoid vision that is to see the surrounding actuality of the cabin with one eye and with the other the bright tables and graphs of the flight parameters slipping across a moving film of the ground in shades of green and grey beneath the roaring rotor-blades of the Apache squadron cowering

objects

can be seen moss-green jade-green rush-green suddenly sprinkled with maggot-like whitish spectres (the brighter the warmer)

COMES LEFT!

the onboard gunner shouts the dazzling blast of the jets of the (Hellfire) rocket and almost simultaneously the impact and hit on the ground the pilot has turned away in time so as not to be temporarily blinded the cockpit is briefly aglow with the heat of the launch

on the ground

distance stops

everything becomes real below the black helicopters flying at 150 feet everything is torn to pieces the trunks of palm trees trucks tanks the bodies of several hundred soldiers of one of Saddam's elite divisions and also the plantations the toolshed the old navy-blue VW and its owner a 40-year-old gardener who used to drive out here from Baghdad every two weeks to look after the garden of his parents' house to which for once he didn't bring his children because he felt the drive along the open road was too dangerous distances blur swallowed up in the clay-coloured ochre orange fronts of the sandstorms soon glowing red then brown and almost black blotting out the sky as they rip along closer and closer reducing vision to an arm's length as if death were happening in a gigantic howling oven but on the next day you have to once more see clearly

what you're killing

in the sights of the tanks the spurts of blood the sudden holes in the bodies the torn-off arms legs heads

up close

you can't make out the masses of Iraqi soldiers eagerly surrendering and all the time promising to give you their superiors back home and certainly not the populace rejoicing at their liberation instead you're shot at from all sides by Kalashnikovs sub-machine guns bazookas old shotguns by men in uniforms and civilians from roofs bridges towers by Russian T-55 tanks that have been passed on and that the Abrams several technical generations ahead and with special ammunition shoot down like lead ducks

in whose bellies the crew are literally cut to pieces

from close to it's

horrible human mincemeat it's

brutally chaotically savagely shooting your way through an extremely hostile environment that is comprehensively armed even if with outdated weapons sending lunatics at you on pickups motorbikes and even bicycles defenders of their country filled with hatred soldiers doing their duty fathers pressed into the ranks by the secret service young fedayeen whose families were given a shoebox full of dinars seen from close to there's no welcome in the south either or in the towns and villages dominated by the Shiites at best a wait-and-see indifference a mute grinding of teeth a passivity lethargy suppressed fury through which you bomb cut shoot your way

but what do I know anyway we're looking at everything from above what did I know then (more than a year ago) in Berlin

by my mother's sickbed I stared at the magazine I was holding at the fine detail of the asphalt-grey satellite photos as if I were hovering 10,000 feet above the thousands of roofs on the chequerboard of Baghdad through which a pitch-black river twists round a tight meander like an intestinal loop everywhere little irregular yellow-rimmed red stars shone out the main targets as it said or (and naturally assumed to be identical with them) the buildings that had already been destroyed or badly damaged in the air raids

today

from Boston

I see myself as such a miniature and feel nothing more than a

satellite pain

when I see myself in the corridors of the hospital or during my last confused conversations with my mother who once took me for the 10-year-old I had been and then again for a contemporary whose name she'd forgotten a schoolmate or neighbour an immense

distance

basically the only thing that saved me was

walking over the whitish-grey linoleum of a Berlin hospital without paying attention to anything as if it were a narrow bridge of stardust out in space which would disappear together with the universe at my next breath but one

without comment

before I tried to read and cry at night finally plunging into the first stages of the war in Iraq so as to sear my consciousness with fluorescent horrors in order to get to sleep I would walk round ice-cold Berlin that I could still remember pretty well but which didn't seem to remember me at all (why should it) apart from my sister and her family whom I didn't want to pester there was no one I could call and in view of all these things these people rather who had completely slipped and were still slipping away from me I sometimes felt a strange cool and cheerless relief

a far-reaching absence of responsibility for my own state

something like a

birth that was of indifference to me

in a bistro where I went on my way back to the hotel in order to warm up I met a tall ash-blonde woman in her 40s with a mole on her upper lip who seemed familiar to me it was one of the nurses I'd seen with my mother she knew a lot about me the 'Herr Professor' including the fact that I was divorced and had lost a daughter (but not how) you must remember

that I hadn't been in a particularly good state for weeks so

I could picture us after a lengthy conversation walking together hastily and in silence

like people who have agreed to a deal and want to get it over and done with in the winter night over the crackling grit of the sidewalks trying out going arm in arm for a few steps during which I (perhaps) held her large cool long-fingered hand (aroused and horrified as if it were one of her sexual organs) it could be

the flash of triumph or was it simply her girlish pride in a special catch that made me even more abstracted and nervous than in the three or four other fleeting affairs in a life containing relatively few women but it could also have been that

the strangeness the warmth the disturbingly real details (the spacious entrance of an old Berlin tenement the chessboard floor of a cramped elevator with manual hinged wooden doors blue-and-white-striped medical handbooks lying round and hydroponic plants with round artificial stones and thin transparent test tubes such as I hadn't seen for decades) sent me back into the past

as if this were an infidelity

in my own earlier life basically it's just a lively

memory

for actually I'm no longer capable of such actions that are set off by false self-induced warmth overlying plain mechanical ease nothing other than the fact that one can simply act in this way can produce nakedness

as a result almost as something

criminal or criminal-like for seconds possibly for minutes

of simple animal happiness

the realization

that you (too) are just like that seeing yourself inside a woman as a simple happy ephemeral animal (warmth the flow of milk rich dung red slits a warm haystack) or could it be

that absinth-like mixture of bitterness and cold arousal which I have seldom experienced just a thorn in the flesh until you rub open little sores

wrestling yourself into tiredness

actually followed by an almost comic mutual lack of understanding talking past each other during which you get up and then go back into bed and see the other's hairy light-pink nipples the drooping behind (the dangling testicles) something like that

happened to me in a prior existence the tall woman with the mole on her upper lip

only came to see me there and

I saw her a few more times in the hospital and I sat by my mother with a guilty conscience as if I'd broken a windowpane or smashed an expensive vase if I

despised or at least mocked myself

I could think of my last visit to Germany with Sabrina without doubling up in pain

we'd only spent two days in Frankfurt then flown on to Berlin where Luisa and I had a hotel room while she stayed with her cousin Lotta with whom she set off on her tour of Europe a few days later it was the first time I'd been in Germany with Luisa and it made me nervous always trying to give both women my attention and grateful to Luisa when as she often did she let go of me and took Sabrina's arm treating her like a sister

she's wonderful she's so precise and modest I think she could be a poet

Luisa said

why's she gone to MIT then I asked to be told that I had to give up trying to exercise any control over my daughter you've got to

let go

how often have I heard told myself that and stuck to it in most cases which in retrospect were only practice for this black absolute letting go that I can't get out of any more I can see her on the Deutschherren-Ufer in Frankfurt standing on the empty ME plinth and laughing (let go) in Berlin I went with her to a late show in a cinema as I did in my own student days and she once (briefly) lay her head on my shoulder (the film has gone to me it's as if we were watching a silent grey waterfall on the screen) outside the entrance to the Pergamon Museum I made the mistake of telling her that Hitler had bought a version of Böcklin's *Isle of the Dead* in fact I wanted to go to Weimar with her as well and visit the Buchenwald concentration camp there but then I let go there was absolutely no need to keep on educating her

today I dream of the black figure in Afghanistan

and you could say that in the meantime I've covered her up but still can't let her go that is I've covered her up so that I'm allowed

to sit in silence at her side

I let go of my mother in the Berlin winter it was a sigh of relief on her part or at least that's what you could tell yourself for the time it takes to draw breath all the things objects windows walls seemed porous so that the bird of her soul could part them effortlessly

her last words were that

it was enough now and that I should keep an eye

on her

but I don't know whom she meant I thought perhaps my sister but she might have been concerned about Sabrina or Lotta after the funeral I stayed for a few more days without exactly knowing why

I did try

to say goodbye or rather to find the right way of saying goodbye (to my mother to my sister it will certainly be some time before I see her again) to Germany too that in its boorish and self-righteous way seemed peaceable to me when are you in agreement with a country when you stay when you go back there while I was still in Berlin I discovered that I was looking for rapport with Lotta whom I hadn't seen since the memorial ceremony in New York

on my penultimate day in Berlin

when everything had been settled (as you can say when it's a matter of nothing left)

we talked about Sabrina for the one and only time after we'd talked about my mother who had grown very fond of her American granddaughter and to the very end had sent her sensitively chosen presents that always arrived on time

Lotta said with a slightly irritated undertone that it must surely have been possible to come to Germany more often

I didn't manage to get any clearer about her relationship with Sabrina I wanted to hear about their trip together round Europe but all I was told was

that at the beginning Sabrina had been 'extremely cautious' but later on had

loosened up

when I look out of my study on the first floor of a red-brick building close to the campus every morning I see dozens of students the same age as my blonde German niece walking past in class (those 16 hours I've undertaken as a replacement at Tufts University in Boston to be nearer to Luisa and to put off any decision for another year) I hardly get any closer to them

I've learnt

to allow them that distance that is to try to treat each one with the same friendliness coming just close enough to leave them their own space but letting them sense their teacher's interest in their progress it's like doggedly staying standing on the threshold

at least that's what it used to be like now I'm just sitting

outside

on a park bench hoping they'll see me and that that'll be enough for them

Maryann Davenport (22)
Michael Berenger (24)
Jonathan Mailer (22)

Stuart jumps down from the Humvee he's driven up close to the contested bridge over the Euphrates outside Nasiriyah in a group of other Humvees and trucks that advanced more quickly than the tanks a column of black smoke rises up (on the right about five o'clock) from nothing with a thunderous explosion and a shock wave that momentarily seems to transform your teeth into shattering porcelain and your body hair into glass bristles standing on end the shrapnel from the mortar grenades has shredded one of the front tyres but appears to have done no further damage the grenades that follow land so near and are so loud that his ears don't stop ringing the ugly furious noise of rifle fire suddenly seems unreal muted as if someone had turned the sound down like on a radio and individual bullets whistle past apparently harmless as in a cartoon then all at once it's quiet as if everyone (friend and foe) were waiting for a third party or power to intervene

an athletic young man in his 20s

in one of the front rows mostly

very attentive indeed almost concentrating too hard too tensed up

as if it were more than just *Werther* a short story by Kleist or Schopenhauer's aphorisms they were dealing with he sits perfectly upright apparently under a permanent mental strain that almost makes him vibrate he's too serious too grimly determined to be original

when you've survived grenades going off at close range they say it's followed by a sense of almost unearthly serenity a dangerous illusion of godlike invulnerability lasting for several seconds or minutes

if that had gone up your asshole! Jonathan shouts from the shallow depression in the sand he has flung himself into he's the second from the right in the photo of the platoon in their quarters that shows him brandishing a large combat knife while Stuart himself (first on the right) is aiming his sub-machine gun at Michael's feet and he's pulled up his T-shirt above his nipples and with an obscene leer is holding his penis almost exactly as he is now pulling it out of his uniform trousers to urinate lying on his side in the sand outside Nasiriyah no one wants to wet themselves like a coward in the middle of the action the stimulants the adrenaline the Nescafé spooned straight out of the torn-open packet the fear the exhaustion of bodies that have been in action without sleep for 30 hours turn

everything

into a hyperreal three-dimensional film in which you feel you can see through a magnifying glass every little pebble every reflection on the metal of the guns the helmets the vehicles your comrades' every drop of sweat every little hair on your own right hand clutching the rifle trigger while the projector showing this crazy reality stops every now and then the celluloid seems to burn (no it's all digitized in high resolution already in billions of pixels from the sandy ground to the howling pure ochre sky) then suddenly starts again too fast flickers in dazzling colours

artillery fire

from their own troops explodes behind them and Jonathan for whatever stupid reason has stood up and is trying to fit a grenade into the bottom barrel of his rifle as if they'd suddenly turned off the sound

perhaps because a skinny dog with its front right leg shot to pieces is running panic-stricken towards the bridge which turns into a black-and-yellow sand caterpillar with the city behind it darkened and veiled in clouds of smoke mostly clay-brick buildings packed closely together looking as if there are no streets or squares separating them so far they've seen nothing

of Iraq

but distant dusty settlements and villages brooding wretchedly in the sand a country apparently only inhabited by sharpshooters lying in ambush bent old women swathed in black mad or completely fearless peasants driving their sheep and goats straight through the columns of tanks and trucks

what do you think

will get better if you join the marines

the Herr Professor asks one day in a seminar room that all the students apart from Stuart have just left he's standing up straight and as always he's wearing a polo shirt that shows off his muscular arms but his hands clamp the edge of the desk in a clothes-peg manner like a grade-school pupil why am I arguing with him but it won't be a proper argument not even a discussion I'm just curious and embarrassed because he has told me he's going into the army instead of just disappearing what does he expect of me

his young regular features below his thick black hair are pale and look somewhat puffy otherwise you could call him a pretty boy at least until you see the touch of bitterness or outrage the signs of a lack of fulfilment (perhaps that alone) that he's presumably now trying to leave behind him

I can never calm down I'm always alone even when I have a girlfriend even when I'm playing sport nothing's enough to calm me down and then on the other hand nothing gets me excited enough when that's what I want there's never anything that doesn't leave a terribly depressing taste in my mouth boredom or loneliness you'd say ennui but I'm not blasé it's just

this ridiculous life and it goes on and on

d'you understand?

at this point one should have (I should have) taken a broader view but no suitable writer or philosopher happened to occur to me whom I could have quoted so as not to make it too personal maybe he found the answer

to this ridiculous life

outside Nasiriyah things becoming compact in euphoria and mortal danger and fear in a minute he'll stand up and run the 20 yards forward to the next Humvee for a moment the stony sandy ground seems to him like that beach at Cape Cod where two months ago they were lying in almost the same formation (Jonathan on the left Michael on the right) in Bermuda shorts with any amount of cans of beer sunglasses the shining tear-shaped mini headphones of their MP3 players in their ears

a tiny animal a kind of sand-hopper or a little mustard-coloured spider perhaps attempting to climb the trickling sand of the side of the depression into which he's breathing

these idiots we ought to—

says Michael who's one of the guys for whom killing and being allowed to kill and having to kill is the great kick the express main reason for his being in the marines

what're you saying we ought to what you can see

is the red hole in Michael's neck you jump up but there's a kind of pink sun in the way which tears things apart and becomes unbearably bright

friendly

fire

is what they'll call it later on

Stuart Weingart (24)

We (Sami and I)

will have to go back to Wasiriya by the end of this semester at the very latest and who knows for how long

at first it was the bombs in the air that drove us together now it's the wolves in the streets who rob abduct shoot down people force you to wear a headscarf call you a whore after they've raped you I'll perhaps be able to go to the university for two or three more weeks before they

hide me again

in our family home

where everything began with Yasmin's wedding with her cowardly bridegroom Qasim and the Major I wouldn't want to lie under the bed and be crushed any more but

on top

with you

Beloved but I foundered I wailed put my fists over my ears gnawed my knuckles doubled up in fury fear pain no more flying up no more fantasy of rising into the air the king's proud dhow would be shot to pieces in no time at all in that crazy sky over Baghdad we had to live beneath black from the burning oil red from the violent sandstorms with dazzling silvery flashes in the bright blue mornings a howling and booming lid under which we sweltered a tombstone pressing down on us nights of murky purple choking on tar dye through which fiery cracks came right into our cramped entrails

we simply could not imagine it

when we sat in the sun (over 18 months ago) across from one another on the roofs of the old houses

and when we said goodbye to one another at school more than a third of the class didn't turn up some they said had fled with their families to the north or to Syria or Jordan I could only write to Eren and Huda gave me one last intense sad furious embrace there was nothing we could do but let ourselves

be bombed into freedom

it'll turn out all right Huda whispered to me your sister

came back too

what a comfort

a black bird feathers plucked silent and trembling

it happened during one of our PRESIDENT'S great amnesties (presumably his last) he had a whole lot of murderers swindlers thieves and completely innocent people released

THE FATHER OF HIS PEOPLE

The father of his people
comes in through the door.
He gives you a new refrigerator.
He cuts open your mother's wrists.
He brings a new television
and electricity
that he wires to your brother's head.
Today's a holiday.
Specialities are tossed into hot fat.
Sing for him.

it was only a few days ago that Tariq showed me this poem he and Uncle Munir had gone to collect Yasmin the prison was almost empty already only a few relations and unkempt prisoners were still wandering round they eventually found

Yasmin as if

crushed on the floor of a cell

she remained silent in her little room beside my parents' in Wasiriya two specialists (friends of my father's) came to see her she remained silent my mother cleaned her wounds her feet had been almost drilled right through her arms and hips were burnt she remained silent entirely self-absorbed although she took all the medicines father could get hold of without complaint sometimes

I sat beside her where she was huddled up on the floor she seemed to like it when I was just close enough not quite to touch her my proud sister all curled up and emaciated once she stroked my face in a clumsy childlike way soon I couldn't bring myself to talk to her and to see the way she started it was better to remain silent as well and in our silence it sometimes seemed to me as if we were hearing the same voice or the same music or as if it were all right now sitting

like this

in a bright room on a clean carpet in a quiet corner

making terribly childlike rocking motions with our upper bodies for hours on end I wondered whether she was looking in bewilderment at her own past at herself as a proud hawk as a feted bride as a scientist in the lab as a wife bored with her insipid husband who out of sheer insane exuberance takes a dangerous lover from the army

every explosion every rocket howling towards us every bomb making the walls of the district tremble was bringing us closer to the day when we could avenge ourselves the Major would soon be nothing more than an ordinary civilian

Sami said a Kalashnikov cost 20 or 30 dollars in Saddam City and it wouldn't be long before he'd bought one leave us

in peace

my sister (as I firmly believe) said

without a word it's enough

to have been spared and to let life go by

without pain

nothing is more wonderful than a flower

that lives on in the fire

perhaps Yasmin could slowly recover get back on her feet again even though her silence tormented us with the thought of the unspeakable torture

but then she suddenly screamed it was on the seventh night of bombing her American

SHOCK-AND-AWE therapist

had thought up something special loud detonations with unpredictable pauses between them the sandstorm howling in through the open windows with blankets over them and at three in the morning there was a surreal hard sharply defined bang of despicable piercing violence that was so close and so inescapable so nasty so excessive and penetrating that we could do nothing but quiver with outrage and then Yasmin finally cried out and after that she spoke again though only in French

she recognized us all and called Farida *Maman* and me *MaSoeur* she also recognized her aunts and female cousins only the men (Sami included) had no names

on one of the days of bombing Yasmin comforted our seven-year-old niece Nuha who clung on to her as she was going past the living room almost all those present were startled without exactly knowing why and when Yasmin called her

MaPetite

and took her in her arms as any other grown-up would have done it occurred to me that she had first heard bombs when she herself was seven during the war against the Persians and that I too was seven when the first American bombs fell on Baghdad

today precisely calculated remote-controlled via satellites with intelligent power modules Sami had announced at the beginning of the attack he was in high spirits cheerful in an almost crazy way as if he simply enjoyed the whole immense computer game we were involved in since he barked at me like that in front of Nabil (why are you always talking to him) I've noticed his downy moustache I'm losing my dear childhood friend bit by bit to my brother who's growing into a man

after a week of war however

he felt like the rest of us in my father's extended family who looked more and more tired more and more drained when we met in Uncle Munir's living room to eat and watch TV he runs the electrical shop if there were too many of us we ate in two shifts and camped out on the big three-piece suite there were power cuts more and more often and then the generator only supplied the core area of the house but the large screen was always on so the women and children gathered in front of that the men too since hardly any of them went out to work any more Uncle Munir and Aunt Jamila held court in their wing chairs Uncle Fuad and Aunt Fatima sat on a couch beside my mother Aunt Aisha who was childless and could do the bookkeeping with her husband Ahmed she at least still had something to keep her busy and often just stood in the doorway cracking her fingers while Uncle Munir's youngest son Abdullah his wife Nawal and their three children lay on the carpets beside Miral and Sara who are my age and their younger brothers Rashid and Mahmud it seemed to us

as if (in this gathering) nothing could happen to us as if we were protected by the communal meals and cooking the crush in the cramped bathrooms the jokes the quarrels the mixing of smells and the worries about a fate like that of the family a few streets away whose house had been destroyed by a rocket (possibly in the hard angry explosion that had made Yasmin cry out) only the father still a young man had survived he kept pointing in bewilderment at the smoking ruins behind him beneath which his wife and his three daughters were buried can you say buried when

in a single second

everything is crushed by a lightning bolt we saw

bleeding and screaming patients in a hospital 10 minutes away from us the TV was like a periscope view of the horrors in the sea of war right outside our door children with legs torn off on Al Jazeera charred soldiers sitting in a jeep looking as if they were made of lava and ashes fire and blood flickering pictures from the BBC that stabilize while the state television became more and more threadbare and insane the PRESIDENT as an old and feeble copy of himself in front of a blue curtain calling on us to fight with our bare hands patriotic dance groups and choirs looking forward to the day when the heads of Bush and Blair would roll across the ground while in between numbers a surgeon in a hospital near al-Hillah (we'd been there not long ago I'd slept by my mother's side outside the ruins of Babylon) brandished his scalpel and shouted at the camera that after 40 operations it was as blunt as a breadknife

the mothers

as long as they still had the strength immediately stepped in and took the little ones out of our Bedouin camp in front of the television from which we couldn't tear ourselves away the crazed eye on the crazy world which was our home the storyteller of Baghdad was al-Sahhaf the

MINISTER OF INFORMATION

Baghdad Bob in his olive-green uniform and black beret sitting in front of a completely white reality-free map of the world announcing terrible losses of the aggressors and the imminent demise of the American boa constrictor in the desert the unbelievable victories of our troops even if a tank were rolling over him he'd still announce that everything was OK after all he's the last Iraqi anti-tank mine growled Uncle Munir in whose powerful old hands I'd never before seen prayer beads

for half days at a time we watched videos of old Hollywood films schmaltzy Egyptian romantic comedies endless Disney cartoons with the children to calm them down one fairy tale after the other until we didn't care at all about any news item and thought the sound of exploding bombs just came from the loudspeakers of our television

my mother didn't watch television she read she looked after Yasmin she cooked and washed up without showing any strong feelings she leafed through the Koran and sometimes I simply sat down beside her on the bed in the narrow room she and Tariq had to make do with we'll see all this through she would say whenever she felt I was looking for comfort

in stories and computer games (Sami and his male cousins as soon as the electricity came back) in Yasmin's hours of rocking motion that often made me want to scream out loud to scream against getting used to her impassive lost trance-like manner to the loss of her arrogant glittering personality

they're not out to get us not the civilians otherwise we'd all long since be dead calm down wait and see

my father keeps saying they're not out to get us we'll see this through we spent hours swaying in the dark clinging on to the shimmer of the screens while the walls of the house trembled they weren't out to get us we'll see this through the double-cuckoo clock of my great invulnerable parents who clearly became invisible out in the streets and the shrapnel and bullets passed through them for Farida went shopping (while there were still things to buy and as soon as there were any again) and Tariq worked almost every day in the nearby practice of a colleague they walked past the burning oil pits machine-gun emplacements and barbed-wire defences of the soldiers and fedayeen as if the men were merely puffed-up self-important toy figures (were they any more than that no one could believe how quickly the whole immense machinery disintegrated after it had pressed down on us for years like a sheet of lead squeezing the blood out of our bodies)

after three weeks

we were as jumpy and crazy as the state television in the iterative loops of the nights of bombing the same repeated stories of my cousins Miral and Sara with whom I shared a room depressed me our brains suffered from interruptions to transmission as well sometimes I talked without realizing we dug out the fitness video of an American supermodel that had been made in Manhattan a few sequences were filmed in front of a red water tank on the roof and you could see all the skyscrapers spreading out in endless echelons and again and again among them the still undamaged towers of the World Trade Center in the cramped room the door of which we barricaded we three 20-year-olds tried to copy at least some of the exercises that didn't require too much space so as not to be completely stiff and ungainly when

we were bombed to death but (they're not out to get us)

nothing

happened to us we only heard

about people who'd been injured acquaintances who'd lost someone loss I thought

when shaken by the detonations I lay pressed up between my cousins with my hands over my ears

was just another thing you had to get used to we'd been through that already

for that was how we'd come into this world I'd stopped reading the Koran ages ago (because I take after my father that's all) but I often thought that it said there that

we'd already been dead

before we were born

and I didn't remember any kind of torment or pain I didn't have to go to school any more or to study or to think about the university or about London or about you whom I'd lost without ever even touching him

the last call

before the telephone network in our district broke down was unexpectedly from you you'd promised Tariq to keep an eye on our house you were calling from friends whose telephone was still working everything was OK in the old house in Betawiyn that we'd left locked up only

Abu Yusuf

the father and gardener from next door who'd planted the orange and ginkgo trees on his roof and occasionally used to pick up stocky squirming little Ahmed as if he were going to smack his bottom

was dead

he'd been found by his parents almost burnt to a cinder beside his blue VW in the garden of their house in Musayyib which he'd regularly tended during the night a group of helicopters had attacked soldiers of our army who were encamped in a nearby palm grove they weren't out to get us here in Collateral-land I couldn't sleep for two nights the thought of Ahmed and Hind were painful as if I were trying to sleep among thorn bushes we're

sitting in the sun on the warm stone walls of the roof and can't imagine anything

Abdullah (my oldest living cousin Nuha's father) was a soldier he had to defend one of the bridges over the Tigris and Nawal gave him a plastic bag with civilian clothes which he was to put on when the time came we couldn't imagine something like that would be possible in Iraq that the generals majors commanders and so on would simply disappear or go home

in place of the little satellite dish concealed under a projection of the roof Uncle Fuad suddenly installed a large brand-new one on the roof until then he'd only been allowed to keep it in store to sell to authorized highups in the party immediately we saw

the chic black security advisor in a carnation-red suit (on BBC) beside her Mr Bush and one press of the button later a 12-year-old Baghdad boy with a bandaged head cursing him he was lying in a barrel-shaped tent his upper body burnt instead of arms he had two stumps wrapped in white he shouted that he'd kill himself if the doctors couldn't give him new hands

Mr Bush didn't need to imagine someone like that (things like that) all the dead and the maimed over whose bodies HE was liberating us everyone in our family hated Saddam Uncle Munir's eldest son Khalid died in the barracks under circumstances that were never cleared up Farida's younger sister Fatima died in 1991 together with her three children when they were after her husband who they claimed had taken part in a Shiite uprising and whom they shot at their house with a tank

only during the nights when we almost went mad at the thought of Yasmin being tortured

did I have sufficient hatred to wish for a war like this

as we heard that the Americans were already at the airport Uncle Fuad came into the living room looking pale and told us that an hour ago he'd seen Saddam himself right outside the Abu Hanifa Mosque in uniform with a gun belt and amber prayer beads round his neck surrounded by bodyguards and cheering supporters

that wasn't Saddam that was al-Sahhaf disguised as a gorilla and it wasn't a gun but a banana my father said and from that moment on

I became confident again for since Yasmin was abducted I hadn't heard any jokes of that kind from him and I began

to imagine

that things might really change

on that same evening they pulled down Saddam's statue in Paradise Square we watched it again and again on three channels almost like the planes crashing into the World Trade Center 9 April as a response to 9/11 only the way it fell off the plinth was

so strangely banal so mechanical and slow you never had an overall view of the wide square framed in its colonnade nor of the toppling itself from any distance so that you couldn't avoid feeling you were watching a staged celebration I'd gone past there so often when I went for a walk with my parents to Abu Nuwas Street or Karrada they threw stones and shoes at the dark statue in its bronze pinstriped suit raising its right arm in its grandiose fashion they'd put a thick hemp rope round its neck and pulled at it presumably to no effect and then attacked the high tiled plinth with hammers or pickaxes which hardly caused anything more than a kind of superficial wound (so much for the Iraqi contribution

Tariq said)

but its hollow legs tore at the knees after the American soldiers had draped a US flag over HIS face and put a steel chain round HIS neck which they pulled on with a tank a little boy used his shoes to beat the cut-off head that some of our people were dragging through the streets by the chain

it was odd that none of us felt any real pleasure in its fall even though we took it as a good omen most of us had an uneasy feeling we were just standing or rather sitting there helplessly perhaps it was connected with the fact that we knew that

HE

was still alive and that morning had strolled across Baghdad not far away I think that Sami and I were most pleased for Yasmin's sake alone and perhaps also because in our house in Betawiyn hardly a day had passed without Tariq cursing Saddam once he was sure we wouldn't let something slip at school or to the neighbours while in the old family home where they sold radios televisions aerials and recently also PCs they had always had to be extremely careful Uncle Munir (the oldest of the brothers) was a real

tightrope-walker

Tariq told us and now the rope was tied round Saddam's neck in the night of 9 April I dreamt that I

would myself fall from a plinth

right onto my rigid right arm but then

there was suddenly a dance going on at which Eren Huda and I were wearing short skirts and dancing rock 'n' roll just as in an Elvis Presley film I couldn't stop

imagining things that were similarly unimaginable like the futuristic Babylon I hadn't managed to construct in my imagination since the war had come so close

but there were enough real good and bad things happening which in the contractions of fear during the bombing I hadn't thought possible even in the nine months during which the PRESIDENT was sought and remained in hiding during that odd absent pregnancy at the end of which he gave birth to himself anew as a coward and a mole

so

for the second time in my life after Yasmin's abduction I saw my father beside himself when he told us that plunderers had taken the bedsteads and mattresses away from under seriously wounded and dying victims of the war

so the day came

when accompanied by my mother I was allowed to leave the house and walked along the streets covered in debris and broken glass and saw the cars that unbridled force had flung over onto their roofs and my first bomb crater right next to a half-demolished restaurant (HE was said to have eaten there) and

so

an actual American tank appeared with rucksacks in camouflage colours strapped to the outside and an open jeep surrounded by children snatching at sweets there was a black soldier in it and one that looked Asiatic and the driver reminded me of one of my

inventions

with whom I had danced on Paradise Square to Elvis Presley music a pretty sweaty boy freckled and with ginger hair under his helmet that was half slipping off

and so

Mr Bush appeared

in a pilot's uniform on an aircraft carrier off the coast of California on which he'd been set down by a fighter plane (as my father ascertained a few days and editions of the paper later such things won't leave him in peace) beneath a huge banner

MISSION ACCOMPLISHED

thus I went back to our school again at the beginning of May and at least heard that the broken desks the blackboards torn from the walls the smashed windowpanes would be replaced by UNESCO and an English aid organization in the sweltering heat

I had my last lessons

firstly school uniform was no longer compulsory secondly no hymns to Saddam were sung in the morning thirdly the Baath man with the X-ray eyes was no longer there nor the headmaster fourthly the

FRIENDLY CONVERSATIONS

of future school-leavers with the PARTY (party) were cancelled and fifthly Mr Basim was the new (interim) headmaster and not as we had hoped Uncle Mahmud nor Mrs Jadallah who however was teaching more and more English and day by day stood more and more upright and soon became un-bearable as if she were exchanging postcards with Tony Blair himself whose terror-struck face

(together with that of George Bush) disappeared behind four rows of neatly stuck posters for long-gone folk concerts together with the sabre-wielding Saddam though we could never be sure he wouldn't soon be cutting with his blade through the thin layer of glue smeared over him and the paper of the posters to ride out as a fedayeen against the Americans and English

the power cuts continued the taps ran dry for hours on end there were new pots of paint by the dilapidated avocado-green walls but no one took the lids off there were only 12 of us left in the final-year class most of us took our headscarves off as soon as we were inside the school building but four kept their abayas on for which Huda would have spat at them but from Lebanon it's too far away even for her spit and fury I

miss her more than Eren for the first time I was furious with Shiruk who as always had organized everything (their flight before the war began) perfectly and like the other directors of the National Museum had left all its treasures that had not been hidden in the store rooms in time in the care of a few hapless minor employees and therefore at the mercy of the plunderers

I took my exam (chemistry: carbohydrates and sugar no oil) the old mosaic in the courtyard showing the Thames and Big Ben was shining again when I left the school building for the last time on the wall of the cinema that had been repainted and had two new showcases fixed to it the spot that earlier on had eaten away Saddam's left eye still kept coming through the blind no

the blind-making

spot which illness does it stand for

there are some things you can't believe even though they're definitely going to happen or at least are highly probable you don't even believe them when they do happen and are there before your very eyes it was like that with this whole war or just on the day I finished school

they'd never have let you go to university the whole family would have been subjected to more and more harassment after what happened with Yasmin

said Uncle Munir the tightrope-walker with the massive nose patient laugh and almost black eyes he occasionally even beats my father at chess in June he suddenly opened a wooden trapdoor in the garden and brought out a little box with 15 brand-new Thuraya satellite telephones each one of which would once have brought a death sentence and now at least a month's income after most of the telephone exchanges had been destroyed people often went to visit one another and wrote letters even though you could never tell how long they would take to arrive I got long disconsolate despairing letters from Hind each one with a closely written sheet from you enclosed

I'd never have thought I would go past Paradise Square (now Liberation Square) and only see the bottom of the president's legs on the plinth with the steel wires sticking out like torn sinews you can see bombed palaces and the shelled headquarters of the secret service like a film in which astonishingly you're (still) living and in which in the middle of a market in Baghdad a suicide bomber suddenly blows himself up

we must turn our faces to the light we must see the calm and perfect sea through the shadows of violence

you wrote to me shortly after I finished school

I won't go to London I can go to university here we'll soon see one another again in Betawiyn I replied relieved happy without being able to show it the bribes for Yasmin's warders and torturers had taken more than half our savings the villa in Mosul that was positively riddled with bullet holes was a worthy mausoleum for Saddam's sons Uday and Qusay (an adolescent grandson lying underneath a bed with a Kalashnikov was also shot who can write his crazy life)

I hope HE's got a TV in the hole where HE's hiding I hope HE sees that Nawal said as if she had been able to see a few months into the future to the night of 13 December on which HE appeared on the screen once again as a

rat-man with a matted shaggy beard old weak cowardly cowering dragged out by powerful arms and hands in blue plastic gloves forcing open his jaws and shining a torch down the monster's maw where the bodies of hundreds of thousands were rotting

it's Nebuchadnezzar my father said but only he and I knew the biblical prophecy pictures of HIM unkempt and in his underclothes appeared in the American and British tabloids that quickly found their way to us that repulsive brute ever since I've been able to think and yet I felt

what? not pity not regret more of a

gnawing embarrassment

a revolting uncomfortable

presence

sticking to you

it doesn't stop and the way it stops isn't good you wrote (Beloved) in one of your beautiful letters that took two weeks for 15 kilometres the distance I used to travel so easily and simply with Huda on the top deck of the bus

now

I'm packing my bag for the university perhaps for the last time Professor Fahmi had something important to tell us today and in general that means bad news

at the end of the semester we're moving back to Wasiriya anyway Tariq made that absolutely clear and the strange household we've been for three months here (the first four weekdays in Betawiyn Tariq because of the practice Sami because of school and I because of the shorter journey to the university) will be no more there were

days when I enjoyed cooking for the two men taking them freshly brewed tea giving them shopping lists in Wasiriya I'll only be able to help the older women there the cooking's mostly done by Nawal and my mother who stayed with Yasmin in the big house all the time (with the exception of that mad expedition)

you didn't come up on the roof (Beloved)

but we'll see one another soon

after this journey on the minibus that's going to stop at the next crossroads I almost

forgot my bag

Ali Baba was here

they ought to have scrawled that on the walls

for more than a year Iraqi civilians and US soldiers have been communicating by shouting Ali Baba at the predation of plunderers even though the worthy Ali was not a robber (at most a robber of robbers) nor they say was he originally a character in our collection of Arabian stories but let's just take it as a comforting symptom of intercultural solidarity though that's not much use to me

given the devastation of my practice

the best I can do is to tell myself that I was going to close it down this week anyway and the Ali Babas stealing my old PC together with its Japanese dot matrix printer the petty cash most of my stock of medicines all the instruments that seemed valuable or were just shiny and even a doctor's coat and a rickety trolley for files

has only speeded things up and made it easier for me and yet you can't stop yourself feeling injured or even raped despite the fact that the violence was directed against things you slump down in your old practice chair at half past eight in the morning and stare at the floor turned into a rubbish heap with torn-out files and the contents tipped-out of a drawer and the broken drawer itself and tell yourself

this is your country and

THAT'S WHAT YOU WANTED

when they abducted your elder daughter from her apparently comfortable life to drag her off to the hate-filled dark interior of the country the Hades of a carnivorous underground world the whole

eruption of violence

we now see every day seems to me to be the underground hatred emerging in a volcanic outburst releasing the lava that had been seething below the surface for 30 years but it's not that easy at the moment everything seems to have become much worse than it was what is easy to see (write the PRESIDENT another pointless letter) is that any country is rotten inside if it turns its prisons into dungeons and its warders into torturers the

orange overalls of Guantánamo Bay

that

hooded man wired up with electric-shock cables on the crate the

pyramids of naked people

in Abu Ghraib

will etch themselves on the minds of the so-called free world like the emblem of the burning Towers and it doesn't help much that it is justified to say that these were just the forecourts (aftercourts rather) of the hell that was Saddam's torture-chamber system with its routine procedures of bestial murders and tens of thousands of victims who can hardly be traced any more but

I saw such dungeons and I'm making enquiries

when after those desperate weeks during which my life consisted of nothing but depression rage self-reproaches and thoughts of suicide that automatically ruled themselves out

I could collect my daughter a whimpering bundle on the bare concrete floor of a cell used for a dozen women I swore two things

to help to count the victims of the (*ancien*) regime and

to rejoice in the bombs

that would get rid of it

I gave up the latter oath when Yasmin started screaming at night during the air raids and went over to gritting my teeth and telling people to look forward to the future which so many no longer have I'm persevering with the investigations for in a villa in Mansur we found the records of torture and destruction of the victims the head count of terror piled up for a fire (all this must sound familiar to you my friend) which we're now sorting through cataloguing recording on computers keeping them out of the arrogant clutches of the Americans after two attacks on our guards we had to take them to a new hidden documentation centre I write reports on the possible causes of death I help with the counting and with proofs

who would be so bold as to answer the question

whether the fall of the PRESIDENT was worth 10 or 100,000 lives George Bush was clearly vouchsafed the answer he even seems to have some reserves however we too will have to answer that question some day and those who come after us

could contradict us (enjoying their invulnerability in this our present)

Ali rings me

he's also working as a medical expert for an organization that is trying to establish the so-called human cost of war and occupation I think that is also indispensable it is my belief that we should

remember EVERYTHING

here in this country of all places we will also for ever think of the

PLASTIC TURKEY

with which the PRESIDENT played at Thanksgiving last November in the middle of Baghdad I wish that afterwards he'd chanced upon one of the provisional cold-storage units where we had to store the bodies among blocks of ice like fish bleeding from the hook and just dumped there

how practical

Ali says when I tell him about my wrecked practice he's going to come round in the early evening so we can have a drink to his Baba namesake from a bottle of Scotch whisky a patient's just given him I haven't touched alcohol since Yasmin was arrested I still feel as if I ought to

go soberly insane (like all those pious types the place has been teeming with recently) when I

can't walk round my own city carrying my doctor's bag because some-one might think I look like a possibly lucrative kidnap victim

my farewell to my practice (says Ali) is a decisive

break

and perhaps he had to say that to make what's happened clearer to me it's as if you could see everything clearly before you but then someone came along and tore one piece of transparent film after the other away from your eyes without the picture of destruction changing there's now no

protective skin

there are too many bodies I've tried to repair with inadequate means I'm simply too old to go on putting myself wholeheartedly and ineffectively under strain give me a fat grateful

PLASTIC PATIENT

and put me on television among these ruins here

one of the last transparent layers separating me from chaos and total inner defeat is

activity

for I have never been a mere onlooker but have tried to heal people even if it often looked as if I were making them just about well enough to plunge into the next battle now

I'm going to withdraw completely to Wasiriya and as the semi-doctor that is all I now want to be spend three days a week running the practice of a similarly ageing and exhausted colleague so that it will leave me time to continue

counting

and to finally take proper care of my family I hardly dare look at them because they see me as a workaholic ghost (but I'm only running away) in a bent frame by my feet and only held by splinters of glass as if in the wide-open jaws of a lion is the colour photograph from 1990 that shows Farida and me behind our three children arranged in order of height with the laughing five-year-old Sami placed (as a man) in front of me Muna seeming strangely gloomy and Yasmin in a nowadays unimaginable European-looking summer outfit with the nowadays equally unimaginable radiant appearance of invulnerability already taller than her mother who in her early 40s seems to me to look exactly the same as now (since I have assiduously stored her like that in my divan of images it doesn't make much difference even when I'm lying beside her) while the black-haired man with the moustache on her right is someone I

don't know or have forgotten I genuinely can't remember

having posed for this photograph even though we must have been in a proper studio I'm sure we wanted to create an indestructible memory a soap-bubble monument before Yasmin went to Paris that could float through the years to our grandchildren as long as it didn't come across a pin a flame a red-hot iron rod

why can't I remember? was I a stuffed dummy or had they found a double like the unselfish committed guy they stuck in a hole in Tikrit while HE was waiting for a favourable opportunity to get his own back on us all (there are at least half a dozen of my patients who believe that)

perhaps my family double (the other Tariq) would have kept closer to my only son who to me seems too confused too head-in-the-clouds too unstable during the last years of the dictatorship I relied on him not to say the wrong thing at school or in the neighbourhood and now he's suddenly telling me that the mass graves in the south that are being opened up with the cameras running don't contain people murdered by Saddam but the secretly buried victims of the first American invasion

when he watches a playing field in Fallujah being turned into a mass grave on the screen you can understand his susceptibility to such ideas I'll talk to him a lot more now I can't just abandon him to the Internet and his dubious friends

I still haven't yet told him or Muna that we'll be going back to Wasiriya this week

for reasons of security and

for good I almost told myself this apparent finality is a result of the sight of my torn-up files, pulled-out drawers emptied packets of medicine

I've had my practice here for seven years too short a time to be really sentimental a fortnight ago I put up the notice that I was going to close the practice (on the inside of the door with three locks Ali Baba obviously read the mirror writing through the wood) but even today incorrigible patients keep coming the whole morning and in the afternoon and so

I sort out the documents on the floor treat a few minor complaints send the serious cases to colleagues receive insults sympathy gifts and can finally ring up my big brother Munir to tell him that Muna Sami and I will be returning to the tribal tent tomorrow or the day after

I find it humbling and moving

how delighted he is to have me back under his wing all I needed was for them to call me Moshel again for the family business was booming as during the Six Day War except that instead of the radios that sent me to study in Paris we now have mobile phones PCs printers scanners routers and so on making our camels and our women fat with the only difference that this war will probably go on for six years after its official end and that I

the scholarly spoilt child

have to find refuge with my tribe again precisely what we ambitious intellectuals and graduates once despised the Berberization of supposedly modern society and now it's happening again and we can't avoid letting ourselves fall into the last safe nets at least

nowadays emails from all over the world arrive and Hussein the wild painter in Paris who had become a not very happy gallery-owner in Nantes bombards me with questions about our white blood-spattered patch in the map across which exile sends its horrified satellites and unmanned probes on the subject of Moshel that occurred to him spontaneously because he likes to remember his extravagant caricatures of poor harassed Tariq with the Israeli mini fighter-bombers buzzing round his head and now he's added the story of Dayan's 87-year-old widow who for decades has selflessly devoted her energies to helping Palestinians in Israel and the occupied areas

so good people live longer or devoting yourself to something (the OTHERS) gives you a long life

I think and I could imagine hanging up this axiom as a motto precisely on the spot where the miraculously dematerialized portrait of the president has left a lighter rectangle above the forced-open and dented metal cabinet with his calligraphic skill Sami could have designed the maxim it's been months since I saw him draw a single character or is it since Ahmed died whose death he had to witness I've

come through three wars unscathed but

my children were burnt

now I'll get back closer to them even if it means my family will smother me with its embraces and entanglements we never imagined anything so tribal (my tribe has more than 10,000 members) in our days as newly qualified smart junior doctors in white shirts and sunglasses at our fish barbecues in the Club forget it

breathe in deeply take your clothes off Doctor outside is the stench of the sewers that haven't been repaired for a year (send a letter cancelling the contract with the big American firm that's pocketed a billion for doing nothing here up to now) we have people infected with cholera and typhoid as in the jolliest embargo days but the new gleaming white toxic-waste incineration plant from Cambridge–Massachusetts behind the clinic in Zafaraniyah is puffing out smoke that is calming as marijuana over the houses as I observed last week when visiting a colleague

dismissing Laila was the hardest part for the patients all keep reappearing in the ever-same form of the downtrodden masses that want to be made immortal by a divine white coat (come on admit that you will miss some of them especially the long-term patients who had no money left and brought you presents) when Laila said goodbye yesterday she once again offered to come out to work in Wasiriya but to expect her to brave Rashid Street or Khulafa Street three times a week would be almost criminal what have things come to O God send something down to us like

the LETTER she handed me as a farewell gift a truly

divine miracle

46 pale and expressive still with firm breasts and inviting kohl-rimmed eyes her flattened nose (you could break it and do it up with a couple of shavings from her pelvis and—*voilà*, who apart from Ali would have

immediately thought up such a neat idea) her only impediment in the beauty contests of her young days she

almost gave me a parting embrace which would naturally have been going much too far so she just swung round while I was standing by the filing cabinet and accidentally on purpose hit me on the arm with one breast and gave me

the splendid LETTER FROM THE HIGHEST AUTHORITY and a come-hither look

to which I gave a mute reply which was however only half honest for my look in return merely said that I'd always simply been too tired

while I ought to have said: too tired and still too much in love with my own wife to want to start worrying about the ranking of the three wives we are allowed if I were asked

what for me had been the eeriest moment of the war I wouldn't hesitate to say that afternoon the previous April when my naive brother Fuad pale with fright had received me in the family home with the news that

Farida had taken Yasmin in order to make

a pilgrimage on foot to Karbala with her (three days over 100 kilometres)

I immediately took a taxi and almost as immediately was stuck in a demonstration of supporters of Muqtada al-Sadr whom the American substitute king here had just outlawed so that they were celebrating Muharram by dancing and waving home-made dummy explosives (some of them real) and singing the praises of the US

we drove along checking the procession of pilgrims that had formed on the side of the highway columns of flag-wavers packs of singing sanctimonious zealots enthusiasts on crutches others barefoot in white penitential robes women in abayas dancing ecstatically with pickups Humvees gravel trucks tanks and the usual rust buckets thundering past at hardly any distance from them

after two hours of this I had to give the taxi driver my last dinar and was forced to join the pilgrimage in the evening sun

shortly before a resting place soldiers of the newly reconstituted Iraqi army appeared and distributed bottles of water I ended up in a band of recreational flagellants in black habits with green headbands who belaboured their shoulders in rhythm but fortunately spared me dozens were crowding round tarpaulins and stalls to grab bread or devotional objects a few guards with Kalashnikovs but no recognizable uniform were standing round then American soldiers also mingled with the crowd in full battledress their rifles pointing at the ground and long aerials wiggling up in the air from their knapsacks and finally

at a field kitchen where as is the custom the locals distributed rice and stew free to the pilgrims

I saw my beautiful thin daughter in an abaya who looked at me timidly but very joyfully strangely relaxed also startled and liberated I couldn't quite understand it and

Farida

standing behind her holding two tin plates similarly in black and similarly

inspired

and dusty enthused or relaxed it was presumably the side effects of her religious sport that were beyond me what

was it I was going to say? I joined the queue beside her exhausted grateful furious what else and what was it I was going to say

oh yes: have you gone mad what were you thinking of bringing our sick abused daughter here forcing her into a three-day journey on foot have you forgotten the television pictures of the attacks in March are you going to set off for paradise in Karbala or give yourself a thorough whipping or split open your scalp with a butcher's knife or a scimitar while the children and religious tourists lick their ice creams

4,000 angels cried day and night at Imam Hussein's grave over his head that had been cut off over his blood that flowed from 34 sword wounds and 33 arrow wounds you could have

said but you just look at me and

we're standing by the river again as before the war I hate this wallowing in wounds this unnecessary blood (everywhere in the country there's a lack of blood for transfusions) this cult of martyrs I'm a doctor at best I see the angels' tears fine grey rain through which the pilgrims stream and the tanks roll in which the fires under the stew pots flicker and in which your face blurs as if it could actually be torn away from me for ever

only here

can we be healed you said I hadn't forgotten it's your country and perhaps you're right about everything about Karbala as well and about it possibly being easier to bear one's sorrow alone so I only said that I hoped that we would see one another again at home in four or five days' time

then I walked back to Wasiriya around midnight a US tank big as a house appeared beside me at the side of the road they say that in a monster like that you don't notice whether it's a tree or a car you're flattening the steel sides roared past me so close that half an hour later I still couldn't breathe evenly and so

almost wouldn't have lived to see this beautiful day with my practice lying in ruins at my feet and myself saying to Ali

we have to throw the Americans out but in a controlled way

an excellent idea my friend! yes, these Americans are getting to be a nuisance we ought to bring the Persians in instead or the Russians or—sorry this little bugger here's making me quite twitchy—or simply throw out the bad Americans who send their snapshots of torture home and eliminate whole families in their night-time raids and replace them with the good guys say a nice black jazz singer or only Indians and female democrats and a few grizzly bears then we ought to have a lot more of them here you can look at it that way as well for everything has two sides just like

this animal here it's

got eyes on stalks with which it sucks two different images into a single head that's a dialectical creature it can even produce the synthesis by putting its eyes together so that the images overlap a Hegelian head then full of glowing scaly warts a real Sufi—where were we now? send Uncle Sam packing but I can see you're less confused than I am

says Ali and swivels round with his burden and its strange jerky movements (they imitate leaves in the wind) on the office chair Laila chose years ago from the furniture dealer round the corner the red imitation leather of the seat has been slit open diagonally which my clearly overworked friend shaken about by theses and antitheses only notices now as a bizarre hand or claw of the pet on his lap reaches down between his legs leaving two fingers on the seat like a thumb while three grasp the edge in a way that looks rather considered the intense colours of its scaly skin remind me of something

you don't look well (I say it sounds more reproachful than intended)

thank you and the same to you

he replies with a kind of exhausted cheerfulness this here really is a bloody disgrace but as I said over the phone looked at from a practical point of view those bastards have made it easier for you to close down here and go to Wasiriya you only have to turn your eyes in different directions like my ground-lion here and you'll see the gleam of a silver lining round the cloud of destruction so what's bothering you now my friend apart from the fact that I brought this little beast instead of the whisky I promised

what happened (he goes on) was that I was about to set off for you with the firewater when a grateful ex-patient came in with a whole 200-litre barrel not of course filled with precious single malt but with that fuel unfortunately so rare in our country for our tin camels suddenly there's so little of it about that people have started battering one another to death with their empty canisters after standing in a queue for hours we'll soon have to exchange it at one to one for whisky so that I'll have to convert my electricity generator and then spend four hours a day

operating with the best fuel in my generator Mister President! (as an Iraqi poet who wishes to remain anonymous put it) We need electricity in our houses and not up our arses and we need clean water and that without boarding

this animal here

Ali grabs the paunch of his giant chameleon and drags it over his knee and thigh back closer to the middle of his own body this animal's better off it survives with little water when it's going to spend some time roasting in the desert sun it simply blows salt snot out of its nose something even the US Army hasn't been able to teach its men so what's your problem apart from the fact that I've forgotten the whisky and now as the good host that you are you'll have to rummage round in this pile of debris to find a teabag or one of Laila's tampons

I'd no problem I said the word didn't mean anything to me any more

all I could say was

that things were simply depressing me above all the aggression and brutality everywhere the plunderers had startled me and the masses of criminals we'd hated Saddam for 30 years and hardly was he in prison than we'd started tearing ourselves apart instead of getting down to rebuilding the country I couldn't stand the sight of all those warrior types polluting our existence neither the US soldiers riding high in their tanks or on the ground in their wired-up hi-tech battledress nor the guards outside every store or office block carrying their Kalashnikovs like umbrellas nor the resistance fighters wrapped up in their headscarves who might be an old Baathist a young idiot or a traumatized man whose whole family had been annihilated the black mujahideen were getting on my nerves with their woolly hats over their faces and those Mahdi people as well with their green headbands which instead of pious quotations ought to have

The worst disease
is the idea
that gave birth to me.

written on them

what can one say to that Ali replies I'm a doctor (like you and that CIA agent they've just made prime minister) it's a virus we'll never be able to eradicate with our little pills and scalpels is that why you're looking for other means is that why you believe in this LETTER look it's going to shoot out its extrudable tongue two flaps spread out at the point grasp its prey and bon appétit—and just as it wants to swallow this fantastic LETTER it also wants to gobble up all the bloodthirsty warriors every one of whom believes his opponent is filled with nothing but foam rubber this animal has a red head a white belly and a black prehensile tail three green stars shine on it and between them the words *Allahu Akbar* but we'll have to wipe those off and replace them with new ones for they say it's the handwriting of the death-row president from the hole in the ground look it's just had a new idea and is showing the sun of Shamash above two blue stripes which stand for veins that can be slit open no for the Tigris and Euphrates and its tail is turning red-white-and-green like Kurdistan and wants to run off with Kirkuk under its arm or held in its prehensile tail Kirkuk that is statistically proven to be inhabited by 70 per cent Kurds 70 per cent Turkomans 70 per cent Arabs and 70 per cent others along with a few Chaldaeans and Assyrians all of whom demand a modest 110 per cent of the sea of oil on which the city is floating however chameleons can't shed their tails they're simply not lizards—what's that you said?

that I could understand him I said that his observations were both amusing and correct but for all that would not help me to answer the question of how I should respond to the LETTER and that seemed to me to be one of the most important questions of all that we were faced with at that moment

in order to clarify something

Ali declares with his emblematic animal jerking and darting its tongue in and out

we ought to start by enriching this peppermint tea with sufficient ethanol (I'm sure that somewhere in all this mess you've still got a phial of the non-denatured stuff after all Ali Baba can seldom read) perhaps it'll help my friend to calm down and then we should remember Jabir by the way did you know that he's been living in Amman since he was wounded by a bullet they shot through his window solely because he's a poet and writer and lived in Sadr City I mean he hadn't even begun to put the works hidden inside his head down on paper it was a pre-emptive strike of these ardent anti-Americans simply on the basis of his hypothetical function as an author and you can therefore assume they'll soon be attacking us simply because we're doctors and have the audacity to patch up their enemies

why did you bring up Jabir

to apply his theory of the giant that's why my friend Ali says holding his glass under the nose of his lap-chameleon but it quickly turns its striped scaly head away which Ali says shows that on the one hand it hadn't much sense of smell (the blasted thing didn't hear or listen very well either) but on the other was a truly refined Baghdadi well read and elegant its favourite books came from the ninth century for example *The Book of Delicate Taste and Complete Education* or *The Book of Elaborately Embroidered Garments or of Elegance and Elegant People* works whose influence one can still study everywhere in our streets today my view is that you have this highly cultured society and then the Mongols come and when the Mongols come the Shiites jump for joy but where was I

the giant or leviathan

which is of course broken burst bombed to bits so that all that is left are the colourful gleaming highly vulnerable insides of the state that has no armour any more a chameleon without protection therefore Ali explains cautiously patting the animal on the back a chameleon with a slug's skin has problems where can it find refuge for the moment there's no one you can ingratiate yourself with for the Americans only destroy things and the others have adopted a wait-and-see-attitude

so (I ask)

so it just drops out of the tree Ali says it's well known for that it can blow up its lungs like airbags so that it doesn't hit the ground hard and once it's down there—

it plays dead

correct: thanatosis my friend it disguises itself as a dead branch and waits to see what will happen

until it feels hungry or a Humvee drives over its tail (I say) but perhaps all that's too theoretical

not at all Ali retorts for if the leviathan breaks it disintegrates into lots of dwarf giants or giant dwarves and if one of them comes too close to our possum-playing chameleon quick as a flash it crawls over to him and then it's back with its family with its tribe with its mosque with its militia with its preacher with its old Baath cell

only that leaves us with the fact that all these little giants make war against one another so that there's nothing for it but to establish a new leviathan to bring the war to an end and that's why I must take the LETTER seriously and can't just wait and hope that everything will sort itself out this here (now I take too a sip of the fiery peppermint-ethanol cocktail and indicate with a wildly optimistic gesture the heap of rubble that is my practice) must be rebuilt by us ourselves after all we did build the Tower of Babel and

this time the Persians aren't going to knock it down and there aren't going to be torture chambers in its cellars I know says Ali but what I don't know is what I should be doing my skin turns red and white and green and blue I can't seen any giant whose arse I could lick with a clear conscience all I can see are the madmen and the dead and the bigmouths who hide in the Green Zone while there are more and more madmen and more and more dead

it's no use I say it's no use always being right and I stare at my oldest and best friend and the slashed seat of the office chair and I say Saddam's gone that at least is something

yes—the only weapon of mass destruction they found that we still had

the Americans will leave

like their Timberland-boot consul who's sorted things out here and is going to withdraw this month I wish they'd send over another 200,000 men and stay for another 10 years or would clear off at once the whole lot of them that's the way we chameleons are Ali sighs what can you do if you can't make up your mind do you know that they're very Arab animals? they need several wives and if there are too many in one place they kill themselves with the stress of all the territorial struggles

they're animals we're human beings

it all depends on how you see things Ali says raising his glass I'm going to go and join my wife and children in England I'll protest against Tony Blair in Piccadilly Circus and tell him nice stories about typhoid in Basra I'll take the chameleon back to my anaesthetist to whom it belongs by the way do you know why humans are mortal? God made them immortal and told the chameleon to bring us the news but it took its time and was so late that it was overtaken by a bird with the message of death but back to you my friend and your message after all the

CALIPH'S LETTER

has come so there's nothing left for me other than to point out that you're wrong I say resolutely it's the joylessness the deadly earnest the terrible burden and at the same time futility of anything we might do that torments us that

makes us furious makes us

drink medicinal alcohol with peppermint tea (the most popular drug in Iraq is still dear old Valium) makes us

after having waited for two hours in vain and with increasing concern as the twilight falls in the summer heat simply

invent

an old friend

Samira didn't come this morning

nor her father who always accompanied her as far as the road then stood there hands in his pockets and an embarrassed grin on his face until she'd got on our minibus and we can imagine reasons we're missing the morning embodiment of lonely courage for Samira was always the first to get out of the cramped bus because she was in the philosophy faculty

is! the present tense!

her institute is in the middle of an area that's been devastated by fighting Samira's our

woman on the moon

every weekday morning she walks in her calm and dignified manner wearing a headscarf light-coloured jacket and wide skirt-like trousers towards a motorway bridge that ends like a piece of torn-off cardboard directly above the top of a tree her obstacle race takes her across a rubble-strewn area the size of two football pitches past piles of rubbish and stones over twisted pieces of metal and debris overgrown with weeds flattened pillars and masonry roof-tiles flung onto the ground all of which scarcely leaves room for a narrow path between vague hedges that are beginning to grow again to a black bomb crater beside the shot-up facade of a building that has otherwise miraculously remained undamaged her institute that recalls a research station on a planet with no atmosphere hopelessly exposed to the falling meteorites in

Samira's case

do we have a new martyr or

another family that's gone into exile because they can't stand our blood-stained planet any more no matter we'll soon have to find someone to take her place in the minibus it costs six families a lot for the reasonably secure daily transport of their daughters to the university we have two young drivers who behave well but unfortunately Ali the better calmer one isn't there today

he's also the one who knows how to use the brand-new mobile phone for shortly before we get off the nervous Naji presses a button at which it immediately rings and Samira at the other end of the line tells him she's tried to contact him umpteen times she had to set off earlier that morning but he's to pick her afterwards as usual

a good start for a hot summer's day

outside the main entrance to the university there are students both male and female walking quickly and purposefully alongside one another or criss-crossing

I used to find the crush more exciting and more promising than anything else and after the war to be able to sit alone or with another girl looking through our books chatting on a bench on the campus lawn seemed absolutely improbable as if every weekday I flew to a different country given the Internet and telephone shops shooting up like mushrooms round the university the newly donated computers the more and more frequent sound of the mobiles ringing in students' bags and jackets and proudly produced we could almost feel it's an international institution although more and more women (like myself) protect themselves with headscarves and all-concealing clothes

as a SuShi

with my longing for the future Babylon

I feel uneasy in the face of the posters and appeals of the Shiite student organizations whose influence is growing more and more I wanted to study

as an Iraqi woman

not as this or that brand of believer (even though I'm in love with a would-be hauza student) I wanted to help to free our memories of Babylon from the Baathist excrement in many textbooks it's enough

if you simply tear out the last 20 pages

said Professor Fahmi for whom we're having to wait today he also showed us a delightful way they had of making Saddam look ridiculous (by including in master's or even doctoral theses long unmotivated extracts from his hollow speeches beside quotations from internationally renowned scholars and authorities on the subject) and that there had continued to be outstanding textbooks free from all ideological ballast that we could still use for example the standard work on scholarly methods in historical research and archaeology that would help us

to excavate Iraq anew

that is to remove the cladding refute the forgeries get rid of the kitsch that Baathism and Mesopotamianism had imposed on past archaeologists and early historians could finally stop tunnelling under Tikrit in search of the massive subterranean pyramid in which Saddam's great-great-great-grandfather was said to be lying right next to the Hidden Imam and they would finally be

internationally competitive and part of the international network in dialogue with the rest of the world about the latest developments in research and part of that was

to denounce the disgraceful disrespectful lack of interest the occupying troops showed for the archaeological treasures of our country tolerating and even themselves committing acts of vandalism and looting

the past

Professor Fahmi cried

was not a sealed-up dead place it was the scene of constant debate a target for those who would destroy it and consign it to oblivion not only modern Babylon had to be protected from grave-robbers and tanks heedlessly crashing through the walls

but also the ancient city that

kept on being invaded by the hordes of the future to daub the tower the temple the houses with the wrong colours or misuse them as advertising hoardings or as theatrical backdrops for absurd and embarrassing performances and not only the buildings the living inhabitants of the past were also at the mercy of future interference and needed us to be alert and self-critical in protecting them

Professor Fahmi declared

with his energetic electrifying smile inviting and spurring on each of us to be at our very best through hard work and concentrated intelligence

Professor Fahmi who actually ought to have begun his lecture or made the special announcement he told us about

30 minutes ago

is a slightly built man and wears crumpled loose-fitting suits with rimless spectacles has a small moustache and thick grey hair parted on the left at first he looks rather awkward almost comic Chaplinesque though forty no seventy years late not just half an hour

as soon as he begins speaking in polished sonorous High Arabic or refined old-fashioned-sounding Agatha Christie English (he could appear in one of her detective novels a mysterious Middle Eastern scholar a double or triple agent) you completely forget the way he looks he lifts us out of the chaotic noisy dangerous sweltering Moloch of the city even the shots from outside that keep echoing round the room as now and making us start only seem

a nuisance

in his presence

there are only 18 of us left in the semi-dark seminar room 12 men and 6 women there's a new ventilator on the ceiling it makes an unpleasant noise when it's running as if you were constantly riffling the edge of a stack of paper with your thumb at the beginning of the year there were 34 of us we rarely hear the reason for a student

leaving

sitting between nervous Fatima perspiring perfume and skinny Iqbal swathed in black apparently not moved by anything I try not to look too often at the door where Akram is sitting in his jeans and aubergine shirt if I weren't so hopelessly in love and so profoundly united with you in the dreamy yearning life locked up inside me I'd talk more often and more openly with Akram he's the best student the most casual and self-confident just imagine being a graduate couple with the same subject studying together doing your doctorates together and so on I say to Huda with whom I'm still in imaginary contact oh you two eggheads in London or Paris she mocks and pow! you'd be incredibly pregnant or he'd turn out to be a coward like that fine brother-in-law of yours who's not shown his face not even once after Yasmin was released

Professor Fahmi's assistant

suddenly comes in gives the squeaking ventilator a pained look and clutching on to a stack of paper in contrast to his usual arrogant manner now goes round like someone distributing advertising leaflets and hands each one of us the certificate for this semester's course credit it

was unfortunately not possible for Professor Fahmi to come personally he says nor was it possible for him to finish his lectures more than that he could not nor would not say

Professor Fahmi was already

abroad

it took three hours for us to find someone on the campus who told us confidentially that Fahmi had received two death threats from Shiite militia or al-Qaeda perhaps both

soon it will be the last time

that I walk round the campus I can feel it for ages now I've had to argue with Tariq after every assassination and every abduction that's reported he wants to bundle me off back to Wasiriya I go into the library again it's been given five new computers but so far no one who can link them up to the Internet and

once more I'm sitting with three other young women on the bus that quickly joins the stream of traffic on the roads that are well-maintained in this area but accelerates too tentatively and brakes too sharply as soon as a traffic light turns red or it looks as if there's an obstacle ahead two American helicopters roar over the roof of an office building not huge Apaches but smaller more manoeuvrable ones though also named after some Indian tribe Sami would know what they're called he might even have the cockpit of one in the Flight Simulator he almost only plays with now in order (at the weekend with his cousin in Wasiriya) to make various types of aeroplane crash into the World Trade Center they fly over the little island with the Statue of Liberty heading straight for the tip of Manhattan it always ends in a tangle of lines and bottle-green splinter-like shapes and an error message

sometimes you expect an error message like that to appear over the streets of Baghdad and you could press a button to make everything (what everything where to) go back what is it that

makes your little brother use the Internet that is finally accessible to watch glorious al-Qaeda attacks on American soldiers jeeps and tanks (does he also watch these beheadings) Tariq is out of touch with him he has friends you wouldn't want to talk to and I don't say anything when he goes to see them instead of

keeping an eye on me (protecting me irritating me)

it was just a journey like this one

in July last year in the sweltering heat along a side street in Ishbilya Sami and Yusuf had gone with one of Yusuf's uncles to help him transport some pieces of furniture in his pickup and little Ahmed had jumped in and and forced his way onto his elder brother's lap oddly enough

he was the first to react correctly when shots rang out some masked figures slipped across the street to be immediately followed by American soldiers in full battle gear and the white

spider's web

that shot with a bang in all directions across the windscreen of the pickup

started to bleed

and it was only because Ahmed was desperately reaching for the door handle and trying to get off Yusuf's lap that Sami realized a bullet had actually hit his uncle in the middle of the forehead and all three of them dropped out of the nearside door to the ground and lay without moving sheltering behind the truck the engine of which had stalled with a violent jerk

not to move

was certainly the best idea Sami was afraid the shots would hit the tank and set the pickup on fire but they were even more afraid that the slightest movement might incite someone to shoot they lay there as if nailed to the ground as if gigantic steel bloodhounds were panting and snorting directly over them and would sink their teeth into them at the slightest provocation until after

20 or 30 minutes they spent flat down on the road like insane sleepers while Yusuf's uncle's blood dripped onto the floor of the truck with the terrible sound of a faulty tap until it was drowned out when a radio with pop music was switched on nearby it was as if someone had reluctantly started to do the washing-up after there'd been no more shots for a while

Come on boys get out of here!

a voice above them finally said a young voice that perhaps even sounded friendly they cautiously got to their feet

The little guy too—oh shit!

Ahmed wasn't moving at all he lay so still and rolled up like a little dead animal

Sami told them after he'd spent two days sitting apathetically in the courtyard and in his room incapable of speech as Yasmin had been for so long as if he were waiting for the bullet with his name on it to hit him here why Ahmed of all people why Yusuf's uncle

the woman on the moon

comes back to us through the ruined landscape she's holding a few textbooks in the crook of her arm and walks in such a matter-of-course way with such measured steps to the end of her path through the rubble against the background of the half-destroyed motorway bridge that even you suddenly calm down and can hardly resist feeling hopeful Samira's studying several languages she's got a brain like a computer or a chess grandmaster and her broad sturdy frame seems to provide the stability it needs to protect it from any shocks

turn the music down do you want to kill us

she says to Naji the driver who looks particularly professional today in his white shirt and black trousers but drives even worse than usual especially off the main roads in the district where our two medical students have to beg set down immediately behind a row of neat houses with gardens and garages you soon get onto wide tracks full of potholes with lots of wrecked cars where people drive round in all directions as if they were on an excavation site

slowly calm down brake gently smile you idiot stop that's a checkpoint not an abduction stop good smile like that let your hands rest calmly on the steering wheel

out of the dust-veiled window I can see as if through mist in the July heat a roll of barbed wire the grey-green screen of an armoured car then uniform jackets and ammunition belts coming closer until they almost touch the glass

but Samira's calm firm voice has remotely controlled the twitchy Naji perfectly he stopped without a jolt

Students! Only women! Baghdad University! These are our books!

in the silence of a mysterious wait (we don't have to show anything else we're not told to get out we're not searched) we just keep our books and jotters held up in the air and think of all the stories we've heard of people being killed at this kind of checkpoint there were pictures on TV showing the bodies of a whole family that could only be recovered from a car riddled with bullet holes hours later my memory is terribly precise

slowly

careful

second gear what

an idiot you are pull yourself together left now watch that taxi calmly calm down now well

done

the woman from the moon leans back the sweat running down her firm face with its discreet make-up she's just saved us all (or exaggerated the danger who can say) at least I say thank you and briefly put my hand on her forearm the trembling of which startles me as much as the view of the scratched muzzle of the barrel of a machine gun that hit the bus window only a minute ago

Ahmed sitting opposite me in the sun on the Rikabis' roof

his fat little arms are bare he's mad about football players he lays his tousled head on his big sister's thighs he only lived for four months after his father's death the quiet gardener's family (Mrs Rikabi and Ahmed's grandfather) had to identify both corpses the

ginkgo and orange trees on the roof are still looked after for Hind can remember every movement of her father's hand in the little garden on the house I have to prune the ginkgo or it'll grow to be a hundred feet high she says I don't know how I always found the strength to answer her sad letters (*my father was so gentle my mother is so alone I miss Ahmed so much I can't bear the way my brother Yusuf gets angrier and angrier every day what does the girls' paradise look like*) but perhaps that helped me as well after all there was a letter from you in every envelope

in the afternoon the two houses are eerily quiet in the heat white bricks in the furnace of the city I'm the last but one to get off the bus my knees are still trembling when I was younger I used to imagine those two Babylonian lions on either side that would protect me but today I'd be afraid of them when I tell Tariq about the checkpoint (and I must do that) he'll send me back to Wasiriya since he's considering it all the time and has already told me that I can stay in Betawiyn until the end of semester at most without Professor Fahmi there's no point anyway but

what then

Sami hasn't left a note Tariq often comes back late in the night

there's no sound from the Rikabis' house things have become quiet there anyway a sour-faced elder sister of the gardener moved into one of the rooms making it possible for you to stay and your uncle to continue to pay the Rikabis the rent they so badly need

the oppressive silence of the two houses it's as if they've been left out of the noise of the city as if there were invisible insulation all round us I wash myself slowly like a baby

the orange trees on the roof have fruits

I can't keep my hands still their soapy smell does calm me down a little I know that soon they'll hide me away again and

protect

me but only imagine if you were to fly (without sails without wings) into this afternoon air

just a short way you don't need any more strength any more imagination

and as you leap something in your body will remember the garden that has been there for 1,400 years on one of the banks of the Tigris in the middle of Baghdad and that only lovers are allowed to enter the grass shines beneath you like whole fields with emeralds scattered over them the trees have white and pink blossom almonds and pomegranates oranges and figs the blossom of undreamt-of unknown fruits catches softens embraces your fall you feel smell see flowers

crocuses narcissi violets roses lilies and hyacinths anemones tulips jasmine

the poppies

of my little nights

the petal-soft smoothness the concealed

mirrors

of my body that open up there's no more day beyond that garden believe me

for today

Beloved! that's why you flew and that's why you're not speaking and why your prayers are on my lips alonetoday what has happened and what is to come is benumbed by the scent of the flowers time is resting in the narcosis of our great

moment

you're falling into

flowers and light into a sea of flowers and light and

never

were you so alive this is your most wide-awake moment and your life before and your life after will forever stay asleep

at some point

it has to happen at some point they all have to have gone and the old houses stand there empty for us as if no one were ever going to come home your heart is pounding with fear but it's not the lion of war making it shake but the female cheetah I am the hawk the eagle

the lamb beneath the lion that is not afraid they

broke my sister but now

I am here

in the fire in the flames on the summit of this afternoon the garden is a
tower above the war a pillar of blossom a green swirling waterfall only if
you leap if you fly and if you fall can you walk in it and never come

back down to earth

THE BALANCE

Does water float in the heat
      of the shimmering air?
Are the wings of the raven before your eyes
      the night?
Can the past read the wishes
      on the lips of the future?
Is the ball rising or falling
      on the balance of photography?
Clues or proofs?
      Drown of thirst.
      Starve in plenty.
      Close your eyes and see!

Even the run-down shabby look of the planes used for domestic flights can evoke nostalgia in the hyphenated American on my flight from New York City to Boston I keep getting stuck (astonishingly fortunately) in an emotional groove in which everything seems to be as it was 10 years ago as if at Logan Airport I could get into my old Ford that's long since been stolen and drive back to Amherst to a life that today seems so intact that it had to burst soon anyway like an overripe grape or a Disney figure blown up too tight

I was really impressed

Seymour said

that you sold the house in Amherst

so there's nothing (no further objects or real estate) waiting for me other than the cramped little apartment by the Tufts campus and I wouldn't have had to spend half the night in

tormented ecstatic

dreams of Amanda but it's a fact (as Seymour couldn't avoid noticing yesterday) that I grieve for Amanda as well that I have to get through the

protective shield of the feeling

that she died in a catastrophe that happened several years before Sabrina's death

to the whole extent of the simultaneous double loss

perhaps I shouldn't have had dinner with Seymour even though my transatlantic flight went from Frankfurt to New York after a two-hour wait I could have flown straight on to Boston but it was what I wanted as well Seymour and I exchange emails once a month and I don't have to feel ashamed of my need to see him even though in his life (reciprocal system of emotional coordinates) Amanda was presumably lost later than my daughter

Seymour (black short-sleeved shirt grey pants closely shaved and well groomed but paler thinner than he used to be perhaps also in better health) met me at Penn Station after the usual civilities we went out into the din of the summer evening in the Garment District at first glance the vertical lines of Sixth Avenue seemed to be out of perpendicular like pick-up sticks falling down and criss-crossing I felt it was at the same time disturbing and familiar almost like Gulliver returning to the land of giants

WAIT

FOR

WALK

SIGNAL

our rapid progress together soothed my guilty conscience it could only be Luisa I felt guilty about where had I read something connected with that in Walter Benjamin I remembered it was a meditation on the dead women of history whose charms and beauty we have never experienced nor ever will had I not come to my *Loving Goethe* project by the same route

on board an ageing plane somewhere over Connecticut I can admit to my loneliness my fear and finally my

(misplaced) annoyance with Luisa

which the previous night had made me desire Amanda again even now with my eyes open staring out of the cabin window into the steel-blue air I can call up brief arousing intermediate images it's a kind of hurried leafing back through my life but this time to the (few) women before Amanda to a few

daguerrotype miniatures

of my former physical passion

how are you REALLY Seymour asked me yesterday outside Macy's

THE WORLD'S LARGEST STORE

and I almost told him about my stupid Berlin affair in the spring of 2003 that joyless animal escape with the nurse which Luisa seemed at first to have forgiven me without making a thing of it (but how could she have got over it so quickly) the jet lag was almost making me feel drunk this tiredness that seems absurd in the early evening the pure alcohol of distorted time was going to my head and making me more and more open and affable in need of a shoulder to lean on due to my intercontinental vertigo (basically my state for the last 30 years) despite Seymour's offer I didn't want to rest but to switch over to local time straight away we could get round easily because I'd put my suitcase in a locker at Penn Station and was only carrying a daypack with the minimum I needed for an overnight stay

the park's much nicer nowadays but otherwise it's just like in the 1970s

Seymour said as we sat down at one of the green metal tables in Bryant Park I almost disputed this because in my state (it was about one in the morning and the July sun was still shining brightly through the leaves of the trees above us and onto the facade of the Public Library) I assumed the 1970s was the time when Seymour and I used to see each other so often here

a precarious economic situation and the war Seymour went on in those days there were mostly drug dealers and junkies here now at midday it's the big lunch with nice clean tourists and nice clean businessmen it's just the war that's getting dirty like the one in Vietnam I have to apologize to you (even more to Luisa) because the threats with Iraqi weapons of mass destruction and links to al-Qaeda did make a big impression on me it's terrible and what really makes me mad is the fact that it's the same people who before 9/11 played down the danger of a large-scale terrorist attack who are now assuring us with the same chutzpah that they had developments in Iraq under control what do you say

the same (I say) rather surprised at my fellow sufferer's development it's THE BIG SHIT he went on

but that was enough for us to float up to the main steps in front of the white pillars of the Public Library where like Dean Martin and Frank Sinatra of blessed memory we performed our

MESOPOTAMIAN WAR DUET

in the manner of an oratorio (entirely without rhymes but not discordant)

SEYMOUR. everything OK? nothing's OK!

MARTIN. the civilian administrator clears off two days before his official departure

SEYMOUR. (the whole country a hot potato hastily put into the bare outstretched hands of the locals)

MARTIN. thus avoiding the danger of becoming one of the 2000 victims of assassination in his last month in office

SEYMOUR. what's happened already?

MARTIN. in three weeks the strongest army in the world conquers the capital of a Third World country drives out the bloody dictator his secret services the army party and police and waits for the applause that doesn't come

SEYMOUR. instead the country breaks up into the pieces

MARTIN. that the experts knew about already

SEYMOUR. most of the inhabitants don't feel liberated

MARTIN. they feel invaded and occupied

SEYMOUR. a guerilla war breaks out

MARTIN. which we were neither ready nor prepared for

SEYMOUR. which our administration ignores or plays down

MARTIN. until the blood spilt and the failure of the civilian and military occupation authorities stinks to high heaven (the international press)

SEYMOUR. but now the china shop really belongs to US and WE're right in the middle of it

MARTIN. with a raging fighting dog a CARE parcel and a blind person's armband

SEYMOUR. don't trip over the empty petrol cans

MARTIN. don't do any body counts

SEYMOUR. but every near-zero value of your non-thought costs the lives of tens of thousands

MARTIN. (a nice Hegelian way of putting it my friend)

SEYMOUR. but only roughly—for now we hand over

MARTIN. to the statisticians historians and judges of the future

SEYMOUR. may they know better than us

MARTIN. who were only looking on

SEYMOUR and MARTIN. Amen

are you asleep? what are you dreaming of? Seymour looked amused and seemed to have forgotten our duet as soon as the final chord had died away

so I had to sort of pinch myself and say: unfortunately I wasn't as strongly against the war as Luisa

how is she?

for four weeks (I had to overcome some resistance to admit) I hadn't heard a word from her and now I didn't know—

Seymour gave me an encouraging look so with a rush I explained that what I didn't know was whether to leave the country or not if Bush was re-elected

the whole of Baghdad will breathe a sigh of relief if you do that and Rumsfeld will put an 'Old Europe goes home' sticker on your suitcase

Seymour raised his cardboard cup of coffee (we'd both bought one during our War Duet) and said cobbler stick to your last don't you Germans say that and where is your last? over there isn't it? (pointing to the Public Library) your students are sitting on the steps waiting for explanations and you can invite me as a guest speaker to tell them that the oil industry has no interest in torturing prisoners

Stuart Weingart ought to be sitting there I thought in the diffuse and somehow dusty summer-evening light but my jet-lagged imagination couldn't conjure him up any more the duet had drained me and everything stayed the way it was only I felt I was threatening to slump in on myself as if something were dissolving my muscles and suddenly I remembered that there must be big operation scars under the black shirt Seymour was wearing yet he was drinking normal coffee

he was still fascinated by the statement of the weapons expert who after a year of investigations in Iraq had explained that they had been taken in by the fact that Saddam Hussein had behaved as if he had weapons of mass destruction and even more by Paul Bremer III who had now retired after a year without a scratch on his missionary self-confidence as God's own man in order to have the time to write a book as had become the norm for people in high office even for the military commander-in-chief who hardly had the war begun had retired to fight on in his memoirs

you're talking like Luisa (and could actually have sung with me) I couldn't resist pointing out

could be—but what do you think

this ability to retire that's what I mean by TOWER I said (as if immured in my travel-weariness) they function as organs of the state then retire behind the walls as citizens the state or Goya's giant that's the Titan operating in history lives off that or by getting its citizens to believe it's the strongest power the greatest of the towers available to them and will supply them with everything without much happening to them

but then it shouldn't make war

not a disastrous war for us—under normal circumstances—but under our circumstances it or WE had to make war so that the whole world would again believe we're the hegemonic tower and can never again be hurt the way we were hurt—some of us—we—

thanks (Seymour said) but I don't like your theory

because it's a theory and therefore something frivolous for you no (he was drinking his coffee in little sips as if in that way it would be less harmful) that's not what bothers me what I don't like is that your theory is a purely formal structure with no content from your model I can't tell whether I live in a democracy or a dictatorship

that's just what I've been thinking about

if we behave like barbarians towards the outside world (says you) how can the others believe that our domestic model is the most civilized?

I said something like that as I looked at the pillars of the Public Library gleaming in the evening light at the large billiard cloth of the lawn in front of it and the people walking round the park gradually becoming calmer and more relaxed oddly enough I was embarrassed by the way Seymour now saw things in a similar light to me perhaps I didn't really believe him or suspected him of excessive politeness since I wanted to stay awake for at least two more hours we headed for a restaurant he suggested on 52nd Street I spoke (to my own surprise at great length) of my researches in Berlin over the last four weeks which had made me abandon Goethe's women but not Goethe himself it was a subject that seemed very relevant to the present with regard to the relationship between literature and war and between progress and barbarity

Goethe was an Arab as I recall Seymour said he was overtaken by progress

he also attacked or rather he went along when the attack was made I told him about the Austro-Prussian campaign against Republican France in which Goethe took part as a kind of *embedded poet* sitting in a chaise or on horseback sometimes well cushioned from the events but also sometimes exposed to and endangered by them an observer of everything from convivial evenings in camp harmless bombardments which then turned bloody drawing-room conversations and sudden bloodbaths to the retreat in mud and misery blighted by devastating epidemics he took his mind off it with physics textbooks and his theory of colour for him it was the republic of the mind and of literature that was reality perhaps he saw himself as the envoy of a more civilized future which has still not arrived

so we are Goethe

if I've understood you correctly Seymour said on the Avenue of the Americas against the backdrop of Rockefeller Plaza

I agreed with him as far as the chaise and the detached observations were concerned embedded consumers of news playing with their colour charts while the soldiers are being slaughtered

mostly Iraqis I interjected

Seymour halted for a moment as if to remind himself that he wanted to have the same opinions as me (looking over his shoulder I'm suddenly plunged back into winter: the huge Christmas tree in Channel Gardens round it giraffe-sized white angels made of wire with wire trumpets Sabrina's six- or seven-year-old hand flying up into mine because she's afraid of them they were like holy skeletons she said) causing the crowd to pile up behind us and we had to move on two old nags pulling their chaise skinny but not for lack of fodder for Seymour had certainly made his million(s) and the new development that had turned the voluble beaming sporting but doubt-less too bulky man in his mid 50s with heart problems into a slimmer and pretty thoughtful 60-year-old with well-serviced bypasses was to be wel-comed—a pleasure—a relief—how come you like him so much he took your wife away from you! something inside me wanted to cry out but it was just a shadow from another life resulting from my

looking back

or from things catching up with me for everything did indeed seem to be repeating itself the Vietnam War (at least in some important aspects) a relationship crisis (at least without a child involved this time) I had jet lag in my life if I were to start drinking again I could perhaps enjoy falling into this vortex—

I'm sure Luisa will have her own opinion about Bush and Mrs Rice Sey-mour said

she calls them Dr Jekyll and Mr Hyde

Mr Hyde as the evil of democracy I can see it's schizophrenia she's get-ting at Seymour was mildly amused I think Bush really does know how to relax he doesn't know what damage he's doing or he somehow manages not to want to know that distinguishes him from Napoleon who cynically accepted and boasted about it

perhaps he'll reach similar levels as far as the number of casualties is concerned the Grande Armée consisted of 600,000 men and 100,000 of them returned from Russia after three or four years

no chance said Seymour horrified we won't be there that long

but why (he asked not long after when we were sitting in the restaurant he'd chosen a pleasantly cool cavern of a place with red leather upholstery damask tablecloths silver cutlery and crystal glasses) are we so quiet? why are there no demonstrations no large-scale student protests no series of angry articles that you (he gave me a somewhat pitying look) as a German (a jet-lag nation) have

certain inhibitions about attacking others

(the Holocaust the Second World War the liberation from fascism) I can well understand but what about me why do I just feel depressed and impotent

because your parents only just managed to escape from Rotterdam to the US in time I should have interjected here but I said we were depressed because we couldn't do anything and told him I was thinking of going to Tel Aviv since I'd had an offer of a guest professorship

without Luisa? and only if Bush gets re-elected? or just because the Israelis are directly affected by the war? what's the point of all this? Seymour shook his head and placed his stethoscope on my chest I think you want to mix everything up so as to give yourself better reasons for being so mixed up

stupid oil-driller! I thought only to assure him unnecessarily that there was an alternative Israel just as there was an alternative America I ordered an alcohol-free beer (in a crystal glass) and tried to relax because despite my befuddled jet-lagged state I could not ignore the fact that Seymour was the only person with whom I could still have lengthy political arguments and even enjoy them (while with my students I dithered inwardly and spoke in a very controlled manner choosing every word carefully) and that he was the only one to whom I talked about Luisa even if I told him hardly anything Tel Aviv to increase my confusion even more of course that's what it was while I'd thought that by going there I'd get nearer to the conflict so as to be able to see more clearly

we think or

we're encouraged to think

that (the beer arrived and I tried to blow away the foam from inside my overtired head) we can't change anything anyway we watched the attack paralysed because whatever we believed or didn't believe we thought we couldn't stop it anyway and because we were unwilling to lift a finger to help Saddam's mass-murderous regime and now on the other hand we think (or on the other hand are encouraged to think) that there's

no choice left anyway Seymour says finishing off my sentence for me he'd ordered mineral water and a glass of red wine for himself (good for the heart) now that we're there and have to see to it that civil war doesn't break out and that the country makes the transition to democracy

in which the Iraqis with little more than war occupation violence and chaos to see round them are expected to queue up as targets outside the polling stations

it's not easy Seymour said a transformation like that's an immense process but basically things can only get better now everyone knows that things have to change the Iraqis know that and we know that we also know that we must improve the way we go about it THEY will have to send more soldiers better people will be in charge (that Petraeus for example) people will write the truth more and more it's politics and it's terrible but there's no alternative or can you see one

I'd never seen an alternative to better people and writing the truth strangely enough I ate with a good appetite in America I'm not alone I thought recalling my lonely weeks of research in Berlin which I could only relieve with visits to what was left of my family (at least a dozen times I'd resisted the temptation to ring the nurse) and when Seymour came back to Luisa as if with his old oilman's instincts he could sense the wildcat beneath the resistant surface

I said that she hadn't wanted simply to go back to Spain either since until the unexpected change of government it had been part of the so-called coalition of the willing and that the train bombings in Madrid the previous March had been particularly painful for her

11-M like 9/11

why do we create these brands of history they're

seals

Seymour assumed something we want to use to seal the envelope not to forget something but to make something comprehensible and to bring closure

Luisa had become very worked up over the debate about the conservative government's insinuations that ETA was responsible for the attack the Francoists she said (as if time hadn't moved on) who were in favour of the war in Iraq now don't want to be saddled with the consequences of an al-Qaeda attack

as a 9/11–11-M couple (a friend of Luisa's and her husband had been killed on the track outside Atocha Station) we got through April with shared grief and mourning but then Luisa took a clear and considered view of the truth or truthfulness of our relationship by

by what? Seymour had asked the previous evening after I had once more unexpectedly opened the bedroom door it was four in the morning in my still-in-Berlin response time so I told him what I'd been meaning to tell him all the time namely that three months before 11-M Luisa had started an undecided but continuing relationship with a colleague in Amherst a historian I knew

what do you mean undecided

Seymour asked with surprising sharpness

it (their relationship) was (presumably) based above all on the fact that I couldn't (any longer) commit myself clearly (enough) to her (at least in her—Luisa's—opinion)

and so you go off to Berlin for a month where of course nothing's become clear to you you'd be making (Seymour said very calmly and so firmly it penetrated the barricade of my wounded male pride) a big mistake if you thought that was a repetition

Luisa is not Amanda

it's that simple (*oil is buried deep in the earth*—it was the same tone of voice) but too banal I was going to object when he went into more detail and explained (presumably correctly) that Amanda had run away from academic life first of all then from me and then (partly—should we send Leslie a postcard) from him while Luisa was fed up neither with me nor with academic life

he himself was now living alone

Seymour said and that would probably never change he'd kept the apartment in Little Brazil Street as well as the house on Long Island and after a blazing argument with his analyst who naturally emphasized the deeply regressive nature of this determination to cling on to things he'd had a simple and effective idea and commissioned an interior architect to completely redesign both the house and the apartment while he was away on a long business trip without having done more than give a general indication of his own taste as a guideline

so now his apartment had a fully refurbished guest room and you would find nothing (immediately visible) to remind you of Amanda or Sabrina for the first time I looked out of the window in the kitchen Sabrina must have looked out of on her last day

a fall past flashing flickering gleaming adverts narrowing vertiginously
on bottomless towers of light

FRAGMENT

The flame I've been since my rebirth,
    Spreads wings to carry me to you,
A being now of air, not earth.
    Framed in the fire your face shines through.

I thought of these lines in Sabrina's sweeping round handwriting when I
woke up in the middle of the night because according to my internal European clock it was already morning I had wanted to recite the poem in my
sleep but kept making some mistake or other so that I now got up to look
for it in the black notebook

    Seymour was sitting on his (neutral) leather sofa in front of a large TV
screen a cup of tea in his hand we were both wearing a T-shirt and striped
boxer shorts and had to laugh is there anything original about the male sex
I had the same herbal tea and like two boys who'd arranged to meet at night
to get up to mischief we watched a ghost film

    from Afghanistan

    that still existed where tough fighting was still taking place where Ger-
man and American soldiers were being killed it seemed to be a never-ending
gruesome round of assassinations skirmishes and political manoeuvring
where international armies and aid organizations diplomats tribal chiefs bandits and terrorists were hopelessly entangled on the backs of the population

    on the screen

    we saw an almost 80-year-old man and a little girl his granddaughter it
said they lived in a place that was nothing but stone and dust they had no
piped water in their village high in the mountains and the whole (remaining)
life of the old man consisted of going a thousand feet down three times a
day and back up laden with two canisters of water and the girl carried two
plastic bottles tied together the man

    took opium chewed it somehow

    so as not to feel all that he said opium and my granddaughter who
always comes with me the seven-year-old child they are the happiness I need
not to feel anything

going up

going down

going up your sweating

grandfather smiling in his opium daze with his hook nose his wrinkled tanned face beneath his grey turban stuck there with no way out in the dust in the heat in the sweat of the ascent and descent and my

only thought (crazily jealous) was at least

they're together

then I was ashamed of such a thought in Seymour's Midtown apartment in the untold wealth of the

TOWER

from down below the noise of the nocturnal traffic was very distant and muted like the signs of life from a drowned city after the Afghanistan film there was a report on nature reserves in Florida and exchanging little more than a couple of words we went back to bed

for breakfast we both had just a slice of toast and black coffee Seymour seemed to have told me something important and very comforting about Luisa the previous evening but I couldn't remember what and didn't want to ask him now we were sitting opposite each other freshly showered and shaved and strangers to each other until Seymour started to talk about Berlin where he hadn't been for ages if Bush should be re-elected we could both go into exile there that would be an astounding historical development

what I find incomprehensible (I said breaking into a sudden sweat but I had to say it) is the ability of these political figures to take personal responsibility for the deaths of tens or hundreds of thousands no one will ever be able to take that away from them not even the appalling amnesty of history they're perhaps hoping for

they just can't comprehend it Seymour said shrugging his shoulders that's their secret and nothing else

an opaque secret the heartlessness of a granite rock I just can't fathom this relentlessness that drives you mad this strength of belief this enthusiasm for liberation or whatever it is is it just a result of our sickened Romantic way of looking at things should we rather not follow Goethe and learn to take a natural scientist's attitude towards the vain undersized mass murderer of an emperor whom he regarded as an unavoidable catastrophe and accepted like a Muslim does the will of God but of course we've had that attitude for ages how else could we live here (just think of the tower theory you proposed yourself)

what had Seymour said to me about Luisa? I would have brought it up again before I left if he hadn't reminded me about Sabrina's blue rucksack with the things she'd packed for her trip to California for a long time now I'd had the black notebook with her poems and diary entries (which have made things so much easier and so much harder for me) Seymour only wanted to know if he could continue to keep the rucksack he wouldn't open it he said or take anything out since the one time we'd been through it the rucksack had been kept in one of the built-in wardrobes which had been reserved for Sabrina sometimes he felt that she simply

hadn't come back yet

even today

we don't know where she spent her last night in New York City we'd never been able to find her friend (Mary) who was supposed to live on the Upper East Side she'd not even called Eric all we have is her farewell from Seymour on 10 September and the call the next morning the message for Julia during which she would have been at her mother's office or even with Amanda herself which I sometimes hope sometimes not why should it have been a good thing that they could have seen each other in those moments (it was a comfort to me)

I once thought it would be impossible for me ever to fly again

but even that wouldn't have meant anything I land in Boston and as every time tell myself that the terrorists who destroyed the World Trade Center checked in on the morning of 11 September in this

perfectly everyday

setting

such as we will be compelled to take as reality to the end of our days

soon the report of the 9/11 Commission for which Seymour campaigned so hard in an action group will appear it will say that the unimaginable attack was unimaginable but with greater care and more luck could almost have been prevented since the terrorists had been known for a long time and countless clues just needed to be correctly interpreted

a year ago (the month the war broke out) the jigsaw puzzle jelled into a concrete picture the originator of the idea of destroying the Towers had appeared in the press a crazy head the brain AL-MUKH a short almost fat man with an angular forehead moderately long dishevelled black hair being dragged out of his bed by secret police in a terrorists' house in Pakistan his thick neck looking as if it were screwed in to the hairy base of his shoulders and chest sticking out of a low-cut undershirt

taken by the CIA to a *Hotel California* a place in a country where they can (get others to) use torture

so AL-MUKH confessed that fire had been breaking out inside his head for many years ever since February 1993 when his nephew with his help had detonated 1,300 pounds of nitroglycerine in the underground garage of the World Trade Center

he saw

airplanes

exploding over America

a magnificent firework display

on the West Coast on the East Coast over the Pacific dozens hitting buildings at the same time being set off in the air as fire-bombs high over the sea or over towns

what does that clear up (what does it make clear to me)

as justification he said

what the other perpetrators and planners who were put in front of the cameras immediately after the collapse of the Towers had said

that Israel committed atrocities and America supported Israel and the Arab regimes that claimed to hate Israel were supplying oil to America that was supporting Israel

just about enough twisted

arguments for the eternal cycle of hatred and violence for the only

perpetual motion

that has ever worked technical arguments for an engineer who had studied in the US (mechanical engineering in Greensboro)

at the luggage reclaim I almost tripped over a folding sign such as you see on the sidewalk outside booths or restaurants in quiet streets five passport photos had been enlarged and name age and rank written beside them with a blue felt-tip

OUR HEROES

are those who were killed the previous day in Iraq with the teeming banal heedless bustle of the airport going by I stand out because I've stopped to look at the sign perhaps they think I'm a patriot who's going to make an unpleasant scene so I hurry on seen from Germany the US is clearly a belligerent state over there that's the primary attribute of the nation while these five dead men here will fade away like the results of some sport which seems to be much less important than baseball that was something I'd forgotten to tell Seymour (or he to tell me) this fading away the marginal and distant nature of the war was and remains its inescapable precondition the brutal mathematical relationship between OUR dead and OUR total population with a further circumstance that reduces the threat to one's own family even more namely that it is a professional army being deployed in it among the over a thousand of the US Army killed in action so far there are said to be 20 or 30 female soldiers in a hostile land they don't understand whose language they don't speak whose culture they don't understand and whose hatred and desperation they only continue to provoke by their lack of understanding

Goethe's women

I imagine having to explain such a woman's fate to them a journey in a uniform with moss-coloured patches in a Humvee along a desert track in the vicinity of Tikrit in a heat of over a hundred degrees you're 26 you have two children in Philadelphia to whom you were yesterday allowed to send an email and a digital photo by the side of the road you see a black bundle a sheep no a dead dog that explodes two seconds later

Bettine with her

over-excitable nature

would have been least surprised I think

and all at once Seymour's message occurs to me or becomes clear for it wasn't explicitly stated first of all I had to try to see Boston Logan International Airport with Bettine's or Friederike's eyes a place you can't get to without motorized transport because only multi-lane highways take you into it and to the terminals

be glad she's alive

his look didn't have to mean any more than that I've tried in vain to find a solution on my own whether I should stay or go to Berlin or Tel Aviv I don't have to work that out for myself if Luisa will give me another chance

to get there more slowly and clear-sightedly (reverently) I take the ferry to Rowes Wharf on which I last travelled in the summer of 2000 with

Sabrina when we were coming back together from my researches in Frankfurt and Weimar and she from her trip round Europe

through the glass of the passenger cabin spattered with drops and flashes of light the view of the waterfront intermittently blurs and becomes intensely clear so that the eye which for weeks has adapted to the confined and smaller dimensions of Europe imagines it's approaching the stone cliffs of Manhattan

outside by the railings Sabrina bronzed by the Italian sun and pressing her heavy rucksack against the metal with her knees says you know I can live here

why not I think resigned and optimistic at the same time she would study here and hold her own even at MIT the trip with her cousin had boosted her self-assurance and adventurousness she'll make it I look across the water and try to suck in as much of the confidence and cool vitality of the Financial District as possible of the business energy and dynamism of the city (the mayor and the biggest gangster could be brothers) Boston is a manageable city it has a solid modernity nothing overwhelming

Sabrina was talking and I should have been listening

the pewter-coloured smooth water of the harbour entrance flows sluggishly and calmly to the arched gateway of Rowes Wharf behind which individual tall buildings rise up set close to one another and somehow belonging together

castle towers or rather like the cliffs of the

Isle of the Dead

for a moment it's

such a compelling visual crossfade of the harbour entrance and Böcklin's painting that I wonder if I'm going out of my mind I shouldn't have talked about Hitler and Berchtesgaden it spoilt her fascination with the picture Sabrina forgets nothing she seeks out and archives details

the little Moor dressed in gold with his black dancing bear on a plaque on a wooden grandfather clock in the Goethe House in Frankfurt

or those

winged skulls that were being carved into the top of the gravestones in Copp's Hill Burying Ground here at the time when Goethe was going to France (in Boston Sabrina no longer remembered the skeleton angels in Channel Gardens) in front of a brick wall a completely white statue of Francis of Assisi with a white sparrow on his shoulder

that bonnet looking as if it were made from a large torn-up paper handkerchief above the blurred yellowish oval face of the oldest doll in America (white North America) in a display case in Deerfield

the next time

I promise

when we've had a good sleep

we'll walk the whole of the Freedom Trail together following its course from Boston Common to Charlestown black and red blood mixed to the paradoxical cockscomb colour of freedom a narrow well-trodden line running along the sidewalks and streets round the corners of buildings and across the parks everything so long ago like that MASSACRE committed against US in 1770 by the English (five dead) outside the Old State House

if you drive over the bridge I say (again and again) you'll get home

it was just intended to indicate the way to academic life to Cambridge what else can I talk about what else do I know about why

didn't she call me

on her last day

take the Red Line across Longfellow Bridge to Cambridge and you plunge unexpectedly into the light you see the skyscrapers of Back Bay and the South End the Charles River becomes an unbounded expanse if you first close your eyes and then open them at the right moment which gave Sabrina the idea of sitting opposite me there were (for two or three seconds perhaps) no immediate earthly surroundings the rails were sloping in such a way that there was nothing but the blue of the water and the sky the heads and torsos of the passengers on Sabrina's side looked as if they were floating in front of a blue screen like biblical figures in a painting by Raphael or Michelangelo just as if

they were

never coming back

At last it's hot enough in the heat of the late afternoon the pale whitish sky is still pressing a gag of humid air down on the city almost like the cushion with an old sheet stretched over it on which Miral spreads out the flat rounds of dough I lift up the stove lid see the blue gas flames spurting up through a circle of holes punched in the floor and plunge into a cylinder of dark quivering air I'm not afraid I sometimes feel like shouting out loud nothing will to happen to you there your bodies are in control just let your-selves fall and watch out because

now the iron sides have reached the right temperature and we can begin we three cousins in our light loose housecoats it reassures me and comforts me as well

to fall down

from the seventh no let's say the fourth heaven the one of short or per-haps just vividly imagined joys

back into the family

I've always played with Sara and Miral (for thousands of years in the shadow of the Tower) and now as well when we're all three in our early 20s we can be a jolly and boisterous threesome as if we were still dressing our dolls or jumping one after another on the hopscotch squares but otherwise nothing's the same as it used to be when we were only allowed to watch the older women the balls of dough on the tray dusted with flour by Sara's place at the garden table form a smooth female landscape wonderful but boring ona snow-covered moon smoothly swelling untouched monotonous perfect you don't know whether you want to seal them in glass display cases or dig your teeth into them just imagine a royal love simple and majestically sump-tuous and dazzling (behind your closed lids sapphires rubies splinters of sky shining spirals under your skin) all with no bought

jewellery at all

this time it wasn't through dangling gold chains that I saw

the Major

but it was in another souk the little food market nearby in relatively safe Wasiriya I'd been allowed to go shopping by myself three times during the last few weeks and the third time he was suddenly there in front of me in jeans and a green-and-white check shirt so unfamiliar that I forgot

to cry out

if you

want to know the truth my little dove then

just listen and stay quiet I stayed because he'd given me such a shock I couldn't have moved anyway it was by a stall with medicinal herbs dried beetles and empty tortoise shells among dangling snake-skins the Major whispered urgently in my ear and held my right arm as if he were my father having to give me a good telling-off something's always grabbing and holding me

you are

the whole person is the women in this country are

are we still nothing but a handful of smooth helpless dough that can be formed into anything I try to stand up straight I wanted him to sense the change in me to realize that I wasn't afraid to call for help

now the dough is taken off the tray and first of all Sara's practised hands flatten it into a pancake then stretch it over her clenched fist and with slightly rocking movements of her outspread fingers spin it out into a thin disc

your sister

the Major says in his civilian check shirt when did he leave the army (during the war or had the American substitute king fired him) if I had a snake's skin I would sink my poisonous fangs into his leg

never had anything to fear from me I loved her and if you're wondering how it came about that

she disappeared

then ask yourselves to whom did that fine husband of hers introduce her he worked it out nicely did that Qasim he himself couldn't have done anything about me because of his wife but he managed to find someone who

knew how to take revenge if he was

spurned

is that clear enough (my little dove) I just wanted

you all to know that goodbye

in the fiery furnace of hell the flat cake of dough goes from Sara's to Miral's hands Miral spreads it out over the cushion I lift the metal lid and she presses the dough firmly against the hot inner side of the barrel stove until bubbles form all over and she pulls it off the side like skin that's been stuck fast and then slings it onto the tray I'm holding ready and I stack the bread in a large tin bowl

Yasmin's scars on her feet on her back and along her hip are slowly turning white

since Karbala

she sometimes speaks Arabic again

if she doesn't say anything herself if she's protecting Qasim or doesn't suspect him or simply never wants to speak his name again what should what must I do with this possible truth or possible slander what danger does it involve if what the Major said is correct and Qasim put someone from the secret service onto my sister so that she would decline his advances and he would take his revenge on my sister and the otherwise unassailable Major as a substitute for my brother-in-law

now

after we have been living through a war for a whole year and have seen nothing of him but the divorce papers I believe

Qasim's capable of that

the way he was so distraught and in shock when he came to see us in our old house in Betawiyn after her disappearance my fine brother-in-law I

don't want to be

responsible for even more hatred and even more death there has to be an end to it some time at some point of time we must learn to float over the gardens of Babylon to soar up to take the sick the heavy-laden the torture victims on board our air-ships to look down and to lie together without fear learn

to be silent

from your tortured sister from your brother when he suffered from shock (after Ahmed's death 10 seemingly endless months ago) even he said nothing

for two whole days

shivering and in need of protection he even took up his pen again to calm himself down he wrote out some lines praising God in calligraphy he was almost changed back into the dear friend of my childhood who looked up to me clung on to me stole horses with me who would have joined in straight away and one night would have jumped out of the window onto the back of a flashing

electrical horse with a metallic whinny for example to gallop off to the stars with me instead of indulging in stupid electronic aeroplane attacks on crude cardboardy representations of New York City in camouflage colours

all I get from him now is his disregard or contempt what do people see in me I ask myself here between Miral and Sara one ball of dough after the other lands flat on the glowing side of the stove and then covered in blisters on a tray humans (where did I read that) are one of the few things that can change themselves completely without any outward signs only God

the greatest player

cannot be deceived why should He be when has He ever killed

a loving couple He only killed

the saint Dhu'n-Nun out of love and wrote that on the forehead of his corpse

that kind of thing was in the terrible first letter I received from you after the move to Wasiriya

we take the bread

to the family table like my cousins I'm proud of our work and like them I swathe myself in long loose-fitting clothes so as to get all of them accustomed to it in time no one seems surprised or bothered least of all the men who clearly have no problem with the whole of female Iraq having to wrap itself up in sheets more and more

Sami's distrust

that evening (the penultimate one) in Betawiyn he tried to get something out of me to press me for an answer with shocking and painful presumptuousness and since then

my brother has become a man an enemy

of my love coolly clearly I reflect his mute attacks back at him

why

am I so afraid

the most likely outcome is that nothing will happen to you would we have all these wars and murders and attacks and weddings if everyone didn't

hope to survive I put out the fresh bread

on plates at either end of the cloth spread out on the floor by now we're all used to being back here again Miral gave up her teacher-training course four months ago Sami has to repeat the final year at school because he was almost never there Sara lost her job in a state printing works and is now working in one of Uncle Munir's shops that are doing better and better since we've been allowed to sell mobile phones cameras PCs and printers even my mother has joined the family business and besides looking after Yasmin and doing her cooking and housework she translates instructions for use for the latest gadgets and appliances from French and English you just have to

be able to wait

you should think the young and the innocent can afford to

insofar as

they're protected I have little appetite and wait anxiously for strange cravings the big lively picture of the family meal blurs before my eyes melting into a colourful printed veil through which I can't see to the bottom of their minds to the marrow of their bones the mirrors of their hearts the reflective heart hides itself best of all

you can see whatever

you want to see I

keep calm by locking up inside it the things I want to conceal from myself memory is the mirror of the searching present hide it as

invented past

the Major in the souk

need never to have existed as long as

only I saw him

in the reflective chamber of my heart you lie among the petals smiling on your back breathless or rather breathing heavily again because you were about to start once more at least that's how I imagine it I'm sure you would want to make the thing that could have

happened

that we once both so passionately longed for part of the (accepted) order instead of making what is accepted part of the order of our love as is right and proper for what was it to him so we ought to you ought to if you still had a mother she would come to see my mother my parents married young (at a time when my grandfather was almost rich and studying abroad was almost easy for people) but I would have been so strangely calm at that moment as if my own resting

Ishtar body

its swellings its scent

had made me lose all my fears marry me for

one more hour (Beloved!)

as is possible in your and in my mother's (unpredictable) faith mut'ah marriage for one hour or for 99 years

for

pleasure

I am very clear about what my parents' reply to us would have been if we'd asked them

wait finish

your studies even if you see

that nothing stops everything's like this war from which the American substitute king in his dark-blue suit dazzling white shirt red tie and desert-coloured paratrooper's boots has flown away after telling us (in a kind of surprise attack) on television that conditions had improved remarkably

the country now belonged to us or

to the wolves

that drive us into our houses on the screen we saw a man shoot another man in the temple just like that between two lines of cars slowly edging forward at four o'clock in the afternoon the old red Mercedes on the right-hand edge of the picture belonged to Uncle Fuad in such cases

you don't get out

it's better to duck down with trembling limbs

Fear shame and do not forget that a partridge is not a hawk

it was so difficult to answer the first letter you wrote after our last meeting in Betawiyn which was no more about love than the previous ones which however radiated comfort and confidence you seem to have been wounded by

a mortal rejection

(when your reception should have been nothing but the embrace of the morning air of the clouds of the petals moist with dew of the soft clear waves of a lake) it seemed the hawk tore out your entrails and choked on your feathers or as if I were the monster partridge from a Japanese horror film that hasn't been made yet it drove not only your heart but also your reason straight out of the window you weren't going to use it anyway but to attain quite different and higher states

in this disturbing letter

states in which every rose seems to you to be

like a gallows

in which crying is like breathing you say for God likes to see His servants cry one ought to make Hind and Mrs Rikabi the mourning widow aware of the example of Fudail who only smiled once in 30 years namely when his son died for

the death of his children was like a sweetmeat to him

poverty instead of riches hunger instead of repletion lower instead of higher humiliation instead of honour modesty instead of pride grief instead of joy death instead of life

is that what you really want is that what I've given you was everything my skin wanted to say to you wrong did it have such a bad translator were my hands skeletal my eyes empty sockets was my hair lying on bare bone did I have no lips any more no flesh do I imagine peaches instead of bare ribs what you wrote about

the death of a child was a kind of

insane panicky running away (I replied agitatedly) listen for a woman

God is a child

my mother sometimes used to read lines from the Sufis to me and only recently in my (as you say) unbelieving family your beloved al-Hallaj was discussed the great butterfly who wanted to be consumed in the candle flame and is said to have danced through Baghdad on his way to the gallows

now that madness is beginning again Tariq cried when the bombs exploded outside mosques Sunnis against Shiites and vice versa as if Iraq had never existed damn it all a thousand years ago my fellow physician al-Razi wrote in his textbook that any religion was harmful to the health if nothing else and moreover no one punished him for it

but they killed al-Hallaj Farida retorted because they couldn't bear him saying that God is love al-Hallaj! he also thought that instead of going to Mecca a journey to the ceiling of the living room was sufficient and you went to the madmen in Karbala and they could have killed you!

no one harmed a hair of our heads they gave us water they cooked for us along the way they opened their guest rooms Farida said and refrained from pointing out to Tariq that the pilgrimage had done more for Yasmin than all his colleagues had managed to do in their hurried visits

so if God is love (I wrote) then I can't understand the desire to be consumed in the flame at all for love is not fire this longing of butterflies of male butterflies rather for death is becoming government policy in this country that's what Saddam whom you all hated wanted for you all to rush off and die for him

sensible 12-year-old Hind told me very clearly that Mrs Rikabi had to tell you to leave their house because Yusuf (crazy jealous brainwashed when did he ever do anything sensible) accused you of working for the Americans at the university it's appalling what could happen to us in this short period of war the walls on which we sat chatting and joking together in the evening sun are stained with blood in my letter

I made every effort to counter your black mood I went so far as to tell you not to underestimate my father his modernity his strength his consistency it was only because she had been forced into an unwanted marriage that Laila bore death within her and Tariq would never do something like that do you hear in our story there's no husband tragically keeping the lovers apart and no deranged lover is going to throw himself on his beloved's grave we just need a little patience and *God is with those who patiently persevere* as you ought to know better than I

perhaps that was what most convinced you for in your next letter in the envelope addressed by Hind

which she sent in a bigger envelope you'd

come back to your senses

you wrote that you'd thought things over that you were very confused that the quotations from the Sufis made you feel ashamed you weren't worthy of them that you were making progress in your studies again and had no idea what had made Yusuf denounce you and that most of all you felt sorry for Hind who had no simple way of talking to you any more but she wrote to your new address you'd found a room not far from the Rikabis' house but you wanted to move out closer to me in Wasiriya and so

I was walking on air again

only a tiny bit above the ground so that no one noticed with silent

fireworks in my reflective heart

my father

comes too late to the family meal Farida gives him a plate and he sits down with it outside in the courtyard from the living room comes the sound of the big television mosquitoes are buzzing round in the still oppressive air I made peppermint tea for Tariq and stood then sat down by the green metal table underneath the fig tree and I'm drinking tea as well and trying to imagine what it would be like if I had

to tell him

something really awful

but I don't believe it and anyway life isn't something awful I can't help but be optimistic and assume the best in 20 or 25 years' time my son will be at university in this reawakening land and he'll know nothing of our defeats

are you reading your books Muna how are you getting on with cuneiform as you know mankind must gradually make progress

now he looks older than he is I think almost everyone would put him in his early 60s he's sitting here before me exhausted and thin with his high bald forehead his completely white hair framing it his moustache has gone almost completely white too because everyone in the family looks up to him no one has the courage to ask how tired he is apart from me perhaps

Yabba you should consult yourself I say

why

because I've discovered that you doctors are mortal

he laughs and asks for another cup of tea

we rarely have much more than that to say to one another who do I actually talk to previously I used to have long conversations with Sami and with my mother and actually I stopped doing so (or they stopped) when I was 15 since then even God hasn't talked to me any more my strong unquestioning child's faith simply disappeared leaving something between Farida's fits of devoutness and the poetic atheism of my father who maintains that the most terrible thing (if one were a believer) is that then what it says in the Koran would be correct namely that the face of God is everywhere you turn

Yasmin looks at me now and then as if

she were completely cured and would now finally speak to me the way I've wanted her to ever since I was a child and she was living in Paris for so long but she remains silent in a way that is even more painful it's only with Eren and Huda in fact only with the rebellious mocking and ostensibly superficial Huda that I've talked about everything in recent years

now I really need her

at night

when I'm lying in bed between my cousins with whom I talk a lot but in an oddly cautious and inhibited way perhaps because we've known one another since we were little it's not easy to change it's as if (just as with Sami) you couldn't become grown-up together yet Miral with her

suspended

teacher-training course is in the same situation as me and has grown into an interesting young woman and I know about Selim the young married man with three children in the neighbourhood whose looks torment her like something

pleasurable you stick into yourself

Huda would say and giggle they're all so serious so reserved we toss and turn in the beds in the humid summer nights sometimes it feels as heavy as lead in my heart in my head the gigantic leaden fist in my belly but sometimes I can rise up become transparent and fly as in my dreams when I was a little girl I tell myself that perhaps you've already moved to Wasiriya when the muezzin calls I have the feeling I haven't slept an hour

no more bombs but shots now and then in this or that night my quiet patient cousins and I dream turn roll over soaked in sweat we keep on hopping into the same squares throw the stone jump don't make a mistake

wahid
ithnain
thalatha
arba'a

that's the way we try to stay the same
in the family
but

everything's changing the whole country's turning upside down hop quicker on one leg

in the morning

another week has passed and it only seems as if nothing's changed we carry on sleeping while we're working or torment ourselves with idleness until lunch once again

we bake bread

once again the gas flames flare up through the grill once again Sara spreads the dough over her outspread fingers once again

there's a letter in an envelope addressed in Hind's handwriting I carry it round like a tender hand on my breast for two hours then I open it and the snake

bites my heart

. . . to put it briefly: My uncle's had a long talk with me. My conscience as well. Most of your family are Sunni, but as you know I want to ask my uncle to support me to become a Shia religious teacher. It will, I hope, help me if I remain true to myself. That means that we should not see one another again. I wish you all the best for the future

Trust in God the All-powerful, laud and praise Him, in whose hands lies the destiny of all men and all things.

Your

Nabil

You think

this can't be ME carrying the CALIPH'S LETTER in the inside pocket of a lightweight pale-green jacket (the weight of that tremendous document would pull me down into the dust at once) how then would I get out of the terrors rejections everyday humiliations and bullets of the RED ZONE of blood of fire that considerable portion of our country where the coalition troops have to carry their guns with the safety catch off that is from Sindbad's harbour through the marshes with their reed huts and wild women across the camp of those occupying the mosque in Najaf the tents of the flagellants of Karbala the ruins and mass graves of Babylon the sea of ordinary mortals' houses in Baghdad all the way up to the north where they roll the barrels of oil over the mountains to Turkey in brief everywhere in this chameleon country of ours where everyone sees RED no matter whether they think or rather try to think green or black before they pick up their Kalashnikov and begin to

argue

however I manage to remain calm and discover paradises beyond the rage and I say

Ali my friend your animal has earned some peace and quiet I'll take it with me to the

GREEN ZONE

even if it just can't be ME (or want to be me) floating along on a pearl-grey seat in a limousine your animal Ali is travelling well hidden inside my head straight into the gleaming emerald heart of the country girt with barbed-wire tank-traps watchtowers concrete stelae machine-gun emplacements

across

on the restored 14th of July Bridge (imaginary balloons with the distended features of Qasim who drove out the English rise up into the golden-boy sphere of Tony Blair whose mosquito nets afford little protection against his bombs) to the safest place in Baghdad the

INTERNATIONAL ZONE

right at the entrance we can see

WAIT OR

YOU WILL BE SHOT!

such prospects always cheer me up and while the limousine brakes its engine falters whines and dies away and all those sitting on the grey seats meekly nod to themselves all of them like me

or rather the person playing me

carrying a hidden chameleon inside their head and perhaps with just as little expectation of really getting through although each and every one of them has a caliph's letter in his grey suit (of eight suits only one is dark blue and that's the one the driver's wearing) for a few crazy moments I can imagine getting through the barbed-wire ramparts of the bridge through the deserts of the glacis through the mountains of the outer walls the series of forecourts through the labyrinth of the fore-palaces up the steps that lead to the steps between the pillars that are only the bases of the pillars to the entrance halls of the entrance halls and the hall of halls itself to the inconceivable interior of the palace right up to the

huge golden puppet

of the CALIPH himself that (inside my crazy mind) suddenly bursts open like a bud and would reveal the unthinkable sight of the RULER if I hadn't thrown myself into the dust my lids tightly closed but I hear

voices I can't help hearing these voices that get louder and louder clearer and clearer until finally I am compelled to understand them

inside the puppet (they say) there is nothing more than an

ordinary American

so I jump up take the letter out of my pocket the scroll with the kilometre-long

COMPLAINT OF THE PEOPLE

on Egyptian papyrus

that I read through silently as we get out between the barriers at

CHECKPOINT II

and grim American guards with ill-tempered sniffer dogs that sniff at everything we have especially our genitals and then the LETTER our accreditation as

Delegates to the Iraqi National Conference

invited by the probably not so transitory transitional government the IGC (Iraqi Governing Council) or iIGC (interim Iraqi Governing Council) alongside the highly provisional CPA (Coalition Provisional

Authority—Children-Playing-Adults Authority—Can't-Produce-Anything Corporation)

beside that we place our folding Kalashnikovs a few mini hand grenades the batteries of our mobile phones our wallets full to bursting with bribes the stings in our tails and wrapped in shiny black-red-and-green sweet papers our testicles in which the dogs are so interested on the table but not

the chameleons inside out heads that don't know whether we really want to ought to be here or not you can see me (or a poor idea of me) Ali as one of seven middle-aged grey-haired gentlemen standing after an unpleasant but expertly carried-out frisking beside the hyperbolic upcurve of a suspension-bridge cable as thick as a tree trunk and looking down through a fence taller than a man at the

morning-grey Tigris

that we used to jump into like merry little frogs today I have the smell of the water from all those years ago in my nostrils as if I had never turned into the grumpy shabbut plodding along deep below the surface in its murky subject's life in constantly growing fear of the angler's hook closer and closer to the muddy bottom are things

changing now

that we're standing on the bridge our ties flapping in the morning breeze after the body search of our scale-armour

some imams (people say) had issued fatwas against eating fish from the Tigris since they'd nibbled at too many corpses so let us put an end to living in the mud let us feel

delegated

let us look confidently across to the Karkh side to that large green tumour of power the river forms with a bold intestinal twist even if it stinks of sewage the air is still fresh up here at seven in the morning

another watchtower rises up before us as we slowly drive on two soldiers together with the barrels of their machine guns look down sleepily at us I wonder if I should get out here already and read out my papyrus-scroll speech for the unknown American that is even before I set foot on the green tumour or hernia set in a ring of quarter- or half-bombed ministries let us hold on to this thought the erection of power as the umbilical hernia of the people Ali you were the best surgeon I've seen in recent years (your heraldic beast inside my head can't bring itself to don red-and-white stripes and white stars on a blue background) so there's nothing left for it but to jump up onto the bonnet of the delegates' limousine in front of one of the countless barriers that protect our country

from us

and break out into the

Declaration of Tariq

which I must read out to the American inside the caliph's puppet as a representative of his whole nation that for some reason finds it easier to cope with 1,000 dead than we can with 100,000 martyrs (since HE's been in the death cell we've become sensitive) what was I going to say oh yes

Americans!

You didn't find the weapons that were the reason you attacked us.

You brought hordes of terrorists from whom you wanted to protect your people into our country.

You plunged us into violence and chaos

by your occupation policy that is as arrogant as it is amateurish.

You—

at this point the delegates' limousine accelerates to full speed so that it's better if we think that we didn't get up on the bonnet at all now we will have to put forward everything I was going to declare (the 17 paragraphs each with three or four sub-paragraphs) at the National Conference after all that's why we're here we're on the other side of the river on our left are the more recent palaces at which we used to stare across full of hatred in the swimming pools of which the GIs splashed round on Al Jazeera (parts of the Iraqi population hoped they would see young naked negresses and were bitterly disappointed) on our right

Coalition Headquarters and the big old palace the core of which still consists of colonial English workmanship while the gigantic wings were commissioned by our EX with the 15-metre high helmeted heads on them that are now lying on their faces some distance away or in the mud fenced off by barbed wire presumably because the *No pissing on the heads* signs were ignored

we (teachers imams lawyers human rights activists local politicians oil smugglers who changed sides at the right moment ex-communists with prayer beads and doctors who are already counting Saddam's dead out loud and Bush's victims quietly still) drive onto the 14th of July Square with the bronze soldiers climbing on the plinth the last time I drove round this monument was perhaps 15 years ago but we came to the area on foot quite often if only out of curiosity and historical masochism in order to gape at the unspeakable monuments that piled up round the Qadisiya Expressway over the years to the eternal terror of the Persians that still unknown soldier for example whose gigantic body was dissolved in a gas attack by a flying saucer so that all we have left is his blood for ever going round and round inside a cube the size of a house or those four chopped-off hands of victory beneath whose crossed sabre blades of genuine German steel every coalition soldier must have posed for his wish-you-were-here-in-Baghdad snap

some

are said to have tried out the Lion of the Tigris as well that 60-metre-high beast of prey (made by an international consortium) into whose marble-titanium head on all public holidays they threw groups of up to 20 enemies whom an astonished crowd could watch being crushed and dissolved through its glass coat in the similarly transparent artificial organs of the wonder beast what

makes me think of something like that

perhaps because the delegate on my left muttered to me that the man-eating pets of our EX had been taken to the zoo that was also inside the Green Zone within the

BUBBLE

as the camouflage-dressed boys outside in front of the tinted windscreen of our limousine call it (I'm a chameleon with sunglasses with a hard impenetrable stare Ali a lizard with an all-over reflective body that throws the self-reproaches of collaboration back at its compatriots

as an accusation of chaos

or roasts itself with them if the lizard's skin should happen to be reflective on the inside as well)

there really are a lot of trees here probably more than in the whole of red Baghdad and that somehow fits in with the irrealities of the power zone Humvees and armoured cars shooting past then oddly deformed and bug-like vehicles with revolving gun turrets that almost knock us off the road so abruptly do they change lanes even here we can almost touch the sign that says we should *Keep 100 yards distance* here the clattering black helicopters that dot the sky over the Red Zone densify as if over a wasps' nest and we gawp at a group of joggers in front of an old wall mosaic with our praying EX above whose head someone's painted an Iraqi flag and over whose lower abdomen he or someone else has scrawled another canonic dictum: *Iraq good—US good—Saddam donkey*!

guards with white helmets and white gloves are standing outside a massive puzzling concrete structure and that reminds us that the

Führerbunker

must be somewhere near here (built by 20 Germans 150 Filipinos and countless unknown Mesopotamians who'd already been employed building the Tower of Babel) the American bombs hit the pseudo-palace that was built as a tortoiseshell over it but they couldn't do any damage to the seven-metre-thick concrete cover of the bunker so that we wonder why our EX wasn't found there in the underground monument of Esser Schutzraumtechnik GmbH (Munich) in one of the marble baths with gold taps not giving a shit about anything

but in his hole in the ground in Tikrit instead

until the answer to the 114-million-dollar question came to us namely that there's no point to a bunker unless there is a certain probability that the enemy will lose and the danger disappear but

the Americans don't seem to be thinking of that at the moment

Ali my friend now you can see me (absolutely nervous and sweating people have never seen me like this and will therefore presumably gradually start to doubt my reality) being driven towards a further checkpoint past a vegetable stall and a pack of local shoppers (aborigines) only now does it occur to me that countless compatriots of ours have been living in the SPHERE for more than a year are they kept as a species of animal or are various methods of promoting international understanding tried out on them before going over to field trials in the Red Zone

in the green heart of power

I would not like to be inside the headroom of our liberators/occupiers who have put a damned stupid head on our country (for it's hard of hearing not very good at thinking and believes its wood is diamond) but somewhere between Camp Dragon FOB Blackhawk Camp Horror (no: Honour) and FOB Trojan House (no: Horse)

I have to jump out of the Odyssean limousine into the brain of the occupier and continue with my *Declaration of Tariq*

Dear Sirs, Ladies and Gents,
Dear Americans,

You declare democracy and take away our voice.
You ought to be forced by ayatollahs to hold elections.
You—

but basically I don't say anything at all again but once more am frisked like
a tailor's dummy (this time they're keen on armpits) and then I find myself
with a plastic name-tag on a blood-red string round my neck among hundreds of people I don't know on the square outside the massive conference
centre (CC) our EX had constructed like a long steel barrel already half
sunk into the ground in which as many speakers as possible from as many
countries as possible in as many addresses as possible would say as little as
possible nothing but glass and dust and aluminium more and more

people come

1,300 delegates have been invited to the conference which is to select a
100-person commission whose task will be to take over the organization of
the elections next year and *to supervise* (whatever that might mean) the 25-
person government Civilian Administration has pulled out of its poker-player's
sleeves and given a beautiful place (SEAT) in the monstrous Stalinist-looking
high-rise building of the former Industry Ministry directly opposite our
wavering standpoint

I'm not here Ali I'm just taking your chameleon for a walk a light
breeze is making the ties the kaffiyehs ghotras and even the abayas flutter
(we're working on a 25 per cent quota of women to which all Farida could
say was that in present-day Iraq it was 58 per cent) actually I could let your
pet walk round freely the prevailing mood here is (for me at least) surreal
red-white-green-and-black camels with copies of the Koran in their mouths
and huge plastic turkeys with stars cruising through the air accompanied
by Double-George helicopter gunships and those patriotic giant desert
spiders that as is well known gobbled up whole companies of GIs outside
Fallujah I mean

we're standing round here in the mercilessly rising morning sun like
oil- sand- or arms-dealers outside a conference centre in Dubai or Riyadh
waiting for a few mortar grenades to come crashing through the bulletproof
glass of the BUBBLE and nothing happens thanks to the EXORBITANT
security measures (everyone's constantly frisking everyone else) I simply feel
wrong or as unrepresentative as the countless enraged critics of the conference say write broadcast

while spasmodic movement starts round some seemingly enlightened (lit up) figures you think you recognize from television and the crowd starts to stream into the half-sunken giant barrel

I'm out of place and out of sorts it's

like having to smile all the time at a funeral and yet it's a

birth

we're bringing about here the blood-stained amateurish forceps and vacuum-extraction delivery of the democracy which has come upon us and which now has to come from us before us the incubator (along with the usual vandals who want to pull us out) for it's clear that this premature baby will not be able to survive on the milk of its starving mother alone she's been subjected to rape for years is covered in bruises and addicted to violence so the American

star surgeons

have amputated her right arm (if we can call the army and the police that which we're reluctant to do) so that she won't stick a knife in their ribs on top of that they've tried to remove half her brain (Baathists Islamists pan-Arabists communists) and at the same time ripped open her belly (the competitive Caesarean technique during which one party drags the child out of the belly while the other tries to tear it out of the womb) oh Ali I

shouldn't be here if I were to follow my feelings at the sight of the returned exiles posing for TV cameras and press photographers after 30 years in Paris London Washington they know very well that a child is brought into the world out of the left ear by remote control

but it's no use it's clear as daylight (by Shamash!) that the exiles have to return even if we don't like those who in the great

HORSE RACE as our American friends and benefactors call it

cross the finish line first (confidence tricksters CIA agents power-hungry tribal chiefs who don't give a damn about the country as a whole)

others will return will have to return above all the thousands of doctors engineers teachers scientists we've lost over all those years and of course it's not so much the first and quite certainly botched elections that matter but the next ones and the ones after that (etc)

just as

it's not the dead that matter it's the way it is in the Shiite scholarly community where they no longer have a voice we have to talk to the living Ali

in front of me

between a group of tribal chiefs and a Kurdish delegation I suddenly see our friend Samir who was relegated from the Ministry of Health to a practice in New Baghdad and

even before the bell sounds summoning us to the biggest conference hall and before the newly appointed president can talk about a great day and the (temporary) prime minister about a first step in opening up the horizon of dialogue (a three-veil sentence) I must tell my (like me) unusually businesslike and excited-looking moustachioed colleague Samir about that evening four weeks ago when I sat waiting amid the ruins of my practice when I drank medical alcohol until I saw the chameleon and took Ali's ghost for the actual person of my friend into whose operating theatre four militiamen forced their way one with a graze on his thigh which they demanded he treat immediately but Ali had a severely injured boy on the table (who had arrived shortly before he was going to set off to see me) and when they pressurized him and threatened to force him he made the mistake of saying he would deal first with the one who would not shoot at others

in the conference hall which I enter together with Samir we're faced with long rows of empty seats mauve folding chairs and narrow desks with little plastic bottles of mineral water on them all with the same blue lid and the same blue label like a battery farm like a conveyor belt on an assembly line in a car factory it's the absolute democracy of emptiness as long as no one sits down there it's

an image of death

and we only sit down (or so it seems to me) in order

to deny that with our irritating difference even if when sitting down I can only think of Ali

I shall die, and shall I not then be as Enkidu?
Sorrow has entered my heart!
I am afraid of death, so I wander the wild,
to find Uta-napishti, son of Ubar-Tutu.
On the road, travelling swiftly,
I came one night to a mountain pass.
I saw some lions and grew afraid

Gilgamesh killed the lion

despite or because of his fear we've hardly begun to argue

1,300 Iraqis

non-representative as Al Jazeera as the Supreme Council of Islamic Scholars as the right half of my brain think

as non-representative (no a little more) as Muqtada al-Sadr with his wild
agitation and attempt to assume authority over the Shiites and who weeks
ago occupied the Imam Ali Mosque in Najaf with his gunmen and now

breaks up the conference just as it's getting going

because the media reports of fighting flaring up again arouse the suspi-
cion among the delegates that the prime minister who is present wants to
join the Americans in killing all the lions

dozens shout

dozens leave the hall

we take a break set up television sets and try to see through their flickering lenses as far as Najaf what can we do we have to get worked up and
debate we'll put a commission of arbitration together or mow down all the
rebels there (thoughts like that flash through your mind when such wretched
tattered lions have murdered your best friend) I

leave the hall as well I

have to breathe I need more

green in the Green Zone and a sphere in the sphere if only for a few
minutes to work off my adrenaline I'm growing old and I'm afraid (amongst
other things of becoming like lots of other people) I'm a doctor and I've
sworn an oath *Whoever kills a man kills all men* but anyone who heals a person heals at most himself as well that's the asymmetry of Hippocrates and
we have to live with it

a few (guarded) bushes a garden path between them a few trees and
already I feel better you just have to

pump enough green blood through your veins

calm yourself or

this organism that claims to be you I have my own shrine to Ali inside
me all he wanted was to go and join his family in London where al-Sistani is
in a cardiac clinic at the moment the ayatollah will have to return and settle
the argument about the shrine to Ali he has true authority with the Shiite

faithful and we will probably have to learn to work together with the believers the Mosque of Ali Ibn Abi Talib with its golden dome and golden facade sticks in my memory but even more the unending grey of the myriads of little grave-domes and gravestones in the cemetery which is said to contain four or five million dead

there behind the graves is the shimmer of the

Sea of Najaf

a shining shimmering expanse of desert like flowing vibrating molten glass fusing with the sky dissolving all contours

for the dead will be more numerous than the living

how many dead can have been laid to rest in Iraq's earth since the days of Gilgamesh

hazy

I sit down on a bench in the Green Zone it's one year after the war and yet just one year into a war and suddenly I notice that

the American

to whom I wanted to speak all the time the person hidden inside the gold puppet of the caliph is sitting right beside me on the bench so that I can finally continue my declaration and can therefore cry out that as a result of their arrogance their contempt for our culture their lack of planning and frightening indifference the peace they've perpetrated is even worse than the war we were afraid of

but when I turn to look

all I see is a young woman a girl almost still very slim delicate she's wearing flat leather shoes jeans and a neatly ironed brown blouse she has dark-brown hair with a straight parting and intelligent almost black eyes she briefly wipes her forehead with her hand and I notice that her thumbnail has a vertical line in the middle

we've done everything wrong here, haven't we (she says it with unexpected vehemence in a voice that belongs to an older or more mature woman)

who are you? what are you doing here?

translating I'm an interpreter

your Arabic's very good I say feeling oddly numbed and although she hardly said anything more perhaps it's the residual shimmer of the memory of the lustrous desert that makes me feel so peaceable or yielding or it's simply this open young face that reminds me of my children of Yasmin before I sent her to Paris and of Muna who can't go to university any more and is morosely baking bread at home

a strangely soft blurring of boundaries that

could liberate us (I think or something

inside me thinks)

have we done everything wrong? the girl asks persistently and gently

yes—many things

then we must do things differently you can do everything differently and better than before

not necessarily everything I say (after all) I still appear to be concerned to maintain certain boundary lines to leave certain dividing walls (at least thin membranes) standing in this shimmering and blurring of things and of ideas about things of course you can look at everything as optimistically as this girl it's all a question of your standpoint

where was something

and where was it not

the place from which you tell the story (Green Zone) could decide its course

what do you think the young woman asks

we

I finally say (because she looks at me so intently)

WE must do things better

Sami didn't come home that night he didn't tell us he'd be out didn't send a message my mother was white as a sheet and stayed up until midnight while Tariq and Uncle Fuad kept trying to tell her that such things weren't unusual for a 19-year-old but it sounded disingenuous

false like this terrible letter that's eating away at my heart I don't even trust the handwriting although you must have been in a state the day before yesterday when you tried to push me into the abyss with these 10 lines were you a Sufi yesterday do you want to be a Shiite mullah again this morning

the call of the muezzin

caught me in the middle of a dream in which it was so dark and quiet that I couldn't help thinking I was on a bier in a mausoleum and when I woke with a start there was only one reason for me to come back to life namely

to save my brother

in the dark

I looked

in haste in panic

for my sword but it was too dark to see anything time was pressing it seemed to be getting even darker the big sword must be close by it was razor sharp I had to be both quick and cautious as I felt for it in the darkness hoping I'd touch the flat of it the handle or the pommel instead of the edge which would immediately cut into my flesh now the sound of fighting came through the walls of the tomb my brother

looked like you I

knew that thought that in the night of this dream from which the muezzin woke me to push me into the darkness of our family worries I ought to have got up straight away to see if Sami had come home after all but I was too tired or was I just being mean did I not want to go and look for him or at least not to hurry to join the search

but my rage

must be directed at you your short icy letter is as arrogant as the mullahs striding past those kneeling on the floor of a mosque in prayer turbaned heads held high (but I once saw an ordinary old man who with an outraged gesture waved away a mullah trying to pass between him and the wall) who else should I direct my rage at where's my sword I ought to

kill Qasim of course I feel I want to

scream with rage and impotence to sleep till the end of all darkness my abducted? brother tortured sister murderous brother-in-law COWARDLY

Beloved I

don't believe it the sword

belongs to

Semiramis

who didn't build Babylon but it was ascribed to her the greatest queens have never existed

Sister it is said that to satisfy her (frequent) nocturnal needs the queen took a man from the army and had him beheaded the next morning so she was like Uday (Huda once said) Saddam's pervert of a son who has met a well-deserved fate

if only Huda were lying beside me instead of Miral and Eren were in Sara's place with sisters like that I could bear more nights in a cramped room but that too is probably an illusion the

sword handle feels amazingly round and obliging it's vibrating of course there

are two handles and

once more I'm sitting in the saddle of one of the red child's bicycles Tariq bought for us when Yasmin flew off to Paris my hands on the handlebar grips looking back over my shoulder I see you my brother like a little colourful laughing reflection oh Sami

why should I bother with Babylon any more what would Semiramis do would she put on a suicide vest and crash into an American checkpoint I don't need a war I've just begun to understand but if the professor who was to teach me how to read the law tables of Hammurabi is driven out of the country then I've no chance I

get up and it

doesn't get light

my mother's face is pale as if you were seeing it in the artificial darkness of a theatre as if it had been made up with lime or chalk I make a list of all of Sami's friends I know everyone tries to phone one of them my male cousins promise to look for Sami track him down bring him home

when the telephone rings around 10 there's no one left in the house apart from Sara and me the oldest women and little children so I lift the receiver what a piece of luck for it's Hind who wants to speak to me

it doesn't get bright on that day the light's like a thin coat of paint over the world that's already peeling off the darkness is bubbling up everywhere and unstoppably smoke from the atoms what should I do Semiramis was sitting at her dressing table when the revolution broke out in Babylon she put it down and returned to her dressing table between my darkness and the murky world outside the door there is only

my sister

half turning away sideways as if

she were about to duck to avoid blows in the last few months she's become beautiful again eerie in the dark long-sleeved housecoats buttoned up to the neck that she wears in silence she can't look me in the eye she's definitely disturbed because in the morning she sensed the agitation over Sami's disappearance and the desperation of our mother who would otherwise never have been out at this time

you've got to tell them the business with Qasim and the Major yourself you've got to make the decision I wanted to tell her to her face yesterday and certainly didn't and now there's this panic that's driving me out as if in a terrible storm or simply

as in the war that's going on round us and

the dams have burst the walls have come tumbling down night keeps flooding farther into the day

Yasmin

listen I'm going to Betawiyn Hind rang me from there something's happened there do you understand

Sister?

her smile is so

distant and absent so terribly unimpressed that the pure horror sends me out into the street

something bad's happened to Sami or to you or to Yusuf Hind wouldn't say any more couldn't say another word but the way she spoke it was clear that everything was over I'm heading for whatever's happened I haven't taken a single dinar only the key to our old house at the last moment I tie on one of Sara's headscarves it's a strikingly bright blue bright dove-blue my little dove you understand your fine brother-in-law I wanted you all to know that

the dove the Kurdish boy ripped all the feathers off at the edge of Saadun Park all those years ago was a sign from the future that would pluck out our fine feathers

the abandoned child

Semiramis

was fed by doves and at the end of her successful wild proud invented life turned into a dove herself what does that mean what does it matter I'm walking across Baghdad in America there are no doves only a kind of squirrel instead who told me that perhaps it was my brother or it was Professor Fahmi who left Babylon in the lurch who went to Beirut

to have his hair done

you overcome the fear choking everyone here by simply

going out

without a sword as a

dove

perhaps tonight I'll give them a fright perhaps they'll take me for a hawk and assume I've got an explosive belt round my stomach because I ignore the rules and don't keep my distance from the city any longer I've put on my old school gym shoes when I go when I come on foot to Betawiyn then

I'll examine my heart examine the city I'll examine

the war to see how far it bears within it the peace we've been promised why am I going alone why did I tell Yasmin where I'm going

just imagine a girl in New York City who one morning in September

goes into the World Trade Center imagine

she was thinking (simply by chance) of a sister in another country in another time in an unimaginable war a satellite view from high up on a big crossroads in Baghdad a sharp precisely aimed and calculated camera shot N 33°20'49.56" and E 44°22'58.85" on the

Life Simulator Sami why don't you play that game

at home on the computer that for so long replaced and improved the world outside for you before you flew off at the Towers just imagine (he would say) a sister the same age with a face like a hamster and a green uniform dragging the Iraqi men by a dog's lead tied round their neck across a prison corridor instructing them to form a pyramid naked a sister with a cigarette in the corner of her mouth aiming an imaginary gun at their exposed penises

clear off

out of yourself

she's sweating it's already hot on this September morning she hurries over the wide street with no lights or zebra crossing across a triangular island on which a soldier waving a flag is getting up on a kind of mud column of grey bodies which for its part is standing on a tank

barbed-wire barricades

WARNING!

COALITION CHECKPOINT!

keep well away from all checkpoints all military vehicles all police stations and police cars but she walks so close past the American soldiers in steel helmets and combat uniforms that they would have had to react if a white car that had already stopped and out of which four big men are getting had not occupied their entire attention

beyond Maidan Square cars can drive again she goes diagonally across an area blighted by broken glass and wrecked cars

then along the central reservation of a wide street completely empty on the right on the left on the other hand soon blocked by dusty battered cars nervously edging forward

Rashid Street you know that

once the old three-storey houses were just the friendly entrance to the old town Huda and I would come from the Karkh side and go from the fish market across Shuhada Bridge to the old souks you have the best view from the middle of the bridge if you can ignore the bawling and hooting nowadays no woman dares stand there one Friday evening Shiruk accompanied us across the bridge as far as the Baghdad Museum where we listened to the musicians playing outside once my father took me down al-Mutanabbi Street in order to show me the bookshops the Ottoman palace the legendary Shabander Café on the corner in those days the professors sold their books on blankets spread out on the ground today there are parts for all kinds of generators I can feel people giving me

looks

which in the past (yesterday even) would have frightened me to death sometimes behind the blinds and bars of the closed shops the boarded-up windows something

snake-like

seems to be moving in the last few months there have been dozens of rapes every woman knows that the wolves are lurking everywhere perhaps even in the cavities of this once modern now bombed-out building don't rush walk calmly get to the next corner turn off the poet al-Rusafi used to stand there relaxed and affable in his lightweight suit on a high white plinth like a fatherly mayor in the middle of a turbulent little square now the plinth is grey and scrawled on with half-full black rubbish sacks strewn about the monument has a circle of barbed wire round it the buildings on the periphery look scorched even the sky with more black helicopters thundering across is veiled by smoke and I don't know whether once you actually or only

in my mind told me about the

black light

in which things (slowly perhaps as now) become invisible

the square the bearded men as shadowy as spectral as the past when Huda and I crossed the copper and clothes markets to the goldsmiths' booths to discover the Major's hands placing a gold chain round my sister's neck

Ishtar must

descend no one can see me in the darkness surrounding me the black light dissolves everything like acid in the air through which I walk and walk never before have I gone so far on my own in Baghdad more and more things disappearing (they disappear because they've nothing to do with me any more) I come to the massive dissolving sugar-lump of the Central Bank with its shadow guards and machine-gun emplacement a wall made of four-metre-high concrete blocks isn't porous enough and the red stencilled

ROAD CLOSED

on it forces me to make a detour towards the gold market in an alley between old houses three women appear in front of me a redhead with a dirty redhead child in her arm and two with black headscarves and expressively made-up faces who speak to me give me a well-meant warning but they're only

shadow-words hardly visible

things I forget having heard because streams of blood are roaring in my ears and the black light makes the images of you and Ahmed and Hind and Sami shine out with such force that even the pompous man of bronze on his triple plinth outside the semicircular arcade of the Chamber of Commerce fades

soon

there won't be anyone standing on columns any more who wasn't a poet who wasn't a good person or at least valuable for the community with black light that's how far I can see into the black tunnel of the future

my gym shoes seem to have become tighter the sides are rubbing

something inside me (disconcerting frightening I don't want to have to see it clearly) welcomes this long walk something that wants and demands it only now does it become clear to me why my mother suddenly set off for Karbala with Yasmin she simply had to push open the door and go out into the open air you can stop me the woman (alone unprotected) and kill me but in order to stop me

you will also have to kill me I

walk

and at last the old Centre for Telecommunications appears in front of me a grey high-rise building that's had a hole shot in it very high up between supporting pillars that have been pulled out of the building like cables for Chinese lanterns you can see people walking round what is there left to steal there or are they perhaps tidying up

wide streets large squares

we marched along here several times with the whole school and had to sing songs for Saddam hold up placards and chant slogans that echoed back from the facades of the high-rise hotels (God bless his buttocks Huda sang) the stone relief with the 10-metre-high portrait of the president is still standing though someone has painted over the area round the eyes and nose with black paint here he can no longer see what's happening in Iraq and on TV he swears and curses without sound will they hang him or not I don't care it would be good if they put him in a glass case in Paradise Square with a stack of tomatoes by it to throw at him for the rest of his life he should just be left to rot in a cell (my father says) so that at last we can show we're a civilized nation what would he say

if Yasmin hadn't survived

if Tariq were to see me now I know he'd be horrified it's just that there's no other way possible there's no

Simulator

any more there's no other place from which I could imagine my life than this one here inside

my skin

on Tahrir Square an American tank abruptly changes lanes it drives the red-and-white taxis and other cars on ahead of it like a mythical giant boar a pack of hounds a smaller faster armoured car overtakes it and pushes a few cars to the side denting them with a bang the drivers hastily veer away but once the Americans are past they're tailgating and hooting at one another again anyone who hesitates for a second is lost and left behind what

do I care

the Liberation Monument

that 30-metre-long white slab stuck into the supporting sidewalls like the blade of a gigantic guillotine

hasn't had paint smeared or sprayed over it yet the dark relief figures on it (the athletic soldier pushing the bars apart and the rejoicing crowd with arms raised) look even more shadowy and charred as if burnt into the white stone

Humvees and armoured vehicles again whizzing round the roundabout and this time all the drivers get out of the way in time as if they'd learnt their lesson although they're different drivers of course

close your eyes

open them

don't let yourself be stopped in the black light the contours of the liberators are

only negatives

with fluid fading edges on a vehicle a sloping metal plate revolves behind it a rifleman with a steel helmet then a soldier

right in front of her he seems to be about to say something

but then blurs in the glare or turns into a tree from behind which a group of boys with toy pistols and plastic swords jump out Ahmed could be one of them he'd jump and brandish his weapons just like that who was it who told the story of the boys who were given spades by American soldiers to help make a football pitch and burst into tears after a few minutes' work because they thought they were to dig their own graves Ahmed your tousled head your chubby arms you're sitting on the wall in front of the ginkgo tree on the other side

is the

GREEN ZONE

previously the palaces of terror dug themselves in there today you find the concrete walls barbed-wire barricades tank traps of democracy everything that has been promised will only come when the wars in paradise are over (Tariq told her about that secret book of the poet without paper)

when anyone

can cross over to the other side of the Tigris as they wish

that's

the way she used to go to school she walked along here so often with Tariq and Sami and her sister to the old house with the lock that's been forced where is Hind perhaps it would be better to go next door first and

shapes

massive shadows hard black glittering eyes this here's this was

your mother's kitchen but now

it's clear what had to happen is happening there are three men stone wolves they waited here or came back to empty the cupboards knock over the chairs slit open the mattresses

if you think

you're not here (under the shadows) or that it's inevitable that you'll enter your sister's

night

(talk to me, Yasmin, your blue-grey face) then perhaps you'll hardly feel anything take off your gold crown take the rings out of you ears untie the pearl necklace round your neck and the brooches on your breast I'll send

my lions to Hind she's only 12 she's to be protected until the immense

onset

of actual and eternal peace I told you (Sister) about the women who were found in the mass graves of Ur human grave goods the king takes his harem with him across to

the other side

but here we're in the house where I lived for so long the cramped rooms the quiet of my thoughtful friendly family is being trampled on and devastated the

house in which we want to live

has to be built by ourselves (not the Americans) they're not here anyway because we ignore them and just go on murdering one another

no more than the stone people who dissolve in the black light King Shahryar was a mass murderer he should have married Semiramis then the next day would belong to

US

close your eyes

in the depths of her body she wants to become a shadow herself that is untouched by anything what happens on the surface is nothing but extreme (external) misfortune but all of a sudden

Yusuf

is standing beside her aiming a rifle at the men he screams with such outrage such fury such fear as she has never heard a person scream and the others offer no words no resistance but

go (unwillingly and agonizingly slowly shadows of stones on a house wall that you've looked at too closely and that for that very reason move away so slowly)

Yusuf's stammering is hardly comprehensible how should she find out

in this state

what he's saying Sami (she finally understands) is alive he hasn't been abducted but has gone into hiding—don't you see it's all your fault why are you so

depraved

these letters

that Sami wrote she can't understand she bundles her clothes together on her chest she can't find the headscarf she staggers along behind Yusuf to the room where her parents used to sleep why there what letter she only understands later after she's left the house and stares at the crumpled piece of paper in her hand painstakingly smooths it out to see strange words in her own handwriting on it they're very skilfully (his astonishing skill) very well-forged lines these letters that Sami wrote

a letter to Nabil in what looks like her handwriting

Meet me one last time, darling. My parents' house is empty!

is a more convincing forgery than the letter in which Nabil told her their love was over

this grave by her parents' bed as if it had dropped down from a crazy murderous planet no one can invent something like that how did you come to be in this house Beloved perhaps everything's different and all you must do is go as a dead body everywhere where you were once loved

but this cushion of coagulated blood below your breast Beloved and the terrible smell

you must

go home Muna and tell them and

′ you must

understand and

you must not

say a word it's a matter of life and death you alone are to blame Muna do you understand that you and not your brother are to blame this man here (even beside his corpse he doesn't say Nabil's name) was only meant to get a warning

what can she understand and retain of all this as she leaves the house stumbles out into the midday heat with the forged letter in her hand has the black light already made things so invisible so undetectable that she doesn't feel anything when she bumps into a corner of the wall everything slips away moves further and further back the district is hazy and colourless all the noises it produces muffled it seems to be pulsating almost without sound everything's like a gigantic ultrasound image she's moving through with indistinct aching limbs the death of her Beloved like a burning bullet in her breast this here

is only

the dreadful embryo of the present in the womb of the future they stick their needles into it they cut it to pieces because they hate the child which they're not a hundred per cent sure is theirs in a kind of

flickering

the colours and smells of the hot September afternoon return she's reached a small square a few red double-decker buses with white roofs are parked between rows of palms behind them there's a market with vegetables pots and pans clothes at first she can't understand why she should be drawn to this surface why she should emerge here from her monochrome half-numb despair and she has to see the purple of aubergines the green and red of cucumbers and tomatoes the cheerful gaudy colours of a silver Mickey Mouse balloon before she realizes

that her sister Yasmin is actually standing there by the fruit carts and is pointing at her and that her mother appears beside her in a black abaya both clearly happy and relieved at first she can't understand why but then she too feels relief and comfort the reason is that

Yasmin leads the way that she's wearing a light-green dress and a head-scarf of a similar colour and looks as resolute and composed as she could only last have been two or three years ago there's no doubt that she has brought Farida here that she's understood everything that was said to her and is herself again in front of this

dazzlingly bright wall of fire

consuming burning dissolving her transforming her into a shadow through an unimaginably violent light an avalanche of flame an exploding comet in the street only

you hear nothing

your ear has been

destroyed

but after a certain (murky how

could it turn dark again so quickly) time she has something like a memory of an infernal bang a minute before from which now a rising whistling noise is left you still

have a mouth to scream you can

open your eyes for the

view of a volcanic landscape full of ash dust smoke everywhere flames licking over the ground

scraps grey debris sharp-edged bent torn objects which should recall something the whistling gets louder even louder painful a burst shining red watermelon perhaps a burning straw basket in which someone wanted to carry red-hot coals a pool spreading glutinously and shining like quicksilver on which a comb of little blue flames settles in an oddly slow way across the rise of a clumsy shoe with a torn-off foot in it a person with no head is lying in front of you and the burning limbs on the half-shredded plastic sheet don't belong to it a

car tyre a tiny dead red bird bizarre imaginary objects covered in a downy grey skin of ash parts of people and machines as if arranged by a sadistic painter

the whistling

nevertheless now you hear shouts and screams you think you must be wrong

just now you saw

your Beloved and you believe (although you know it can't be right) that he must be here among all the dead the whimpering injured you see the naked completely hairless torso of a large doll a kind of yellow down floats past you

can move your arms you can feel your fingers your legs

move

it's like a preliminary exercise for an (as yet unknown) swimming stroke how come you're on the ground anyway and what

have you forgotten what are you always forgetting

right next to your left cheek is another shoe you venture to raise yourself up on your hands elbows knees the whistling it's not stopping it's swelling again so

that for a while you can't hear any human sound until you've overcome a wave of sickness dizziness and strangely enough shame and now on your knees hands with your arms stretched out look in front draw up one leg as if for the start of a race

all the things

you have to think of! your hand (after standing up what have you forgotten) feels your uninjured stomach straight ahead through the debris the layers of ash the shattered market cart there was

something there

they

were coming towards you behind you

there are people lots of people now who are coming even closer helpful people that you can feel Farida and Yasmin ought to be there

you feel these people like a large cloak laid across your shoulders something comforting loose calm you will now

go straight ahead
in this direction you
raise your head and now you see the
second explosion

RETURN

Smash me, my body flees
into a mirror, my face
dances on the wave,
flows into fragments.
I do not breathe.

Lightly I go, lightly I return,
lightly I fit myself together,
circle after circle
in the glass of the deepest of all seas,
of the lake on which every image
appears anew
and remains.

Sabrina Dies
–
Martin + Seymore try to
reconstruct 9/11 + deal w/ grief

Iraq
trying to serve the community (Pre-9/11)
{ where to go w/ life
⌐ precarious & dangerous
  ∟ → death

EPILOGUE

September 2004

Word vomit :)

many interpretations of
the vagueness

You don't need to

    wake up any more

    that is an immense relief just as you will never get tired again

    what you are still aware of (instead of activity and sleep) is just a flicker of attention or of the degree of presence at a particular place or at different places and times

    where you've been taken or perhaps you're directing everything the way you want (but would that be a release)

    you're still there

    only with a fragile presence that leaves no imprint you can imagine such a mode of existence better by mirroring it in external things by first of all

    reducing

    the apparently firm and solid nature of things what you might call their optical state

    to the very edge of transparency (if you should be absent)

    and then intensifying it (if you should return) to such a perfect breathtaking luminous incontrovertible presentness as if the whole world were made out of metals of unbelievable weight and unbearable radiance then you would believe yourself incapable of leaving any place at all any more due to its annihilating force of attraction

    the present

    even the most fleeting and fresh moment turns old and brittle beneath your stare it's this (unimaginable) distance in your look the chest of a person sleeping next to you from which the blanket has slipped off looks to you like the torso of a statue thousands of years old covered in cracks and scratches its skin (a lime-marl layer) like the bottom of a lake dried out by the sun a mosaic of the most delicate shards a highly complicated jigsaw puzzle that your undreamt-of new state allows you to fit together in a fraction of a second

    behind the glass of a tall display case

    the statue of a woman with no arms

    that is tangible

with the large almond-shaped blind stones in her eye sockets she stares in vain at our times and her cry doesn't even arise for below her vaguely defined nose there is no mouth (as if these fractions of a second had been shaped like that leaving no time to fill the lungs with air)

it was because of these skulls (genuine human skulls) which had been covered by a layer of clay and given stone eyes for an everlasting horrified look that I plunged back into those days in Manhattan to the torsos marked with the sashes of the safety belts on the World Trade Center Plaza

if you were to see it now perhaps only with a faraway look

so that the whole city would appear as if made of glass or celluloid

even its noise would be transparent so to speak only present as white noise as a kind of acoustic fog in which now and then blurred voices whisper or fragments of sentences appear

you pass through the walls as if they were curtains that can be parted at any point everything is transparent hazy and light when you look

back

in this way (at a distance of 7,000 years) nothing is distinct any more but it becomes easier to picture or sketch something you haven't possibly got the strength for a painting or a film (to create and bear something like that)

the possibilities that arise in the flowing city of glass are translucent like a thin film the one and only life turns into a swarm of ghostly existences it's only this peculiar colourlessness that makes you think that and the great distance at which everything now happens (or has happened) for these are not fish lives there's nothing cool or indifferent about them it's more as if you were viewing

touching highly dramatic melancholy and heart-rending scenes in black-and-white films that were never made

the possibilities you have like tickets to various plots and genres

you call your mother again and she tells you to go back right away and have dinner with her (second) husband you are to spend the night in his apartment everything will be as normal and according to expectations and the next morning you are to be in her office in the World Trade Center at nine

you don't call anyone none of your friends neither your father in Amherst nor Eric or Iris the housekeeper in Long Island with whom you were able to talk about everything you're alone at last (bewildered) and drift round the city you watch time passing in it until it's night and early morning girls are murdered in parks under bridges in shabby hotels or they're accosted and involved in strange perhaps terrible perhaps only repulsive and ordinary glassy transparent nebulous matters it

could be

that you spend a whole warm summer's evening sitting on a bench by the East River (a fragile girl self-absorbed writing in a notebook) and nothing at all happens to you

your first reaction in Little Brazil Street when you suddenly become aware of your loneliness is to take out your mobile and one after the other you dial all the numbers of students who live here and somehow or other (at a party at a college event etc) have ended up in your address book

a boy studying at Columbia replies he has a room in a student residence and is delighted at your call he very clearly remembers a conversation with you of which your memory is as hazy and fragmentary as that of the boy himself only when you see him does he come back to mind he's a smoothy a clown who imagines himself a poet a simple-minded sportsman a business careerist a

guy who puts on a show of being affable and sensible on the short side but sporty proud of his dazzlingly white teeth and the cup for the last college triathlon or fencing or judo championship (you didn't look that closely) now he's happy and embarrassed at the same time for this evening he absolutely has to go to a birthday party his best friend's whose parents are really loaded and have this phenomenal penthouse on the Upper West Side you could simply come along (which suits you down to the ground) when we get back or at the party there'll be no problem finding a room in the residence or with some acquaintance

you stay at the party until three or four you've left nothing in the room of the boy who's taking you and and with your ability to stick by a decision can simply shake him off or get rid of him and then you could approach a girl or a young woman of your age and go home with her for a quick forty winks (wouldn't that be the simplest solution) or you could keep going until dawn and walk back through the streets have breakfast in some deli or on the other hand

you could come back with the boy who only has his own room of course at your age there's no problem sleeping side by side in the same bed like brother and sister it's so easy to have a distorted picture of young people who will be (must have been) just as lustful and tender and wretched and generous as you were and even if it should happen that you despite your romantic love for Eric or precisely because of that or for no other reason than the opportunity and the simultaneous activation of a robust irrepressible biological mechanism were to sleep with him it would

only be one moment in the life that belongs to you alone

whatever happens at that

place of glass where the future and the past touch in destruction and conception

it will never be compact and clear it's nothing but the buzz of transparent phantoms inside your head it's a glass knot in the glass city that tears apart

what remains are the hard final colours in stone glass asphalt are the sweat and scent of your youth in the inexorable reality of your last evening the few

moments before things become transparent or are hypothetically liquified at the moment when you on Sixth Avenue as a reflex action and almost in panic take out your mobile and do not press a button but stand still in the stream of people as if a magic hand (the hand of the djinn) had set you down on the top of a solitary pillar you're surrounded by an invisible rumbling abyss and you can feel the heartlessness and the grandiose nature of the city in the same breath with a mirror of all possible states in front of you at any time you could contact someone you know your mother your father your new boyfriend all your friends and fellow students in Boston but

you remain silent you don't press a button

thus

transforming the city into a city with no name therefore of necessity without your name either

there's no more

to be said about you

no further thoughts beyond these moments or

you simply take a hotel room even if so far you've only done that on rare occasions it reminds you of your trip round Europe with your cousin Lotta perhaps of Paris as well the last trip together with your parents because then (you were 13) it was the first time you had a hotel room of your own even on a different floor from the couple who are having to make a great effort to keep themselves under control in front of you and whose attempts to mask their bitterness with activity (the Louvre Montmartre the Opera the famous cafes Shakespeare & Co) torment you and who by quarrelling

erase your name

once you woke up long before they did and simply went out into the street a cobbled street in the Latin Quarter like something from a film set no one took any notice of you no one stopped you no one asked you anything the city seemed so immensely indifferent and liberating fear and excitement balancing one another out just as now on Sixth Avenue

after you'd

been walking for five or ten minutes

past bookshops bistros shops with gold signs on a black or red background

you started again (after years) talking to the Arab sister you'd once invented and you saw her here in Paris as well at a table outside a nearby cafe it was a Middle Eastern family or rather a father and his two daughters the man had a black moustache a high forehead and thinning hair he looked very kind but also worn out he was having an agitated discussion with his elder daughter a very elegant young woman in Western clothes almost like a model holding a cigarette between her

fingers and arguing with him vehemently while the younger one

a girl of 11 or 12

looked upset but then preoccupied again she was a bit chubby and short very reserved and pretty in a way that's not immediately striking (like yourself perhaps) but also somehow self-confident you suddenly felt drawn by curiosity to know more about her and at one point your eyes met

it gave you both a strange little shock which made you open your lips wordlessly at the same time

what

could you or would you have said how

does one greet the apparent reflection of a long-cherished daydream what did she represent in her completely impenetrable Parisian life

the hotel room

in which you wake up doesn't fit the Latin Quarter it's the second time you've come to that morning and seeing a Moorish moulding on the wall up by the ceiling you remember that the first time it was actually a muezzin's call to prayer that woke you from your sleep

you're

in the country (one of the possible countries) of your Arab sister no doubt about it open the curtains and your eye will plunge into the light of bright concrete dried palm leaves dusty cars neon signs in Arabic still illuminated with a weak glow like embers beneath ashes

the wrinkled torsos looking like burnt and cracked clay skin the heads staring at your time with stone eyes

belonged to the Neolithic statues in the museum on Citadel Hill in Amman

even yesterday afternoon

you were standing there in front of two massive Greek columns with the Caesarean view of the hills of the city dotted with grey and ochre houses futuristic high-rise buildings tower up from one district over another the country's flag is flying from an absurdly high pole on the baked structures of the old-town houses the water tanks shimmer as if a swarm of wingless artificial insects or an army of jolly robots had descended on the thirsty city and were sucking the water up instead of releasing it the Roman theatre lay like the impression of a gigantic shell immortalized in sandstone at the foot of Jaufa Hill there's no doubt about it

you were here in as many times and circumstances

as you want to imagine

the elevator to the breakfast room is jam-packed with package tourists who mustn't miss their bus so you take the stairs

Luisa's already at the table beside a little wall with green plants on it she needs her tea as soon as she gets up in the morning she waves sits back as you approach after the second night in Amman she looks relaxed with her brown skin black hair and dark eyes she could easily disguise herself as an Arab you think it's the South the warmth and the sun which make her blossom like this perhaps the two of you should transfer to a Californian university after all

everything seems to be connected with everything else in a way that's almost embarrassing or eerie but as you walk towards her this has the form of a return to happiness once more you feel the sense of profound relief that her decision had gone in your favour

for just one second before you also sit down at the table and as on almost every morning together feel this sitting-opposite-each-other as a perfect interlocking in an ideal (dual) state like something technical almost or rather chemical perhaps two hydrogen or oxygen atoms forming a bond that is stable and more efficient in terms of energy the surprising unpleasant realization hits you like an electric shock that

the table is only set for two

it makes no sense to be startled at it even less annoyed but it

distances you and you can't do anything to slip out of it (where to) and although it's great and also a deserved happiness that's been earned (encouraged) by confessions honesty and determination (responding to an offer of a one-year guest professorship in Tel Aviv with a trip to Jordan and Israel to make up your minds whether you want to have a year here together)

you have to spend the whole day struggling to get close to this couple who keep being lost in swirls of dust in clouds of sadness and apathy (bodies you think tearing each other to pieces in an unutterably faraway place without feeling any clear pain until they come to resemble the armless statues in that museum on Citadel Hill)

you see them get out of a taxi and go round a kind of fort or little castle that has fallen straight out of the sky onto a putty-coloured desert

they're standing by a cage with ostriches and are being badgered by souvenir sellers

the cloud of dust swallows them up again in the next brighter phase a structure like an aqueduct appears and the tall almost thin middle-aged man with glasses and grey crew-cut hair says something to the woman in the straw hat white blouse and inky-black trousers which she doesn't seem to understand immediately but then you see her laugh

then come out-of-focus houses on the hills and in the narrow streets of the town like a still life painted in thick oils there's a souk in front of crumbling masonry with pastose fruits dully gleaming copperware bulging sacks of spices and old silver a mosque

denser movement in the narrow squares of the old town children and youths jumping over sacks of garbage lying round

the white tents of an UNHCR refugee camp

the couple beat a retreat (embarrassed you think ashamed perhaps or even afraid the taxi driver had hardly had a good word for the Iraqi refugees) they hesitate however again the man with the crew cut stops and the woman clutches his arm not to drag him away but to let him know she's still there clearly his attention has been gripped by another man appearing who could be in his middle or late 50s visibly Middle Eastern with receding hair and a grey moustache a gaunt man who seems measured and dignified in the heat of the afternoon he's wearing a grey suit and to go by the old leather bag he's holding in his right hand he could be a doctor

I met him again

you say in the evening on the left (western) side of a big double bed Luisa turns her head in surprise the frame of her reading glasses is the same shiny black as her shoulder-length hair she's puzzled by the urgency of your remark almost like a confession so you quickly explain that you meant the man with the doctor's bag

while she had a rest in their hotel room for an hour before dinner you went out again at first just for a few minutes because despite your full programme of things to see you felt adventurous or restless rather then you took a downhill street with a melodious swing to it that reminded you of San Francisco and drew you on farther and farther down so that

for the second time during your short stay in Amman you were in the scrubby park outside the Roman theatre you were just wondering whether to go up between the rows of seats to the highest gallery to enjoy the view of the early-evening city

when you saw (believed you recognized) the man the same age as you with the high forehead and the moustache

this time he wasn't alone but accompanied by a young woman wearing a blue headscarf jeans and a loose-fitting long-sleeved blouse both were looking closely and affectionately at a very worn animal on a stand a ride for children it was a fat red elephant with a saddle and even as you were wondering how you could approach the man (for you felt a positively burning desire to do so a curiosity set off by another physically given existence that is usually completely alien to you)

he said in French that

the elephant was his daughter's favourite animal she'd called it Hannibal when she was 11 and had seen it there for the first time

and so

you got talking (Luisa asks)

we stood by the elephant for 10 minutes then the young woman left us and we had a coffee with cardamom at one of the tables by the stalls

what prompted him to tell me all the things he did (so much but without any vagueness or elaborate detail it was just the headlines of his drama which no longer seemed to affect him) is an absolute mystery to me

you perhaps thought

that this man of the same age from the West seemed more patient and interested than most of those you'd seen during the last few weeks

or you

simply wanted to give him an insight (concisely without being maudlin) because he irritated you with his aura of officialdom he'd register everything conscientiously but nothing would follow from it (you thought) he could have been French or American an engineer or teacher certainly married with a son or daughter of Fatima's age

but what did he tell you Luisa asks gently

she puts the guide book down on the bedcover on the open pages you can see the cracked armless 7,000-year-old statues from Ain Ghazal again bluish-grey now like pottery in the light from the lamp on the bedside table

he came here from Baghdad two weeks ago he's an Iraqi doctor his family survived three wars but last month his wife and elder daughter were killed in a terrorist attack by some miracle his younger daughter the one who liked the elephant so much survived the attack she was 20 and he suspected she was pregnant by a student who had been murdered by insurgents he was going to ask her about it very soon but they'd actually come to a wordless understanding it was because of this presumed child in her womb (perhaps even more than the death threats he'd received which had to be taken seriously) that he'd left Baghdad even though a large part of his family were still there amongst others his son who'd disappeared in the underground

did you tell him anything about yourself?

it seemed to me—

inappropriate you're going to say but why did he give you this report what did he hope to achieve by it

nothing really nothing I think he just wanted to—

carry on

yes he wanted to put something into words to keep hold of it and bring it to a close

just like you no? when you completed Sabrina's poems and when you wrote down all your pain instead of finishing the book on Goethe's women Luisa takes off her glasses and gently folds the sidepieces what were the man and his daughter called

Fatima and Mahmud

I think

deep in the night

a memory returns

it comes from a happier day in another country you're once more completely secure intact of course normal you're just two tourists the god of chance has sent you alone into the Court of the Lions in the Alhambra your shoulders touch lightly as you walk toward the basin of the fountain in the middle borne by friendly looking lions

the narrow canals radiating from the centre in all four directions have a dry shimmer

for a moment

silence

Luisa's firm breasts a seemingly unshakeable warm figure at your side

the tears of the Nasrids fell over 500 years ago a coach party pours in

black drops fall

from the future into the marble of the watercourses very quickly and more and more until a ring of gleaming oil has formed round the lion basin and

bursts into flame

I hear (in the fire as if you could walk round in the flames as in a field of high corn or between silk scarves blazing orange and yellow on a washing line) Luisa say

always the same device

the motto

is repeated a hundred times on the walls ceilings columns between the arabesques and ironwork I see her soft hand with the slim fingers the nails of which are painted cherry red on that day gently cautiously she touches

the elaborately carved letters in the light-coloured stone the tip of her finger
moving from right to left

ولا غالب الا الله

Wa la ghalib illa-llah
There is no victor but God.

The poems quoted in the text are from the following:

AL-AZZAWI, Fadhil. 'Nothing Happens in My Dreams Anymore' in *Miracle Maker: The Selected Poems of Fadhil al-Azzawi*. Translated by Khaled Mattawa. New York: BOA Editions, 2003, p. 108.

DICKINSON, Emily. *The Poems of Emily Dickinson*. Edited by Thomas H. Johnson. Harvard: Harvard University Press, 1998.

The Epic of Gilgamesh. Translated by Andrew George. London and New York: Penguin Classics, 2003.

GOETHE, Johann Wolfgang von. 'Zephyr for Thy Humid Wing' in *The Poems of Goethe*. Translated by Alfred Edgar Bowring. Whitefish, MT: Kessinger Publishing, 2004, p. 554.

———. 'Power that O'ermasters' in *West-Eastern Divan*. Translated by Edward Dowden. London: J. M. Dent and Sons, 1914, p. 67.

The Quatrains of Omar Khayyam. Translated by E. H. Whinfield. London: Routledge, 2001.

WHITMAN, Walt. *Leaves of Grass*. Edited with an afterword by David S. Reynolds. London and New York: Oxford University Press, 2005.

I have translated from the German the verses by Hafiz; the lines from Abu Nuwas, al-Mutannabi and other Arabic and Persian mystics such as Rumi, Djunaid and al-Hallaj; the lines from Adonis' poem 'A Grave for New York'; the verses from Friedrich Rückert's *Kindertotenlieder*; and the lines from Goethe's *Campaign in France in the Year 1792*.